A DANGEROUS SECRET

"All is not settled between us, Miss Belanger," Lord Wycke said. "I am not a man who turns a blind eye to mysteries. I will uncover everything I need to know about you before you leave my employ." He raised an eyebrow. "What, no foolish declaration that you will leave Eastcott this very night to protect your bloody secrets?"

"No," Tessa said quietly. She fought the sickening dread of becoming completely ensnared in her lies. She searched Reave's face, but he concealed his feelings too well. Did he truly desire to help her, or was she only a challenge to his injured pride?

"No, you will not leave, or no, you have no secrets?"

"Curse you!" she spat out. "You know I would have left if I had been given a choice."

"Why did you not leave with Viscount Turnberry?"

"Because there was no one to care and nowhere to go," she cried. She shoved his blocking arm out of her path and ran from the room.

She was so damn haughty—and too beautiful for his own good, Reave thought. Nonetheless, for the first time, he believed she was telling the truth.

BOOK YOUR PLACE ON OUR WEBSITE AND MAKE THE READING CONNECTION!

We've created a customized website just for our very special readers, where you can get the inside scoop on everything that's going on with Zebra, Pinnacle and Kensington books.

When you come online, you'll have the exciting opportunity to:

- View covers of upcoming books

- Read sample chapters

- Learn about our future publishing schedule (listed by publication month *and author*)

- Find out when your favorite authors will be visiting a city near you

- Search for and order backlist books from our online catalog

- Check out author bios and background information

- Send e-mail to your favorite authors

- Meet the Kensington staff online

- Join us in weekly chats with authors, readers and other guests

- Get writing guidelines

- AND MUCH MORE!

Visit our website at
http://www.zebrabooks.com

A DESPERATE GAME

Barbara Pierce

Zebra Books
Kensington Publishing Corp.

http://www.zebrabooks.com

For my husband, Todd. Thank you for your unwavering faith and pride in my accomplishments. Also, my gratitude to Barb, Carmel, Ellen, Gaelen, and Jan. No one could ask for better friends.

Prologue

London—1814

"Well ... well ... what a rare event to have my countess visit me in my private chamber." The insolent gaze of Edmund Tratton, the fifth Earl of Lathom, slid from his wife's pale countenance to her breasts. "Forgive me if I cannot believe you have developed a sudden desire to satisfy your lust in my bed—that is, if I could imagine your unyielding body has ever felt such needs."

"You know me better than that, Edmund. I would never accept the leavings of a whore, be she highborn or servant," she said in a voice much calmer than she felt, but the slight tremor of her lower lip hinted at darker emotions. A month had passed since her husband had first flaunted his latest and most notorious mistress to the ton—her beautiful, faithless mother. Vain and very much out of her depth when playing with debauchery, Mrs. Hone had been ripe for Edmund's twisted seduction. Their betrayal had extinguished what little love she had left for either of them.

"So, Lady Lathom, what curiosity tempts you to my chamber this evening?" He languidly stretched. When she remained mute, his impatience ruined his pose. "Well?"

"I had hoped to chose a more acceptable setting for this, but you have been rather difficult to locate lately," she said, her words fading at his arrogant smile.

"Pray continue. You possess my full attention."

Finally, noticing where his attention was focused, she crossed her arms over her breasts. "Our five-year union has borne nothing but hatred, disgust, humiliation . . . and—perversion!" A warning glint flared in his eyes. He sat up, easing his legs off the bed. She edged away and moved closer to the fire. "I think it best we annul this mockery."

Edmund's laughter echoed, disturbing the quiet tension of the room. "So the little mouse has convinced herself that she's a she-wolf." Oblivious of his nudity, he rose off the bed and strode to a side table. Choosing a crystal decanter, he removed the stopper and poured himself a drink. Amused by her unwavering expression, he offered with uncharacteristic courtesy, "Some wine to steady your nerves? Reaffirm your hollow mettle?" He saluted her and raised the glass to his lips.

She wet her lips in a nervous gesture, never taking her gaze from his glass. What would it take? One swallow. Perhaps two. She never confessed to having the skills of an apothecary. Not that the distinction would matter if she succeeded. It would, however, still make her a murderess. A lump of panic tightened her throat as sure as any gallows noose. What was she doing? To proceed would only prove her soul was as barren as Edmund's. Clearing her throat, she attacked, hoping the words she chose would discharge her desperate attempt at escape. "I do not need that poison to sustain my courage. However, please, quench whatever thirst you have, sir, for it will not be slaked from my blood this eve!" Her mouth curled upward into a triumphant smile when he lowered the glass to his waist. "Besides, a drunken fool is much easier to manipulate," she purred.

"Bitch!" he cursed. Again he raised his glass to his lips,

but he hesitated to drink. Grimacing, he issued forth a strangled roar, then smashed the glass against the wall. Splintered shards of crystal and drops of wine skittered across the rug. As if the act had not satisfied him, he swept his arm over the table, sending the numerous decanters crashing to the floor.

Seemingly unaffected by his wrath, she turned from him and stared into the fire. "You have given me more reasons than not to seek this." She risked a sidelong glance when she felt the heat of his body near her. He looked as if he would kill her if she dared to speak again. She closed her eyes. "Let us end this before someone truly gets hurt." The hair on the back of her neck prickled when he moved behind her. He used silence as other men would use a rapier to slice and puncture her confidence and composure. She remained motionless, withstanding his subtle attack. It was his warm breath against her ear that almost completely undid her.

"Did you know when you stand in front of the fire, like this, all rosy and golden, your muslin gown offers me the most delicious silhouette of your naked body," he taunted.

"No!" She did not know which was more horrifying, his revelation or the erection he pressed against her backside.

"Did you think to tease me with your delectable form, believing I would grant you anything as long as I was bewitched by your charms?" He spun her around to face him and shook her, squeezing her upper arms, grinding flesh to bone. "Did you?"

"No. Edmund, you are hurting me!"

"What? You have my attention, and like a fickle strumpet you deny me your wares." He rubbed his chapped lips across her brow, down the angle of her nose, his ultimate goal her mouth. As he drew nigh, she turned her face away. Angered, he bit her ear. Her cry of pain pleased him. Licking the salt of her flesh from his lips, he gripped her chin and forced her to look at him. "You will not leave me. Never," he rasped with violent emotion. "I think it is time to claim what is mine by

God and law." One hand slid up her side until it cupped the warm weight of her breast. He squeezed the pliant flesh.

She spat in his face.

Taking advantage of his shock, she broke free, her eyes wild, and searched for a weapon to fend him off. Skidding on shards of glass and spilled wine, she stumbled, landing face first on Edmund's bed. A wooden bowl filled with red apples toppled over with the motion, revealing a small knife. She seized the scarred handle and whirled around, halting his angry stride.

"I would reconsider your decision, husband," she panted, cradling her injured ear. "Place me in your bed, and I vow my blade will split your devil's heart!"

Chapter One

She was free of him. Never would she cower in his presence again. That morning she had shed her title of Countess of Lathom as easily as a butterfly its chrysalis, and in its place she chose the simple name Tessa Belanger. The name belonged to a long-dead ancestor, but no one knew enough about her family to recognize it.

She looked up at the blustery black clouds surging overhead. Snow. As the word faded from her mind, tiny beads of ice fell from the sky, stinging her wind-burned cheeks. If she had been superstitious, she would have considered it a bad omen.

"Ginger nuts, miss?" A low but decidedly feminine voice rasped behind her.

Pulling the edges of her brown and cream cloak together, she spun around to confront her unwelcome companion. It was difficult to identify the gender of the person wrapped from head to foot in tattered clothing that even the rag-and-bone man would have been reluctant to accept. Still, she assumed the muffled creature was a woman. The multicolored fabrics and textures were out of place on the frozen London streets, almost mocking to the gloomy setting. "I beg your pardon?"

"Nuts, pretty."

The woman removed the ragged scrap of cloth from her face. She was several heads shorter and many stone heavier, but she had a kind smile when she exposed her blackened teeth.

"Wurmed nuts t'ease an empty ache in yer gut on a biting morn such as this." She beckoned for Tessa to follow. "Me bones clank like brittle sticks in the wind." As if to emphasize her discomfort, she rubbed her back. She cocked her head to one side. "I left me cart near the wall. Come, miss."

Nervous, Tessa glanced down the street, noting with dismay that they were alone. She had chosen a less traveled street to await the stagecoach's arrival to avoid discovery. Now she wished she were sitting with the rough company of the public inn. "I have little coin," she confessed, resisting the persistent tug at her elbow.

"A pence, miss, surely ye 'ave that?"

"Well, yes . . . I suppose."

"Good gel! 'Tis a fool that spurns a friendly-like act o' kindness." The woman patted her on the arm as she pulled her down a narrow alley.

Tessa could feel the woman's light grip subtly tighten. She opened her mouth to suggest that she preferred to remain where she was, but a beefy hand silenced her. Before the horror of what was about to occur marked her face, she was shoved against the wall. The sharp point of a blade pricking her throat held her there.

"Nary a peep, o' this won't be friendly," the woman threatened. She whistled twice. From the shadows another vagrant appeared.

"Ye cot a fresh one, Sallie! An' wit looks too!" He leered, tugging the brown bonnet from Tessa's head, revealing her features. He clucked his tongue in appreciation of the prize they possessed. Sallie punched him in the throat. Choking, he stumbled backward to avoid another attack.

"Arse!" she hissed. "The likes o' her stick close like tykes. Rattle yer cock-loft, ye gull, an' pinch the strings."

The man removed a wicked, sharp knife from the back of his worn trousers. He chuckled, and his bearded smile showed an absence of teeth when Tessa could not prevent herself from whimpering. Raising the knife to her face, he brandished the blade before her terror-filled wide eyes, then slipped it into her cloak and deftly cut the reticule from her wrist. He shoved a grimy hand into the soft velvet opening and pulled out her watch.

"No!" Tessa cried out, but Sallie's knife dug into her flesh, reminding her that she was not in a position to protest. The man grinned as he tucked the watch into his trousers. He dumped the remaining contents of the reticule into the street. A lace handkerchief, a small ivory comb, and a few silver coins fell into the half-frozen filth.

"A pittance, Sal," he grumbled, picking up the comb and coins and stuffing them down his shirt. "Seems she should be the one wit the blade."

Sallie grabbed Tessa's jaw and shoved her head against the stone wall. "Ye think me a fool, gel? Spat, hold yer pick to 'er flesh."

The sharp nails digging into her cheeks were replaced with the lethal coldness of Spat's knife. Tessa swallowed the scream threatening to rise with her bile as he lightly caressed the sensitive area behind her ear with the tip. Her frantic gaze shifted to the alley's entrance, even praying for Edmund's timely arrival.

"Perhaps I may be of assistance?" a masculine voice calmly interjected, startling them. He wielded a walking stick that bore a deadly steel daggerlike point at the end. "Release her at once!" His piercing gaze expected nothing but obedience.

Without a word to his cohort, Spat ran down the alley, disappearing into the shadows. Sallie roared with rage, surprising the man by swinging her heavy fist at his head. He blocked the blow with a sickening crack of his stick. The woman screamed in pain. Heedless of the consequences, she rushed him with amazing agility, knocking him to the ground. She kept running until she, too, was out of sight.

"Damn," the man swore. With a grunt he sat up gingerly, testing his ribs. "I handled that rather badly," he muttered to himself.

Tessa slumped against the wall, relieved she had escaped unscathed and fully clothed. Her relief was brief as she watched her bruised champion rise from the mud. He was a large man; the width of his shoulders alone seemed to be twice the size of Edmund's. His hat had been knocked to the ground in the struggle, exposing slick black hair suggesting he had just finished his morning ablutions. With another curse, he reached down for his hat and slapped it against his cloak before placing it on his head. Her eyes widened when he strode toward her. He knelt in front of her, retrieving her ruined bonnet and reticule. She opened her mouth to thank him, but the cold blue gaze he pinned her with when he stood killed any thoughts of gratitude.

"Lady, what maggot do you have rattling inside that hollow head of yours to make you even consider walking down a street like this unescorted?"

He shoved her possessions into her hands, then marched up to the main street as if searching for someone. Returning, he removed his hat, then threaded his gloved hand through his hair. His gaze settled on her. It was the first time he had actually looked at her, and what he saw made his lips thin into a grim line.

"Where is your maid?" he asked, noting the expensive cloak she wore. "No proper woman would be alone . . ." he began, the dawning that she probably was not one showing plainly on his face.

He assumed she was someone's mistress.

"Your protector is a fool to allow you so much freedom. Come, tell me his name so I can thank him for this inconvenience.'' He reached for her cheek, assessing the crescent-shaped wounds on her face. She surprised him by slapping his hand away.

He smiled, though there was little humor in the expression. ''If you were mine, I would take better care of you.''

''Then I consider myself fortunate, sir.'' Tessa edged her way along the wall to the street.

''I did not rescue you from those footpads only to release you unescorted so they may chance upon a second opportunity.'' He started after her.

''They have already taken everything I valued,'' she lied, unconsciously touching the gold locket concealed beneath her walking dress. Inside, it contained a miniature, the only remembrance of her dead sister. She was grateful the thieves had not found it. ''I possess nothing to tempt the simplest of rogues.''

''It is a matter I would not lightly wager, Miss—?''

She halted in the middle of the street, her attention froze on his carriage. Her disposition switched rapidly from shock, confusion, and recognition to certain distress. She turned her wide eyes to him. ''You are an earl,'' she said, not pleased with the revelation.

He did not bother to acknowledge or deny her claim. ''The equipage is mine. If you will tell me where you live, I will see that my man takes you home.''

''That will not be necessary.''

He might as well have offered to give her a ride in a used chamber pot. *God's teeth, another earl!* The thought of sitting next to one of her husband's peers gave her a slashing pain through her skull. She pivoted and walked away in the opposite direction.

''You will break your neck at that pace,'' he yelled.

His warning only made her lift her skirts higher and run without glancing back. She would not return to Edmund.

* * *

"Ungrateful wench!" Reave Alden, Earl of Wycke shouted to her retreating figure. He was tempted to leave her alone on the streets.

Quite tempted.

She deserved her ruinous undoing for not having the common sense to accept his offer. Unless, he began to rationalize, her encounter with the thieves had addled her senses. Certainly, her reactions toward him had been odd from the start. Regretting what he was about to do, he stepped up his pursuit. She was only a few buildings ahead of him, but the smooth-soled boots he wore could not keep up with the iron pattens she had attached to her shoes. His heel struck a patch of ice, throwing him off balance and his feet from under him. He landed on his back in an awkward heap. When Reave sat up, he was cursing an empty street.

Chapter Two

"Good God, man, I know he is in there!"

Reave raised his head, wearily focusing on the closed door of his study. He recognized the exasperated voice of his lifelong friend, Kim Farrell, Viscount Turnberry. Tossing aside the document he was holding, he awaited the explosion. He was rarely disappointed when it came to his friend's deviltry.

Kim considered himself a part of Reave's small family, a notion that had not set well with his manservant, Maxwell, who along with most of the staff considered himself an adopted relative. The two battled at every opportunity, and Reave was, in general, too amused to intervene. Unfortunately, it was the pain in his back rather than his souring mood that prevented him from ending their argument.

Reave ground his teeth together every time he recalled the mishap that morning with the irritating wench. She had unmanned him without laying a soiled gloved hand on him.

His fist propped against his jaw slipped at a sudden thud. The image of his servant's head striking the door came to mind. Before he could rise to intervene, the heavy oak door groaned on its hinges as it swung open. Kim drifted in, unaffected by the altercation. Reave leaned to one side to check on the welfare of his servant. The man was not in view.

"Not to worry, ol' boy." The viscount brushed at the dark stain on his sleeve. "Maxie is unharmed, and most likely sulking." Kim stopped fussing with his coat, and his lower lip lost a little of its aristocratic stiffness at the sight of his host. Reave's unexpected condition caused a moment's hesitation before he dryly remarked, " 'Tis a pity, I cannot state the same for you. Been run over by a carriage lately?"

"Feels like it." He shifted, stifling the groan the movement urged. "Actually, I rescued a woman from two footpads this morning. It is damn embarrassing to discover I am too old to act on my chivalrous principles." It was depressing to be brought low at the age of two and thirty.

Kim chuckled and winked. "Knuckled you to your knees, did she?"

"I either confess to that or admit I was undone by a chunk of ice." Reave rubbed his eyes, blurry from the long hours of reading. Suddenly, he recalled the manner of his friend's entrance. "Have you ever considered trying to oblige Maxwell by just waiting to be announced?"

"And spoil my fun? Never!" He dropped into the nearest chair and tossed his hat. It landed on a small marble-surfaced table, where it slid across the smooth top and fell to the floor. Kim shrugged, then gestured toward the pile of books and papers on the desk in front of him. "An upcoming trial?"

"No, I am settling a few details on the MacAllistor case before I leave London."

Kim raised a curious brow at this revelation. "Good God, at this time of year? Whatever could entice you from your old dusty texts and dull contracts to travel out to the country? I warrant you'll have frozen your arse to the seat before you leave town."

"Most likely, but I cannot dismiss my obligation this year. If you were an attentive uncle, you would recall that Jason's birthday will be upon us soon." The awkwardness of mentioning his son made Reave reach for the nearest stack of papers. Work had always dulled the pain.

"By the bye, how old is the runt this year? I never seem to keep track of such things."

"Six. He will be six," Reave replied, his brusque tone matching his actions. Realizing he had destroyed the order of his drafts, with resignation he allowed the papers to slip from his hands. Distracted, he rubbed the sharp pain in his left temple. "Why are you here?"

"Have you always been this forgetful, or was it an intentional slight?" Kim blandly inquired while pulling at each finger before removing his leather gloves.

Puzzlement wrinkled his handsome features. "Kim? What the devil are you about?"

"I said, my inattentive companion, that you forgot about our meeting at the Clarestines' rout."

Grateful for a less threatening topic, Reave widened his smile as he replied, "Ah, but I did not say that I would attend the engagement. I merely commented that I would meet you later." He sat back in his chair and waited for Kim to react to his baiting.

"You, sir, are a scoundrel and a liar!" the viscount charged with mock outrage. "Philmore was present with us at White's when you confirmed you would attend the gathering. You even remarked that you cherished the talents of Miss Amelia Clarestine and anticipated a reintroduction."

"You misconstrued my words," he explained. "Would you care for something to drink? Brandy? Port? Something warm? Perhaps some tea? If Maxwell has recovered from his injuries—"

"To Hades with Maxwell, and cease this prate of courtesy!" Kim jumped up, bracing his palms on the desk that separated them. His eyes narrowed. "I know you too well. Wycke. It is unlike you to play with words."

Reave interjected a harsh laugh that seemed only to incense

his friend. "You do not know me as well as you charge. My first duty may be that of Earl of Wycke; however, I am also a barrister. I am a man whose very profession is to play with words. My days are spent manipulating and interpreting words, which we call *law,* to the better of my patron. From my reputation, I think I have proven myself adequate to the taskwork."

Kim pushed off the desk and returned to his chair, shaking his head. "I confess you are a credit to your craft, but alas, we digress. I believe we were speaking of your absence from the soirée."

Reave's eyelids narrowed with predatory coolness. He sat back and studied his friend. "Why was my presence so important to you this evening?"

"No reason," Kim replied, attempting to meet Reave's intense scrutiny, but failing. "Damn your eyes! Your unsettling manner of dissecting a man with that stare may be extremely useful in your profession but a damn nuisance when it comes to more casual exchanges." Slapping his gloves against his palm, the viscount gave up his pretension, confessing, "I concede, there was a small deception—this, given your nature, you have already surmised."

"I look forward to your explanation." Reave crossed his arms, giving him a look a father might give to his errant son.

"It began as a sport of matchmaking betwixt Philmore and myself. You had mentioned that you admired Miss Clarestine's voice, and I—"

"I made no such comment."

"The devil you did. You said that you had admired her talents, and since the chit was supposed to sing tonight, I assumed . . ." Kim's voice faded at the incrédulous expression on Reave's face.

"This is rich, my friend, and so unlike you to be so dimwitted," he chuckled. "I have regrettably endured a few evenings with Miss Clarestine's voice in attendance. I do not think I am unjust by likening her singing to a squeaky axle joint." Reave lost the shuttered expression he usually cultivated, indulging in a moment of unconcealed amusement.

"You jest!"

"Think, man. Philmore is a distant cousin of the irritating chit's, and it would have been offensive if I had spoken otherwise. Besides, what I said was not altogether false." Reave rubbed his knuckles against his jaw while he paused. It was a dramatic gesture he often used in court and found it difficult to keep such affectations from bleeding into his private life. "There is much to admire about Miss Amelia, and none have anything to do with her voice."

"So you are attracted to her. Philmore was correct."

"Not exactly, but I am neither dead." Reave shrugged, the slight smile thinning at the irony of the statement. It had been six years since he had been ruled by his heart. However, his body was another matter. "So, how much did you lose?"

Stunned by his accurate deduction, Kim could only stare openmouthed. "How did you know?"

"It was your insistence that exposed you. How much?"

"Lady Pratt laid down a monkey that you would not attend, and the cursed gambling soul I possess could not leave off from accepting the wager," he grudgingly confessed.

"Maggs shall enjoy collecting your silver. Knowing her well, I predict she will make it a public spectacle."

"Maggs?" Her name was barely a whisper upon his lips as Kim considered the ramifications of Reave's acquaintance with the beautiful and recently widowed Lady Pratt. "You bastard! You knew about the wager and allowed the cunning witch to taunt me into accepting the bet." The look on Reave's face confirmed his suspicions. "Damn. You have abused our friendship. By rights I should call you out," he said, more amused than angered at being caught.

"Ha! Roil in your criminations, but it was your advantageous knowledge of my plans that led to your lighter pockets. You would have unconscionably cozened her money without hesitation, yet you condemn her for the same crime." He shook his

Barbara Pierce

head, muttering, "Both of you should be chastised like children for wagering on my personal affairs."

"So that is the way of things," Kim wondered aloud.

"Maggs is a grown woman and sees our relationship for what it truly is." He studied his hands momentarily before continuing. "Elise is gone. I doubt she would fault me for succumbing to my baser instincts after all these years?"

"No, no, she was a good woman. 'Bout time, actually. I was beginning to think we had placed you in the mausoleum with her." There was an awkward silence. Clearing his throat, Kim said, "Say, I am off to search for your Lady Maggie and bear the humiliation of my loss. Perhaps she will be kind if you are there to distract her?"

"I wish I could witness your humility; unfortunately, I have another engagement." Reave walked around his desk, stopping only to retrieve his friend's hat that covered the spidery legs of the small serpentine table. "I plan to leave tomorrow. You are welcome at Eastcott if you would consider joining our celebration." The ghost of a mocking smile faded as quickly as it surfaced "Your visits stir Jason in a manner that I never seem to do." He offered the hat.

Embarrassed, Kim gave him a sheepish smile. "Oh, I suppose I am a novelty to the boy." He tucked his hat under his arm, then tugged his gloves over his hands. "If it is possible, I will join you at the end of the week." He walked to the door, hesitated, then turned back to his friend. "Jason has a fine example of a father. You have just been remiss in showing it."

An hour later, Reave sat in the cold darkness of his carriage, thinking about Kim's parting words. Damn, he knew his relationship with Jason vacillated between cool detachment and suppressed hostility, but he could never find a way to reach the boy. If truthful, there was a part of him that did not want to, the part of him that found the pain was still there if he dared to press the wound.

It had begun otherwise, when his beautiful flaxen-haired Elise had confessed that she was increasing, but then, he had been a different man seven years ago. They had been fortunate, theirs had been a love match, and the prospect of her bearing his children had filled him with euphoria. He had insisted that they settle in the country at Eastcott, his ancestral home, and Elise, so radiantly pleased with her growing condition, readily agreed.

Reave squeezed his eyes tightly shut, wishing he could banish the memory playing only for him in the darkened box of his carriage, the hideous tale always continuing until its mortal conclusion. With the passing years, it had become easier to suppress the vivid memories, cruel and gruesome in their details of his private agony, but this time of year was different. He could not hold back the demons, as much as he could not have her back. Allowing his head to fall against the cold leather seat, he opened his mind, welcoming the hateful specters that held his head, pried opened his eyes, ever gleeful that he was forced to watch.

The uneventful yet cherished months after her announcement flashed in his mind, then slowed to the final month of her confinement. He had been summoned to town, and Elise had encouraged him to go. Reave recalled that she had kissed him to still his protesting tongue, but her kisses were never successful in quieting any part of him.

Sometimes, when he concentrated, he could still feel the gentle pressure of her lips pressed to his own, still smell the sweet scent of her flesh, though he had learned to leave such recollections buried. The insatiable hunger remaining after the memory had faded like summer morning mist, left him shaken and so alone he was certain he would go mad. He never knew when she had kissed him that day, it would be the last time he would be able to look into her eyes and see the love she held for him in her heart.

Her labor had begun two days later. Not trusting a midwife, Reave insisted the physician be summoned. He felt an educated man would be better able to care for his precious wife than a woman, who would simply sit by his suffering wife's side and work on her stitching. Not wanting to concern her husband, Elise followed his instructions, sending a servant into the night to find the man, but the night was early, leaving her many hours to suffer alone until the man her beloved husband trusted could aid her.

When the man did arrive, he was drunk, having been called away from a small gathering. He assured the wide-eyed, frightened staff that he was quite fit to handle the birth. Everyone was too grateful to have someone alleviate their lady's suffering to contradict him. The birth had been messy and difficult, Reave had been told. Elise's screams echoed the halls through the night, and a silent vigil for her release was kept on bent knees. He learned later that the child had been caught inside her. The man used a strange instrument unknown to the frightened yet watchful maid to coax the babe out of the womb. With clumsy drunkenness, he pulled the baby from Elise's bloodied, writhing body, inadvertently crushing the fragile skull with his actions. His wife had not been aware of their daughter. With haunting screams that bordered on madness and a rush of her life's blood, she pushed out another babe. A son. As if knowing she was through with her work, she then lost consciousness.

When Reave arrived the next forenoon, she was almost gone. Walking by the servant holding his flailing, red-faced son, he knelt at his wife's bedside. He knew as he hugged her against his chest that his Elise was dying. Her once-rosy-tinted lips were blue, an unnatural contrast to her deathly pale skin. Whispering promises of life and love he knew he could not keep, she slipped away from him as easily as her blood had spilled from her ravaged body. She was dead.

A wheel dropped into a hole, causing the carriage to lurch to the right, jarring Reave from the grisly image of his dead wife. He had not noticed his tears until they had begun to freeze on his cheeks, leaving stinging trails. Wiping a woolen sleeve over his eyes, he tried to stanch his bitterness, crying in anguish, "Forgive me, my love." Reave reached out into the unyielding blackness, grasping at the grief-induced phantom, allowing the coldness to engulf him.

A half hour later, the carriage halted at the residence of Lady Pratt. A composed Reave stepped out, inhaling the crisp night air. The broken, embittered man had been neatly tucked away as if he had been made of linen. It was the passing years that now eased the ache, making it easier for the mind to sweep aside the sad memories when they visited him.

"I was beginning to think I would retire alone," Maggs drawled from the open doorway. Something in his expression arrested her sulk. Giving up her pretentious role of siren, she drew him into the foyer. "Reave, darling, what is amiss?"

He knew he did not love her, and he cursed himself for a fool as she gazed up at him with eyes clouded with concern. Desperate, he crushed her to him, attempting to quell the dark, tormenting whispers that reminded him that love was something now absent from his life.

"Reave?"

He lifted her chin as his lips descended to her soft, inviting mouth. "Make me forget," he whispered before hungrily claiming what was so eagerly offered.

Chapter Three

"The food looks bland but edible."

Tessa nodded to the man across from her, although her own bowl of soup remained untouched. She had passed the morning within the public inn. The angry earl she had escaped must have thought her cracked, but she had not been inclined to explain her aversion to earls, nor her reluctance to return home. Remaining would have forced her to answer questions she had not been prepared to address.

Initially, she had avoided the inn, afraid Edmund would send men out in search of her. However, the harsh lesson of being alone in the streets forced her to reconsider her decision. Still, she could not find comfort within the crowded room. Every patron was a potential enemy. Her gaze flickered to the man across from her.

Vivid green eyes reflected genuine concern as they strayed from her eyes to the wounds on her cheeks. "Has some man hurt you? Your face?" the handsome stranger asked.

Self-conscious, she covered the marks with her gloved hand.

"I was foolish enough to fall for the ruse of some clever footpads."

"How did you escape them?"

The image of her reluctant champion flashed in her mind. "A noise in the street frightened them away," she improvised, deciding not to complicate the tale by mentioning the earl. She had learned from Edmund long ago that the best lies were the ones told in the simplest terms. "I wish the stage would arrive soon." She glanced wistfully at the closed door before remembering her curious companion. "Forgive me. I have been eager to leave London, and my violent encounter with those footpads has heightened my desire for haste."

"I quite understand, Miss—?" He gifted her with a smile meant to charm even the sternest countenance.

"Miss Tessa Belanger," she said without hesitation. Her past was dead; it was time to try her new identity on someone. "Mr.—?"

He slanted his head and bowed. "Kim Farrell, just Kim if it pleases you." His smile dimmed as he grew thoughtful. "Pardon my interest, Miss Belanger, but why are you alone? Your speech and dress have all the markings of gentle rearing, yet you sit in this establishment without a chaperone, nor servants."

Tessa sniffed into the handkerchief. Her mind was spinning with several plausible explanations, but she was too nervous to grasp more than an image or two. There was a certain thrill to this latest game she had chosen to play. Her blood pounded in her ears, and her skin tingled with acute anticipation of being caught. She glanced again at the door. "I was on a quest. Now it is over."

"You have whetted my curiosity, Miss Belanger. A quest, indeed!" Kim lifted his pewter tankard of ale and took a hearty toss. He gestured for her to continue with a wave of his fist.

"I speak not of a tale that one tells others on a cold night before a blazing hearth. Rather, mine is one of those nasty snippets of gossip that is bandied about a crowded ballroom or a gentleman's club.'' She shuddered, an aftereffect of her tears. ''Six months ago I discovered the woman who had raised me since birth was nothing more than a common blackmailer.''

''Your mother?''

She shook her head. ''No, my aunt. I was told my mother and father had been killed by a fever, but that, too, was a lie. After my aunt's death, I discovered letters confirming that fact. My mother had run off to Venice with a lover, leaving me in the care of her younger sister. My aunt dedicated her life to raising me to be a proper lady while she blackmailed my father. He paid for her silence, so it was never revealed to his wife and children that he had a bastard—me.'' All things considered, she thought her fictitious past worked quite well. There was no one to verify or impugn it. *Except for Edmund.*

He tried to ease her obvious torment. ''It must have been a shock to learn the truth.'' He took her hand and gave it a comforting squeeze when she nodded. ''You are not the first to have an ignoble birth. Do not allow the shame to ruin your life.'' Kim paused as a revelation struck him. ''You came to London to find your father,'' he said more as a fact than query.

''Yes. I wanted to see him, to tell him that no one would ever ask him for another groat, that his secret was safe, but I was too late. I was told he had died.''

Kim tapped his steepled fingers on his nose, digesting this bit of news. ''I assume your father moved within the ton and did not feel secure enough to weather the scandal.''

''Very few do, sir,'' she replied, thinking bitterly of her own experiences.

''What was his name? Foster?''

''No. I—I . . . his name is of no consequence. Let the man have the peaceful repose he was denied in life.''

She turned at the sound of the door opening. The northern wind burst between the four men who had entered, chilling the conversation. Unaware their entrance had interrupted the comforting warmth of the room, they argued with the quiet man who walked one step ahead of them. Ignoring his companions, the man strode to the hearth to warm his hands. A barmaid handed him a tankard of ale.

"Aw, Tom."

"Out wit' it!"

"We all want to hear the news."

Tessa gave Kim a questioning look. He shrugged and took a sip of his ale. The room had hushed. Everyone was straining to hear the stranger's news.

"Settle yourselves an' all may hear," the man called Tom said, striking his tankard on a table to gain attention. The gesture was unnecessary. They had been observed since their boisterous arrival. "Gents, an', er, ladies. I bear news of the vilest lot. Ladies, I think it best that the weak-hearted close off their ears." He emptied his tankard, pausing to allow a kind girl to refill it.

"Miss Belanger?" Kim queried with a raised blond brow.

She did not realize he had spoken until he touched her on the sleeve. "Pardon? Oh, nonsense," she whispered back, ignoring the unsettling feeling that fluttered in her stomach. Silly chit! No one knew her whereabouts, and within the hour she would vanish from this town, ending Lady Lathom and her miserable existence.

". . . this very morn." The man's voice interrupted her thoughts. "There he was in his own house, a man of the peerage, found dead! Stabbed he was, in the heart, a thousand times over, and his throat had been ripped open as if a vicious hellhound had pried it open with its lethal jaws." Tom demonstrated with his fingers. Several of the women cried out in horror. One caused a stir by collapsing to the floor in a dead faint. Tom's eyes glittered with excitement. "An' he was nude, defenseless against this monstrous brutality. An' there's more," he said, nodding his head to confirm his own words. "His fancy piece met a similar fate. The poor wench was stabbed in the back as she tried to flee from the murderous butcher!"

"Who was the chap?"

The question was shouted from someone behind Tessa, startling her. Despite the warmth of the hearth, she suddenly felt cold.

"I'll be telling it in my own way, man! There's more to the patient ear," he yelled back, angry that he had been interrupted. Lowering his voice, he went on. "They say it was the wife, yea, the wife who struck the fatal blows, bloodying her lily-white hands." He waited until the numerous gasps and murmurs from the patrons had quieted before continuing. "There be witnesses who will swear she threatened her kind husband with a scathing vow that could wane a randy cock. All agree, she had the ice in her blood to wield the blade." He took a swig of ale, pleased he had been the first to carry the tale to the inn.

"So who was snuffed?" someone demanded, which was punctuated by several words of concord.

Tom, enjoying the attention, took his time wiping his wet whiskers on his sleeve before replying. "He was Edmund Tratton, Earl of Lathom. May God have mercy on his soul." He raised his tankard in salutation.

Kim almost choked on his ale. "Good God!" he exclaimed.

"Sweet mercy! This is madness!" Tessa cried out, then stuffed her fist into her mouth, smothering the scream that threatened to surface. Without thought to the man beside her, she blindly ran to the door, pushing her way through a group of men before disappearing into the light. She managed a few steps, then fell to her knees and vomited. Dead! Murdered! Condemned villainess! Her mind screamed the words as her throat strained convulsively. Her mother. Her mother was dead. She must have joined Edmund sometime that night after their fight. She clutched her stomach and heaved again. The weight of her cloak fell gently across her shoulders while Kim's soothing voice in her ear coaxed her to stand and accept his comfort.

"Shhh, the worst has passed." He rubbed her back, allowing her to cry into his chest.

"He is dead." She shook her head in disbelief.

"Aye, that is the ill rumor."

She pulled back, her gaze searching for something akin to understanding in his kind face. "I—I did not—"

"I know," he said with a trace of pity. "The man was vulgar to repeat such news in the presence of a lady. Your reaction is not surprising." Espying his carriage, he raised his cane to signal his coachman. "However, I fear your tears are misplaced, Miss Belanger. Lathom was said to be consumed by a savage nature, and unworthy of your compassion."

"He said the wife—the wife," she stammered, too upset to continue.

Kim shrugged as he attempted to guide her closer to the street. "If one believes the gossip, then the lady had good reason to carry out the deed."

She gave him a malevolent look before tugging her arm from his grasp and marched off in the opposite direction. Fear had dried her tears, sobering her to the notion that if she was recognized on the streets, she had little chance of being justly tried.

"Tessa! Miss Belanger!" Kim pursued her, catching her with ease. He knew what he was about to do was insane, but he never could resist a woman who needed protecting, whether or not she was aware of it.

"Take your hands off me," she hissed, trying not to draw attention to them as she struggled to break free. "I must leave." She thought of the stagecoach that could have taken her to her father's estate. It would be searched, she was certain. There had to be another way she could leave town without being noticed. Panting from the strain, she stared at him with a contemplating expression on her face. She reached under the collar of her gown and pulled out her gold locket. With a violent jerk she freed the chain from her neck. "Here. Take it." She pressed it into his unresisting palm. "I will leave London now, with or without your assistance. Is it enough to pay for my journey? The thieves took everything else."

He gave the locket only a cursory glance. "What of the stage, surely—"

"After what has occurred, do you think I could tolerate this town another minute? The stage could take hours, days—oh, never mind!" She snatched the locket from his hand and turned to walk away.

"Please hear me out," he said, weighing the anger of his friend against the need of this unprotected beauty. "I understand your desire to leave, but where will you go? Will you live off the blackmail money that is left, or did you use it to fund your trip to London?" She opened her mouth to speak, but he held up a hand to silence her. "I suspect we both know the answer to that. Now, I propose a solution to your plight. I cannot in good faith place you unescorted on a stage. However, it is your good fortune that I am on my way to the Earl of Wycke's country home. Not only is he a good friend, he is also a barrister who could discreetly look into your father's estate."

She was speechless. The slight widening of her eyes was the only indication that she heard his offer. Finally, she uttered, "I cannot ask this of you, sir."

"He has the finest reputation," he resumed, ignoring her reply. "The man enjoys this sort of business. Consider the matter settled."

"Sir!"

"Kim," he corrected her as they approached his carriage.

"There is no propriety in—" she sputtered.

"Ah, but we have yet to follow the sways of convention. Why dull this maddening adventure with decorum?"

Tessa glanced at the people about her, expecting one of them to point and shout "Murderess!" They walked on, concerned only with their own affairs. Kim halted in front of his carriage. Her gaze met his as he waited for her to acquiesce. She stifled a groan when she saw the crest. "You are titled also?"

"Viscount Turnberry," he confessed, critically appraising her paling complexion.

"A viscount and an earl. I am indeed fortunate." Her tone implied she felt otherwise. Sighing, she offered her hand, which he took without hesitation. "I predict you may regret your role in this entanglement."

Unmoved by her warning, he gave her a brilliant smile. "Never! I relish playing the role of the chivalrous protector to your virtuous lady."

"Kim, you have permission to call me by my Christian name," she said, quietly settling in the seat opposite her foolish new friend. "Any man who blindly accepts a role without first reading the play certainly deserves to walk beyond the bonds of etiquette."

Chapter Four

"No, absolutely not." Reave pushed his fingers through his black hair, clenching the slight curl at the ends.

"But—"

"It is not a case that would interest me. Moreover, I have made other plans," he said, dismissing the subject. His pride and backside were still stinging from his encounter with the thankless chit, and this had precipitated into an irritable disposition and no tolerance for his friend's persistence.

Hayden Quinn frowned, his brown eyes troubled as he contemplated an argument to sway his friend. Being a solicitor, he could only bring the brief to Wycke's attention. His kind were not allowed to go before the court. This should have bothered him more than it did, but until this day, theirs had been a mutually satisfying arrangement.

Although a barrister could not have a partner, Hayden considered himself as one. They had both become quite renowned with Reave's successes, leaving him to collect the fees for their services. "Consider the attention this one will create. Your name will be on everyone's tongue within a day."

Reave cared little for invitations to balls and even less for the gossip. "You know as well as I that my time is spent in the Chancery Court. You should be seeking a sergeant for the King's Bench. I am certain Hartcord would welcome the honor."

"This concerns you more than you believe. Lathom died intestate! There is no heir apparent as far as anyone can prove." Wycke, damn him, did not even bother to appear interested with that bit of information. He tried another tactic. "Besides, I need your talents to help me put this one together. Let Hartcord argue the damn thing, but I need that perceptive mind of yours to sort through it all. You are wasted here, my friend, unless you have the aspirations of becoming a bencher or lord chancellor?"

His brow rose at the thought of becoming King's Counsel. It was an honor and a goal he did not consider lightly, but he had to agree with Hayden that he did enjoy plying his intellect to preparing the briefs of the more complicated cases. This was not the first time he had been asked to assist with a criminal case. The missing elements had always intrigued him. He had an aptness for rearranging those missing pieces in his head until they fit perfectly in place like a child's wooden puzzle. "Praise works well on women and dogs. I suggest you seek out your wife."

"Claire is too spoiled to appreciate the difference between praise and manipulation, and you—you are just too damn intelligent!" Hayden gnashed his teeth at the earl's low chuckle. Disgruntled, he looked out the window at the activity below. "The snow will keep you in town if it worsens."

"Possibly. It won't change my mind."

"We knew the man. Do we not owe him justice?"

Reave brushed aside the question with a dismissing wave of his hand. "The man might have moved in the same circles, still, I would be hard pressed to call Lathom my friend. His habits were sickening to even the most stalwart of bowel. No, what amazes me is that he lived as long." He paused, thoughtfully tapping his finger to his lower lip. "Did you know the wife?"

Hayden shifted, leaning his shoulder against the wall. "Countess? Well, yes, as you mentioned, the same circles and such." He crossed his arms and shifted his stance.

"Do you believe she murdered him?"

"I cannot look inside a woman's mind and know the thoughts of a woman betrayed," he deliberated. "Were you aware Lathom had been flaunting her mother as his latest mistress for a fortnight? 'Tis a pity, for she died for that assignation."

"I assume the ton is ready to hang Lady Lathom, ignoring the fact that she has not been formally charged." He did not need Hayden's confirmation. This was the type of gossip that set everyone to whispering. "Where is she being held?"

"Nowhere, or, rather, she has yet to be found."

Reave did not bother to conceal his amazement. "Has it been considered she, too, might be a victim?"

"Of that I have no doubt. Edmund was a bastard."

Hayden's dimwittedness was beginning to irritate him. "Perhaps, she has met a similar fate?" he clarified. Had no one contemplated the notion?

"If true, her body would have been found in the house," he insisted.

Reave gave him a look of contempt, then he took up his greatcoat and hat. "I believe you have convinced me to look into this case for you after all." Slapping his hat on his head, he shrugged into the black wool greatcoat. "If Lady Lathom must hang, then let it be for her guilt and not because of the passionate cry of retribution from the ton. Condemning an innocent woman nauseates me." He turned to leave.

"You forget yourself. You will be helping those who wish to prosecute her."

"Exactly." He grimaced. "I fear her only chance of justness will be by my hand. The rest of you have already found her guilty."

* * *

Standing in Eastcott's entrance hall should have offered more warmth than the chilly coach ride she had shared with Lord Turnberry. Unfortunately, the gloomy hall offered no relief. Although the exterior of Eastcott, built in the early 1700s, was a fine example of the Palladian style, some ancestor had not been satisfied and had added a Gothic touch to the hall. Elaborate plasterwork and delicate wood-beam cross-hatching competed for space as the two styles climbed the walls and fanned out in a scallop design overhead.

"Cold?" Kim asked behind her, returning from his trip outside to make certain the horses were in the competent hands of the grooms.

Eyeing the weapons of war, body armor, and animal trophies mounted high on the walls as they stepped deeper into the hall, she shivered. *A hunter.* She wondered silently if the ruthless metal and gloating prizes were the present lord's contribution or another ancestor's attempt to leave his mark.

"I am certain I am no colder than you, my lord."

"Kim."

"Yes." She walked ahead, stopping at the bottom of the stairs that led to the next landing and two very ornate balconies. Petting the mahogany balustrade, she tried to think of something polite to say. *Eastcott is a grand old house. Is that gold leaf on the balcony? I have never seen the equal to this marble floor.* She could not tell him her true thoughts. *This place is filled with shadows and ice and something very, very dead.* Without revealing her thoughts, she gestured to a battered tapestry of a hunt. "Is it genuine?"

Kim, knowing Eastcott as well as if it were his own, did not bother to glance at the tapestry. "Most likely. The Aldens have had the title for generations and to my knowledge have never lacked for funds."

"Generations of hunters to hone their skills," Tessa mused. If Kim had heard her, he did not comment. A noise to the right caught his attention. "Ah, there you are, Thorne. You are slipping in your duties. Miss Belanger and I could have made off with half the items in this hall." He affectionately cuffed the elderly man on the shoulder. "This place is as soundless as a crypt. Lucky for you, Miss Belanger and I have arrived to stir up the household. Where is the master of this rustic museum?"

Puzzled, the butler slowly replied, "He is not in residence at this time, Lord Turnberry. Is he expected?" The thought seemed to terrify the man.

"Why, yes. The boy's birthday, you know. The snow must have caused his delay. We had a beastly time getting here ourselves."

The servant's attention focused disapprovingly on Tessa. "Does his lordship know that there will be two of you?"

"No, but I'll straighten out the matter when it comes to light."

The elderly man grunted, not looking very confident in the viscount's abilities. Excusing himself, he left to see to their rooms.

"Uncle Kim!" An excited voice echoed all around them.

"Captain Runt!" Kim returned in lieu of a greeting before the young boy rushing down the stairs launched himself into Kim's open arms. Pretending to be bruised by the assault, Kim painfully struggled to lift him up. The boy giggled at his exaggerated groans and winces. Setting the boy on the floor, he gave the child's black hair an affectionate tousle. "So, imp, how does it feel to be an old man of six?"

"I won't be six till tomorrow." He laughed, tugging playfully on Kim's coat.

"How utterly rattlebrained of me to forget! Remind me to pose the question to you later, then, when you have achieved the proper age."

Tessa watched their exchange with a slight smile on her lips. There was true affection between them. As an outsider, it healed and broke her heart in one stroke.

"Have you come for a visit? How long this time? Did you bring me a surprise?" The boy squirmed with excitement at the prospect for having a playmate.

"Questions, questions." Kim chuckled. "For answers, I must confess, yes . . . I regret only a day or two . . . and, yes." Kim, anticipating the next logical question, added, "No, you may not open it now."

He gestured toward Tessa, who had remained in the background. "I have brought you a new friend. Tessa?" He beckoned her to come closer. "Jason, this is Miss Tessa Belanger. Tessa, may I present Master Jason, Lord Wycke's son and heir."

"An honor, sir." She executed a polite curtsy.

Jason gaped at her with an owlish expression. Taking a step backward, he leaned against Kim's legs. "Uncle Kim, why is she covered in mud? Mr. Luke says it's common work to roll in the mud like livestock."

"Good God, your manners are insufferable!" he scolded lightly, a silent apology shining in his expression as he glanced at Tessa to access her reaction. The trembling smile she gave him worried him. Jason tilted his head back with a questioning look. "In plainest terms, imp, it is rude to comment on a lady's appearance when she is not quite herself." He bent down to the boy's ear. "Apologize."

"Miss Bel—" Jason looked to Kim for assistance.

"Miss Belanger."

Jason bravely took a few steps toward Tessa. "Miss Belanger, I apologize." She met his uneasy gaze. "I think you wear mud very well."

"Jason!" Kim yelped, more from amusement than anger.

Tessa stopped trying to conceal her amusement and laughed, startling both males. She touched Jason's chin so that he could see for himself that she was not upset. "I usually try to restrain myself from rolling in the mud when I plan my calls, but I fear there was little opportunity to change after—" She almost revealed her unidentified hero. "After I chased the footpads away. You see, I had nothing—"

"You were set upon by thieves?" Jason interrupted. "How many were there? Did you use your bare hands or a pistol to fight them off? Did you see any blood?" Her status of importance had risen considerably in his estimation.

Kim clapped a hand over the boy's mouth. "Enough! Miss Belanger can answer all your questions later, when she has a chance to settle into her chamber."

Undaunted, he smiled at his new friend. "Your word?"

Tessa, already half in love, placed her hand on her heart. "On my honor."

Kim lifted Jason up and placed his arm around her in a friendly embrace. "Welcome to Eastcott, Tessa."

A clock somewhere within Eastcott was chiming four when a sleepy footman unlocked the door for Reave. After handing his damp greatcoat and hat to the servant, he took the branch of tallow candles from the man and, with a dismissing grunt, limped off toward the library. He considered the room his private sanctuary, a place to warm his frozen feet. To his surprise, the room had a lingering trace of warmth. The hearth contained remnants of glowing coal within the white ashes. Bemused, he wondered if Thorne had been helping himself to the port. It mattered little to him, since the old man had lived in the house longer than he, and for that he could make allowances.

Once the fire was ablaze, he sat on the edge of his chair and removed his boots. It had grown colder, if that had been at all possible, and the small heating grate in the coach could not compete with the bitter winds. He felt near frozen, but he had arrived in time to celebrate his son's birthday. That had to count for something.

Stretching his legs in front of him, Reave thought about the past two days. They had been hell. His decision to help with the Lathom brief had been impulsive. It was a decision he now regretted. After he had walked out of Hayden's office, curiosity had prompted him to seek out the Lathom residence. It was doubtful the grisly vision of the earl's chamber would ever leave him. The last time he had seen so much blood was when he had held Elise. Reave shifted, recalling the memories of his own past. They were as disturbing and vivid as the dried blood he had seen on Lathom's fine Axminster rugs. He had seen and smelled enough death to last him for eternity. Rising to his feet, he groaned and stretched before heading for the door. He was too exhausted to do anything except briefly wonder why his steward had permitted the large pile of correspondence to amass on his desk. In the morning, he would remind Lawson of his duties, but for now, he was too weary to think.

He had reached the second landing when a muffled sound from overhead made him forget about his warming bed. Instead, he sought out his son's room on the third floor. It was probably the wind rattling a pane, though he felt obligated to confirm his suspicions. The heavy feeling of weariness vanished, and his senses heightened at the sight of the door ajar. Quietly approaching, he could see the shadowy flickering of candlelight dancing off the polished wooden floorboards. Reave licked his finger and thumb, then he pinched the sputtering flames of the silver branch he held, masking his presence with the darkness. He pushed the door open to accommodate his large size, but what he beheld within froze his movements. His heart ceased its steady beat as he tried to make sense of the vision.

His first thought was that she was a ghost.

Her slender form was sheathed in flowing fabric of the softest cream. A golden cascade of waist-length hair shielded his hungry gaze from what he imagined were soft full breasts, a narrow waist, and the inviting curve of swaying hips. Spellbound, he watched her move about the room with unworldly grace. Reave stepped deeper into the shadows, and she paused to look in his direction. He was afraid the vision would fade into the frozen night if she discovered she was being watched by a mortal. When the taper she held permitted a glimpse of her features, he decided she was an angel from the heavens. Seized with the desire to view more of this delicate beauty, to see the color of her eyes, he took a step forward. Hot tallow from the forgotten candelabrum splashed on his hand, awakening him from the spell she had woven around him. Who was she? Somehow it disturbed him to accept that this woman was of flesh rather than of spirit.

She adjusted the blanket Jason had kicked off, then leaned over his head, showering him with her tresses. Reave's throat tightened as he wondered what it would feel like to have those fragrant silky strands caress his face. Horrified by his thoughts, he retreated into the passageway, and waited for her to emerge. Soundlessly, he set the candelabrum on the floor, anticipating that angels were not so easily captured. Minutes ticked by, and she did not appear. He began to believe he had dreamed the nocturnal visit, when the whisper of fabric brushing against wood warned him of her approach. She was within an arm's reach as she backed out and closed the door. Turning, her foot became entangled in the silver detailing of the candelabrum, and she fell, extinguishing her taper.

He caught her, but not before her head struck the middle of his chest. She stiffened at his grunt. This mysterious woman had a few questions to answer in order to gain her release. He could feel the warm, laborious pant of her breath against his chest. Like a wild animal caught in a snare, she twisted and strained for her freedom.

"You are soundly caught," he taunted. He was about to ask her how she came to be in his home, when she kicked him in the instep. The abusive attack on his frozen foot was enough to break his hold. Pain shot up his leg. She screamed and ran toward the stairs.

He pursued her, trailing her by the light footfalls sounding on the wooden flooring. She stumbled more than ran down the stairs to the second landing. Knowing the house even without the benefit of light, he caught up to her with ease when she stopped and struggled to open one of the doors. She screamed the moment he touched her. A door opened farther down the passageway, and a small sliver of the emerging light warmed the darkness. A man clothed only in a dressing gown bounded out. He held a candle in one hand and a pistol in the other. Reave immediately recognized his friend.

"Tessa?" Kim shouted at the two straining figures in the shadows.

Reave slackened his grip, giving her the chance to break free. She ran straight into the viscount's outstretched arm. "Oh, Kim!" she sobbed, the rest of her words indistinguishable against his shoulder.

Kim pushed her behind him. He peered into the darkness at the intruder. "Come out of the shadows, man!" he brusquely ordered. His face reflected his disbelief when the man limped into the light. "What the devil? Reave, what are you doing here?" He lowered the pistol.

"I might turn the question on you, my friend," Reave drawled. His attention flickered to the woman hiding behind Kim.

"If you recall, you invited me, you arse!" Kim moved aside, drawing the woman forward. "You are trembling. My dear, you have nothing to fear from this brooding hulk. This is our overdue host, Reave Alden, the Earl of Wycke. Reave, may I introduce Miss Tessa Belanger."

" 'Tis you," she mouthed, her voice barely an audible squeak, when he stepped closer so she could see his face. From his expression, there was no doubt he had recognized her also. Red-eyed and obviously miserable, she appeared to have thoughts of flight.

"Indeed, you ungrateful waif!" Reave glared at his friend. "Turnberry, have you lost your head? Bringing your mistress here—"

"Mistress!" Kim and Miss Belanger protested in harmonious outrage. His friend explained, "She is under my protection. Nothing more." He shifted his gaze to Miss Belanger, who was glaring at her host as if she wished he would be struck by lightning. "She has lost her family and home. I thought perhaps you could help her inquire into her father's estate," Kim added when Reave appeared unconvinced.

"Kim!" she wailed.

Reave did not know if he wanted to learn the details of how she came to be in his household. His backside was still sore because of her reckless flight from him, and his leg was throbbing from her most recent assault. The woman was a curse! "I have a charitable disposition to the unfortunate, but I do not run a shelter for orphans. Dammit, Kim, she is not a stray cur you can merely feed and shelter at whim then turn back on the streets when you have become bored."

Miss Belanger's chin rose, as did her temper. "How dare you liken me to a cur, you arrogant, self-righteous whoreson!"

Kim clapped a hand over her mouth, silencing her tirade. "I believe what Tessa is attempting to say is that we are all tired and should save this complicated discussion until the morning. Is that not right, my dear?" Her eyes narrowed rebelliously, but she had the intelligence to remain mute and nod.

Reave scratched the beard stubble along his jaw, rudely staring at his unwelcome guest. He blinked twice when she crossed her arms and met his brazen glare. Who was she? Was it a coincidence that brought them together again, or had someone arranged their meeting? Kim was correct, he was too tired to listen to explanations or play childish games. He glanced down and frowned when he noticed her feet were bare. "I assume you are not taking the role of protector entirely to heart and have procured separate rooms?" He knew the question was insulting. If he did not, her gasp and Kim's stony expression were telling. Regardless, he was not in any mood to be courteous. His eyes lifted heavenward at the soft thud on the landing above. "Jason, go to bed!" he roared. There was the distinct padding of retreating little feet, then a door slammed overhead.

"Fear not, I can be honorable when I choose," Kim smirked. *Unlike you, you arse!* The unspoken words were as loud as the crackling tension between them.

Reave raised his hands in mock surrender. "For once, I agree. If you would care to enlighten me to the reason Miss Belanger is in my household, I will be available after breakfast." He began to walk toward his chamber, then hesitated. "I still have a chamber, do I not? You have not given it to another unfortunate soul?"

"No, you will be quite alone," Kim replied with a coldness that rivaled the passageway. Whispering words of comfort, he escorted Miss Belanger to her chamber.

Later, as Reave drifted off to sleep, his last thoughts were of his unexpected guest. Beneath heavy lids, her image teased him. He could still see her proud stance, daring him to insult her further, while her cold bare feet kneaded the equally frigid floor.

Fire and ice.

An inner voice warned him she was trouble, but mysteries always intrigued him. He rolled to his side, burying his face into a feather pillow. Drowsily, he realized he had the answer to one of his many questions—that defiant angels possessed startling eyes of blue.

Chapter Five

"Shall we call a truce or would you rather call me out?" Kim casually inquired. His back was to Reave as he helped himself to a portion of poached eggs and kidney pie. "Well?"

Reave peered over the paper he held in his hand. "I have not come to a decision."

Kim glanced about the room. "Have you seen Tessa?"

"If you are referring to Miss Belanger, she has been blessedly absent." He raised the letter higher to discourage further conversation.

"For a man who seeks fairness within the confines of justice, you have a rather one-sided, vulgar imagination. That woman has suffered her fair measure the past few days and your nasty comments about her questionable character were unfounded." He slapped the paper from Reave's hands to the table. "Damn me, I confess appearances last night wove a bleak representation of us all—including you! All I ask is that you listen to the events that led to our unexpected presence. If, withal, you find our companionship unwelcome, then I will take her elsewhere."

Returning to his chair, Kim picked up his fork and turned his attention to his plate.

Reave picked up the letter. Staring blankly at it, he tossed it aside and crossed his arms. There was no doubt Miss Belanger would have to leave. Having her in his home had already disturbed the household and, if he was truthful, his own peace of mind. He had spent the past hour pretending to be interested in the variety of correspondence stacked in front of him, but with every sound his muscles tensed, waiting for her to enter the room. It did not signify what misfortune befell her, he kept reminding himself. He would not tolerate her presence an hour longer than necessary. "How did you meet her?"

Kim needed no further encouragement. Recounting their encounter, he told Reave of her desperate plea to leave London and the reasons of her upset. Reave did not interrupt, his expression as impassive as his thoughts. Only when Kim mentioned that his son had met the woman and an immediate friendship had sprung up between the two did Reave's features betray the tension within him. It never occurred to him that he could be jealous. He decided it had to be outrage. Yes, that was it, pure outrage at the audacity of a young woman who would use a motherless boy's affection to worm her way into his household. She had also beguiled his best friend. Reave's expression grew forbidding. It was fortunate for all that he could see through her deception.

"Where do your feelings stand with this woman?"

Kim raised his cup to his lips and swallowed, grimacing at the coldness. "I am her friend. No more than that." He shoved the cup to his lips, poorly concealing his grin.

Reave was not clear on the reasons for his friend's amusement, so he chose not to be so ambiguous. "Well, let me speak as a friend who has known you more than a few hours. Remove yourself from this woman's life. Even you must realize that she was probably not wholly truthful in her facts. We can only speculate the reasons for her secrecy."

"If she lied, then it was motivated by fear. She awoke one

morning and discovered the life she had known was gone. She
was alone and destitute, possessing unanswered questions about
the people she once loved. I think we could help her.''

Tessa paused outside the breakfast room, unabashedly listening to the two men argue. If she had not felt so miserable,
she would have laughed at the entire situation. They were
discussing the fate of a woman who did not exist! The earl,
despite his friend's assurances, did not welcome her presence.
Considering the circumstances, she could not fault the man for
his astute judgment. She was a pariah to the life in which she
had once meekly existed.

''You appear lost, Miss Belanger,'' Thorne observed as he
approached her. Before she could form a reasonable reply to
her presence, Lord Wycke's baritone roar shattered all thoughts.

''Once again you have allowed a pleasing countenance to
manipulate what little common sense you possess. Then you
have the effrontery of expecting me to fix the matter! The little
strumpet has gulled you. I pray at least you were recompensed
for your services last night!''

''You bloody bastard. Again you have twisted—''

She heard only a few words of Kim's defense, its volume
matching the earl's vehemence before it dropped to an angry
undertone. A warm wave of humiliation rushed through her.
Her gaze flickered to the butler's compassionate eyes. It was
her undoing.

''I—I forgot—if you will excuse me.'' Her trembling fingers
covering her lips muffled any further explanation. She dashed
in the direction of the stairs. This was all her fault. Was it not
enough her own life was a sinking wreckage? Did she have to
ruin a friendship between two men because each had opposing
beliefs about a woman who in the kindest of terms was a
criminal and perjurerer!

Tessa hurried into her chamber with the purpose of collecting
her meager belongings. After all, she did possess some pride.
She would leave before she was thrown out. She retrieved her

locket from its hiding place in a drawer and dropped it into her reticule. Once her prized possession was secured, Tessa drew up her pelisse, not bothering to fasten the tapes. Her cloak and newly cleaned bonnet followed in her haste to dress, all the while her gaze fixed on the closed door.

She would go to the village. It was a practical plan. The miniature could be traded for a seat to anyplace except London. Never London. Her original plan of contacting her father for funds was still possible as long as news of her husband's death had not reached his ears. Where she would go next she did not know. Quickly, she moved down the stairs, careful not to draw attention. It was fortunate the servants were more interested in the argument than in keeping to their duties.

"It's my birthday."

Jason's quiet announcement froze her movements. Tessa turned to find his sad little face pressed between two of the lower balustrades. She had forgotten it was his birthday. Forcing a cheerful expression, she knelt beside him. "Joyous tidings to you, little one."

"Why are you leaving?" he asked in a manner that expressly told her he was wary of her reply.

"Forgive me, Jason. It is impossible for me to remain. I—" What was she to tell the boy?

"It's him, he's sending you away."

"Who? Oh, no, this is my decision," she explained. With a nervous gesture, her head snapped in the direction of the angry voices.

"You lie! He's sending you away. He sends everyone away!"

"Jason!"

He ran out of the hall, not waiting for her to deny it. Now she could add breaking a little boy's heart to her list of escalating sins. Straightening, she wrapped the cloak around her and slipped unnoticed through the door and out of the house.

* * *

"Thorne, has Mr. Lawson arrived?" Reave inquired, not bothering to glance up. He scribbled something on a document.

"Not likely under the circumstances, milord," Thorne replied. He glared at the smiling viscount, promising retribution.

"What? Has the weather hindered the roads?"

" 'Tis always a possibility this time of year, milord, but doubtful considering Mr. Lawson's posture."

"Which undoubtedly is prone," Kim muttered.

That comment resulted in another baleful stare from Thorne.

"Will someone tell me where I might find my steward?" Reave demanded, finally looking at them.

Recognizing his lord's impatience, Thorne cleared his throat. "I believe you will find him in one of the small sheds near the stables." From his incredulous expression, this was unquestionably not the answer his lordship expected.

"What the devil is he doing out there?"

"I would think it would be obvious to you. The man is dead," Kim bluntly stated.

Lord Wycke stood up, kicking the chair from the desk with a little more force than necessary. It slammed against the wall.

"Why was I not notified of this? Did no one think that I would find this information of interest?" His tone was as rasping as a metal file against cold steel.

"Leave off the man, Reave, before he has a fit," Lord Turnberry interceded. "From what was told to me, your Lawson recently succumbed to lung fever. A message was sent, but you had already left town."

The earl nodded, accepting the explanation. Bracing his palms on his desk, he considered the work upon it. "I suppose Mr. Luke can be excused from his tutorial duties to assist with the imperative matters. . . ." He broke off at the viscount's sudden coughing fit and muffled a groan. "Lord, don't tell me the man is residing in the shed too?"

Lord Wycke's exasperation caused his friend to laugh outright. "Not to worry, Thorne, I will relieve you of the telling of this one."

Thorne grimaced, his lips thinning a fraction. Everything was a bloody game with that man.

"It was a far worse fate than death. The man married."

Thorne interjected, "Word was sent out to you, milord, as soon as we learned of the marriage."

"Then I assume he will be returning with his bride?" The earl stroked his jaw.

"No, the young lady's father is a bookseller and expects his son-in-law to join the family business. I would expect his resignation is somewhere on your desk." His lord's contemplative gaze shifted to the desk.

"If there is nothing more, I shall return to my duties." Relieved his part was finished, Thorne stiffly bowed, then retreated from the room.

"Yes, yes." Reave waved the butler away. "The man has been in my employ for years." Losing both a steward and tutor would delay his return to town.

"May I suggest a temporary solution to your staff predicament?" Kim asked, interrupting his thoughts.

"It depends," he replied warily, suspecting he knew where this conversation would lead them.

"Tessa requires—"

"Unequivocally, no. I will not consider it." He shook his head. "The woman is unknown to me, and placing her in my home without references would be nitwitted."

"If that is your only problem, then I shall be willing to write one up." Kim swung his legs off the settee and jumped to his feet. "However, if I were you, I would examine the true reasons for your decision. She is a kind woman who has no one, and neither does your son."

"Get out."

"No need to growl, I'm leaving," Kim grumbled. "You have chosen to be a cynical, cold bastard, but for once consider your son. He happens to like Tessa, and perhaps she can provide a woman's warmth—a love, if you will—which you seem incapable of expressing.''

Reave's urge to strike him down warred with his control, reminding him that even their friendship had boundaries. Kim must have sensed it also. Sighing, he relaxed his battle stance, then casually walked to the door.

"We will remain for the celebration, then depart." Kim paused at the open door. "You did happen to recall today is your son's birthday, did you not?" he sneered. Without waiting for a reply, he closed the door.

Three hours later, Kim burst through the door. "Have you seen Tessa?" he demanded.

Reave rubbed his eyes. The passing hours had dulled the desire to test his pugilist skills on his friend. Still, the mention of that woman's name brought up a surge of irritation. "No."

Plainly upset, he began pacing. "No one has seen her for hours. Not only that, your son has barricaded himself in the nursery, permitting no one to enter." Scowling, he must have realized Reave would be the last person who would want to help him find Tessa, so he turned to leave.

"Wait!" With reluctance, Reave rose to his feet, mumbling to himself that this woman had become a damn nuisance to all. "I suggest we question Jason first. Perhaps he saw something."

When they reached the nursery, Reave pounded on the door. "Jason, I demand you open this door!" Kim's sniping remarks and the unexpected trip to the nursery had fired his temper. "This is trifling away valuable time. The boy has inherited your stubbornness; he will not listen."

The lock was undone and the door opened a crack.

Reave pushed the door open, walking by his son while he searched the room. Everything seemed in order. "Why was this door locked?"

Jason sat down in the middle of the room, where he had been stacking large wooden blocks. Ignoring his father, he picked up a red rectangle shape.

"Well?" The boy remained silent but flinched when Reave took a few menacing steps closer.

"Leave off, Reave, it is unlikely he knows anything about her whereabouts."

"She liked me," Jason whispered, his voice choked with emotion. "She promised to stay." His eyes shone brilliantly with tears and hate. "You made her cry. She left 'cause you didn't like her!" he cried, swiping at his tears.

"Son, you barely knew the woman," Reave began, slightly stunned and hurt that a brief acquaintance could have made such an impression. His pride was also bruised because a stranger could experience a closeness with his boy he could never attain. Damn the woman!

"Did she mention where she might go?" Kim gently questioned as he twisted his leather gloves into an unrecognizable contortion. Jason shook his head.

"Kim, if your benevolent angel has a pence of wit, she has headed for the village. We can gather a few men and search the area for her." Reave frowned when he saw the tiny flame of hope in his son's eyes. Initially, he had hoped the woman would not be found. The expression on his son's face changed his expectations. "Go on ahead. I will alert the men," he said to Kim. He knelt beside Jason. "Son, I—Miss Belanger will be found." There was more, but his throat ached too much to proceed. He reached out to touch his son on the head. His hand hovered inches from the boy's unruly locks before he clenched his fingers into a fist. He stood and strode from the room.

"Thorne." Reave encountered the butler at the base of the staircase. "Have someone gather a few of the men to help Lord Turnberry search for Miss Belanger. I will join them after I have changed."

"The lady is missing, milord?"

"I thought it was common knowledge. Viscount Turnberry certainly turned the house over to find the troublesome wench."

"I confess her hasty departure does not surprise me, milord. I came upon her this morning near the breakfast room. The nature of your conversation could not be avoided.'' His features had their usual bland appearance, but his tone implied Reave was at fault. "I will promptly see to the men.''

Bemused, Reave gaped at the spot where his loyal servant had stood. Within a number of days, Miss Belanger had won the loyalty of his closest friend, son, and even his butler! This was no angel; the woman was a witch. He marched upstairs to change his clothing, attempting to think of a method of exorcising her from his household before he, too, was touched by her magic. Or was it too late?

Chapter Six

"I must leave this day," Tessa addressed the village blacksmith while she shifted her well-nigh-frozen feet. The small confines and the fierce heat billowing in her face made her a little light-headed and her exposed flesh burn. She might have departed Eastcott high in temper and determination, but the hours of walking through ice-crusted mud and slush, then the small salvation of a local man and his horse and wagon, had left her subdued. Tessa arrived in the village cold and damp, and she soon added frustrated to her list after receiving terse replies from the several villagers she had engaged. "Surely there must be someone traveling south?"

"The weather is foul. No man travels if he has some mother wit."

The man was a wealth of information. He struck his hammer against the anvil, sending a shower of sparks from the glowing metal between. Tessa jumped back, fearing her clothing would ignite from a spark. Realizing the man would offer nothing more, she pulled her cloak tightly closed and stepped out of the shed. The icy tendrils of the wind pulled and twisted her clothing, forcing her to grasp a hitching post to prevent herself from blowing away. She fluttered her lashes to clear them of the clinging snow. As she made her way down the road, thoughts of returning to Eastcott invaded her lofty resolve. Tessa banished them with an unladylike shudder. She would never humble herself to Lord Wycke. She had spent too many years crawling on her knees to satisfy an unappeasable devil to subject herself to another.

"Logan said you were in need of the Lord's help, child."

She had not noticed the approaching man. His black attire and hat marked him as a member of the clergy. Through numb lips she asked, "Do you know of a man traveling south today?"

The old man shook his head. "The roads will be impassable by morning. I know of no one who would attempt to leave this late in the day with a gray tempest overhead. Have you lodgings to pass the storm?"

She glanced in the direction of Eastcott. The words that would assure her a dry bed and warm meal would not come forth.

"Mrs. Leach, my wife, that is, and I have a small cottage. You are welcome to pass the night until we can find someone who could take you south." He shouted over the burst of wind that threatened to knock them both to the ground.

"I have nothing to repay your kindness, Reverend Leach."

"To help a soul is payment enough for me," he replied, gesturing in the direction of his dwelling. Grabbing his offered arm, they began to walk. "By what name shall I call you?"

"Tessa. Please call me Tessa." She was relieved when he had not pressed her for her full name. Tessa was certain lying to a holy man would hasten her soul to hell if the many lies she had uttered the past few days had not already secured her position.

"Have you journeyed very far?" He shouted the question twice. The roaring wind seemed to snatch the breath from his lips, carrying it high into the heavens.

"London," she confessed, then cringed at her foolishness. "Do you think I might find a ride tomorrow?"

The man shrugged. "The weather is uncertain, but I will say a special prayer for you this eve. Come, this is the place."

Mrs. Leach and a blazing hearth greeted the frozen pair. Tessa smiled at the older woman, allowing her to peel off her outer garments. She was guided to a chair to enjoy the spreading warmth of the fire and the wool blanket in which she was wrapped. Her pride almost killed her this day. What would the morning bring? she wondered. That evening she would accept their hospitality; to involve them further would be sinful. At first light, she was determined to find the means to leave the village, even if she had to do it on foot.

"Any sign?" Reave patted his agitated stallion. It stomped the frozen earth, emphasizing its disapproval with a steamy snort.

Kim guided his horse closer so they would not have to raise their voices. Large snowflakes were falling from the sky, muffling each man's voice as it accumulated on the ground. "No. I thought we had picked up her trail but then lost it. This accursed snow and wind have succeeded in covering what remained of her trail."

"It is almost dusk. Perhaps we should call off the search until morning." Even as he spoke the words, he did not believe he could leave the foolish woman out there alone.

"And discover her stiff body in one of the fields in the morn so she can partner your inflexible steward in the shed? I'll pass." Kim scanned the horizon. "I cannot help but feel responsible for her. Damn, where is she?"

"I suggest you check the western boundaries. There is a small cottage there. It has been abandoned for years. I'll ride back to the house in hope that she has found her way back. If she has not returned, then I will have the coach hitched and head for the village. There is the slight possibility she found the means to travel so far."

"I suppose," Kim replied with a grim expression.

Reave tugged the reins, turning his stallion's head toward the direction of the house. "Return to the house after you have checked the cottage. The snow and impending darkness are a deadly combination out here. I would hate to have you placed next to Lawson."

Kim grinned. "I fear such a demise would give Thorne and Maxwell too much pleasure!" The men separated, each determined to find Miss Belanger.

"You have a beautiful voice, Mrs. Leach. My pianoforte accompaniment pales considerably in comparison," Tessa complimented her hostess. The quiet evening spent with the couple had restored her wilting spirit as much as the warm stew had filled her empty stomach. She had found it increasingly difficult as the evening progressed to keep her silent pledge not to involve them into her web of lies. Unfortunately, the vicar was persistent, forcing her to carefully evade each question about her background.

"Bosh!" Mrs. Leach exclaimed, as a light blush blended with her ruddy cheeks, making her entire complexion pink with delight. "The Lord has blessed us both with praiseworthy gifts. Jacob, would you honor us with a passage from the Bible?" She addressed Tessa, but her adoration was bestowed on her husband. "He speaks the holy words with a pure resonance that could make the angels weep!"

A pounding at the door disrupted all thoughts of a reading. The iron hinges rattled with each stroke. The vicar set aside his Bible. The door burst open, swinging wide on the raging currents of the storm. Snow danced on invisible whirlwinds, settling on the rough pine floor when the doorway was filled by a man dressed from head to foot in black.

"My, Lord Wycke!" The vicar stepped aside, allowing the heavily clothed man to enter. "Is someone ill?"

Reave removed his hat, shaking the snow from the fur. His gaze immediately settled on Miss Belanger, who upon recognizing him had grown considerably pallid. Without taking his eyes off her, he replied, "No, all is well, sir." He took a step closer to the hearth, acknowledging the older woman with a nod.

"Jacob, our manners need attending. Lord Wycke, may I introduce you to our guest."

Reave's blue eyes darkened slightly as Miss Belanger uneasily rose from her chair. She did not appear to be enthused to see him. "I can see you are well despite your foolish flight."

"There was no need to follow, for I will be leaving the village in the morning," she stiffly replied.

So she planned to be difficult. What did he expect? That she might be grateful he had come for her? The haughty little baggage did not seem to have a remorseful disposition in her soul. He would have left her to the Leachs if not for the anxious faces he would have to confront upon his return. Bloody hell! "Gather what possessions you have. The journey home will be arduous," he said with a sigh, accepting he would have to take her back to Eastcott.

"I think not."

"Child, are you acquainted with his lordship?"

Reave startled everyone by laughing. What pretty trimming to such an ugly mess. "Tessa was impatient because of the delays I had placed on her, and in her usual indiscriminate fashion she stalked off, heedless of the consequences." He gave her a look that dared her to contradict him. Gratefully, she remained mute.

"I did not realize. She did not mention . . ." The poor man was confused as he looked to Reave, then Miss Belanger.

Reave wondered how long it would take Miss Belanger to understand the lurid implication of his statement. He was about to suggest they take their leave, when she suddenly gasped, her hands reached out catching air.

"Sir, you m-mis—" she stammered.

"Nonsense, m'dear. I believe the vicar understands perfectly. Further explanation would only delay our departure," Reave smoothly interjected. He took her cloak and reticule from the

openmouthed Mrs. Leach. He placed the garment efficiently
around her rigid shoulders as if he had always seen to the task.
She slapped his hands away, which only made him laugh and
pinch her cheek. It left a small white mark that quickly faded
into the soft pink suffusing her face.

"Your generosity was well appreciated," she said in a hoarse
voice. "I will always remember your kindness." She accepted
Reave's arm, allowing him to drag her through the door.

The vicar held the door, bracing it with both hands so the
wind could not tear it from his grip. "The roads will be heavy
with snow. You are welcome to find shelter here till morning."

Miss Belanger turned back to the vicar when he shouted,
but his words were lost in the wind. Before she could delay
them further with idle chatter, Reave lifted her by her hips and
pushed her inside the coach. The winds had picked up since
he had entered the vicar's cottage.

So had his temper.

Purposely, he sat beside Miss Belanger only because he knew
it irritated her, and after tonight's ordeal, he wanted her to be
as miserable as he. With half-concealed amusement, he watched
her carefully pull her skirts tightly about her, then she sat on
the folds so not one thread would touch him. He could tell
from her movements she was furious. She waited until he
secured the door before she unleashed her temper.

"You did that deliberately!" she accused him.

Ignoring her outburst, Reave struck the trapdoor twice. The
coach jerked forward, beginning the journey to Eastcott.
"Whatever are you screeching about?" He knew what was on
her mind, he just felt like goading her.

"I will not tolerate being handled like a bale of hay. Touch me
on"—she struggled for a polite word concerning an indelicate
subject—"in that manner again, and I will repay in kind."

Before he could reply to her absurd threat, she charged forth
with another accusation.

"I am not—you are well aware of what I am referring to.

You allowed those decent people to believe that you and I are more than casual acquaintances!''

''Perhaps.''

His immediate concurrence stunned her momentarily. She sucked in her breath as if bracing for a scream.

''What is your game?'' she finally asked in a tight, controlled voice.

''Pardon?''

''Is this part of it? Must I guess your intentions?'' she practically shrieked.

''I was wrong earlier; your duration in the cold has addled your senses. Do us both a favor by closing you mouth and eyes. I know I need the rest.'' He shifted his position, wishing he had chosen the other seat. She muttered something unintelligible and shifted next to him. As far as Reave was concerned, Miss Belanger deserved her discomfort, since he had certainly been experiencing the sensation from the first moment he had encountered her in his son's room. He almost laughed as he watched her struggling to keep from touching him. The task was virtually impossible with the interminable rocking of the compartment, which slid them from side to side.

''They think I am your mistress.''

She sounded like she was about to cry. Reave could not abide tears, so he tried to ease her fears. ''Not necessarily. My explanation could lead them to several conclusions. It is doubtful they will repeat the meeting to others.''

''Ha!'' she huffed, then, as if she had not expressed her feelings on the subject clearly, she continued. ''You know very well what they thought when you hinted at a more intimate relationship. What confuses me is your motives.''

''Nothing mysterious, I assure you, Miss Belanger. The hour is late and I had no desire to explain the trivial circumstances that resulted in your flight. The vicar is a curious man, and I am one to keep personal matters private.''

''Why did you not name Lord Turnberry as my dearest friend?'' She leaned closer, straining to see his expression.

"That way you would have remained detached from the situation."

Reave pulled back from her scrutiny. "Generally, my word goes unchallenged here," he laconically replied. Thankfully, those haunting blue eyes retreated into the shadows. He shifted, trying to shake off the tightness in his chest that had repeatedly occurred since he had first stumbled across her. If there had been a seat next to the coachman, he would have gladly taken it. "I was the one to discover you, which was quite by chance, and to involve my friend would have proceeded to other questions, none of which either of us would have deigned to answer. Am I correct in my summation?"

"Partially," she admitted. "We have one thing in common, I suppose—the need to keep our affairs to ourselves." She grimaced at her word choice.

"Is that your reason for your selective truths? To protect your family?"

"I believe I will follow your earlier advice, Lord Wycke, and rest." She leaned the side of her head against the opposite wall from him and closed her eyes.

He knew the moment she was asleep. Her reticule slipped from her slack hold and fell to the floor. Slowly, Reave bent forward to retrieve the cloth bag. Banishing the quick flash of guilt pricking his conscience, he reminded himself she had brought it upon herself by being so damned secretive. He did not like secrets. Widening the drawstring opening, he pulled out the contents with disappointment. A soiled handkerchief and a gold locket. Neither revealed the inscrutable lady beside him. He opened the miniature, holding it closer to the glowing grate. He ran his thumb across the image. The detailing was impossible to discern in the soft light. He assumed she had planned to use the piece to pay her passage, but to where he could only speculate. He dropped the items back into the bag. Inspiration caused him to pull the linen back out of the bag. Smoothing out the crumpled fabric, like a blind man his fingers moved over the delicate embroidery. Within the oval border of what he guessed were flowers and vines, his sensitive fingers traced the bold *T* in the center. He did not know what he expected. Defeated, he stuffed the handkerchief into the reticule and pulled the strings tight. If he was to discover who she was, it would have to be from the lady herself.

The coach jolted to the right, sending the slumbering Miss Belanger against him. She shifted and snuggled her head against his rigid shoulder. He waited for her to awake, to flee in horror of the intimate contact. She definitely reacted when she was conscious, as if he were a carrier of the plague.

Minutes ticked by, but she remained where the damnable coach had placed her. The depressing black bonnet she possessed had loosened, exposing her fragrant blond tresses. They almost appeared dark brown in the darkness. However, he held a vivid impression in his mind of her leaning over his son, her hair a redolent cascade of wheat and honey. He almost growled aloud as his body betrayed him.

He tilted his face closer to hers. This eve she wore her tantalizing tresses in a plaited crown about her head. It affected him nonetheless, the braid teasing him inches from his nose. Giving in to the temptation of her placid attitude, he leaned closer, his nose lightly touching her temple before he inhaled. Elise had always smelled of lavender, while his mistress, Maggs, smothered her body with the heavy scent of roses. Miss Belanger's scent bore no resemblance of a hothouse bloom. This woman smelled of rain, hay, and something he had trouble identifying. His nose twitched. Horse? The combination was not at all unappealing, which surprised him.

Pulling back, he chided himself for the foolish fancy of his actions. He was acting like a callow lad on his first outing with a female. There was no need for a woman in his life except for an occasional dalliance to ease a physical need. He had had a wife, and he had his heir, so there was no logical reason to chase a mysterious vixen who possessed full pink lips that made her look as if she were frowning even when she was not. He did not need the madness the likes of her would bring to his life. Reave sighed, stretching his long legs as far as they could extend within the cramped confines. Miss Belanger was Kim's responsibility, a fact he would remind his reckless friend the moment they arrived at Eastcott.

The coach slowed, skidding to a stop. Overhead, the coachman called out. Gently, Reave extricated Miss Belanger from his side, tucking his beaver hat between the cold leather seat and her flushed soft flesh. Thinking about the possible causes for their delay, he climbed out of the coach to check on their progress.

The door slammed shut, waking Tessa.

"Edmund?" she whispered, a thread of fear making her tremble. Her throat hurt. She shifted, attempting to revive her cramped muscles. Where was she? The sudden clarity of her circumstances hit her as if someone had poured a pitcher of icy river water over her head.

Edmund was dead.

Pushing open the door, Tessa cautiously peered outside. The snow still fell silently from the sky with intermittent bursts of wind to scatter the frozen lace. There was little to see beyond the small realm of the lantern attached to the side of the coach. A cough drew her attention to the horses. Leaning out, she could see the dancing shadows of a lantern, but its source was past her vision. Before she could decide whether or not to descend the steps, three men walked around the horses. She assumed the large one was Lord Wycke, since he seemed to be the one issuing orders. Sensing he was being watched, the earl turned and saw her poised at the door. Abruptly ending the conversation, he dismissed the men, then headed back to the coach. The snow was almost knee-high in places, she noted as he strode toward her.

"You may be witless enough to stand out here, freezing, but I prefer the shelter." He guided her back inside with a firm grip and slammed the door.

"Why have we stopped? Are we near Eastcott?"

"No." He stirred the embers in the grate, cursing aloud because there was nothing more to add to the perishing glow.

"Are we trapped in the snow?"

"No."

She turned to face him in the darkness, although there was little to see with his back to her. When it was obvious Lord Wycke was not planning to elaborate, Tessa said, "I realize you have little patience for civil conversation. However, if you would give me some reassurance, I promise to refrain from further dialogue." The smoldering fury she beheld when he finally turned his gaze on her made her regret any attempt to speak to the infuriating man.

"What do you want to hear, Miss Belanger? That we are within the gates of Eastcott? No, we are not." He kicked the grate with his foot. "That there is an inn to warm our frozen extremities and revive our spirit? Hardly. The truth is, we are wending on a road so covered in snow that it is difficult to distinguish road from pasture. Our horses are nigh spent and we must pause from time to time to thaw their noses with the warmth of our hands so they may breathe." His features twisted into a scowl. The shadow of a beard enhanced his sinister appearance. "Have I given adequate explanation to temper your incessant chatter?"

"I was not aware of our perilous situation, my lord."

"Obviously. If you had not been inclined to press your face to doors to overhear conversations not meant for your delicate pink ears, then we would not be in this predicament!" he shouted. "How old are you?"

"I do not see—one-and-twenty. Why do you ask?"

"You behave more like a schoolgirl with braids. I swear, my son has more sense than you."

Stung by his insult, Tessa retorted, "I am surprised you know anything about the boy, considering you do everything to avoid him."

Immediately, she regretted her words. Lord Wycke was not helping matters by attempting to pressed her back into the corner. She refused to let him know his intimidating tactics were working. Audibly gasping, her hand covered her mouth. "Oh, no, Jason's birthday!" She had forgotten.

"Finally, you see the consequences of your selfishness," he growled, his fury barely reined. "Kim and many others have endured the cold to find you, and a little boy locked himself in the nursery because you told him I was sending you away."

Nothing could assuage her guilt about being the cause of Jason's grief. In an unconscious gesture, Tessa placed her hand on his chest. She did not know whether she was attempting to ward him off or offer comfort. With a little breathy sound of surprise, she pulled her hand back, dropping it back into her lap. It was disconcerting to discover touching him was more intimidating than his presence.

"No—I swear, I said only that I could not remain. He ran off before I could further explain." She gripped and twisted a handful of her skirt. "I thought if I left, then Lord Turnberry would be released from his pledge to protect me." Tessa paused, considering her unspoken thought. "I must confess I found some small satisfaction by withdrawing the small pleasure it would have given you in seeing me thrown out," she added quietly.

She thought he might have smiled at her confession, agreeing he would have relished her departure. However, when she dared to look at him directly, she saw, instead, his lips had thinned into a grimace.

"I am not an unreasonable man. Nor am I in the habit of tossing ladies out on their skirts," he said, though they both knew that was exactly what he would have done if given the chance. He cleared his throat. "I confess, I am opposed to your presence in my household. All the same, you are welcome to remain at Eastcott until the severe weather passes. My son has a certain fondness for you, and perhaps your visit will lighten his spirits in spite of my presence. I will leave your departure to Kim."

"You have my gratitude," she murmured, not quite managing to sound grateful.

Lord Wycke bristled. "I require nothing from you except your prompt departure."

Lord, he was a rude man, Tessa thought, albeit an honest one. She tolerated the awkward silence, using the time to mull over the day. Finally, she could not resist asking, "One thing puzzles me, my lord. If you find me intolerable, then why did you attempt to find me? You could have left me at the vicar's house and no one would have known until I had departed."

"I am not in the habit of explaining myself, Miss Belanger," he snapped. "I have explained why we have stopped. Now I suggest you uphold your promise and refrain from further chatter."

The coach lurched as the horses slowly plodded through the snow. Neither spoke the rest of the journey, each lost in thoughtful turmoil. London seemed far away to Tessa. She listened to the wheels crunch through the powderlike snow, wondering how far she would have to flee before she could find refuge.

She strained in the darkness to see Reave's expression, but his face was blank as slate, so she laid her head on the leather cushion and closed her eyes. She was too tired and cold to contemplate his words. Nor did it signify, since she would soon leave Eastcott. As for Lord Wycke, she mused, he could go to the devil as far as she was concerned.

Chapter Seven

It was well past three when Reave and Miss Belanger stumbled into the foyer, yet the house was bustling with activity. Everyone had been waiting for word of the earl. A little dazed by the warmth of their greeting, Reave squinted at the brightness of the cheery interior. Everyone eagerly rushed to their aid. Kim shouted orders for warm food and extra blankets before he greeted them.

"You both look hellish," Kim observed. He placed a supportive arm around Miss Belanger and guided her into the library.

Thorne and a footman attempted to help Reave. His gait was a bit unsteady as he entered the room. Since his pride was at stake, he waved them away. "I'm tired and half frozen, Thorne, not a weak babe," he muttered, then slumped into the nearest chair, wondering if he would ever be able to feel his legs. Thorne pressed a snifter of brandy into Reave's hand, then snatched it back when it was apparent he could not make his hand grip the glass. Disgruntled, he opened his lips when the rim touched them and quickly downed its contents.

"How is she?" Reave asked, his gaze for the first time since they entered the house resting on her. The warmth of the brandy was already creating a comforting burn in his stomach. It also brought on tremors, afflicting his entire body.

"I live, with little thanks to you!" Miss Belanger replied through trembling blue lips. "Kim, I question your friend's sanity and my own for allowing you to bring me to this place."

Kim opened his mouth, but it was Reave's angry retort that made her flinch.

"I saved your life, you ungrateful waif!"

"I was quite protected from the storm"—she pointed an accusatory finger at Reave as she spoke to everyone in the room—"when this lunatic strode into the vicar's cottage—"

"I did not know you were there!"

"—and intimated at an outrageous adulterous relationship, horrifying all people present, most of all myself!" Bright eyes turned on Reave, daring him to deny her charges.

"What the devil?" Kim began, confusion and something akin to anger replacing the concern and amusement that had played upon his features.

Feeling caged by everyone's frozen interest, Reave scowled. "Miss Belanger, I explained my actions."

The sorrowful beauty drew herself up to full indignation. "I unmistakably recall you roaring at me that you were not of the habit of explaining anything."

"I never roar!" he yelled back.

Tessa cocked her head and sniffed, "My point exactly."

"This would have never transpired if you had not run away like a child with hurt feelings." His retort lacked the anger he felt. He was just too damn tired.

Miss Belanger sat back and closed her eyes. "I was brought here because I was told you could help me. I would have never come if I had had a choice." Her eyes snapped open. This time she focused her ire on Kim.

"And she calls me the lunatic." Reave staggered to his feet.

Kim stepped between them. "Neither of you has a vein of

rational thought. I suggest you both sleep off the brandy and chew each other to pieces in the morning.'' Kim and Thorne each clasped one of Miss Belanger's arms and pulled her up. She hung between them like a limp cloth doll. ''I must say, for your first day together, you have gotten on better than my highest expectations.''

Wearily, Reave limped behind the trio, cursing his friend's odd sense of humor. ''Remind me tomorrow to beat you bloody, as I had promised.''

''Are you hiding?''

Tessa placed the small pillow she had been hugging back on the settee and stood to greet Jason. Holding out her hand, she smiled at him. ''No, I was just appreciating the beauty of this room.'' The explanation sounded suspiciously weak even to her own ears.

''Cook says you're hiding.''

It was true she had spent the morning avoiding Lord Wycke after their parting. She sank back onto the settee, amazed how quickly it had become servant gossip. ''How does Cook know so much?''

''Oh, Robbie told him,'' Jason replied, tracing the floral pattern in the fabric with a grimy finger.

''Who is Robbie?''

''Oh, he's a footman. He helps in the breakfast room. He told Cook the earl was angry you were hiding from him. Are you hiding?'' His blue eyes widened. ''I know a good place to hide, even better than this!''

''It matters not what he believes.'' Coming to a private conclusion, she returned to Jason's side. ''I fear my blundered flight overshadowed your celebration. Dare I beg your forgiveness?''

He looked away, scuffing his shoes on the carpet as he considered her question. He nodded. ''I was mad for a time, but Uncle Kim said we could pretend today was my birthday. See?"

"Yes, indeed. A very good notion, I think." She patted him on the shoulder and gently led him to the door. "You must excuse me now, for I must prepare for your father's audience."

"Will he look for you like Uncle Kim does when I hide under the stairs?"

"No, sweet, the game the earl chooses to play calls for higher stakes and a more perceptive presence of mind. He knows where to find me when he is prepared." She opened the door. "I will see you later, then?" She smiled when his head bobbed with the eagerness of a puppy. "Off with you!"

Tessa closed the door, resting her forehead on the cool surface. She had been foolish to utter such nonsense to the boy. He did not understand. She was definitely becoming rattled.

Spineless bitch.

Edmund was still bedeviling her even from his moldering grave. He better than anyone would know how undone she would have been by his demise. A part of her believed this was all a terrible lie. Perhaps Edmund was still alive, laughing at her and wondering how mired she would become in this mischief. Oh, if only she could summon a small portion of the courage she thought she possessed. She would march into Lord Wycke's chambers and demand the proper respect he owed her. But Edmund was dead, and what little courage she owned withered at the proclamation that he died by her hand. No one would believe her now.

"My lord?"

Lord Wycke set aside the correspondence and stood to greet her. His gaze lingered rudely over her shabby black gown. He regarded her with silent contempt. Tessa felt a rush of warmth to her face. Having a fresh gown on hand had been the least of her concerns, considering the trials of these past days. Nevertheless, it did not remove the sting from her hide, making her feel like common baggage.

"You surprise me, Miss Belanger."

"I do not understand, my lord."

He gestured for her to sit. "Considering our inability to maintain civility, I half expected your method of choice to confront me would be by force."

"You amaze me with your perceptiveness, my lord." She sat down, then paused, a sudden insight striking her. "I must confess I was surprised that even you would condescend to use your son as an artifice to manipulate me."

"Be quick with your meaning, Miss Belanger," Lord Wycke said, his voice deceptively soft.

"My words are as clear as glass, sir! Did you not send Jason to my chamber to repeat your horrid comments so I would be honor bound to directly address you?" She started to rise. He stilled her with a hand gesture.

Stroking his jaw, he paced before her, possessing the grace of a caged wild beast. "If my son visited you, it was by his choice alone. It seems you are not the only one who has picked up the unacceptable inclination for eavesdropping."

"I told you before, I—"

"I know. My ears still ring from your endless excuses."

Tessa stood up. Her lower lip trembled with frustration and anger. If he had been any other man, she would have thought he was trying to provoke her. She immediately dismissed the thought, because Lord Wycke was hardened, emotionless. "Where is Lord Turnberry?"

"Prowling around, I suppose. Why?"

"If I may summon a man to locate him, we will depart with your blessing."

"Not possible."

"I beg your pardon?"

Lord Wycke returned to his desk and picked up the discarded letter. "Rightly so, but you must remain my guest for another day or two."

He sounded absolutely appalled at the notion. Confusion knitted her brow as she tried to understand this exasperating man. "Why would you wish for me to remain?"

"I don't," he bluntly confessed. "Somehow you have endeared yourself to my son, and it would please him to have you remain for his celebration." He gave her a look reminding her that he had not forgotten she was responsible for them missing Jason's birthday. "I see no reason why I cannot tolerate the situation for a few days more."

"Tolerate!" She choked on the word.

"Reave, I have just—" Kim burst into the room. "Tessa! My dear, have you mended from your ordeal?" Kim took up her hand and gallantly bowed to kiss it. His actions gained a disapproving glare from the earl.

"A night's slumber has revived me, sir. However, I cannot help but feel our prompt departure would not improve everyone's dispositions."

"Is something amiss?" Kim looked to Lord Wycke to explain the urgency in her tone. "Have you not told her?"

"I have not been gifted with the opportunity," the earl dryly replied. "If she were a spring, I would never die of thirst."

The man was baiting her again! Even so, she would not act like a pet fish, rising to the occasion just because he tossed stale bread upon the water. Instead, she asked. "What was he to have told me?"

"The snowstorm continued throughout the night. All roads are void of man and beast."

"No! I must leave." She twisted a gloved finger. "I place the blame entirely at your feet, Lord Wycke."

"Has she always shown a tendency to being non compos mentis?" he wondered aloud.

Tessa ground her teeth. "I am not a bedlamite."

The earl rubbed his jaw, observing the flush heating her cheeks. She felt like she had been scalded with hot water.

"A poor waif who knows her Latin. Really, Kim, your talent for finding an original astounds me."

His sarcastic observation snapped her mouth shut tighter than a clam out of water. What was she thinking? This man was a barrister and fully capable of recognizing a fraud when he met one. Here she was, about to tell him about the fine education she received to prepare her for the aristocratic husband of her father's choosing. *Fine, Tessa, tell him the truth and the hangman will soon place moldy hemp around your neck!* She took a deep breath, praying she appeared composed. "Will it be possible to leave tomorrow?"

"It is difficult to predict these matters," Kim remarked. He clasped his hands behind his back and looked as if he wanted to say more. She tried to keep the wariness she felt from showing in her eyes.

"Tessa, you have reiterated daily your desire to leave Eastcott, but where do you plan to go? Your family is dead, the estate gone. What are your prospects?"

Flustered, she glanced about the room wishing she could find the answer tucked between two books and as accessible. "I have not considered—what does it signify? Within a fortnight, neither of you will remember my name." She did not like the unnatural gleam she saw in Kim's eye. He was up to mischief.

"You smite at my heart with your cruelty, my lady." His dramatic protest drew a groan from Lord Wycke and a reluctant smile from Tessa. "Have I not proven myself worthy? Even Reave risked his life, defeating the ravages of a wrathful blizzard to return you to the protection of Eastcott."

"Save us from this theatrical turn and explain your motives," the earl demanded.

"I must agree with his lordship. Where do you lead us with your verbal play?"

"I am rather surprised neither of you has considered the good fortunateness of your meeting. Tessa, you are without a home and funds. Reave, you are without a steward and tutor. I put before you a solution to both your needs. Hire Tessa until the positions can be filled."

"No."

Both of them had protested, but it was Lord Wycke who continued. "This was unsporting of you to force the issue, my friend. Miss Belanger would not find this household satisfactory."

"You owe the earl an apology for placing him in this awkward predicament."

Kim shrugged. "I cannot repent something I feel could help both of you."

Satisfied they would at least consider his idea, Kim released her arm and disappeared through the doorway, leaving them to quietly consider the merits of accepting his proposal.

Chapter Eight

Eight days had passed since the night Tessa had participated in Jason's birthday celebration. Eight endless days of waiting, wanting, needing to escape. With each day, the tension within the household became as frigid and brittle as the ice that clung to the barren tree branches surrounding the house. Everyone was aware of it. To some, it seemed it had evolved into a physical entity, its long, icy fingers impatiently tapping the frosted glass windowpanes while it bided time until it disrupted the harmony.

Lord Wycke spent the days locked within his library. Tessa was not certain what he did all those hours, but he assured everyone very loudly one evening that he indeed did have obligations when Kim accused him of hiding. Regardless of the earl's excuses, she felt inclined to agree with Kim yet remained mute on the subject. Instead, she did her best to avoid the man and spent her time in the nursery with Jason.

Lord Wycke had been correct when he had said that she would find residing at Eastcott unsatisfactory. Life with Edmund might have been unsavory and unavoidable, but all

the while he had become predictable. Her encounters with
the earl were teaching her that the unknown could be equally
unsettling.

A platter of fish was placed in front of Tessa, startling her
from her musings. She waved the footman off with a remote
smile, a soft sigh escaping her lips.

"The mice eat more than you do," Kim teased, suddenly
finding his tongue. " 'Tis no wonder half the females of the
ton faint at a little excitement. You women never eat."

"Oh, but we do, sir. We devour our meals behind closed
doors so we are the model of female propriety when escorted
to supper." It would not do to tell him the true reasons for her
fading appetite. "Women are expected to be as perfect and
emotionless as the Greek statues they emulate."

"You speak like one who has moved within the beau
monde," Lord Wycke observed.

His casual comment caused her to choke on the wine she
was sipping. Coughing into her hand, she blinked away the
tears clouding her vision. She took a few ragged breaths. "One
does not need to move within the circles to know of its shal-
lowness," she said hoarsely. "There are many to retell such
incidents at the local assemblies."

He nodded, saying nothing more. Tessa stood, gesturing to
the men to remain seated. "I believe I will retire, leaving you
gentlemen to your own amusements this evening."

Kim rose to escort her to the archway. "We shall miss your
recitation, my dear. Your voice is as smooth as Wycke's best
brandy, and as intoxicating."

"As usual, my lord, your praise is too bold."

"But justly deserved. Is that not so, Reave?"

Again she felt his blatant perusal. She burned under his
scrutiny.

"You know of these things better than I." This time he
slurred a few words. He staggered to his feet, joining Kim at
the door. Together they watched her regally climb the stairs;
the gentle sway of her hips was not lost on either man.

When she was gone, Kim's demeanor radically changed from engaging to one of animosity. "It was not enough to humiliate her. You had to prove to her that you are a bastard."

"I can't seem to recall my legitimacy ever being in question. Can you say the same?" Reave turned his back, ignoring the thunderous expression on his friend's face, and returned to the dining room in search of a drink.

"I think you would like nothing better than to have me bash that bloody noble face of yours, but I won't oblige you this time. I am curious to know what has caused this sudden desire to empty your stock within a fortnight. You have never been one to touch too much of the stuff, and lately you reek of it."

Reave raised the snifter to the light, squinting at the amber liquid. "This—this is the reason for your maiden-aunt looks of disapproval at supper?" He laughed and shook his head in disbelief.

"It isn't the drinking as much as the reason behind it. You thought you could scare her off."

"I think you've had your fair share this evening to invent this nonsense."

Kim did not give up his attack. "You thought a good proper lady would never risk her reputation residing in the home of a lecherous drunk. I congratulate you on your subtle plan. I doubt she will accept a position here even if it means being thrown into the streets."

"If she's so wonderful, why don't *you* keep her?" He did not need this, not tonight. Kim could be relentless when he was living the role of the valiant knight.

"I would if there was a place in my household. I thought you would at least consider keeping her for Jason's sake. He needs someone like Tessa."

Someone who can give Jason what I cannot.

Reave was not drunk enough to confess the true reason for his odd behavior to his friend. He was trying to frighten Miss Belanger away, not to protect her reputation but, rather, to keep himself from confronting what he had suspected the first night he saw her.

Despite her frumpy black gown and numinous background, he was attracted to her. She had entered his home and without effort had enchanted the household, including the reserved Thorne, who did not like many of his friends. He kept thinking about the glorious mane of honey hair she kept confined in a braided crown. What would be her reaction if he had given in to his impulse the night in the coach and plucked the pins from her hair, releasing it from its confines. He imagined it felt like the softest silk. He knew how it smelled, a heady essence of secular elements and woman. The simple reminder aroused him, heightened his senses.

Closing his eyes, he could see her rolling her eyes heavenward at one of Kim's witty remarks, gifting him with one of her rare sincere smiles. Reave doubted he had ever given her a reason to smile. No, the truth was, he prayed the liquor would numb his tongue to prevent him from giving in and asking her to remain.

"No decent woman would want to live here. Take your Miss Belanger somewhere safe," he growled.

Kim gave him a measured look before he spoke. "Put your fears aside, we will leave tomorrow. However, 'tis a pity."

Reave pinched the bridge of his nose, attempting to block the ensuing headache he assuredly deserved. "How so?"

"Jason has become very attached to her. They have been steadfast companions. Well, you know best how to handle the boy." He yawned, then patted Reave on the shoulder. "We will have an early day, so I shall leave you to your drink. I am certain I will see you in London soon."

This was too easy. He expected an argument; hell, he even wanted one! "Is that where you plan to take her?"

"London? No, I thought Pike might hire her on."

Reave vehemently shook his head. "She's too soft to withstand his household. The man runs his home the same way he ran his men. He will have her weeping within the first hour."

"Have you another suggestion?"

The room seemed too small for Reave. He loosened his cravat while tossing his friend a malevolent glare. The smug expression Kim was attempting to hide, and doing a poor job of it, too, told him he had been manipulated. Damn the meddling fool! If he had not been drinking, he would have recognized the ploy at once.

"The hour is late. I wish you a safe journey."

Reave was satisfied to see disappointment flash in the bastard's eyes. Good! Let him think he failed. He closed his eyes, listening to the retreating echo of Kim's boots.

Reave gazed upward, wondering if she was in bed. He imagined she was appealing even when she was warm and puffy from sleep. Groaning at his weakness, he banished her fair image from his hazy thoughts. The decision had been made long before Kim had tried his hand at matchmaking. The mysterious Miss Belanger would remain at Eastcott.

"Oh, where is it?" Tessa knelt down and dumped the contents of her reticule on the bottom step.

"Something amiss, my chick?" Kim asked, grinning as he watched her invert her reticule and shake the fabric.

"I have lost my locket. Do you see it?"

He scanned the marble floor, seeing nothing on the reflective cream-colored surface. "Not even dust, love. Did you search your chamber?"

"Is this the reason my guests are polishing the front hall with their clothing?"

Lord Wycke's voice resonated above them. When she glanced up, she saw her gold locket tangled in his grasp.

Tessa could not keep the mistrust from surfacing. "My locket. Where did you find it?"

He joined them below before answering. "I didn't steal it, Miss Belanger. One of the servants found it in the hall. Have a care, your precious bauble would be safer around your neck."

Bristling at his patronizing advice, she smirked, "The chain is broken."

Apparently not interested in her little trinket, he dropped the locket into her outstretched palm without comment. "I thought I was too late," he said, turning to Kim.

"Would it have mattered?" Kim challenged.

"Would *what* have mattered?" She looked to each man for the answer. Neither deigned to reply.

Chuckling, Kim slapped his gloves against his left palm. He reached down and pulled Tessa to her feet. "Well, my dear, you may return your meager possessions to your chamber."

Confused, she tentatively queried, "But you said the roads were passable."

"True, but unnecessary for you this day. His lordship has agreed to take you into his household."

She turned to Lord Wycke, expecting him to deny Kim's preposterous statement. All she saw was resignation in his dark gaze. "Why?"

"Tessa, the man has offered you a home. You should be thanking him, not interrogating him." Kim cuffed the earl on the shoulder. "A wise decision, my friend. You have my gratitude."

"Well, you have not gained mine!"

Both men started at her frosty indignation. Kim tried to approach her. "You are upset."

Upset? The man was a dolt! "You speak of passing me to this man as if I were your chattel. I am not a piece of clothing you can cast off merely because you have grown weary of the sight of it. Curse you for not leaving me to the London streets, where the felons are at least more apparent!"

"Don't be a fool," Kim snapped. "Your well-being has been my utmost concern. You are hurt and have no place to go. Here you can heal and find peace."

Her laugh was choked with frustration. "He does not want me!"

Tessa thought she saw a mixture of pain and derision glint in the dark blue depths of Lord Wycke's eyes. His angry command made her think she had been mistaken.

"Miss Belanger, we have given the staff enough gossip to last the winter. I suggest we remove ourselves to a more private room to vent our spleens." Lord Wycke did not bother waiting for them to follow and headed for the morning room.

"I see no need for a prolonged discussion, my lord," she said, matching his stride by running every few steps. "I understand perfectly. Your friend has coerced you into accepting my presence." Tessa glanced back to give Kim a withering glare to force him to confess. Lord Wycke stopped without warning. She slammed into his back and bounced back a step. She took another step backward for protection.

"Now you are speaking like a weak-headed chit. Do I appear to be a man who can be manipulated?" He towered over her. "I could have left you in the care of the vicar and his wife, but I brought you back here. I decided even after you aptly proved you had the common sense of a stick that you needed someone to take a firm hand." He continued into the room.

His insults could not be borne! Who did he think she was? *A nobody. Someone beneath his class.* And to keep his thoughts in that direction she would have to learn to keep her mouth shut! Tessa bit her lower lip until she tasted blood. "What position are you offering?" she managed to ask without screaming.

Some of the tension eased from his posture. "My son has lost his tutor. The position is yours if you want it."

She shook her head. "I could not accept your generous offer. I have not the training to guide him through his studies."

"You are conspicuously well educated," he stated, his back turned to her while he poured himself a cup of coffee. "I thought a woman of your class would choose the position of a governess rather than the fate of a toad-eater." He shrugged, and the strength of him rippled under his brown coat. "I am mistaken."

Tessa colored at his cruel barb. She wanted to tell him she

had never been a burden to her family; in fact, she had sacrificed everything for their welfare. However, Miss Tessa Belanger had lost her family, so she had to be satisfied with the murderous glare she gave him. "I am not qualified." She gritted her teeth.

"I lost my steward. Could you manage this estate?" She laughed. It was a high, nervous sound. "I can assume that means no." Lord Wycke glanced at Kim. "This might have been a foolish idea, after all."

"Tessa could assist you where she is capable until a suitable replacement is found." Kim suggested before the earl could withdraw his compliance. "Is this agreeable?"

Bleakly, Tessa felt there was no alternative but to accept. It was likely word had reached her father of Edmund's murder, leaving her alone and without the funds she desperately needed. Working for the earl would give her the means to flee. Lord Wycke assented to the compromise. She knew they awaited her decision.

"I will accept your offer, my lord. I pray you will not come to regret your generosity."

Dismissing Miss Belanger, he addressed Kim. "Will you remain?"

"Mayhaps another day or two to make certain all is well."

"Fine," Reave said, irritated at the speculative grin on his friend's face. He stared at the vacant spot where she had stood recalling the concern he had seen when she said that she hoped he would not regret his decision. It was too late. He had.

"I'm glad you are staying here with me," Jason said, bouncing on her bed. "I promise to be good."

"Jason, this is only a temporary arrangement until your father can find a more suitable replacement." She sat on the bed next to him. "I really do not understand why I am here." Tessa jumped up, trying to shake the unsettled feeling in her stomach. Well, there was nothing to be done until she was summoned. A light tapping at the door interrupted her next question to

Jason. The door opened and Kim peeked through the gap. "Have you no decency, sir?"

"Hang society. I wanted to talk to you." The viscount strolled into her chamber and leaned against the wall. "Any chance I can speak to Tessa alone, runt?"

"Sure, Uncle Kim! Just don't let her leave. I like her." Planting a quick kiss on her hand, Jason scampered out of the room.

"I suppose you taught him that?" Tessa laughed, bringing the hand he kissed up to her lips. She was becoming extremely fond of the boy.

"No, I am learning from him," was the good-natured response. "Despite appearances, he is a lonely boy. You'll be good for each other."

"Are you implying I am lonely?"

"Anyone who closes themselves off from others eventually becomes afflicted. But that is not the reason for my visit." He avoided the bed and chose to sit in a crimson and gold brocaded chair. "I will be leaving in the morning."

"Leaving! Why?" Unadulterated fear knotted in her throat, making it difficult to breathe.

"I know I have given you the impression I live a blithesome existence, but I do have obligations, my sweet."

Forlorn, she grabbed the drapery for support as she stared out the frosted window. Everything was a blur.

"Here, here. Wycke is not as bad as all that. I know he has acted like a wretch, but I swear, I would never leave you with a man I could not trust with my own life."

"What of mine?"

Kim came from behind, wrapping her in his warm embrace. She flinched yet did not struggle. "Have I not taken my role as your protector with zealous fervor?" She bumped his chin with her nod. "Well, then, trust me when I tell you, Wycke's household is as safe as your mother's bosom."

She released a strangled sob, then broke away from his touch.

"Forgive my hysterics, my lord. I have not been able to trust many in my life."

Kim pressed a clean handkerchief into her palm. "Wycke is trustworthy and honorable. He has had his own tragedies to face, which have left him a little roughened for the delicate sex. Besides, the man spends most of the year in town, so you will rarely have to endure his presence."

"There are no women here."

That mischievous glint sparkled in his eye when he firmly grasped her arm and whirled her around to face him. "I have to go out for a short time. Do you think you and Reave can avoid getting into fisticuffs before my return?"

"Possibly, if I hide in my room for the duration."

He pinched her chin. "Clever girl! I will see you this evening if all is well." He leaned over and placed a quick chaste kiss on her forehead.

There was much to be done.

Reave was irritated. Kim had left hours ago, and no one seemed to know his whereabouts. The man was definitely up to something. He stopped his pacing and stared down at Miss Belanger. She was curled up in one of the drawing room chairs, absently chewing her thumbnail. She clasped a book in her other hand. Her pose had not altered in the last hour. He suspected she was keeping something from him.

"What were his last words to you?"

Her gaze shifted from the book to him. She seemed annoyed, not that he cared. She would repeat it one hundred times if that was his inclination.

"He said if all went well, then he would see us this evening."

"Damn the man! He is as irresponsible as a wo—" He swallowed the insult when he saw her stiffen. Her posture was already straighter than the chair she was sitting on, if it was at all possible. He resumed pacing, only to stop again when he noticed the book she was holding. It was written in Greek.

Sensing she was being watched, she brought the book closer to her face. It was obvious he was intimidating her again, but, damn, he could not help it. Kim was out there doing something Reave would most likely have to suffer the results and he did not like it in the slightest. The rustling of a page being turned brought his attention back to the book she was holding. He would not have been surprised if she was cross-eyed with the book so close.

Lacking the true target of his vexation, he could not resist snarling at her. "Miss Belanger, I have discovered Greek is best read when the book is right side up." He seized the book, righted it, then, ignoring her discomposure, he stalked out of the room.

Another hour had passed before the viscount returned. Tessa bounded out of her chair to see what was causing the commotion in the front hall. She did not know where he had come from, but Lord Wycke was several paces behind her.

"Turnberry, what have you done? Miss Belanger has been frantic."

"I—" she began, only to be ignored by both men.

"My apologies to both of you. There was a slight indelicacy to the arrangement I needed to rectify," was Kim's ambiguous reply. He shrugged out of his greatcoat, handing the garment to a footman.

The earl's eyes narrowed. "What the devil are you referring to?"

"Lady Brackett."

Horror dissolved the remaining traces of irritation. "God's blood, you haven't!" Reave brushed past a footman, then froze at the entrance. A large woman blocked his path.

"Lord Wycke, a pleasure as usual," she said in a tone implying the pleasure should be all his. She shoved a generous hand in his face, which he took and bowed over. He guided her into the room, giving Kim a bloodthirsty stare as he walked by.

"Is this the gel?" She waved a heavily jeweled hand in

Tessa's direction. "Why, she is almost a child herself, the poor dear."

Kim stepped forward to do the proper introductions. "Madam, may I present to you Miss Tessa Belanger. Tessa, this is Lady Simona Brackett. She will be your chaperone while you remain at Eastcott," he announced.

Everyone in the room hushed, awaiting Lord Wycke's protest. The wait was brief.

"My lord, perhaps we should speak in private," Lord Wycke interjected. His feelings on the subject were quite evident.

"Of course." Kim signaled the butler. "Thorne, is Sims's chamber prepared?"

Thorne cast a wary glance to his lordship. "Yes, milord. This way, ma'am."

"It is kind of you to stay at Eastcott, Lady—" Tessa rushed forward, attempting to make the woman feel welcome, since all Lord Wycke could do was scowl at everyone.

"Call me Sims, my dear child. Just my husband dared to use Simona, may God keep him."

Flustered, Tessa nervously placed her hand to her heart. "I am sorry. I was not aware of your loss."

"Pardon?" Her ladyship squinted, leaning forward until her nose was inches from Tessa's face. "Oh, no, the only place Lord Brackett has departed is to town. He cannot tolerate the country, you know."

"Or you," Lord Wycke muttered under his breath.

No one except Tessa had heard his comment. Her quick intake of breath shifted the earl's ire from Kim to her. She shook her head, feeling helpless she could not make him understand she had nothing to do with the older woman's unforeseen arrival. He grunted, then went after Kim. The viscount had pressed the boundaries of friendship with his high-handedness; now it was the earl's turn to do a little pressing of his own. She would not allow them to fight. After all, it was her fault. Kim had brought her ladyship to protect her reputation.

"Thorne, you may proceed. I will see you all at breakfast."

Lady Brackett declared, mounting the stairs with the help of a footman.

"I need not ask you twice," Lord Wycke said to Kim, then headed for the sanctuary of the library, leaving the others to follow.

It was not until the door was closed that he glanced up and saw Tessa standing in the middle of the room, her hands tightly clasped together.

"Fine, Miss Belanger, do join us. This way you will not misunderstand any insults directed your way."

"Leave off, Wycke. Take your anger out on me. Tessa did not know my intentions."

The earl raised a dubious brow. "Indeed? What exactly were your intentions when you invited that creature into my household?"

"To maintain a certain propriety, I asked Sims to look after Tessa while you reside at Eastcott."

"Why the devil did you chose her of all people? The woman is intolerable; even her own husband flees to London to escape her."

"Being rather limited on time, she was the most respectable woman I could charm and make short work of it." Kim grinned. Lord Wycke looked like he wanted to beat him. "You never remain longer than a day or so. I trust you can endure her to protect Tessa's reputation?"

Tessa stiffened, her face a cool mask of indifference while she prepared herself for the earl's insulting reply. She was well aware her behavior up to that moment was far from exemplary. It would not be astonishing if the man just laughed outright at Kim's insistence that she be treated like a respectable woman. She did not deserve it. When the insult did not come, she slanted her gaze toward him and found him staring back with a unreadable expression.

"She is a drunk. I hear she laps up her nightly sherry like a kitten laps warm cream," Reave finally said without much heat.

Kim shrugged. "So she sleeps soundly at night."

"I will wager half my stock will be consumed before there is a hint of spring."

"If it is, then I will personally replace it."

They were at an impasse, and neither man spoke for a few minutes. "If there is a way to repay you for this, Turnberry, I will not procrastinate," he grumbled, then quit the room.

"He may never forgive you for this," Tessa whispered, afraid the earl was still within hearing.

"Wycke knows when he is trounced." Kim winked and offered his arm, which she accepted. "He will come around eventually, so do not allow him to frighten you. I confess, Sims is an odd creature, but she has a kind heart. You will like her."

"Again you are my champion," she sighed. It was a mockingly feminine noise. "How will I requite your kindness?"

Kim paused, and his visage grew thoughtful. "Allow Reave to help you. You may be just the risk he needs to help him piece his own life together."

Chapter Nine

"Now, where was I?" Lady Brackett adjusted her wire-framed spectacles and studied the chain stitches she had just sewn into the fabric. Clucking with disapproval, she pushed aside her tambour. "Never get old, my dear. I swear I am nigh blind, practically a tragedy for someone of fifty!"

Tessa made a small sound in her throat to concur. Not that she truly believed such nonsense; Lady Brackett possessed a keen sensibility for details. However, she had discovered in their brief acquaintance that the lady enjoyed drama, and one could not have it if one's life was not fraught with one or two tragedies.

"You were speaking of your husband, my lady," Tessa reminded her. With a pen poised in her right hand, she deftly copied out another series of notes on a sheet on paper. Her ladyship had expressed a desire to possess this particular composition of Haydn's, so she had offered her hand.

Whether or not they actually were discussing Sir Walter Brackett, Tessa could not be certain. She had never encountered anyone who could switch topics as ofttimes as her companion.

"Ah, yes, dear Lord Brackett." Her ladyship went on without taking a breath. "A wonderful man except for his disagreeable bowel. It is the boiled onions, you know."

Lady Brackett repositioned her tambour frame, then stabbed a fine needle into the muslin. The scratching of Tessa's pen filled the rare absence of conversation.

"Do you think it will last?"

Tessa halted her work and looked up. "His indigestion?"

"Dear me, no," she chortled, her ample bosom heaving with effort. "This bout of weather. My fingers ache horribly when the temperature drops."

"Have you tried a camphor liniment?"

"For Lord Brackett? I was not aware it would help. Generally, he eases his discomfort with a cup of weak tea and peppermint."

Tessa continued her work while Lady Brackett prattled on about her husband's bowels, her swollen joints, and a personal female problem she was too frightened to discuss with a man she kept referring to as the local butcher. She assumed he was the closest the village had for a surgeon. Her ladyship was certain the two of them could solve her ailment with the proper dosing of herbs. After spending the morning in Sims's company, Tessa concluded the older woman was more in need of a chaperone than she. A discreet cough from the doorway brought an end to their conversation.

"Forgive my intrusion, ladies. His lordship is requesting Miss Belanger's presence in the library."

"Thank you, Thorne," said Tessa, smiling at the retreating butler. "It is time I learn of my duties." She stood and brushed the small pieces of colored silk clinging to her skirt from Lady Brackett's embroidery. "If you need me, ma'am, have one of the footmen summon me."

"Not to worry, my dear. I spend most of my days alone," she replied merrily, waving her off. She adjusted her spectacles, returning to her work. "Lord Wycke is an impatient man. It is not wise to tarry."

* * *

Lord Wycke was staring out one of the large windows when she entered. A large gold-embossed book rested on his hip.

"You wished to see me, my lord?" He was frowning again. She had the urge to knead his lips into a more pleasing form. He was too dark and formidable with that grim expression.

He moved away from the window, placing the book on the leather-covered tabletop nearest him. He made a vertical movement with his hand, taking her in from head to toe. "Is this rag your complete wardrobe?"

Tessa looked down at her black bombazine gown. She agreed the coloring was not flattering, nor was it in the best condition, from daily use, but in an ironic twist of fate it had definitely become appropriate.

"As you see, I have precious little."

He stroked his upper lip, his eyes still regarding her. "I suppose I shall have to purchase a few gowns to keep you from wearing that hideous thing again."

Having him bestow charity upon her pricked her pride and her temper. She managed to keep her face a perfect study of serenity. Unfortunately, her voice would not cooperate. "I will remember in the future to pack an extra bag of clothing on the chance I am set upon by thieves again. It is so difficult to pack for these encounters, you know."

"Are you in mourning?"

"No." The word was from her lips before she realized her error. She gripped the sides of her skirt with clammy hands.

He stroked the shallow cleft of his chin, considering her reply. "Did you not tell Kim that your aunt had died recently?"

"I—I have mourned her for five months. That is more than an acceptable amount of time."

Was she perspiring? Tessa resisted the urge to rub her temples. The room was stifling. She looked to the window, longing to throw open the sash, but thought better of it. Her answer was plausible, she thought. Three months was the beau ideal observed by the ton. The fact her aunt had raised her would explain her extended mourning.

"Indeed." He halted in front of her. "Regardless, no one in my charge dresses like a street urchin. I will arrange for some gowns." Her chin went up a little higher. "And when they arrive, you will wear them. There is no need to thank me. I know any woman would appreciate the gift."

Tessa cleared her throat and clasped her hands together. "You may associate with women who blindly accept your gifts, my lord. However, I am not cut from the same cloth. You will take whatever allowance necessary out of my wages."

"Ah, yes, your position. Where precisely do your talents lie?"

"I must remind his lordship, I did not seek this arrangement. If you are seeking a reason to release me, do not bother. I will oblige you."

"Miss Belanger, Tessa, if I may gain your permission to be so informal?" He continued when he received her wary nod of consent. "From my perspective, I see the scales tipped in the other direction. You have done your best to leave this house and persist even now to provoke me to break my word to my friend and cast you out. What intrigues me is the reasons for your outlandish behavior. A sensible person would consider herself blessed during these times to gain employment without a single reference. For all I know, you could be a murderess," he laughed.

Lord Wycke grabbed her before she hit the floor. "Turnberry was correct. The rodents eat more off the floor than you do a plate," he muttered, guiding her into the nearest chair.

He strode to the decanter on a small table and poured a healthy portion into a glass. Kneeling beside her, he raised the glass to her lips. She could not stop trembling.

"N-no," she said through chattering teeth. Watching him pour had reminded her of another time, another man. "No, thank you."

"I insist. You will be of little use to me if you are ill."

She took a tiny sip, then gagged and coughed. The liquid burned her throat. "This is vile!"

His expression was one of feigned outrage. "You insult my finest stock. Try a few more sips. Once you get used to it, it is actually quite good."

"I have no intention of drinking more." Finally noticing his proximity, she scrambled out of his reach. "Thank you for your concern. I am feeling better."

"You are a poor liar, Tessa." He used her Christian name as if he had done so a thousand times. "At this moment, even Lawson, despite his stiff repose, has better coloring than you. Sit down and we will continue our discussion."

She slid into the chair, grateful he chose to sit on the other side of his desk. Her attention settled on the corded movement of his shoulders. They flexed when he tossed the remaining contents of her glass to the back of his throat and swallowed. She glanced away when he turned to face her. "I suspect when you use the word *discussion* you mean I will listen and comply to your dictates."

Lord Wycke chuckled softly. "Yes, I suppose you would see it that way. Would you believe there are those who consider me quite an agreeable man?"

If he heard her whispered "ha," he had elected to ignore her insolence. Tessa studied her hands. She had twisted them into a bloodless grip in her lap, feeling it was all that was preventing her from falling apart.

He cleared his throat. "You never answered my question."

"Pardon?" She snapped her head up, meeting his direct gaze.

"Your talents, experience?"

She sighed, then shrugged. "I have none."

"Ridiculous! All women have talents, although some are more difficult to ascertain."

He circled the desk until he was standing before her. It was an intimidating pose. It was also working.

"You have dealt well with my son, and everyone else in my

household is charmed by your presence. Come, now, what other virtues do you possess?''

"None that would intrigue you." She held his piercing stare. He seemed more predator than man as he stalked around the chair, trying to reveal her secrets.

"Tell me," he coaxed. "What position were you raised to tolerate?"

Tessa became thoughtful. Before that moment she had never given attention to the culmination of her father's efforts. It had not been her place to challenge his direction. She had been a lonely, unappealing, overweight child who had been grateful for the opportunity to gain her father's favor by marrying a titled gentleman. Beyond that she had not considered herself of any worth. At least that was what Edmund had repeatedly told her.

Lord Wycke was awaiting a reply. She feared the truth would disappoint him. Well, it did not signify, because it was unsatisfactory for her tale. What she needed was a reply that would keep him from prying, something to scare him off.

Laving her lower lip with her tongue, she gave him a look she prayed was closely akin to sultry. Once at one of the numerous balls she had attended, she had seen a woman act in the same manner to entice a gentleman. Aware of the earl's dislike for her, she hoped her actions would achieve the opposite and repulse him.

"I was bred and educated to be the pretty asset of a rich gentleman such as yourself, my lord" was her low, breathy reply. With more boldness than she felt, she stepped toward him. The heat and scent of him assailed her senses. "Have I answered your query?"

He wavered, moving closer as if tempted by what she was pretending to offer. Slightly amazed and a little horrified he was not offended by her brazen behavior, she stood there like a garden statue. He came to his senses before she did. Tensing, his eyes took on a cynical light as he pulled back.

"So you were bred to be a man's whore?"

"Some men call these women *brides;* however, use whatever word that pleases you." Tessa tried to walk away, but he squeezed her arm.

"You once accused me of playing a game. Now you are the one who appears to have a fondness for them."

"I have answered your question, may I please leave?"

"All is not settled between us, Miss Belanger. I am not a man who turns a blind eye to mysteries. I will uncover everything I need to know about you before you leave my employ. What? No foolish declaration that you will leave Eastcott this very night to protect your bloody secrets?"

"No," she said quietly. She felt the sickening dread of becoming completely ensnared in her lies. It almost stole her breath. The truth would damn her, yet her silence seemed a grimmer hell. She searched his face. He concealed himself well. Did he truly desire to help her as Kim had said, or was she a challenge to his injured pride?

"No, you will leave, or no, you have no secrets?"

"Curse you! You know I would have left with Kim if I had been given a choice."

"Why did you not leave with him?" he persisted.

"Because there was no one to care and nowhere to go," she cried. She shoved his blocking arm out of her path and ran from the room.

She was so damn haughty—and too beautiful for his own good, Reave thought. Nonetheless, for the first time, he believed she was telling the truth.

Reave was not surprised when Thorne told him Miss Belanger would be unable to join him for dinner. She had used her low servant status to decline his request. The entire situation was ludicrous, since she was the first servant he knew who retained an aristocrat as a chaperone.

Following supper, Reave extricated himself from Lady Brackett's zealous attention and went in search of his neglectful servant. He knocked on her chamber door. Tessa did not answer. After their discussion earlier, there was no doubt she would not willingly engage him in another. Deciding anything said between them would most likely end with someone raising their voice, he walked away.

Reave heard voices, soft and vague on the night's air. Curious, he searched for their source, pausing at the door to the nursery. Peering through the cracked door, he saw Jason was not alone.

"Not another. You should have been asleep hours ago. If we are caught, I will be the one who shall be reprimanded," said Tessa, pushing the boy toward his bed.

"No one checks. Ever. Our secret is safe. Will you read another story?" Jason pleaded, his expressive eyes entreating louder than his voice.

"How do you know they never look when you are supposed to be asleep?" She ruffled his hair and lifted the covers so he could scoot underneath.

He crossed his arms. "The servants don't care."

"And what of your father? He strikes me as a man who would be more than mildly interested in your nocturnal habits." Tucking the blanket around him, she sat on the mattress.

"He lives mostly in town an' doesn't care what I do."

They were brash words for one so little. Despite his attempt to appear unaffected, there was a wealth of hurt spoken, and Tessa's heart could not bear it. She did not like the earl, yet she would not vilify him to a boy who so desperately needed his attention.

"Ah, that is where you are wrong. He may not be obvious, as some people might, but he marks your activities." She kissed him on the cheek.

"Truly? How is it done when he is gone so often?"

"Oh, fathers have their own way of learning what they want to know, love. Now, 'tis time to dream." She picked up her taper and headed for the adjoining door.

" 'Night, Tessa."

"Good night, Jason."

Neither heard the door on the level below them click shut.

Despite the distance of a night's repose, the image of Tessa and his son drifted into Reave's consciousness like perfume assailing the senses even after the wearer had quit the room. He saw them as two souls wary of the world around them, but they had found solace in each other's company. To be excluded made Reave's throat ache.

He turned the corner and saw her waiting by the door to the breakfast room. Well, perhaps *waiting* was not the proper word.

"Eavesdropping, Miss Belanger?" He almost laughed when she jumped as if she had scorched her skirts. "It is amazing you ever sit down to a meal."

"My slipper loosened," she improvised. "I had to adjust it."

He walked into the room. "Are you eating or sulking?"

Hunger overruled Tessa's pride. "I never sulk." She sat in the chair offered.

"And never lie?"

"Certainly." A plate heaped with a delectable assortment was placed before her.

"Careful, Tessa, I have my own way of learning the truth about you."

She gave him a startled look, perhaps recalling the words she spoke to Jason the night before. Clearly dismissing his remark as coincidence, she resumed buttering her bread. "I must apologize for my behavior the other day. Running out of the room was childish."

"I agree. Although, I will go as far as to say that my own behavior was not beyond reproach."

She hesitated, a piece of toasted bread poised at her mouth. "Is that an apology?"

A smile teased his lips. "I expect it is the closest I will come to one today."

"Then I will accept it as such." She sunk her teeth into the crust. Her eyes unconsciously rolled heavenward with the pleasure of it.

"Good." He was pleased to see her eating with some enthusiasm. "We have a few things to discuss before I leave for London."

She reached for her coffee, quickly swallowing to wash down the bread. "When will you leave?"

"Tomorrow. There is a case needing my attention."

"Have you come to a decision concerning my station here, my lord?"

He looked up and was surprised to find her brow furrowed with doubt about her future. "I was under the impression we had an agreement. You will look after my son."

"But, my lord, I explained to you the other day I have not the skills to tutor Jason, certainly not to ready him for Eton. Perhaps there is something else—"

"My decision is final," he interrupted. "I have discreetly viewed the two of you, and you handle him well. Better than Luke ever did. If it will put your mind at ease, then we will consider it a temporary arrangement. I will make a few inquiries for a replacement when I return to town. Until such a man can be found, I suggest we hold to our agreement."

His words did not erase the uncertainty, so he felt compelled to add, "I doubt you could do worse than I when it comes to governing the boy." Embarrassed, he opened his paper.

"Will there be other duties?"

He raised a dark brow. "I would think a young boy would be enough to fill your day?"

"He is. Well, you did say that you also needed to find a replacement for your steward. I thought there might be other work to be done before I leave."

He had never thought about her departure. Most servants lived out their lives within their households; he assumed she would remain, since she had no other home. "I see," he said slowly. "I was unaware we were detaining you from your destination."

Chagrined by what he probably considered rudeness on her part, her gaze shifted to her plate. "Oh, I have no specific intentions, my lord. My loss of funds at the hands of those footpads encourages me to remain. I swear I will not impose upon your generosity for long."

"It is not kindness nor charity but honest work I offer. Each of us will be compensated."

His bluntness gave her a start. One minute she was demure, the next looking like she wanted to poke her fork in his eye. Thankfully, she did not give in to her fancy. Setting down her fork, she met his bold stare. "In plain terms, sir, my presence was forced on you and your household. For this, I apologize. I never did understand why Kim brought me here, knowing of your feelings as he did."

Ah, but Reave was beginning to understand the mischievous workings of his friend's mind. He did not care to enlighten her. "What has passed is irrelevant, Tessa," he said with resignation. "Now that I think on it, there are other duties for you. I assume you know your letters? Yes, yes, of course," he concluded at the flicker of affront deepening the blue in her eyes. "There is correspondence needing attention, perhaps you could respond to the various inquiries, naturally under my guidance. Then we will continue from there."

"Very well, my lord," she acquiesced. "If I may have your permission to leave, I will see to your son's lessons."

"Before you depart, I have one other matter to discuss."

"Yes?"

Reave stood then, leaned forward, bracing his arms on the wooden table. "The next time you are asked to join me for supper, I expect your presence at my table. You and I both know you are about as common as gold, and this subservient demeanor tries my temper. Have I clearly expressed myself?"

Her eyes widened, but she uttered nothing except a perfunctory "Yes, my lord."

He nodded, returning to his seat. "I will see you at three to help me with my business correspondence. Lawson's untimely demise has left this estate in disarray, blast his soul!" He glanced up and found he had been talking to himself. She was gone.

"Forgive my tardiness, my lord." Lady Brackett swept through the room, yards of plaid kerseymere adding to her presence. "I have not been much of a chaperone as of yet. Has there been a need?" She pinned him with the question.

Reave scowled at the woman. "I must attend to work," he grumbled, escaping the room before she could ply him with other questions he had no intention of answering.

Sims raised a brow at his abrupt departure. Signaling the footman to serve her breakfast, she smiled. "La, the charming viscount was correct." The air fairly tingled with scandal. With enthusiasm she contemplated the possibilities. This promised to be better than one of those maudlin little novels!

Chapter Ten

"Wycke! Rumors were circulating you had disappeared to the country. Who was she?"

"Do not answer him, Reave. He is incorrigible this evening, and most likely the one responsible for spreading these scandalous tales!" Melissa Savant, Duchess of Densmore, rapped her closed fan across her husband's knuckles, causing him to yelp. She bestowed a disarming smile upon Reave.

He accepted her offered hand and gallantly bowed. The young duchess was breathtaking, wearing a simple gown of amethyst and silver cord. It enhanced the violet hue of her eyes. He raised his head and winked at her husband. "Bryson, you are foolish to release such a fair beauty among the depraved and licentious. Someone might be of the mind to steal her away."

The duke smirked, pulling his wife from Reave's side. "To you, my friend, Melissa may appear to be a demure, uncomplicated fragile bloom"—he received an elbow in his ribs from his delicate duchess, causing him to grunt—"in a room full of ragweed, but I would be remiss not to clarify that appearances can be deceiving." Bryson laughed, placing his arms around his outraged mate. "She has led me around the countryside at a pace to cause even the strongest to waver. If I survive, it will be because I have made a pact with old Nick himself!"

Melissa snapped open her fan, using it to conceal her laughter. "Good Lord, you make me sound like a brassy piece of horse-flesh." She squirmed to escape his compromising embrace, but Bryson held her possessively to his chest.

"I agree with the brassy part," the duke murmured, brushing his lips behind her ear.

Reave's smile was bittersweet seeing the love play between his friends. To show affection openly was considered vulgar by the ton, but the duke and his duchess were too much in love to follow convention, nor did they care. A twinge of envy tightened his throat.

In fairness, he knew Melissa and Bryson had endured their own trials of misery and loss, though in the end, they had prevailed. They would share a lifetime that was full of love. He had not been as fortunate.

"So what calamity summoned you to Eastcott?" Bryson asked, remembering Reave.

"I trust Jason is well?" Melissa added, her blue-violet eyes filled with concern.

"Yes, the boy is thriving. I had some personal obligations to address before Hayden involved me with the Lathom brief."

Melissa's smile faded at the mention of the name. She looked to her husband, seemingly struggling whether or not to speak her mind. "Reave, I love you dearly for helping Bryson clear my name. However, I will never forgive you if you help send that poor woman to the gallows!"

"Lis," Bryson invoked.

Reave did not bother to conceal his surprise. "You know the countess?"

Melissa appeared uncomfortable at his sudden interest. "Naturally, she was introduced to us," she said, glancing about. Her voice dropped to a whisper. "Lathom moved within the same circles. 'Tis a pity such a gentle, spirited creature was married to a man who sullied his family name often enough to make them both palatable prey for the gossips. The countess barely managed to hold a smile at these gatherings.''

Reave stroked his jaw, attempting to pull the woman's image from his memory. Finally, he said, ''I cannot recall her.''

''Well, Lord Lathom brought her into London society almost six years ago as his bride. I remember it distinctly, because my brother Marcus and I had decided to remain in town that winter. Where were you?'' She clasped her hand over her open mouth, realizing her blunder. ''Oh, Reave, I am a thoughtless softhead. I did not mean—''

''I know.'' He had been burying his wife when Lady Lathom had been introduced. ''What can you tell me about her?''

She was flustered for a moment. Reave guessed from Bryson's thunderous expression that he planned to chastise his wife for her brashness. Melissa did not bother to acknowledge her husband. Instead, she fingered the large emerald-cut amethyst suspended from her throat. ''Sad. She had the saddest eyes I had ever encountered.''

''Nothing more?''

''Our association was not intimate. I am certain we most likely discussed the fripperies of the hour. I doubt I have helped, and honestly I am pleased. She does not deserve to hang for the death of that lowlife, even if he did die by her hand!''

''Lower your voice,'' the duke growled in her ear. ''There are people present who feel inclined otherwise, my love, and I will not have you risk your neck again. Think of our child.''

''I did not—congratulations to you both.'' Reave clapped Bryson on the shoulder, then kissed Melissa on the cheek. ''I believe I have asked all the questions I dare on this subject for now. Perhaps I will have better luck at the tables.''

Reave was forced to greet a few more acquaintances before he escaped to the gaming room.

Sad eyes.

It was not unusual for an arranged marriage to have reluctant participants. The knowledge did not bring him any closer to learning more about the woman. Suddenly, his thoughts switched to another lady he found equally mysterious. Disgusted a single day had not ended when he had not thought of her, he straightened his waistcoat with a violent jerk, then went in search of a safer game of chance.

Several hours later, Reave traveled to White's to play a few hands of whist and listen to the latest news circulating through the club. His face was shadowed by a straw hat, which was worn by all the players at the table to shield their eyes from the bright lighting. However, it did not prevent Hayden Quinn from recognizing him.

"It is you. The Duke of Densmore suggested you might play here." The solicitor leaned against the wall to watch Reave play out the hand. He lost.

"I must remember to thank Densmore," Reave muttered. Bidding "good evening" to his companions, he walked away from the table without bothering to glance back at his friend.

"See here, I have not been running about town, searching for naught, only to be dismissed like a common servant, Wycke."

Reave accepted his coat and hat from an attendant. "This is not the time to discuss anything of importance. See me in the morning." He walked out the door and into the street.

"More than a sennight has expired and still I have had no word from you."

Reave signaled his coachman. "I told you then I was leaving for Eastcott. The weather prolonged my stay." He climbed into his carriage, hoping their conversation had ended, but Hayden was persistent. He climbed into the seat across from Reave.

Exasperated, Reave demanded, "Hayden, what has you so agitated that it cannot wait?" The man was acting damn peculiar.

The solicitor removed his hat and smoothed the stray blond

strands from his creasing forehead. "Everyone is in an uproar about this Lathom trial."

"Trial? So the countess has been found?" Odd, no one had told him this at the club.

"No, she has yet to be located. Still, her absence has caused the mobs to find her guilty. They cry for her blood."

"Jesus, the last thing we need is to worry about the masses breaking into the court and taking her away, all for the mere pleasure of seeing her hanged."

"Reave, it is not only the mobs, but the ton as well. The shock of one of their own, a woman, no less, has everyone screaming for justice."

Reave grimaced. "Someone has a loose tongue and should be silenced. The countess will be brought in dead before she can be properly tried if the fervor for reprisal cannot be allayed."

"What you desire will not be easily attained. We are at the mercy of the mob, for I have yet witnessed a comparable balance of power to halt their frenzied fury when they have tasted blood."

"Then for her sake I pray she has found passage from the country. She deserves more than a rabid crowd cheering for her death."

Hayden hesitated. "I thought you were not acquainted with her."

"True, even so, I cannot abide a sloppy execution of justice. From what I can ascertain, the entire situation has been handled badly, so if I do not appear enthusiastic about her capture, then forgive my indiscretion."

Densmore was correct when he had commented that there were many who wanted to see this woman hanged, including Hayden. Reave wondered what type of woman could incite such hatred in her peers. "Shall I have my man drop you somewhere, or do you intend to sleep with me too?"

"Very amusing," he replied dryly. "No, my carriage is close." Hayden put on his hat, then stepped down. He paused, gripping the door. "I have collected a few documents concern-

ing the investigation you might find of interest. You know—
statements from the servants and the like. If you are still prepared to help me with this one, I can have a boy send them to
your house.''

Reave nodded and tiredly waved him off. As the wheels of
the carriage rattled over the cobblestones, slicing through the
slush, he closed his eyes and allowed his head to reel with a
colorful swirl of ill-defined thoughts and fragmented images.
Tomorrow he would begin to build his case against Lady
Lathom. The first step would be to learn more about her background. What was it that pushed her to the violent pinnacle of
murder? If she was guilty, he would see she was punished.

"My lord, I am honored.'' Melissa warmly greeted Reave
at the doorway to her winter garden. "If you are to see Bryson,
he is at Tattersall's, admiring some new bloods. And I, as you
can plainly see, am not fit to be viewed by any man.'' She
laughed, trying to conceal her hands blackened by charcoal.

Despite her protests, Reave thought she looked charming with
her mussed hair and the gray streak across her cheek, the messy
result of attempting to tuck a wisp of hair behind her ear. He
knew her to be a talented artist, and it was clear Densmore had
continued to encourage his wife, regardless of her position.

"Duchess,'' he began, casually strolling behind her as they
walked among the potted flora. Halting beside a bench, she
knelt to retrieve a rag to wipe the blackness from her hands in
earnest. "Melissa,'' he amended when she gave him a look
that told him they had been through enough to warrant the use
of their Christian names. "It was you I came to visit.''

"Oh?'' She stopped cleaning her hands and tossed the rag
back into a wooden box.

"Please, there is no reason why we should be so formal
about this. I would enjoy watching you sketch as we talk.''

Melissa glanced down at the sketch she had been working
on before his interruption. A lily had been lightly outlined.

"I'll agree, as long as you do not tell anyone of my atrocious manners. I still have not learned to be the proper hostess." Sitting on the bench, she leaned down, took a small piece of charcoal from her box, and began to add detail to a bud.

"A proper hostess entertains her guest in the manner expected by the guest. This setting appears to be agreeable to both of us." Reave sat in a chair brought out to him by the butler.

"You are too kind to say otherwise, my lord." She cocked her head. Her cinnamon-colored curls tumbled to one side. "Why have you come?"

"Lady Lathom." He noticed her hand stilled at the announcement.

"Oh, why would you want to discuss the lady with me? Does it not break one of your laws or something?"

"There is no trial at present, so there are no laws to be broken. I have reason to suspect you can tell me something about the countess.

Her gaze snapped up and met his. "I told you, I did not know her well. I cannot help you."

"May I?" he asked, then sat beside her. "You have that expression again."

Bewildered, she asked, "What expression?"

"The same one you had last evening, the same one you had when I needed information concerning your brother."

"You speak of a meeting two years ago," she said lightly. "I barely recall the conversation."

"You were afraid everyone thought your brother was a traitor—"

"I know what I thought," Melissa interrupted, speaking over his explanation. "I said, I cannot recall the words exchanged."

Reave reached over and stilled her hand, holding it until she looked directly at him. "You were afraid of what I would learn of him. Just as now, you fear I will discover something about your friend that might destroy her." He softly entreated, "She has few friends in this town. There may be something you can tell me that will save her from hanging.''

"You think I have forgotten you represent the prosecution?'' She smashed the fragile charcoal into the paper. It fragmented into powder. " 'Tis like whispering in the devil's ear!'' she scoffed.

"I seek the truth first, then justice. Madam, the ton has already found her guilty. You know I am no villain. At least allow me the opportunity to prove her innocence, if she is indeed innocent.''

Melissa allowed the sketch to fall to the ground. Her face betrayed her concerns as she rose from the bench. She took a few steps, pulling the sagging shawl over her shoulders. "It isn't what you suspect. I do not know where she is . . . w-whether or not he has finally killed her.''

"You believe she is dead?''

Melissa spun around unexpectedly. "I do not know what to think.'' She hugged her arms to her breast, kneading her upper arms. "I suppose I was as close to a friend as she had. Lathom had a way of discouraging anyone from becoming too familiar. Even Bryson was against the friendship.''

"Why?''

"Is it not obvious? Lathom was insane! What other reason was there for the cruelty he inflicted on her and others.'' She shuddered.

Recalling her delicate condition, Reave gently clasped her upper arm and led her back to the bench. He felt like a bounder for upsetting her, but she was the only one who could give him insight into the woman's character. "Did he beat her?''

"If he did, she never confessed it to me. Though it is not surprising. She did not speak much about him, you see. It would have given Lord Lathom great pleasure to know he had hurt her, so she guarded her feelings well.'' The duchess grimaced as if remembering something distasteful. "The night of the Keels' ball was the first time I had ever seen her lose her composure. But who would have expected the man to be so despicable? Gracious me, the man seduced his own wife's mother! He humiliated her, which undoubtedly had been his intention all along.''

"Was she angry? Was it enough to provoke her to murder?"

Melissa smiled like one would to a child who did not understand. ''The countess was strong, she would have to be to endure six years of marriage to that bastard. If she was planning to kill him, she would have done it years earlier. Odd, you would have thought the time with him would have made her cynical and bitter. Up to the last day I saw her, she believed there was good in everyone. Even him.''

"When did you last see her?"

She tapped her first finger to her lips, attempting to recall. ''The Keels' ball. Almost two months ago. She refused to go out after Lathom's scandalous behavior. One could not blame her. I tried calling several times, but I was told she was not receiving visitors. Regardless, Lathom continued to scandalize the ton, parading the old witch around like she was a prized mare. He took perverse pleasure in flaunting it to everyone.''

"If Lady Lathom wanted to murder him, why would she wait more than a month?" Reave posed the question more to himself than to the duchess.

"You are assuming she is capable of the crime, which she is not!"

"I am not so narrow-minded as you believe, Melissa." Reave squeezed her hand, then stood. "You have told me enough for the moment. I should leave before Densmore calls me out for upsetting you."

"I do not understand. I thought you wanted to know more about her?"

"Another time, if I may. I have made other inquiries, and you have confirmed what I already know." He anticipated her next question, adding, ''The tales of cruelty are the same, only the name of the, ah, lady, vary. All things considered, the man was rather unimaginative. Lady Lathom's reaction to each humiliation was the same. She consistently closed herself off until the gossip died to a whisper, then she would resume her quiet routine. Something broke her icy regard the night Lathom introduced his new mistress to the ton. A month later the adulterous couple were slain. It's a damnable coincidence, is it not?''

"You are as predictable as boiled potatoes," Kim drawled, finding Reave preoccupied at his desk later that evening. "I'll wager you have not moved from this room since your arrival, which, I might add, you did not bother to announce." He threw his cloak, stick, and hat unexpectedly at the motionless butler, startling the poor man. The items fell to the floor. "Miss me, Maxie, ol' man?"

The rancorous servant grunted while he collected the viscount's possessions and stomped out of the study.

"Because of you, I will be fortunate if I get my supper. That man holds a grudge longer than your stretches between baths." Reave snapped the book he was holding shut and tossed it to Kim.

Turnberry smoothly caught the book and turned it to read the title on its spine. "Very dull." He threw it on the nearest piece of furniture. "How is Tessa?"

"I do not know. Perhaps you should have remained a little longer to see how your matchmaking progressed." Reave grimaced. "Your timing was off, ol' man. Pushing a chit off on a man who wanted to pass the anniversary of his wife's death in solitude was incredibly thick-witted, even for you."

Kim raised his palms upward and shrugged with an air of innocence. "You bestow me with too much credit. I did not set those footpads on her so you could rescue her. Nor did I conjure the snowstorm that kept us at Eastcott. I will admit that I took advantage of your misfortune, what with Lawson dying and the boy's tutor running off, but I felt having Tessa remain was amicable to both of you."

"What of Lady Brackett?" The thought of the woman made Reave's chest burn with acid.

"Oh, her. Well, I invited her on your behalf. If Tessa threw herself at your head, although why she would want you is beyond me, then you could depend on Sims to save your virtue. Lord knows, she could match me any day."

The image of her ladyship wrestling the petite Miss Belanger to the ground in attempt to foil a seduction was too ludicrous to ponder. Would he truly want to be saved? Laughing, he rubbed his brow and shook his head. "Are you ever serious?"

"You are serious enough for the two of us," Kim said, then sobered. "You realize there would have been speculation in the village. I wanted to make certain her presence was respectable. By the bye, how is she getting along?"

"Fine. She appears to have an affection for Jason and is competent enough to see to his studies until a proper tutor can be hired."

"I thought you might allow her to remain once you understood she was no threat to that crystalline specimen you call a heart."

Oh, indeed, the bewitching beauty was a threat! "It was not my decision, she has insisted from the beginning I consider her presence pro tempore. From her perspective, I doubt she feels you have done her any kindness by leaving her in my protection."

"Have you discussed this inheritance business with her? She was tight-lipped when it came to telling me the name of her father. For all we know, she could be giving up a bloody fortune!"

An heiress. This thought conjured his parting image of her in the schoolroom, still wearing that god-awful black gown. She and Jason had not been aware of his presence. They had been too busy; their heads bowed close, thick as hops playing their private game. It seemed so easy for her to revert, to understand the wiles of a child. Perhaps it was a simpler task for those who sampled more of the pleasures of life rather than be burdened with the pain. He had known both. The latter had almost destroyed him.

"I have complete trust in your abilities to ferret out the family name."

"Kim, Miss Belanger's petty domestic issues are not my concern. She may keep her secrets. If you haven't noticed, I have several cases that need my attention." He gestured to the paperwork and books on his desk.

"I assume it is this Lathom business that is inducing your present black mood. Very nasty, but it makes delightful gossip." Kim settled in a stuffed leather chair, then bound from it. "Say, leave this for later and come with me to one of the clubs or all, if you prefer."

"You go," Reave replied, his mind more on the Lathoms than his friend's suggestion. "Did you know the countess?"

Kim rolled his eyes with exasperation. "Nothing else matters to you when you have the scent of a new investigation. You are hopeless, my friend." He shook his head with dismay. "Well, I may have been introduced when the lady first arrived in town, although if I was, I cannot recall the encounter."

"You cannot remember? You never saw her later at a ball or the theater?"

"Christ, Reave, you speak of an incident that occurred over five years ago! I have trouble remembering events from a sennight past."

Reave opened his mouth to agree, however, Kim silenced him by raising his hand to surrender.

"All right!" Kim closed his eyes and thought. "Nothing. No, wait, I do recollect hearing the usual vulgar observations. They called her a plain little puff-guts. She was not really the type one would have expected Lathom to choose, but the rumor circulating at the time was that her father was well breached. Made his fortune in shipping, I think."

The viscount frowned when he saw Reave make a few notes. "Do not consider the information reliable, as I said, I cannot recall meeting her. Besides, gossip is the muse of knaves and half-wits."

"You must be confusing her with another lady. The Duchess

of Densmore described her as delicate and fair, hardly a puff-guts,'' said Reave, irritated by the conflicting description. Kim was mistaken. "Her looks are irrelevant. What I need is more information about her relationship with Lathom.''

"Sorry, I never knew her.''

"You and most of the ton. How could she live under the speculative eye of the fashionable, with few to truly claim or at least admit to an intimate association.''

Kim shrugged, dismissing the subject. "Leave this till morning. You need to clear your head and enjoy the pleasures of the evening.''

"Perhaps you are right." Reave summoned his manservant, then collected his briefs and dropped them in a desk drawer. He closed and locked it, depositing the key into his waistcoat pocket. Documents and books would not reveal the secrets of Lady Lathom. He needed to return to society, something he had spurned years before, to learn more of Lathom's unsavory past and his tormented countess.

Chapter Eleven

"Bump the pins!" Jason chanted behind Tessa while she focused on her target at the end of the hall. This was their second game of skittles. He had trounced her soundly once and appeared to be the winner of this game too.

"Sims, you should be playing, not I. I have neither the skill nor the eye for it."

"Tut, my dear. All you need is a little practice," Sims encouraged. "Go on, throw the ball."

Jason cried out again for her to throw the ball. Closing her eyes, she released it. The red-and-green-striped ball rolled down the passageway, its wobbly gait due to the uneven floor. She could hear the energetic cheers of her companions as the ball rolled toward the wooden frame. She turned away at the last moment, unable to witness the results. The ball struck the pins, toppling them over. They rumbled across the hard surface.

"That's five. Tessa, you knocked over five pins!" Jason exclaimed.

His enthusiasm was contagious. She scooped him into her arms and spun him. "I attribute my good fortune to my excellent tutor, sir. Why, without your guidance, my ball might have pocked the plaster, then rolled toward the stairs. By chance, Thorne might have been making his way up those same stairs to announce nuncheon, tripped on my ball, and cracked his skull, which would have turned Eastcott to ruins. Indeed, you have saved us from despair!''

The two of them collapsed to the floor in a fit of giggles, each taking a turn composing short tales about the damage her misguided ball might have wreaked.

"Enough!'' Sims begged. "Tessa, dear girl, cease tickling the boy and dust off your gown. Jason, be a good child and summon Thorne for refreshments. Now the both of you may help me rise and we will remove ourselves to the drawing room.''

"Yes, ma'am,'' the two dutifully replied. Each locked an arm around Sims and helped her stand.

Tessa winked at Jason, who with the jauntiness of a tosspot returned her wink before scampering off in search of the butler. "He is merry as a cricket!''

"We have you to thank for that.''

Tessa halted their progress to the drawing room. "Me?''

Sims looked about to make certain they were alone, then she leaned forward so her words would not be overheard. "On the day of his birth, the poor lad lost both his sweet mother and father.'' She waved off Tessa's attempt to assist her. "Thank you, I can walk alone.'' She took a tentative step down the stairs, gripping the banister with each breath. "There are those who are alive in flesh and dead of soul. Wycke was devastated the night he arrived home to find Elise barely warm. The gossip bandied said it took five men to pull him off the physician. I believe Ross was his name. Reave nearly crushed the man's throat. Not that I do not think the man deserved it, for it was his ineptitude that weakened and eventually ended Elise's life.''

"I was not—Lord Turnberry had not revealed intimate details of Lord Wycke's loss.''

"His lordship is a private man and abhors idle gossip.''

They entered the drawing room. Despite the dark wood walls, it was a pleasant room. Absent was the clutter one usually saw in this particular room, but this household had lost the woman who commonly would have chosen the various plates and objets d'art that would have covered the surface of every shelf and table.

"Jason appears to be a happy child. And the earl's relationship with the boy . . ." Tessa pursed her lips and thought for a moment. Actually, she could not recall a time when the earl had spoken more than a few sentences to his son.

"Exactly my point!" Sims exclaimed as if she had read her mind. "Never a more difficult crevasse to traverse." She clucked her tongue in dismay.

"Are we speaking of Lord Wycke?" Tessa wondered if they were skipping topics again, like one played pitch and toss. No one could predict which topic would be closest to the mark and be grabbed up, only to be tossed out again.

Sims gave her an odd look. "I speak of your presence here, my dear. Has anyone remarked about your scant attentiveness? Now, heed me when I say you are just the person to restore heart to this household."

Tessa could only stare. She did retain the propriety not to allow her mouth to fall open. Thorne interrupted by greeting them and directed a servant where to place the cart. She nodded, not daring to trust her voice. Goodness, whatever did Kim tell this woman?

"Sims, Lord Wycke did not bring me to Eastcott." The words slowly came forth while she tried to think how to explain her circumstances.

"Nonsense! That charming viscount told me Lord Wycke literally snatched you from the vicar's cottage." She reached for a sweetmeat and popped it into her mouth.

"Well, I suppose you could describe it in such a manner." She bit her lower lip, attempting to think of another approach. "I lost what little money I possessed, so his lordship has provided a respectable means for me to replenish my losses."

The older woman clapped her hands together. "Marvelous! The chase can be as stimulating as the capture. A man should appreciate his prize."

Tessa jumped up, planting her fists firmly into her hips. "I am no man's 'prize,' nor will I engage him in any sport! That charming viscount should be horsewhipped for the lies he has uttered, and if I am fortunate, he will suffer by my hand." She marched toward the door.

"Wherever are you running off to?"

"Jason has lessons to recite." The door slammed shut.

Sims reached for the teapot handle and poured the hot liquid into her cup. What a twist! Was the young lady so innocent she was not aware of her predicament? She smiled and reached for another sweetmeat. Later, she would write Wycke to see if she could stir the embers of their obvious attraction. After all, it was rather difficult for them to fall in love if they were not together to recognize it.

Tessa found her charge in the kitchen, dipping his greedy little fingers in Cook's pudding batter. With the morning quickly spent, she ushered him off to his chamber to rest. Entering the upper hall, she walked through until she came to a window. Frost obscured her vision, so she used her fingernail to scratch a small circle.

She peered down at the withered remains of what she assumed was a sunken rose garden. Roses always reminded her of her mother. She wondered what vivid hue would burst forth from the stringy, shrunken tendrils when kinder climates warmed the countryside. Pulling back from the window, she crossed her arms. Dash his prideful honor for returning her to this place! She could have been—well, she did not know where she would have gone, but it had not been his lordship's decision.

Since her arrival, there had been little time to contemplate her mad-brained decision to remain. Spending her days with Jason had reminded her there would be an aftermath to her selfishness. The boy liked her and it was too easy to love him. She had always wanted a child of her own. Even that had been denied her. And now Sims believed her to be the salvation to this family. Madness. She could not save even herself!

She had wasted most of her life on trivialities chosen by her family. Everything she learned, wore, ate, thought, were the calculated ambitions of her father. She had not discovered until later that her mother had had her own personal docket which she had immediately set to the moment the banns had been posted.

Astoundingly, Tessa did not despise her mother. A part of her understood how easy it was to succumb to Edmund's dubious charisma when he had seen fit to ply it. She would never know if her mother had foolishly fallen in love with her daughter's husband, although she was certain Edmund's choice in mistress was another one of his amusing forms of punishment. Whenever she had dared to disobey him, she gained his malevolent attention.

Several days before the ruinous ball held by the Keels, she had suggested to Edmund that she would prefer residing in the country instead of London. If it had been his idea, he would have had her packed off to some moldering ruin without her approval. It was when she dared to speak her mind, or made a decision without his consent, that pricked his ire, and the consequences were left to his sadistic imagination.

That time, he had used her mother to attain his revenge.

His instincts had been correct; she had almost fainted the night her mother arrived at the ball hanging on his arm with a look of intimacy that could still make her retch violently. Her father never knew. She doubted he would care much. The man would have sold her himself if he had thought he could have turned a profit.

Tessa inhaled; her breath frayed into a shudder. She would not cry. Tears ultimately made her head ache. Besides, she was too numb to feel grief. She wondered if, had she reacted differently the night of the ball, her mother would have lived.

She had been a fool to confront him at the ball, yet she had been too humiliated with his latest revelation to restrain herself. Edmund had been waiting for her in the gallery. It had been a dreadful argument. She was certain there had been witnesses to the quarrel, but no one interfered. Perhaps such melodramatics were allowed given the provocation. She did not know. In the end, she had threatened to leave. He had only laughed. He had studied her well and knew her fears. She would never leave him. To defy him so publicly took courage, something he knew she did not possess. His assumption had been correct—for a month.

Tessa thawed the windowpane with the palm of her hand. Her attention returned once again to the frozen dead garden. It was true she had been desperate enough to attempt to poison him. Should it not count in her favor that she had realized her mistake before the results had been fatal? Her forehead fell forward until it rested on the cold glass. She relished the slight burning sensation. It intensified the longer her flesh remained pressed to the pane.

The tightness in her chest made it difficult to breathe. There would be witnesses to verify she had threatened to kill him. She doubted her maid would hold her tongue. Was it coincidence Edmund had died in the very manner she had threatened? There were too many questions she could not answer, nor was she in the position to seek them out.

''Miss Belanger?''

She heard the butler, understood what he was asking, though she could not raise her head from the glass. ''Not to worry, Thorne. Just a slight headache.''

''Shall I mix a powder for you?''

''Yes, a powder. That would be fine,'' Tessa said, her voice barely audible. ''Thorne, the roses below. What color will they be?''

''Red, miss, bloodred—'' He abruptly ceased, rushing forward to catch her before she slumped to the floor.

* * *

"Just another bite, my dear," Sims cajoled. "I swear I will not leave your side."

Tessa dutifully swallowed another spoonful of the clear broth she was offered, grimacing at its blandness. "I am grateful for your tender ministrations, but I am well. The dizziness has passed and I need—" She pushed the spoon in her face aside and attempted to rise from the bed.

"You will remain here the full day even if I must summon a footman to restrain you," the older woman threatened, setting the spoon on the tray. "A fit person does not faint." She leaned closer, her voice dropped to a horrified whisper. "Did the butler make an unseemly overture to you? I am shocked, for it is so difficult to recognize these rogues!"

Tessa could not imagine the kind, elderly butler doing anything remotely rakehell. She laughed and settled back onto the pillows. "No, no, Thorne was beyond reproach. If not for his timely presence, I most likely would be nursing a rather nasty bump on my head."

Sims looked unconvinced. "Thorne mentioned you were behaving oddly before your collapse."

"It was the headache, I suppose. I could barely think," she murmured, hoping to end their discussion. She felt foolish to have succumbed to that particular feminine affliction, and was of the mind not to repeat it.

"Oh, I almost forgot with all of the excitement. Several trunks arrived for you." Sims reached for the spoon, only to halt when Tessa wrinkled her nose and shook her head. "Did I mention Jason has been scratching at the door, wanting to see you?"

"No," Tessa replied, confused about the arrival of the trunks. "Allow him to enter the next time he knocks." She bit her lower lip. It did not take long for her to give in to her curiosity. "There are trunks for me?" She had left a small trunk behind at the inn, but no one had been aware it belonged to her.

Sims smiled as she walked over and pulled the gold bell rope. Her eyes sparkled with the prospect of viewing the contents of the trunks. "The earl has been generous to his lady."

That comment snapped Tessa from her lethargy. Groaning, she recalled the earl had warned her he would be sending her attire befitting her new station. Sims had misinterpreted his charity. She swore silently to get even with Kim if he ever had the courage to visit Eastcott again. "Lord Wycke is generous to his staff." She emphasized the last word.

"La! Here you are, my dear man," Sims greeted the butler. Her apprehension concerning his fictitious forwardness disappeared as quickly as the thought. "Miss Belanger is improving and I feel a peek at his lordship's gifts would prove restorative to her spirit."

"I do not think—"

"Nonsense. Sit back and I will bring everything to you." Sims nodded approvingly when her patient sunk back into the pillows.

"Thorne, you have the earl's confidence. Would you please explain the relationship between Lord Wycke and me to Lady Brackett?" Tessa was irritated to see nothing dampened the woman's disposition, while she was feeling rather temperish. Crossing her arms like a sulking child, she waited with a certain smugness for the loyal servant to clear up the misunderstanding.

Thorne regarded her request for a moment. Clearing his throat, his brown eyes warmed with approval. "It would please his lordship immensely if his gifts were favorably received. I understand he saw to each choice personally."

Her eyes widened at the unexpected reply. She gave the helpful man a chilling stare. A glimmer of satisfaction coursed through her when he looked uncomfortable. He deserved every unsettling moment for collaborating with Sims. She punched her pillow with the enthusiasm of one of Gentleman Jackson's prize pugilists, then plopped on her side, facing away from her unwelcome visitors. The labored breathing of several footmen as they carried in the trunks filled the room. Tessa refused to acknowledge their presence.

"Where is that lazy maid of mine? Thorne, be so good as to send the wench to us. There is much to be done. La, where do we begin?" Sims stroked the leather surface of one of the trunks. "Size!"

"Pardon?" Tessa asked, then reminded herself she was ignoring them.

"You there." Her ladyship pointed to one of the men. "Open the trunks beginning with the largest." She expelled a wondrous gasp and clapped her hands together as she peered over the man's shoulder. "Indeed, his lordship has been generous!"

Tessa squeezed her eyes shut and covered her ears with two pillows. The gesture did not succeed in blocking out Sims's murmurs of surprise and delight. Much to her dismay, curiosity was supplanting her pride. Reluctantly, she dropped the pillows and sat up so she could see the amazing contents of those blasted trunks. "I trust the gowns are satisfactory?" If she sounded like an ungrateful chit, she did not care.

"Gowns?" Sims frowned, appearing confused. "No, my dear. Come and behold your wardrobe."

A fragile cane chair was placed near the trunks so she could admire the contents firsthand. Her eyes widened at the size of the trunks. There were unquestionably more than a few practical gowns enclosed within them. She watched as Sims removed bolts of fabric from the largest trunk. There were cottons of various textures, wool, satins, and even silk! The colors and patterns were as varied as the fabrics: spotted, striped, prints, all enhanced by a spectrum of colors. She reached out to feel the cool smoothness of the Caledonian silk Sims was holding out to her. It was checkered amaranthus on white. She knew it would look lovely on her because she had chosen the pinkish hue of purple for herself in the past, in what seemed a lifetime ago. This was the wardrobe of a lady.

Or a man's fancy whore.

"We will summon my favorite modiste from London, for

we could not trust just anyone to work with these delicate fabrics.''

Tessa's throat felt dry and tight. "Is there no black? No gray?''

The question dimmed some of the excitement animating the older woman's countenance. "Are you in mourning, Tessa?''

"No. These fabrics''—she made a sweeping motion with her hand—"the colors. They do not fit my station. There has been some mistake.''

"Flaming impudence! How can you dismiss the man's generosity? Look at the other treasures he so thoughtfully bestowed upon you. Here are three gowns he had prepared in advance. By the looks of them, they need to be altered; still, one must appreciate the attempt to properly clothe you until the others could be made. And here—''

She moved to another trunk. "Beautiful slippers. Admire the exquisite beading and embroidered bow knots.'' Sims brought the slippers closer, inviting Tessa to make a closer inspection. "Thorne told me his lordship had your old pair traced while they were being cleaned so he could have the proper size made.'' The older woman dropped the pair in Tessa's lap, exclaiming, "Oh, goodness, there are also numerous pairs of half boots of satin and brocade, and here is a pair of nankeen.''

She stared down at the sturdy boots Sims held in her hand and did not know what to say. Verily, Lord Wycke had been generous, too much so, if anyone was interested in her opinion. From the puzzled expressions on everyone's faces, she realized no one understood her wariness. She tightened her grip on the blanket covering her borrowed bedclothes and rose to inspect the contents of another trunk. Inside, she saw white silk hose decorated with embroidery and others with open insets. She colored slightly as she picked up a "zonas,'' or Grecian brassiere, consisting of bands covered in silk. There were also petticoats, stays, small bustles, and even pantalettes! Had the earl truly chosen each article himself? She looked at all the trunks in disbelief.

"The smaller trunk contains ribbons and combs to adorn your hair, not to mention plumes for bonnets, fans, and even cosmetics. There is little he did not consider."

Indeed, Tessa frowned, stroking the ivory ribs of one of the fans. She picked up a bottle of perfume and was stunned to recognize it was one of her favorite scents, lily of the valley. She tried to recall if she was wearing the fragrance the morning she left Edmund. She could not remember.

All of this attention from a man who did not want her in his household made her feel overwhelmed and suspicious. A man would never send gifts unless he expected to be rewarded. She tossed the fan back into the trunk. Well, he was sadly mistaken if he thought she would allow him to toss her skirts for a few trunks! She wanted to rebuke his gifts, but she craved to rid her flesh of the itchy gown she had worn daily since her arrival at Eastcott.

In truth, she had never been without her personal comforts, and at one-and-twenty she was too old to begin. Upon his return, if he dared to even glance at the hem of her gown, she would spit in his face! Uncorking the perfume vial, she inhaled its fragrance. The scent took her back to a time when she knew nothing of Lathom, murders, knife-wielding footpads, or a brooding earl whose haunting eyes bespoke of wicked pleasures.

Chapter Twelve

He was bored. Slanting a glance to Kim and his soon-to-be-former mistress, the Dowager Lady Pratt, Reave realized he was the only one in the group not enjoying the play. The plot did not interest him, not when there was a real-life drama being played out. He should be meeting one of his contacts, attempting to glean more information about Lathom. There were rumors circulating that the man had not always played above the board with his business associates. It was a reasonable motive for killing. He knew men who had killed for less.

A minor character strolled across the stage, her blue train a shimmering cascade behind her. He imagined the color would have favored Miss Belanger's complexion better than the brunette below.

Tessa.

The woman had a way of creeping into his consciousness when he least expected it. He wished he could have seen her face when the trunks had arrived. Using his hand, he rubbed the sardonic curl of his lip threatening the polite bored expression he wore. He could envision her stiff little spine stretched a notch when she inspected the contents. Reave expected her anger, her pride, would have demanded it. He also hoped the lady in her appreciated his gifts. To be sure, what decent woman would not have suspected his motives?

When he had entered the shop, he intended to purchase the most practical, lackluster gowns he could afford. Viewing the latest imports, a different Miss Belanger overtook his thoughts. This fantasy woman wore vibrant colors to match her tempestuous disposition. He saw a woman who was confident, quick-witted, whose eyes were rarely overshadowed by fear or sadness. He chuckled softly. It was foolish to believe a few pretty gowns and incidentals could erase what years of pain and loss had inflicted.

"Where are your thoughts, my lord?" Maggs whispered.

Reave stared at his mistress. This was a woman who possessed all he imagined for another, and yet he did not desire her. He wanted Tessa. Leaning to the side so that his lips brushed her ear, he replied, "You know I have none when I am with you."

"Such pretty words, but your actions play you false."

"How so?"

"Your hands, my love. They are forever stroking your face when you are perplexed." She boldly reached for his hand and teased his palm with her nails. "I can think of other places where your hands may roam if they tire of the rugged planes of your face."

Reave smiled at her enticing invitation. He would not accept her offer. A sennight past he had not been so reluctant, believing a night with a willing woman would quell his interest in Tessa. To his grim surprise, his night with Maggs only fueled his desire for the elusive Miss Belanger. The release had been empty, and he felt all the worse for using Maggs as if she were a whore.

Somehow he suspected if it had been Tessa in his bed, it would have been different. He could not explain his feelings, he simply knew them to be true. His smile warmed as he imagined all the unflattering adjectives she was probably uttering in his name, the maddening ungrateful waif. The truth was, he deserved every one of them.

"Why do I feel that smile is not for me this evening?"

"I was thinking of our time together," he lied. "Regretfully, I cannot accept."

The smile vanished from her face as she understood the words he did not say aloud. "You need not speak further, my lord. You have imparted your most honest discourse this eve by your gestures alone!" She turned to Kim, who watched their exchange with interest. "Please escort me to my carriage, Turnberry. This is one wager I have lost." She left the box.

Kim glanced at the swaying curtain, the only evidence of Maggs's hasty departure. He rose, his expression pensive and uncharacteristically sedate.

"You know as much as I, so do not press," Reave said. "See she gets home without incident, if you do not mind." Kim nodded before slipping through the parted curtains. Reave's cool gaze scanned the theater. He was certain the little scene they had just played out had been much more interesting than the drama below. At least Kim had kept his opinions to himself. He was not in the mood to verbally parry his friend's numerous questions and observations.

An actor's exaggerated moan resonated from the stage. Disgusted, Reave rose. He now recalled why he had given up his box after Elise's death. He lacked the tolerance to indulge bad theater.

Dismissing the idea of finding solitude within one of his clubs, he told his coachman to take him to the town house. Kim would be seeking him out, expecting him to explain his odd behavior. Well, let him search and come up wanting, he thought sourly.

"Good evening, m'lord. We had not expected you so early this evening." Maxwell greeted his lord in an age-worn voice.

"The play is not worth your attention, Max. I think I will work awhile before I retire. See I am not disturbed." He handed his greatcoat and hat to the servant. His hands burned from the cold.

It reminded him of another journey when he had lost the feeling in his fingers. Tugging at each finger's covering with his teeth, he removed the leather gloves and tossed them into his hat. Damn the woman, did she always linger so close in his mind? He briskly rubbed his bare hands together.

"That's what I told him," the servant muttered. "Still, he insisted on seeing you. 'Tis obvious the only resemblance he maintains as a gentleman is the fine cut of his coat."

"How did Turnberry arrive before me?" Reave marveled. "He could not have escorted her home so soon." He turned on his heel and headed for his study.

"No, sir, it not be the viscount who rudely waits for you, but another gent."

"Well, who is it?" Reave demanded.

"He claims to be Chester Hone."

"I do not recognize the name. Get rid of him." He headed for his study.

"He says he's the father of Lady Lathom."

"Where is he?"

"I placed him in the drawing room, m'lord. I trust—" The servant never finished his question, for the earl had rushed passed him in search of his unexpected visitor.

When Reave entered the room, he caught the man helping himself to a generous portion of port. Mr. Hone tossed the liquor to the back of his throat and gulped. He jumped when he noticed Reave quietly observing him. Wiping the back of his hand across his wet lips, he extended his hand in greeting. Reave stared at the offered hand before his gaze traveled upward, meeting the red-rimmed eyes of his caller. "Good evening, Mr.—"

"Hone, Lord Wycke, Chester T. Hone. I heard you've been asking questions 'bout my Countess, so I thought you and me should meet."

"It is rather late to call."

"That I know, sir, but I thought it best under the circumstances," he said, walking to the door. He opened it and seemed pleased to find the corridor empty. Shutting the door, he glanced wistfully at the bottle of port.

Reave gestured toward one of the chairs. He knew little of Mr. Hone with the exception that the man had gained his position in society by his daughter's auspicious marriage. "Might I inquire into the specifics of these circumstances?"

Mr. Hone scratched his balding head, seemingly amused by the question. "Well, she's done herself up well and tight, now, hasn't she? A bit of muslin, yet has London crying for her blood."

"So you believe she murdered her husband and your wife?"

"Hell, no." He colored and tugged at his cravat. "Sweet as damsons, she was, too timid to cut anyone with cruel words let alone a blade, but that won't save her from the gallows." He reached for the bottle and poured himself another drink.

Reave leaned back and studied the older man through steepled fingers. "Mr. Hone, why have you come?"

Mr. Hone swallowed the contents of his glass before responding. "You have a good reputation in town. Solid. Respectable." He cleared his throat and reached for the bottle when he realized his praise had not softened Reave's harsh expression. "Countess—"

"Countess?"

"Aye, I named her myself despite my wife's protests. Countess Saffron Hone. A real lady's name. A name to force people to give her respect. I never dared dream she would find herself a true blue blood and make it official!"

Reave flicked an imaginary irritant from his sleeve. "From what I have gathered, you were the one who found her Lathom," he said, appearing bored by their conversation.

"Well, uh, why, aye, I had met Lord Lathom through a business venture. I say, nothing odd 'bout that. Considering her looks, all fat and weak-kneed, she made a cow seem aggressive." He wiped a trickle of sweat from his temple. "She should have been grateful for the match."

"I understand from various sources she was not particularly elated by your efforts."

"What girl knows of these matters? She was reluctant, but she did her duty."

"Was she happy?"

Mr. Hone blinked, surprised by the question. "Why—I suppose she was. I never thought to ask." He emptied his glass and set it on the floor. " 'Twas not my business once they married, as I see it."

Reave smirked, although he remained silent. So Hone did not care about the private hell his daughter endured as long as his social position was secure. The man repulsed him. He sat there in his foppish attire, the finest coin could provide, yet all Reave could see was the man's baseness and greed. He would have liked nothing better than to toss the bastard out on his selfish arse. Reave stifled the urge, since Hone might be able to help him find her. "Has she contacted you?"

The older man puffed out with indignation. "No, and it would do her little good since I would be forced to hand her over to the magistrate. I must consider the family name."

"Why have you come to me?"

Hone studied his nails, then chewed off a rough edge. "We are both men of the world and understand the way of these things. I am certain we can reach a favorable agreement to a grave situation."

"Are you bribing me, sir?"

Oblivious to the silky menace in Reave's tone, the older man winked at his host. "Come, sir, do not act the green lad with me. If you can assure me the shadow of suspicion cast upon her will vanish, I will be generous."

"Are you so certain she is guilty?"

"It is of no consequence, man! What matters is my business. No one will trade with a man whose daughter is a bloody murderess! I must think of my own." He rose and held out his hand. "Do I have your word?"

Anger prodded Reave to his feet. He towered over the man

by at least twelve inches. "You speak of your family, but whom do you truly represent this eve? Your daughter? She is missing, sir, mayhaps dead. What of your wife? She lies cold in her tomb. That leaves you with your precious good name and money."

"You have no right to speak to me in this manner, regardless of your position," the older man yelled, taking a step backward.

Reave would not allow him to retreat. He matched the distance with a threatening maneuver. "You gave me the right the moment you intruded upon my privacy and dangled your reward for making the scandal disappear. Sweet Jesus! I thought you had come to protect her, but you would rather bury her than bear the disgrace." He pulled the bell cord, summoning his servant. "Get out before I call you out."

Mr. Hone's face contorted with frustration and impotent rage. "There is a price for every man's honor. I wonder what you value more than gold?" He tugged the bottom of his tight waistcoat. "If you care to discuss the matter further, you know where to find me."

"Sir?" Maxwell stood in the doorway.

"Remove this man from my house. See to it he never gains admittance." Reave, a tempest of disgust and outrage, grabbed Mr. Hone by his coat, pushing him against the door. "I pray my people find your daughter. I know if given the choice, I offer a safer refuge." He released the sputtering man, then strode out the door. The door of his study slammed shut before the indignant man could utter a coherent reply.

"Maxie tells me you had an unexpected visitor last evening," Kim commented, watching his friend finish his morning repast.

Reave swallowed the sausage he was chewing and reached for his coffee. "Then I assume I do not have to reiterate the conversation, since Maxwell undoubtedly had his ear pressed to the door." A distant clatter from the next room made both men grin.

bordered on the obsessive. He thought if he could see her, he might put to rest the haunting visions that had taunted him since he had left Eastcott. One usually found reality disappointing when compared to fantasy. God, he hoped he was right!

"My visit shall be brief. I will return once I see to my satisfaction that the woman you pushed off on me is able to function in my household. I will summon you if I find anything to the contrary." The decision had been made. He would travel to Eastcott and end his infatuation with Miss Belanger.

Chapter Thirteen

It had not snowed for almost a sennight. Still, the wind moaned with chilling gusts to create an icy crust upon the frozen earth. Tessa disturbed the frozen surface, her shoes ruining the sculpted white drifts as she plodded by the dormant hedges and headed for a small group of buildings in the distance. She paused. Gritting her teeth against a bitter gust, she decided it had been foolish to indulge Jason with this outdoor game of hide-and-seek. When she had originally suggested they play the game inside the house, the boy had thrown a tantrum.

Lately such scenes had become common, causing her to doubt her abilities to handle him. She had questioned Sims on the very subject, but the dear lady dismissed the topic, pleading ignorance. Even the servants did not appear to be upset by his displays of temper. Perhaps she was being too sensitive. Nevertheless, she felt helpless and needed guidance. She considered writing Lord Wycke, though Sims had advised her not to bother him with trivialities. A boy was expected to exert his power from time to time, and she should allow him such freedom.

Tessa pulled the wool scarf from her face, then wiped away the wetness accumulating where her lips had touched the coarse wrap. Shifting it so a drier section covered her face, she sniffed the air. With a determined toss of her head, she strode toward the buildings.

Jason would have avoided the stables, she concluded, dismissing the largest of the three, because the stable master would have run him off. What of the small shed?

Cautiously, she approached the building. Slowing her movements, she hoped he could not hear her approach. She tried the door. It was stuck. The little imp was wrong to think a barred door would deter her. After a few straining tugs and a frustrated kick, it screeched its protest when she opened it far enough to slip through the opening.

The interior was dark save for the muted daylight filtering through the cracks. Tessa took a few tentative steps forward. A bolder step took her to the edge of a table. Or, rather, she assumed it was a table. Its rough edge snagged her wool gloves as she slid her hands up and down it. She pulled the scarf from her face, allowing her eyes to adjust to the darkness. In the corner to the left of the room she listened to the steady squeak of a loose board while the wind whistled an eerie melody through the various cracks. She shivered, feeling more than the cold.

After she found Jason, the game would end. They would return to the house even if she had to drag him back high with temper. At the moment she cared not one grain if he was the heir.

"Jason," she called out to the darkness. "I am wet and cold and tired of this game. If you do not come out from your hiding place, I shall leave you alone."

Taking a step to the right, her hand fell across a blanket. She tugged at the fabric, meeting some resistance, but it finally gave way and slid off the table. Wrapping it around her, she continued her search for a candle.

"Jason, I do not find this amusing in the slightest. If you do not answer me, I shall write your father," she threatened. The wind replied with a crescendoing mournful wail.

Her elbow brushed against a tinderbox, knocking it to the floor. She reached down and picked up the round tin box, eagerly prying off its lid. Her fingers closed around a small candle stub. The familiar hardness was a comfort. She twisted it into the holder serving also as the box's lid. Further searching within the tin rewarded her with a flint and steel striker.

"You are horrid to do this to me," she muttered, striking the metal against the stone. After several attempts, the sparks ignited the wadding of torn linen within the tinderbox. She coaxed the smoking rag with her breath, then touched the candlewick when it glowed orange. The fragile flame brightened her cloak. Tugging one glove off with her teeth, she cupped her bare hand around the flame.

Raising the candle high so as not to ignite her clothing, she clutched the slipping blanket and headed back to the darkest corner of the shed, where even the faint daylight could not warm. She froze when she saw him. He was on a table, the shadows drawing his small form to almost the size of a grown man.

A gasp of relief escaped her as she silently moved closer to him. The game was over. They could return to the house. Almost to his head, she could see his black hair glisten with golden highlights from her candlelight. Odd, she never realized he had so much gold in his hair.

"Now I have you, my little mischief!" She seized his head before he could roll off the table. Instantly, she knew movement would be an impossibility for either of them. Her own body slowly become as petrified as the skin she was handling. Fear coursed through her blood until it reached her heart. Its pounding beat in her ears muffled her sporadic attempts at breathing. Holding the candle over the body, she peered over the shadowed face. The sharp, sculpted nose and shrunken shadowed sockets conjured the image of a man who would haunt her forever.

Dear God, Edmund had found her!

She heard a scream, not aware she had opened her mouth. Backing away from the table, she whirled around and ran into a support post. The candle sputtered, extinguishing when it struck the dirt floor, plunging her into darkness. Ignoring the stinging pain prickling her face, she staggered to the door. It swung open before she could reach it. One instant she was standing, the next she was in the arms of Lord Wycke. She was too upset to lecture him on the impropriety of their embrace. Clutching fistfuls of the wool covering his broad shoulders as if she never planned to release them, she allowed him to carry her outside.

"Why were you in my shed?" he demanded, pressing her trembling weight to his chest.

Tessa brushed her wet cheeks against the rough gray-and-white twill coat, reveling in his blessed living warmth. "A game," she struggled for the words. "I was supposed to find Jason and . . . and . . . there is a man in there." She pointed back at the building to clarify. "I believe he is dead!" She hiccuped and choked back a sob, recalling with horror the feel of his gray skin.

He was not Edmund.

"Mr. Lawson is indeed dead. He passed away a week before your arrival, I was told. A proper burial has been impossible with the ground as impenetrable as granite." His grip tightened when she shuddered. "No one expected you to walk out here."

"I was looking for Jason." She pulled back so she could see his face. His usual austere visage was reddened by the wind, and his eyes lit with compassion. "I thought he was lying on the table."

The earl tentatively touched her pale face, tracing a wet trail left by her tears. Tessa did not protest his tender ministrations. She was too grateful he had found her.

"Jason is well and drinking hot chocolate with Lady Brackett," he said, giving her a wry smile. "Thorne deterred him from leaving the house. Only later it was discovered you had left without being told. When I arrived, they were sending a few men out to search for you.''

All at once, each became aware of their proximity. He allowed her to stand. Removing his coat, he placed it around her shoulders. ''You will shake yourself into pieces if we do not get you inside. Are you well enough to walk?'' She nodded. Leaning on him, they made their way back to the house.

''Why are you here, my lord?''

The simple question brought them back to the reality of the situation. The intimacy of the moment shattered.

''There will be time to discuss my presence when you have rested, Tessa,'' he replied enigmatically.

Not certain she truly wanted to learn the motivation behind his unexpected appearance, Tessa looked straight ahead toward the main house. They continued their walk in silence.

''When I am forced to risk something I refuse to part with, then I play to win. Such games I have never lost. I keep what is mine and win what I wish to attain.''

His words resounded in Tessa's head, although another day had passed since the earl had uttered them. She had come across him playing billiards. Uncertain of the game, she had asked if he had ever lost. His reply had offered her no comfort. Since then, the feral fire she had seen glowing in his eyes last evening haunted her, stalked her as surely as if he had pulled her into his arms and undermined her intentions by fulfilling their hidden promises. Some unknown spring within her surfaced, bubbling with anticipation, wondering if he sensed the yearnings his hungry stare had breached. Fortunately, fear and regret had been her familiar companions longer, and like the timid mouse Edmund had once called her, she had excused herself from his presence and scurried to her room.

He probably thought her unbalanced. From her behavior at present, she was beginning to doubt her sanity as well. All his talk about games—she frowned with disgust, then planted her fists onto her hips at some spectral challenger. They played a game the other night that had nothing to do with billiards.

Tessa sank to the floor and pressed her head into her lap of plain cream muslin. She had thought her years with Edmund had prepared her for the dangerous game of deceit she had chosen to play with Lord Wycke. Curse him, he was good! Even she could not recall when he had taken up the challenge in earnest and became master of the rules.

"Is this the correct way?" Jason asked, his small body barely able to contain his eagerness.

Tessa studied his watercolor rendering of one of the stable dogs. Since her frightful encounter with Mr. Lawson, he had transformed into the perfect ward. She would have preferred to believe he had felt remorse for his role in her mishap, but Tessa suspected a stern lecture from his father had more to do with his easy compliance.

"This is a fine attempt, Jason." She smiled, noticing he had more pigment on his clothes than on the paper. "Remember, there is no correct method to watercolors, only interpretation." Affectionately, she tousled his hair and whispered, "If you find pleasure with your results, then that is what matters. Do not let others influence you."

"Does this apply to math as well?"

"Ah, mathematics. Although useful in art, it does not rely on interpretation entirely. There is structure with a sound base of equations to . . ." She trailed off, noting his attention was focused beyond her. Turning to see what had captured his interest, she was mildly surprised to find Lord Wycke in the doorway.

"My lord?" She curtsied, bidding him to join them. Tessa sensed his disapproval when he saw his son's efforts. "Jason, it is time to change your clothing. We will resume your other studies upon your return."

"Yes, Tes—Miss Belanger." Jason looked to his father to

countermand her request. He quickly left the room after receiving a dismissing nod from his father.

Her movements felt awkward under his silent regard. She thought her bones would crack from the tension. Slapping down the cloth, her lower lip curled behind her teeth. "I know you disapprove. However, there is more to learning than books and recitation."

"I do not think the delicate art of watercolors is something I wish my son to learn. I do not expect to find him painting again." His tone brooked no disobedience.

"Since when is transcribing images from your mind to paper something unmanly? He is actually quite good at it." She held the wet paper out for him to view. He made no attempt to take it.

"You are under my employ and I expect you to follow my orders, directly or indirectly. See to it that you remember your position next time."

Tessa set the paper down and placed her hands on her hips. "And what are the consequences if I do not heed your command? Will you let me go? Need I remind you I did not want this position. I told you I could not instruct." She gave him her back while she picked up the rag and resumed her cleaning. "Watercolors," she murmured, knowing he was listening to every word. "I dare him to call one of our great masters umanly for creating beautiful works of art!" Lord Wycke placed a warm hand on her shoulder, stilling her tongue.

"Enough. I will allow the painting if this is as far as you will educate him on the delicate arts. If I find him tatting—"

"Oh, no," she rushed in, not wanting to hear another threat. "Only watercolors. We will allow the others who have the talent for making lace to their work." She smiled, even if it was not more solicitous than a grimace. "Thank you for ignoring my impertinence."

He leaned against the table she had just cleaned, and he sighed. "Tessa, the humbleness of a servant fits you as badly as the ready-made gowns I sent you. It irritates me to see you try.'' He raised an eyebrow at her abrupt movements. ''You have been avoiding me.''

She raised her head at his casual observation. She looked directly into his eyes to see if he was angry. She learned nothing from his shuttered gaze. Warily, she said, ''I was not aware you had summoned me. I will mention this to Thorne.''

''That is not what I meant, and you know it.''

Tessa could not deny she wished him gone. The man was a threat. ''I work hard to prove to you I am worthy of your—esteem.'' The word *trust* in her throat like charred bread. ''For your son as well, until you find a suitable replacement.'' Hope brightened her eyes. ''Have you found someone? Is it the reason for your unexpected return?''

''No. Are you eager to leave Eastcott?''

She could not bear his concern. ''I am treated well, my lord. However, I fear Jason needs a firmer hand than I. He is a—a willful boy.'' Her statement brought forth an unexpected laugh from him. She blinked in surprise. The man was rather handsome when he was not staring her into a fit of tremors. The revelation did not please her. She glanced down at the rag she had wrung into a twisted rope.

''Forgive me, dear Tessa, but my son has never been considered willful in nature. Most describe him as a shy, withdrawn child.''

''Perhaps he is lonely for his papa?'' She believed the anguish and frustration he revealed at that moment was the result of her impertinent tongue again. She stiffened for his fury. The blow never came. Instead, he crossed his arms over his chest, his gaze focused on something beyond her, his visage full of self-derision.

''No, Miss Belanger. If you remain here, you will learn the boy hates me.''

''I do not understand. When he speaks of you, it is always with the highest regard, the manner it should be with one's father.''

Lord Wycke dismissed her comment with a frown while he

absently stroked the small cleft of his chin with two fingers. "Oh, I have his respect; fear of me has taught him that much. I have not his love."

He sat there, sullen, lost, like the little boy she had come to know over the past weeks. This side of him seemed approachable. She proved it by walking over and lightly touching him on the shoulder. Her gesture startled both of them. Still, she remained by his side, resisting the urge to pull away.

"I believe he misses you, my lord. Perhaps you have misunderstood his reaction. It might be his resentment is leveled at your actions, your absence from Eastcott, rather than you." His eyes narrowed, compelling her to add, "Oh, I am certain you have visited when you have been able, but with his mama gone, he has no one." Tessa sighed. "I have done it again. Forgive me, it is not my place to speak so freely." She began to pull away. His hand reached out, settling her action.

"I am not in the habit of telling strangers about my personal life. Oh, hell, I was the one who began this conversation. Forget my ramblings. I am tired and perchance indulging in a bit of rue." He clasped her hand tighter while he gently caressed her skin with his thumb. "It is I who should beg your forgiveness for taking advantage of your compassion."

Tessa was certain it was not intentional. The way he stressed *passion* sent chills down her spine. When he brought her hand to his mouth, rubbing the sensitive fingertips with his lips, the quickening of desire was quelled by the sharpness of self-preserving suspicion. There was motive behind his seduction. There had to be. Edmund had reminded her often enough that she had nothing a breathing man would want. Snatching her hand away, she cradled it as if she had been burned.

"You are the vilest of miscreants I have ever had the displeasure to encounter!" She slapped him across the face with the wet rag she had been clutching in her other hand. Disbelief gave way to anger at her sudden attack. She did not hesitate to take advantage of his shock and fled the room. He caught her in the passageway.

"What she-demon possessed you to do that? I thought—" He took a deep, savage breath. "It does not matter what I thought."

"Do you think I am so weak-minded not to understand what you were doing in there?"

He sneered. "Since you consider yourself a bloody authority on my life, why do you not just set me straight!"

"It was one of your vicious games of manipulation, was it not? The all-important Lord Wycke. You cannot tolerate that I prefer to keep to my own affairs. But I thought even you were above seducing a—a servant!" She looked at him with such loathing, then turned away.

"From where do you contrive this tripe? Have you been reading those frivolous novels I have seen in Lady Brackett's possession?" he roared back, appearing genuinely affronted she could think him so base. "If I want to pry into your inconsequential background, I can do so without resorting to the tricks of a courtesan. You insult me to think otherwise."

Tessa shook her head, not certain if he spoke the truth. "No," she said, clearing the hoarseness from her throat. The intensity emanating from him frightened her.

"You little fool. Are you so innocent not to discriminate attraction from a deceptive ploy?" He grabbed her hand. Ignoring the little squeak she made, Reave placed it to the apex of his trousers, allowing her to understand his increasing torment. "Now do you understand? Here is your proof, you bewitching minx! Even I could not feign my desire to have your body pressed against mine." She could not prevent the soft, frightened sound from escaping with each panting breath.

"Please."

"Please what?" he coaxed, holding her firmly against him. "Please hold you closer. Or please whisper in your ear and tell you of my desires. Or, please . . . kiss you?" Even as he said the words, his lips drew closer to hers.

"No," Tessa protested, too fascinated to prevent his lips from touching hers. Their contact was subtle, almost reverent.

When she did not push him from her, his moves became more possessive. Biting and sucking her tender flesh, he kissed her with a passion she could have never imagined. She tentatively returned his kiss, which caused him to groan and renew his assault. Rhythmically, he massaged her upper arms, while thrusting his hardened arousal against her. Tessa slowly linked her hands around his neck, relishing the complete possession of his kiss.

It was when he attempted to probe his tongue into the moist crevasse her slightly opened mouth permitted did she fear she had trespassed into dark waters beyond her experience. There was no one to save her, even if she was not so certain she wanted to be saved. Her second initiation into passion soured, as it had with her wedding night with Edmund. She pulled away, but his hands were caught in her hair. He held her fast. Feeling overwhelmed and panicked, she did the only thing she could think of and bit his tongue. Wounded and successively tempered, he released her.

Holding a hand over his mouth, he growled, ''It took you long enough to decide you did not enjoy my kisses!'' His body shook with bridled passion. With another growl, Lord Wycke slammed his fist against the wall.

''Forgive me,'' Tessa sobbed, her own body aching, strangely wanting. She saw the pain in his eyes, or was it a reflection of her own? With nothing left to say, she heeded his silent warning and retreated.

Chapter Fourteen

"What dreams have removed you from us, my dear?"

Sims's question wrenched Tessa from her thoughts. She glanced back at the table where her new friend sat patiently and smiled. Tapping the edge of her spoon against her plate, she added another dollop of elderberry preserves to her plate before joining the older woman at the table.

"Forgive me, Sims, I am out of sorts this morning." She stifled a yawn. "I did not sleep well." For once, she could be truthful. It had been difficult to fall asleep when all she could think of was the embarrassing predicament she had placed herself in with Lord Wycke. Her hysteria last night would probably result in her termination, and frankly, she decided it was for the best. Living in the residence of the very man who could see her hung had her strung tauter than a harp.

Sims made a tsking sound, and her hazel eyes twinkled in merriment. "This has been a common affliction for you since his lordship's return. I know my heart would be racing if I had gained his favor."

"Really, Sims, you know nothing of the situation. I can

assure you I am far from his good graces this day.'' She raised her hand to silence her companion. ''Truly, if you ask me one question about it, I shall leave this table immediately.''

Sims shifted in her chair, barely able to contain her excitement concerning this new development. Ignoring Tessa's threat, she could not resist asking, ''Was it a lover's quarrel?''

''Sweet heaven! Have you no propriety?'' Tessa, half exasperated and more than a little impressed by the woman's audacity, stood, preparing to leave the prying biddy to her own counsel.

What she did not expect was to find the very source of her distraction calmly lounging in the doorway. Her eyes narrowed on him, wondering how long he had been watching them. When he raised a brow in reply, she decided she would not walk out of the room like a churlish peasant and promptly returned to her seat. She doubted her feet could have treaded the distance past him, when he stood there looking at her with a mocking challenge on his face. Blast the man for looking so handsome this morning too!

''Good morning, ladies. Do you mind if I join you?'' Lord Wycke asked politely as if he did not have the right to intrude.

Sims chuckled at Tessa's stony countenance while motioning with a fleshy hand for him to join them. ''Plenty of room, my lord. We were just discussing Tessa's affliction.''

''Sims!''

Lord Wycke surveyed her from head to foot. ''Tessa, are you ill?''

His concern seemed genuine enough; it was the casual use of her name that thickened her tongue and had her stammering. ''I—I am well, my lord.'' She glared at Lady Brackett.

Frowning at her, he grumbled, ''I believe if you can call my closest friend by his Christian name, then you should undeniably be bloody able to call me by mine.''

After what has transpired between us!

He had the decency not to speak the sentence aloud, but he made certain she understood his meaning. He looked directly at her, an arrogant smirk erasing his imposing frown. It was enough to make her squirm.

"Lord Wycke, this is highly improper." Sims drew herself up, prepared to protect her charge's reputation.

"Thank you, Sims, but his lordsh—Reave is correct." Tessa tried to smile, letting her friend know that she was not upset. "After all, R-Reave rescued me in London and has opened his home to me. I would be honored to call you by name, my lord." Liar, his eyes silently flashed, but she would not challenge him here.

"Well, I suppose there is no harm." Sims relented, regarding Reave, then Tessa. "We are more informal here in the country than in town, you know."

A silent tension descended upon the group. Sims was the only cheerful one, and she ate her meal with particular relish, whereas her companions appeared sullen and mute.

Reave downed the contents of his cup, then broke the silence by querying, "So, dear Tessa, over and above your irritating habit of sidestepping my questions, what else afflicts you?"

She blushed at his reminder of the conversation before his entrance. "Lord—"

"Reave will suffice. I have enough people around to remind me of my status in society."

"Ah, well, as you wish, my lord—Reave," she amended when she saw the warning fire banked in his eyes. "If you desire to know the embarrassing truth, Lady Brackett came upon me while I was spinning thoughts. I am certain a speculative man as yourself has at one time or another been caught in similar circumstances."

"Indeed, I have," Reave agreed. He signaled the footman for more coffee. "Your explanation relieves me. I was expecting you to confess your illness had worsened."

"Illness?" She looked to Sims, who was not looking so smug at the moment. "Whatever are you referring to?" she demanded.

Obviously puzzled by her anger, he replied, "Why, your

collapse. Lady Brackett wrote me directly after you were confined to bed. Were you not ill?'' he asked when she groaned
and caged her face with her fingers.

"Sims, how could you?" Tessa closed her eyes, an attempt
to gain her composure. She inhaled, finally meeting Reave's
curious gaze. "Sir, you have been gravely misled. For reasons
I cringe to gather, her ladyship felt the need to summon you.
However, I can assure you, I am fit for my position."

"To Hades with your position. Did you or did you not
collapse?" he pressed, slapping his linen on the table.

"Yes, a headache, nothing more. I was a trifle warm, and
wearing a corset laced much too—oh, never mind. I suffered
a dizzy spell. Sims ordered me to bed for only the day."
Frowning at Sims, and more mortified than she cared to admit,
she asked, "Am I wrong to suspect that you received a letter
stating something a bit more life threatening?"

"No, you are not," he replied curtly, glowering at both
women.

"My dear Tessa, I thought it best Wycke know of your
situation. It would not have been proper form to brush this
under the rug," Sims argued.

"There is no way you can varnish your mischief, madam.
You purposely misled the man into believing I was one step
to joining Mr. Lawson out in the shed!"

"Mr. Lawson?" Sims wrinkled her nose at the unfamiliar
name. "Whatever is the man doing in the shed in this weather?
He is most likely to catch his death." Her innocent, albeit
accurate observation diffused the mounting tension in the room
quicker than any explanation. Reave laughed unexpectedly. His
hearty chuckle was contagious, forcing a smile out of Tessa
before she let go of her anger and joined him. Eventually, Sims
could not resist laughing at their private joke, since even the
footmen seemed to know their source of amusement. "Did I
say something amusing?"

Reave was the first to recover. "Lady Brackett, you have an
unusual way of disarming a hostile argument." He glanced

over at Tessa. "The letter is inconsequential. We should be gratified Tessa is in good health and hopefully will remain so." He raised his cup to salute her.

"Thank you, my lord. Indeed, I am confused by what I have done," replied Sims. Mystified, she sighed and rose from her seat. "I have letters to write, so if I am needed, please do not hesitate to call me."

Minutes ticked by before Reave attempted to salvage the conversation. "Do you ever eat? I swear, I could afford a hundred more servants if their appetite was as absent as yours."

Tessa was thankful he had decided not to comment on Sims's advice, so she chose to do the same. She stared thoughtfully at her untouched plate. "Odd you should say that"—her voice became soft with reflection—"for there was a time when my eating was all anyone could speak of." Purposely she took a bite of her eggs and swallowed. "I think I was almost as large as Sims by the age of two and ten."

"You jest!" Reave blurted out, but when he saw there was no mirth in her blue eyes, just a distant sadness, he rephrased his thought. "I am certain you were not as large as you think. I have rarely met a woman who truly sees her image properly despite the improvements of the looking glass."

Tessa gave him a side glance, noting only mild curiosity in his expression. He did not even seemed repulsed at the thought of her at almost twice the amount of her present weight. Nevertheless, a man with his distinguished looks and breeding would have never cast a second glance at someone as plump and timid as she had once been. Her eyes met his expectant ones. "We may lie to ourselves; however friends and family rarely lie, sir. I was fortunate enough to have someone remind me of my disgraceful condition daily," she explained without a trace of malice. "Nor did I have gentleman callers ready to whisper flirtatious promises in my ears."

He gave her an assessing look. It spoke of complete male appreciation. "You will never convince me you have ever lacked male admirers. When you are not cutting a man into ribbons with your sharp tongue, you are a rather charming companion. A man who could not see that is a fool.''

She discreetly studied Reave through lowered lashes, attempting to understand why this man could easily draw her out. It did not seem he was trying to trick her. Touching her napkin to each side of her mouth, she set aside the cloth before she clasped her hands together.

There had been a time when she had wondered if any man would find her attractive. She recalled the day Edmund had brought her to London. After the half-day's journey by coach, she had learned her husband could barely tolerate her presence.

'' 'Tis a pity, your sister is dead. I was told what she lacked in constitution she favored in looks. I would have rather had briefly a comely bride with death's kiss upon her lips than an ugly bride I would simply wish dead.''

Edmund had refused to speak to her the rest of the journey. He had not even bothered to approach her on their wedding night, or the lonely nights that were to follow. Only once . . . her hands tightened as if in prayer. She banished the memory from her head.

She gave Reave a small smile. ''You are generous to think so, my lord. I cannot fault the gentlemen when it is I who have changed. Experience has seen to that.''

He nodded, seeming to understand the tinge of bitterness in her statement. ''It must have been difficult to accept your aunt's deception and your father's identity.''

And the lies I have told to protect myself.

''Yes. I believe there were moments I wanted to give up and die.''

''You are too stubborn to allow yourself to be beaten,'' he said. The teasing gleam in his eye dimmed as he cleared his throat, adding, ''There was a time I, too, would have welcomed death. It would have been easier not to have awakened each morning, if only to recall I had survived another day, and that there would be another, and another. I endured in spite of myself. It was necessary.''

Tessa's eyes burned with suppressed tears. "For Jason?" her voice cracked.

Reave nodded, his throat convulsing as if to swallow an unwelcome emotion.

Sensing she had stirred up some difficult memories, she rose to leave. "We never seem to be able to progress to pleasant discourse. Our undoing is you and I do not stick to the proper guidelines society sets," she chided lightly.

Amusement usurped his haunted expression. "You know of these rules?"

"Well, I have it on good account one never discusses matters of importance. If we focused our attention to safer subjects such as the weather, horses, and the latest *on-dit*, we might actually become friends."

"Friends?" Reave pretended to consider the concept. "The idea has merit."

"Now, with your permission, I shall leave and seek out Jason. I fear my employer displays a formidable temper when his servants tarry." She curtsied, bowing her head to prevent him from seeing her smile. The door clicked shut behind her.

Reave relaxed in his chair, thoroughly enjoying the image of Tessa smiling. It had completely transformed her; even her nose wrinkled while her blue eyes sparkled with merriment. She was exceptional, a truly refreshing combination of teasing innocence and wit without the bearing of a frivolous whimsical creature. Tessa was a lady of substance.

His benevolent feelings toward her did not linger beyond the warmth of his coffee when he realized he had been outwitted by her again. Somehow the little minx had switched tactics. She dazzled him with a beguiling smile, hoping he would forget the true reason he wanted to talk to her.

Something had happened between them last night, and she artfully hid behind verbal byplay. He would not have been too surprised if she had maneuvered their conversation to more painful memories just to keep him off balance!

With his hand tightly clutched around a delicate china cup,

he started to follow her. Stopping after a few steps, he pivoted on his heel and returned to the table. Reave slammed the cup into its saucer with a clatter. He refused to go after her like a lovestruck schoolboy! The feeling of being manipulated wrenched him like a baker pilloried for having short-weighed his wares. Later, at a time of his choosing, he would summon her. Reave picked up a copy of *The Times*. It was almost two weeks old, but he did not care as long as it kept him from running after her.

It was late afternoon before Tessa had time to herself, which was well and good considering the direction of her thoughts lately. Her arms still tingled when she thought of his warm hands rubbing and kneading her flesh. It was almost too much to bear. What had she been thinking to allow him to touch her like that?

Almost nothing, you weak-minded chit!

Her inner voice scolded her now, but where was her common sense when it could have done her some good? Sighing, she drew her covered knees up and rested her chin against them. Her posture was inappropriate for a gentle-bred lady, yet she was too wrapped up in her latest blunder to worry about it.

Sims suspected something had transpired, or she would not have been so interested in her whereabouts last evening. Her ladyship was a keen-minded woman when she chose to be. Tessa knew she had left her companion disappointed with her vague replies, but she was not about to give her a confession that could be used to manipulate Reave. Tessa already sensed he anticipated the worst in her. Why not? She was a stranger to him.

A stranger who willingly fell into his arms like a doxy.

"Will you please keep quiet. You are not helping me," she said aloud to the empty room, then laughed at the absurdity of her actions. "Goodness, now I am speaking to myself."

This was truly too much! She whirled around the room in

search of a distraction. Noticing one of the books she used to plan her lessons for Jason, she snatched it up and eagerly scanned its contents. The words blurred and another more disturbing visage came into focus. His deep blue eyes studying her, as they had three hours before.

He had summoned her to his library, and although she had no doubt the meeting would lead to trouble, she had excused herself from the nursery. She knew before he had uttered a command the lighter mood they had shared at breakfast had been replaced with a removed deliberateness. He stared at her so intently when she entered the room, she glanced behind her to make certain his rudeness was not meant for another. It took her two attempts to stir him from his pose.

Curtly, he reminded her that her duties at present extended beyond the nursery when necessary, as was the case. Shoving various statements at her, he told her to add the bills for the monthly accounting. Not wanting to provoke his temper, she demurely accepted the papers and moved to a small writing table across the room.

His request was ridiculously simple and she had set to her task immediately. After she had totaled several pages, she glanced in his direction and was startled to find him in the same brooding position. He did not appear apologetic at being caught, nor did his eyes return to his own work.

She had wanted to ask him what she had done for him to treat her this way. The question remained locked in her throat. Confused by his renewed hostility, she reluctantly returned her attention to her work. She did not have to raise her eyes again to know he was still staring her, trying to penetrate beyond her combination of flesh and bone. What he expected to find there, she could only speculate.

Twenty minutes later she rose from the table, set the paperwork on his desk, and without his permission, returned to Jason. He had not bothered to stop her.

She was still perplexed by his actions, the feeling vexing her pleasant humor even as the hours passed into the evening.

Lord Wycke had been conspicuously absent from dinner. The fact soured any inclination for eating. Sims did not consider his absence odd nor did she allow Tessa's low spirits to deter her from enjoying the meal.

After supper, Jason persuaded them to enjoy their evening entertainment in the music room. A mahogany pianoforte was placed in the corner of the room to allow space for dance instruction. Tessa reverently touched the ivory keys; a note or two sounded.

"Do you play?" Sims settled into one of the ribbon-back chairs positioned off to the side.

"It has been some time." Tessa bit her lip, this time allowing her slender fingers to splay across the keyboard. She hit a chord. "I was never considered good enough."

The older woman waved her hand, dismissing her comment. "I suspect the person who made that cruel observation had not the proper ear for music. The boy and I are a kind audience and would like to hear you play."

"Please, Tessa? I doubt you are any worse than me," Jason earnestly confessed.

She laughed and adjusted her skirts over the small bench. "I have warned you both, so please ask me to cease my feeble attempts if it is painful on your ears." She offered a weak smile.

"We care not to hear the excuses, just the music." Sims shifted forward for Jason's ears alone. "My hearing is poor when it comes to music. I miss most of the notes, so you will have to let me know if her playing is passable."

"All right, Aunt Sims," Jason agreed cheerfully.

Tessa began to play a short, lighthearted piece from her childhood lessons. The name escaped her, although the memory of her finger positions remained. She glanced over at her companions. Remarkably, they were listening to the music with rapt attention. Somewhat taken aback by their reaction, she stumbled over the next few notes. Gaining confidence, Tessa soon lost herself within the melodic spell of the song. When she finished, she was gifted with applause. Jason, her most ardent admirer, jumped up and down while she curtsied.

Sims whispered to Jason, "Did she play well, boy?"

"Quite."

Her ladyship rapped her walking stick on the floor. "Not passable, Tessa? Who uttered such lies?"

"My mother," replied Tessa softly.

"Nonsense. The woman was deaf," she decreed, qualifying it with several nods. "Would you play another?"

Tessa complied, refusing only after a fourth was requested. There were few songs remaining in her memory, and she feared she would embarrass herself if she attempted to read off the sheet music. She was about to ask Sims if she could play, when she noticed Reave had entered the room.

"Good evening. I see I have missed more than dinner this eve."

"Good of you to join us, my lord. We have just exhausted Tessa's talents. Would you care to entertain us?" Sims offered when no one else bothered to invite him into the room.

"I was not aware you played, sir," Tessa said, rising from the bench. He took her place. When she tried to find a seat near Sims, he simply reached out, easily capturing her wrist.

"I thought I told you to call me Reave?" he said, his gentle admonishment for her ears alone. He flexed his fingers in preparation to play.

She almost gawked at the changes in him. The lines around his mouth and eyes seemed softer, and his eyes had warmed to a bluish-gray. He behaved as if that afternoon had not occurred.

"Considering the circumstances, I thought it best to return to a more formal address."

"You get us both in trouble when you think. Help me with the music sheets, enjoy the music, and, for once, close your mouth." He smiled to gentle the command. When she did not protest and stilled her twitching, he spread his hands over the keys and began to play.

It took merely a few notes for Tessa to know his talents were

beyond passable. The man truly had a gift! She absently saw
to her task of turning over the played-out sheets. Instead, she
concentrated on the haunting melody flowing through her, leaving her sad and wanting. The song made her think of faded
dreams and lost youth. By the time he had struck the last notes,
she was digging for her lace handkerchief. His music somehow
found a means to unleash the reckless emotions she kept buried.

"You are forever surprising me with your talents, my lord."

Pleased with her response, he smiled. "It was my mother
who possessed the gift of music. I was the privileged one to
study with her," he modestly replied. He took her hand, his
thumb brushed across her fingers. "Tessa, I—"

"Well done, Lord Wycke," Lady Brackett interrupted.

Reave dropped Tessa's hand, although he did not bother to
conceal his annoyance at the older woman's intrusion.

His irritation went unnoticed as her ladyship blithely continued. "I am most certain with a little practice you will be up
to your usual degree of excellence."

"Sims," Tessa chastised, outraged her ladyship could find
fault with his playing. "I am not surprised the Regent himself
has not asked him to play!"

A warm, appreciative light gleamed in Reave's eyes. "I hold
your high opinion of my talents dearly to my heart, Tessa.
Although it was my mother who had the ability and privilege
to play for kings, not I." He patted her hand. She dodged his
attempt to grasp it.

"Grandmama played for the Regent?" Jason interrupted,
visibly impressed he was related to people who had actually
spoken to royalty.

"No, son, it was his father, King George III, who had the
honor to hear your grandmother play. She was quite a sensation
in her youth."

"How come she don't play anymore?" Jason had moved
closer to the bench until he bumped against it with his thighs.

"Well, it is her hands, you know. They do not work as well

as they did when she was younger. I remember how sad she
was when she announced they hurt too much for her to play.''

''Oh.'' His voice threaded with disappointment as he twisted
in one spot. ''If her hands still worked, I could have learned
how to play as good as her, like you.''

Tessa was about to meddle. She generally took great care
not to involve herself in private matters, but she feared the earl
was too blind to see the opportunity presented to him. She
reached out to the boy. ''Here, Jason, take my place next to
your father so you may inspect the keys. Reave, I fear I am
weary of standing, so you shall need a new assistant.''

Jason began to strike the keys at random. Tessa, taking a
step backward, held her breath. Reave quietly observed his
son's enthusiastic off-key chords. From the back it was difficult
to read his expression. Would there be anger? Indifference? Or
perhaps hope?

''Do you—'' Reave cleared his throat. ''Would you like me
to show you how to play? If you like, we could hire someone
to instruct you.''

''Truly?'' Jason spun back to face her. ''Tessa, Sims, my
father is teaching me how to play!'' He banged on the keys as
if his notes were actually a song.

''How lucky you are to have such a talented papa,'' Tessa
replied, sitting down next to Sims. She felt like crying. Reave
had not turned him away.

During the hour that followed, the ladies chatted congenially,
occasionally stopping long enough to make a comment or two
about Jason's playing. Father and son sat hunched over the
keyboard, thoroughly enjoying their efforts despite the fact that
most of it sounded like a leathered boot striking the keys.

Tessa sat in front of her dressing table hours later, reflecting
on what had transpired that day. She was confused about most
of it, though she did not need anyone to explain what had
occurred in the music room. She had witnessed the healing of

a relationship. "What a watering pot I have turned into," she muttered, leaning forward to blot the mistiness from her eyes.

"If you must cry, cry for yourself." She picked up her brush and briskly attacked one of the many tangles in her hair. When she completed smoothing out her waist-length tresses, her stomach gurgled, reminding her she had skipped supper.

Her appetite had been nearly absent the last few days, but now it gnawed at her insides with determination. Knowing she would not be able to sleep unless she ate something, even a small crust of bread, Tessa reached for her shawl to cover her shoulders. The servants would have long since retired. She would not need to wake anyone for the small portion she desired. Cupping her hand around a single taper, she made her way down the chilly passageway and stairs, searching for the kitchen.

She froze at the threshold when she realized she was not alone in her quest for food. Reave stood in the middle of the kitchen, clad only in a silk dressing gown that had indecently come undone in the front. The candle lit the room enough for her to see a well-formed chest matted with dark, curling hair. She swallowed at the sight.

"Well, Tessa, it appears I am not the only one who missed a meal this eve." His rich voice filled the quiet room. It was as warm as the candle dripping beeswax on her hand.

Chapter Fifteen

"My lord," Tessa executed a perfunctory curtsy, making no attempt to enter.

Reave noticed she was barefoot again. Her toes curled and unfurled in an agitated manner. It was a feeble exercise to ward off the cold.

"If you plan to continue these midnight rendezvous, I would suggest covering your feet, Tessa," he said, recalling the first time he stumbled upon her in his son's room. "Did I not send enough fabric to dress you from head to feet?"

Her gaze dropped to her bare toes. In an embarrassed gesture, she shifted her nightgown over them. "You were more than generous, sir. I have been meaning to express my gratitude."

"You may do so at your convenience." Her gaze snapped up, meeting his, attempting to judge his mood. Reave had given her provocation in the past to make her wary, so he tried to disarm her with a smile. She visibly relaxed.

"I am usually a very thoughtful person, but our encounters since your return have been tumultuous at best. There never seemed to be a moment to thank you properly, even though you took it upon yourself to dress me like"—she hesitated, searching for the proper word—"part of your family."

"Are you expressing your appreciation or complaining?" Reave teased.

Tessa laughed, her eyes warming at last. "I suppose I would sound ungrateful if I was."

He beckoned her to join him at the long pine worktable. "Perhaps you could consider the wardrobe an advance toward future services."

She leaned against the table as confusion wrinkled her nose and brow. "A payment? I have done nothing to warrant your generosity."

"I beg to differ. This evening you gave me my son."

Shaking her head, she rubbed her nose, creating the intriguing combination of humility and embarrassment. "You bestow me with too much honor. I only offered my place to Jason."

Reave reached across the table, capturing her right hand. He turned it over, admiring its unblemished smoothness. "Do not belittle what I know as truth," he admonished her. "I have spent many an hour thinking of elaborate methods to bring down what I considered an impenetrable barrier between my son and myself. You felled it with a simple act of compassion. My lady, I am humbled."

Tessa withdrew her hand from his. A rosy hue stained her skin. He noticed even her shoulders were delightfully pink when the oversized neckline of her nightgown slipped, revealing one alluring curve. Almost as quick as the baring, her hand came up to adjust the errant fabric. Her eyes glittered, full of censure when she caught him staring where most gentlemen, at least not so blatantly, would dare. "You are no more humbled than I, my lord."

"I am pleased we are in agreement." He opened the door to the larder. "Before your arrival, I was about to raid this. Care to join me?"

She nodded, her full lips parted almost in invitation as she peeked over his shoulder. "I am ravenous."

A DESPERATE GAME   163

His hands balled into fists when her ill-fitting gown slipped off her shoulder again. He wanted to reach out and stroke her smooth, alabaster flesh. "Something else we share in common." Reave shoved a plate of apple fritters and lemon patties into her hands before she could adjust her gown again. It was not very sporting of him, he thought, nor was he feeling very much the gentleman this evening. "Do you cook?"

"Only if you want to spend the next three days purging your insides with senna and molasses." She used her chin to push the neckline up over her shoulder.

Ignoring her sigh of frustration when the fabric slid down her shoulder again, he cheerfully continued. "So we will have to endure a cold supper. Next time we will warn Cook of our intentions."

Tessa showed no reaction to his hint to future nocturnal meetings. Instead, she set down the plates she was holding, adjusted her sleeve, and left the room. A few minutes later she returned with a large basket. "I found this in the footmen's anteroom," she said, placing it on the table. "I thought we could use it to carry our food into the—which room should we use, the dining room or the breakfast room?"

"Neither," he replied. He began to fill the basket with his selections from the larder. "There is a fire warming my chamber as we speak. We shall enjoy our repast there." He discerned her reluctance even though she had not voiced her protest aloud. "Is the notion of entering my private chamber unchaperoned too much for your maiden modesty?"

"It is highly improper," she admitted, her attention drifting longingly to the food in the basket. "All the same, I am too hungry to refuse." Tessa picked up her taper. "It would not do to have Sims learn of this." She halted at the doorway, preventing him from passing.

Reave winked, giving her a playful nudge. "On my honor, Lady Brackett will not hear about your shameful behavior from my lips."

The comfort of familiarity made their journey to his chambers swift. Nor did Tessa hesitate when he opened the door to his domain. This was his private sanctuary, forbidden to all women but most assuredly to beautiful, beguiling virgins. Extinguishing her taper, she set it on the veined marbled chimneypiece, then knelt to warm herself.

"We will eat by the fire if you have no objections," Reave said, setting the basket on the floor. He removed a white wool blanket from his bed and shook it out in front of the fireplace. Once the blanket was in place, he began to unpack their meal.

Glancing up, he realized she had not moved from her position. At first, bafffled by her remoteness, the reason for her odd behavior suddenly became clear. "Tessa, my chamber is no different from yours: a toilet table, a washstand on a tripod foot, a wardrobe, and a bed. There is nothing in here that will strike you daft or offend your sensibilities if you dare lift your gaze from the fire and look about the room." He tried not to smile, fearing she would think he mocked her.

"I apologize for my foolishness," she said, turning her back to the fire. "But I—oh, this is quite charming." She took a few tentative steps away from the fire, her hand rested lightly on a haircloth chair.

Reave looked about the room, actually seeing it for the first time in years. The indigo sprig-and-striped painted paper had covered the walls for more than ten years. The matching bed curtains on his tester had been cut into rags years before. In their place was a solid indigo wool trimmed with gold fringe. He had not given the room much thought until he saw it through Tessa's eyes.

"I have never seen such a large bed!" Tessa exclaimed, then slapped her hand over her mouth, horrified by her improper remark.

"My grandfather had it made a lifetime ago. I was told he was a lusty gent who preferred to have his wife in his arms each night." He uncorked a bottle of wine.

"How odd."

"Actually, I thought his sentiments quite appropriate." He

reached into the basket. He withdrew his hand when it grasped air. "We forgot to collect a pair of crystal." He took a swig of wine from the bottle. Offering it to her, he asked, "Would it offend you to place your lips where mine have kissed?" He knew his question would lead her to recall the passionate kiss they had shared the other day, an image that rarely left his thoughts.

She pulled her hair together, allowing it to settle down her back. Taking a deep breath, she moved to the blanket and sat on the floor beside him.

"It is my finest Madeira," he coaxed.

"Very well," Tessa sighed, then took up the bottle he offered and sipped. She handed the bottle back. In its place, he offered a plate of veal patties. Thanking him, she took one.

Too hungry for polite conversation, they ate in silence, speaking only to thank each other for the bottle of wine they passed between them. It was only when the bottle was empty and Tessa was finishing her gooseberry tart that Reave spoke.

"I have never seen you so mellow. Generally, you are as jumpy as a wet cat in a spring thunderstorm."

Tessa laughed at his observation, her eyes were unusually bright. "It is not surprising, since you are either raging at me or—"

"Kissing you?" he succinctly completed.

Her lashes lowered, her gaze focused on her discarded tart. "In truth, I had not considered the incident worth mentioning."

She was giving him absolution for his crude mauling in the schoolroom. They could both ignore the encounter and continue on as lord and servant. However, neither seemed fit for their chosen roles, nor did he feel inclined to ignore their attraction.

"You smite at my manhood with your cruel words," he said, appearing insulted. "Does my face offend you?"

"No" was her faint answer.

"Or my kiss? Perhaps my lips felt as cold as melon soup?"

"My lord," she implored.

"Was the taste of me soured like pickled grapes?" he continued, delighting in her flustered gestures.

"Reave!" Failing to keep her expression stern, Tessa covered her mouth to prevent him from seeing her smile. He reached over and pulled her hand away. She gave up the ruse and laughed.

"A kind word might take the sting out of your lack of denial," he said, thinking for a moment that she truly might find him unappealing.

Sensing his insecurity, she reached out and took his hand. "Oh, Reave."

"Kiss me."

Her face turned up to his, her sweet breath teasing his lips. He pulled her closer, then used his eyes to coax her nearer. The emotions warring within her played across her face. Just when he thought she was about to refuse, Tessa closed her eyes and leaned forward.

"Sweet," Reave whispered as her lips drew nigh.

"Wickedness," she avowed.

Their lips touched.

The taste of her was as various as the many facets of this bewitching lady. Her lips held the sweetness of the wine they shared. With great care, he laved her lower lip, then enfolded it between his own, savoring the nectar she offered.

Encouraged by her soft moan, his hand came up to her face. Gently, he massaged the smooth flesh below her cheeks until her mouth opened wider, allowing him further exploration. He tasted the tartness of the gooseberries she had eaten when his tongue swept over her teeth, seeking her tongue. She stiffened but did not sink her teeth into his flesh as she had to stop him in the schoolroom.

"Trust me," he whispered, pulling back to kiss the tip of her nose.

"If it could be as simple," Tessa murmured, her blue eyes dilated with passion. Even as she spoke, she brushed her lips across his, encouraging him to continue.

"So beautiful," he said, awed by her response, then deepened their kiss. This time, he would cultivate her passion as a gardener would a rose garden. Eagerly, her tongue mated against his. Without his encouragement, she had linked her arms around his neck, her warm body unconsciously moving against him.

It was more than Reave could tolerate. His breathing ragged, he pulled back to regain a little control. Her moan of disappointment was his undoing. While he kissed the frown from her swollen lips, his left arm was pushing the basket out of their way. Once the blanket was cleared, he pressed her to the floor.

Her hands explored his hair. His were intent on caressing the flesh beneath her nightgown. Never before had an oversized neckline seemed a blessing. Reave slid it off her right shoulder. He kissed every inch of flesh he exposed, wanting nothing more than to rip the gown down the front so he could view and taste all of her.

Patience.

He could take only what she was willing to offer. He reached into the neckline and cupped her breast. She tensed. Defensively, she placed her hand over his to halt his action.

"Trust me," he said, his voice hoarse. "Allow me to pleasure you with my touch." He kissed her hand at her breast. "I will stop when you order me to do so."

"No." Tessa shook her head, her blond hair fanned into a halo. "You will say I was playing games."

Leaning over her, he wiped a small tear from the corner of her eye with the pad of his thumb. "If we play a game, I confess to being a willing participant."

Reave moved her hand away, then kissed her before she could think of another excuse. None was uttered. Ignoring his straining arousal rubbing against her thigh, his only thought was to give her pleasure. Slipping his hand through the neckline of the nightgown, he cradled her breast in his hand, savoring the weight.

He gazed into her eyes, showing her there was nothing to fear from his actions. Tessa's breath came in faint pants, not certain of what was to come next. Easing one breast from the neckline, then another, he greedily buried his face into them. Turning his face to the side, he sucked one rosy nipple until it hardened, then switched to the other. She gasped. Whether it was from the shock of his actions or pleasure, Reave did not know.

Boldly, he slipped the neckline off her other shoulder and began to tug the nightgown down until she was bared to the waist. She stopped him when his hands slipped to her buttocks to ease the fabric over her hips.

"Hush, love. Grant me the pleasure of beholding all of you," he requested, pushing the gown to her thighs. Reave lightly trailed his fingertips from her collarbone to the soft, downy curls he would sell his soul to bury his arousal within. Prim little Miss Belanger had the body of a siren. The scent of her was enough to make him forget his promise of restraint.

"W-what are you doing?" Tessa panted when his hand moved between her thighs, rubbing the velvet folds of her sex until they gave way, allowing him to stroke the sensitive flesh within.

"Keep your eyes open, love. I want to see them darken when you reach the pinnacle of your pleasure." Reave slid his fingers lower, testing the portal to her very core. His fingers became slick with her arousal, and she was tight, so wondrously so. Desire coiled and churned within him. His shoulders trembled. It was the only release he would permit for himself now.

"Should I touch you?"

"Christ, no!" he said vehemently, pained by the erotic images assailing him. "I would never survive." Pressing his face into her neck, he inhaled. "You may explore my body at your leisure later. For now it is my turn."

The rhythmical movement of his fingers caused her to arch against his hand; her head thrashed from side to side as if trying to deny the pleasure he was giving her. It became increasingly difficult to override instinct, watching her body ripen for his.

Damn difficult. Reave tried to swallow the dryness from his mouth. Gritting his teeth, he tasted blood from his inner cheek.

Her climax came swift and violent. Finding her voice, she cried out. Gripping his arms, she rode the dark currents of passion until they ebbed across familiar shores. Exhausted and frightened, she clung to him. Reave held her tightly. He swore to her that he would never let her go. He doubted she heard the promise whispered into her hair over the steady pounding of his heartbeat.

Tessa staggered from his embrace. Picking up the nightgown pooled at her feet, she pulled it over her hips, slipping each arm into the sleeves until she was covered again. With trembling hands she reached for her discarded shawl.

Reave gripped her slender waist and pulled her down until she was on her knees. When he pushed her tousled hair from her face, he saw the tears clinging to her lashes. His waning desire left him strangely hollow inside as he stared at her.

Uncertain how to approach her, he warily inquired, "Tessa, did I hurt you?" He released her wrist, half expecting her to spring from his reach, but she remained at his side.

She squeezed her eyes shut. When she opened them, her haunted dark blue gaze was clear of tears. Her tone evoked a calmness her appearance did not. "Tonight was a night of gifts. I never expected—I did not know it could be that way between a man and woman."

"It was only the beginning, love. We could spend the entire night exploring—"

"No," she said, shaking her head. "I do not understand why I could not bring myself to say the word sooner."

She appeared so small and lost. A burst of anger shot through his gut. He would be damned if he would feel guilty despite her propensity to deny herself anything pleasurable.

"Perhaps I should remind you why you found it so difficult to speak." He moved to drag her into his arms again and show her what she was denying both of them.

"You promised." Clutching her shawl fiercely to her throat,

she wiggled from his grasp, not that he was making much effort to hold her. "You promised to stop when I commanded. You swore you would not be angry if I did."

"Then leave," he growled. "Take your precious virginity and guilt and leave me the hell alone! Forget this night ever happened." He turned away from her. The door quietly shut behind him. "I, however, will not," Reave vowed to the empty chamber.

The frigid morning air in the gallery did nothing to still the tremors in Tessa's hands, nor did the condemning stares of Reave's ancestors quell the uneasiness she felt as she padded past each portrait. She had told Sims she had letters to write when she excused herself from the morning room. It took her only minutes to recall a murderess rarely engaged in idle correspondence. The thought made her laugh aloud. Humor bordering on hysteria had forced her to find a quiet place to collect her wits.

The gallery ended with a wall. Tessa turned to retrace her steps. Counting the brick and blue-colored wreaths and tulips stenciled on the floorcloth, she tried to calm down.

Tessa had spent the remainder of the night after she had left Reave fearing their morning confrontation. His absence in the breakfast room seemed to unsettle her more, confirming his anger.

She straightened the dark-green-and-cream-striped gown she had put on especially for him. The gesture was frivolous. Child-ish. It was something she would have done for Edmund to appease his need for revenge against whatever transgression had transpired. Except she was not that frightened, needy child anymore. Or was she?

With a groan of frustration, she pivoted and increased her pace. Why could he not remain an unfeeling ogre in her mind and heart? Behind his fierce facade, there was a man who loved life, viewing it with a cynical yet humorous slant. Nevertheless, he surprised her by risking rejection from his son and including him in his life. Tessa did not doubt Lord Wycke would try to be a true father to Jason.

It had been safer to hate him.

Last night changed everything. How dare he show her an innocuous version of the man she was fated to despise? In another life, they might have been friends, perhaps even lovers. She put her hands to her ears, mussing the lace cap on her head. Since she allowed him to touch her, were they already lovers? She was too innocent to know for certain. What she did understand with frightening clarity was that when Reave was not pressing her about her life or lording his authority, she found him inordinately appealing.

In the few hours they shared, he revealed there was more to him than a relentless barrister. She thought of his hands on her body, his mouth pleasuring her in places she had never imagined. It would have been easy to melt into his arms, accepting all his carnal pleasures.

It was his indifference she could not abide, or, worse, his handsome face contorted with rage and disgust when he learned her true identity. Reave was not a half-wit, nor did she possess the skills of a cunning liar. It was a miracle he had not surmised he sheltered the very woman he sought to destroy.

Tessa tucked a stray curl back into place and climbed the stairs to the nursery, where Jason would be awaiting his lessons. This was not the time to run off in a panic. A sound plan was needed and funds too. All she had to do was be patient, and she had years of practice.

Approaching the nursery, she heard the low rumbling of Reave's voice. Was he waiting for her or visiting his son? Fool, she chided herself, there was a motive behind each executed action. The man hardly would be paying a social call. She stood at the threshold, debating whether or not she should enter. Without warning, the door swung open. Their gazes locked, each surprised to encounter the other. Tessa parted her lips to speak. It was Reave who spoke.

"I was just about to check on your whereabouts. Are you well?"

He seemed terribly cheerful for someone who had been rejected.

"Fit and ready to instruct your son, my lord. Is there a reason for your presence this morning?" She could not keep the hint of suspicion from her inflection.

"I need no one's permission to speak to my son, dear lady. However, I did wish to have a few private words with you as well."

His words sounded too ominous even though they had been spoken calmly.

"N-now? I have to begin our lesson and—"

"Later will suffice." He dismissed the subject with a wave of his hand. "The library at one." He slipped by her, hesitating long enough to kiss her lightly on the forehead. She frowned at his departing figure. Reave was furious, all right. He was just waiting to punish her in private.

The various clocks in the house were striking one when Tessa rapped on the library door. She had changed into a simple muted blue gown, and after rearranging her hair several times, she slapped her lace cap back on her head before she pulled most of her hair out in the struggle.

Reave grunted his leave to enter the room. Pulling the latch down, she pushed the heavy door open. He sat at his desk, engrossed with a letter, oblivious to the shuffling and clattering of the footmen removing the remains of his meal.

"Reave?" Anxious, she stood quietly in front of his desk, awaiting a proper greeting. He ignored her. She had been correct. He was angry.

"Damn!" Reave slammed the letter he was holding on the desk. Tessa flinched. She must have gasped, for his attention was sharply riveted on her. "Tessa." His anger melted as he greeted her with warm appreciation. Rising from his chair, he said, "Forgive me. I received word of a case I have been reviewing, and I forgot about our meeting." He walked around the desk and held out a chair for her. Once she was settled, he sat in the one beside her.

"Was the news what you expected?"

"Not entirely. My men were equally inept as the Runners investigating the case." He grimaced. "Perhaps I misjudged her. I grant you, she is more cunning than I credited."

This was not about last evening. Or revenge. She did not know she was holding her breath until it rushed out of her. Feeling a little light-headed with relief, she said, "My, I am intrigued by this mysterious woman who has brought you low. Who is she?"

"The Countess of Lathom. Ever hear of her?"

Her vision dimmed to the size of a pin. "No, I do not mix with the fashionable ton," she managed to murmur.

Reave did not seem to notice her discomfort. Agitated, he rose and began to pace. "No matter. Not many can recall this remarkably unassuming female, not even the ones who swear that they knew her well." He took a calculating deep breath. "She murders her husband and mother in the most brutal fashion, then vanishes in the morning mist. No one has seen her—well, lately there have been a few who believe she has been sighted in Bath, but I must doubt their character if this letter is any indication."

"Is there no uncertainty to the poor woman's guilt?"

Reave shook his head. "Now I know you are untouched by London's cynicism, love. There is nothing more vicious when one of their own falls out of favor. It sickens me to know this woman is another one of their weekly sports. There will not be much of her left to stand trial if they find her first."

"They?" She uttered the word, not understanding its meaning.

"The masses. I need not explain the unholy blood lust that can bestir the rabid lot." He stopped pacing. "Christ, you look like you are about to faint." He took her hands and began to rub them. "There is no need to humor me by feigning interest in my unpleasant work. I am pleased to discuss other subjects."

It seemed it was veritably too late to return to London to prove her innocence if what he said was true. "Is there no method of deduction that could prove her innocence or guilt?"

"A witness to her whereabouts when the murders occurred," he replied without hesitation. "No, that will not work. A maid has come forward stating the countess had threatened Lathom the night of the killings. Such damning evidence is likely to get her hanged."

"But what if there is no one to speak on her behalf?" she persisted. "Are you accountable for every hour you live each day?"

"No," Reave conceded, "but I have not been accused of murder. Tessa, I realize all of this sounds unfair, and to a certain extent it is; still, the law works, as imperfect as it is."

"Have you ever prosecuted anyone, knowing he was innocent, and yet he was sent to the gallows because the telling accounts were against him?"

He gave her a measured look. "I have upset you with all this talk. We will discuss something more pleasant. How are Jason's lessons coming along?"

Tessa gripped the arms of her chair until she thought she could squeeze blood from the wood. "I must know. Have you seen an innocent man sentenced to death?"

"Tessa?" He turned away, as if debating whether or not he should reveal the truth. "Yes."

Too horrified to speak, Tessa rose and walked almost trance-like to the nearest window. She stared blindly at the frosted panes. Only minutes passed before she felt his warmth enfold her and the small comfort of his chin resting lightly on the crown of her head. She accepted his warming embrace, feeling too frozen inside to walk away.

"I should not have told you the truth." His warm breath tickled her ear.

"Lies rarely alter the outcome, they just delay it." Her voice was barely audible. "Have you also accepted this woman's guilt?"

"No," Reave replied, the burden of his position carried in his voice. "I am a fair man, but I must also do my job. I sent my own people out because I suspected there was more to the Lathom incident than was revealed."

He turned her around and tilted her head back so he could see her face. "I have never sent anyone to Newgate I did not honestly believe deserved it. However, I am not the person who decides the outcome, I only present the evidence. There are injustices, and it angers me as much as it does you." He wiped a tear from her cheek, then leaned over to kiss the spot. She turned her head.

"Please, not just now."

"I did not ask you here to discuss principles of justice."

Her rebuff angered him. She could almost hear the grinding of his teeth as he tried to remain civil. Good, she thought. Anger was something she could manage. Nonchalantly, she strolled the length of one of his bookshelves, gliding her fingertips over the numerous volumes.

"Temper your wounded bellow, I know you are not to blame," she said lightly, but she could not prevent a shudder to pass through her. "If not justice, then what did you wish to discuss with me?"

"Last night."

Tessa removed a book from the shelf, hoping the action concealed her distress. The man was full of disconcerting topics this afternoon. Replacing the book, she spun around, smiling a little too brightly. "How rude of you to remind me! I imbibed too much wine with too little food to sustain it, which resulted in the most unacceptable behavior. Please put it from your mind."

He looked like he had been struck.

"So the yielding woman in my arms the other night, and the fact that we almost made love, was nothing more than the accidental soddening of your bloody proper disposition?"

She pouted, attempting to further provoke him. "Now I have made you angry. I am ashamed by my behavior. It appears you summoned Lady Brackett for naught, for somehow I have placed my reputation up for speculation." His gaze burned her back as she strolled beyond his reach.

"Speculation? The last I heard, servants are rarely afforded such regard," he sneered.

She lost some of her composure with his cruel remark. Her eyes blazed when she faced his contempt by delivering a glare of her own.

"Who are you?" Reave swept his hand from head to foot, scrutinizing her as if she were something he did not understand. "You are an impostor."

"No," she denied. Every nerve in her body was acute, her muscles tensed for flight. "I am simply what you see."

"Tessa, there is nothing simple about you. I only wonder where you have hidden the woman you were last evening. She was by far more truthful than you." He moved closer, matching each step she took backward until she was pressed against the bookcase.

"Could we not just forget about the entire matter and continue forth with our mutual indifference?" Tessa suggested. He was an arm's length from her. The scent of his skin sent her heart racing again. He was so enticingly warm. Dangerous too. It was a combination she found difficult to resist.

"It is not so neatly wrapped as you desire, my dear." He braced his arms on the bookcase, capturing her. "Our relationship has altered. I just have not decided if I like the outcome."

"It would never work," she blurted out. "We would chew each other to bits within a fortnight."

"Perhaps, but what risk is there in trying?"

"Risk? Dallying with you is like handling a poisonous snake. I may not have your high pedigree, but I was raised to be a lady, not your whore," she hissed. She brought her hand down on his arm to break his hold. Reave deflected her attack with ease, then gripped her shoulders and held her against the book-case.

"You accuse me of belittling you," he mocked, his face a cold mask of controlled rage. "I warrant you couldn't have cared less if I thought you a lady or a whore when you rode my fingers last evening, begging me to—"

"Enough!" Reave's closeness and the reminder of what they shared was too overwhelming. His sarcastic retelling made her feel soiled, which had been his intention. "I cannot love you." His harsh laugh made her regret her confession.

"This is lust, Tessa," he explained, treating her as if she were a naive child. "I seek the pleasures of your body. Nothing more." He released her, curling his hand into his left palm in an absent gesture. "You are not some green girl who does not understand the ways of a man and a woman."

"I will not be your mistress."

"You think too highly of yourself. You do not possess the skill."

"Ha! Now who is the liar." Feeling provoked, Tessa stepped closer and pressed a kiss to his lips. Insanity ruled her actions, she thought, that and the unspoken challenge of exploring their attraction. At first still angry, Reave did not respond. She laved his lips with the tip of her tongue, lightly teasing the outline of his sensual mouth. He surrendered before she reached his lower lip, capturing her tongue with his own. It was a kiss of hunger, carnal, all-consuming. Her body ached with a needy sensation, an exquisite torment she felt only Reave could assuage. There would be consequences. This time he would expect her to ease his lust.

Abruptly, as if sensing her inner conflict, he pulled away from her, his expression intense as he studied her face. "Have a care about what you toy with, you may get more than you bargain on." His breath came out in short pants, as if he had been chasing her through the halls of Eastcott. "What were you attempting to prove with this display of affection?"

"At this moment, I do not precisely know," she said, slightly out of breath herself.

The blue in his eyes darkened. "I know it was unintentional, but you have just proven my point. I want more than a passionate kiss. With one word, I would undo the fastenings of your gown until it pooled around your feet. Then I would pull you down to the carpet, where I would spend the rest of the day instructing you on the many pleasures one may give with one's mouth and hands. I doubt I would stop there. Not until I have buried myself into you and watched the passion unfurl within you."

"Must you make it so difficult?" She shoved at his chest, a futile attempt to free herself. He was unmoved by her feeble flight. "I will resist you."

He laughed in his usual humorless fashion at her pitiful vow. "You speak as if I am your downfall. I assure you, I am not pleased with the latest turn of events, but I see no reason to ignore it. Fight it if you must. In the end, we will both get what we truly desire." Her widened blue eyes feverishly followed the casual caress his fingers trailed from her temple to her swollen lower lip. "What is it you fear?"

Her lower lip quivered. "Myself," she replied.

It was almost midnight when Tessa heard a knock at her door. Her first thought was Jason was ill. She tossed aside her bedcovers and went to the door. Throwing it open, she was surprised to see Reave standing at the threshold.

"What are you doing here?" Realizing she had not taken the time to shrug into a robe, she pressed her body against the door, praying he had not noticed. Oh, but he had, if the appreciative leer was any indication. Her whole body began to tingle from the bold regard.

"I thought we agreed to become more intimate?" Reave walked passed her into her chamber.

He still wore his evening clothes. She gave him an appraising look, suspecting he had been drinking, although he appeared to be sober. After their argument in the library and his curt dismissal, Tessa had thought he would keep his distance. Obviously, she was wrong.

Checking the outer passage to make certain they were alone, she glanced back, whispering, "Seriously, why have you come?" She closed the door, then, realizing she was giving him an ample view of her backside, she squeaked and dove for her robe. Holding it in front of her, she said, "Any decent man would turn his head."

"Any decent man would not be knocking on a lady's door at all." He reached over and helped her into her robe. "I forgot to mention earlier that my business partner wishes me to return to London."

"Oh?" Tessa felt a sharp pang of disappointment. "So soon? Well, I wish you Godspeed."

"I figured you would be wishing me to Hades after this afternoon." If he expected her agreement, she did not comply. He appeared awkwardly endearing, like a boy trying to make amends for breaking his mother's favorite vase. "I had rather thought you might like to join me in London." Stunned, she allowed him to guide her to a nearby chair. He added, "I really do not have the time to look for a new man to replace Jason's tutor. If you traveled with me, you could assist me with the interviews."

"I do not see how it is possible." She picked up her brush from the dressing table and began stroking it through her hair, forgetting she had completed the task almost an hour past. "There is Jason, you know."

"Jason is the reason I want you there with me," he argued. "My work allows me little time to pursue this, and your help would be most desirable. At night, we could enjoy the pleasures of the town."

"Your offer is most generous. Even so, I cannot accept."

"Damn you for being so difficult!" He rubbed his jaw, soothing the tension. "If this is a means to punish me for what I—"

"It is more than Jason," she interrupted. "What of my reputation? As Sims mentioned, such indiscretions would not be tolerated by the ton. I refuse to have everyone thinking I am your latest paramour."

"Forgive me for thinking of myself. Naturally, you may bring along Lady Brackett. I am certain her ladyship would love to reacquaint herself with the general, though I doubt I will have his gratitude. You know they have quite an odd relationship. He remains in town whilst—"

"I will not go," she said stubbornly.

"What have I forgotten?"

The silky tone in his voice worried her. "Pardon?"

"Come, come, my dear. Is this a ploy to sweeten my offer? Do you want new gowns suitable to life in town? I am not clutch-fisted. In fact, the mantuamaker here did a fair effort, but her work could not compete with the mantuamakers in London. Will my offer satisfy this latest bout of stubbornness?"

Tessa swung her hand to slap him. Reave swatted it away. "Leave me alone!" she shrieked.

"Not good enough, eh? Well, what more do you want?" He paced in front of her. "A dashing pair of blacks? Or is it the ton you wish to conquer? You have the arrogance for them, and your looks are passable."

"You are wretched to believe I would take these things from you!" She strode away from him, thinking to leave the room. Reave slammed his palm against the door, blocking her movement.

"You have accepted my house, my food, even clothing, how could I not think otherwise?" he cruelly taunted.

"I have had a bellyful of cruel bastards like you in my life. Get out!" she commanded, not caring if she raised the entire staff.

His words had been calculating, malicious, and she questioned if he believed what he said. She ran from the door and threw herself on the bed, allowing her tears to fall freely. It was unbearable to allow him to see her cry, to let him know he had succeeded in hurting her. Unfortunately, she could not stop. Curled up in the bedding, she openly sobbed.

"I am leaving in the morning. I trust you will see to Jason's care until my return?" His question renewed the intensity of her sobbing. "Very well," he muttered, and without waiting for a reply, he marched out of the room.

Tessa raised her head just as the door was about to close. "Reave!" she cried, her plea meeting the finality of the latch clicking shut. Her head rested on the feather mattress, his name a quiet litany against the bedding.

She should be rejoicing, so why did she feel like she had lost? Tessa had never encouraged Reave, but somehow he had won her affections. The thought of him hating her was devastating. Her mind whispered it was better this way, that love had come too late for her. It was her heart that begged her to run after him, make him understand it was London she feared. Not him.

She wiped her eyes with a blanket, attempting to collect herself. It was foolish to cry. She could have never given in to the dreams of love and family. Goodness, the man had not even offered that much. He had offered only lust; the rest was childish daydreams.

Her body still trembled from her outburst. Tessa took another swipe at her eyes. Let him go cold hunting in London for Lady Lathom, she grimly speculated. She hoped each blank day drawn tormented him as much as his absence would devastate her.

Chapter Sixteen

Reave followed the Quinn's elderly butler, Gotch, up the stairs to the drawing room. Since his return to London almost ten days earlier, Hayden had been oddly elusive despite his enthusiastic missive, forcing Reave to seek the man out at his town house. It was not the informal setting that bothered Reave. Rather, it was the risk of encountering Hayden's wife, Claire, alone. Beautiful, intense, and bearing a sexual appetite to rival most men, Claire had chosen him as her next conquest.

Gotch opened the double doors to the drawing room, pausing at the threshold to permit Reave to enter the room first. A cursory glance at the mustard-colored walls, the Hepplewhite chairs, and the Turkish bird rug covering the polished bare floor revealed the room was empty.

"Does m'lord require my services?" the butler intoned.

"Not at this time, Gotch," Reave said, stepping to the fireplace to warm his hands. "Just inform Hayden of my arrival."

"Very good, m'lord." The butler bowed, backing out of the room.

Reave remained by the fire, enjoying the warmth. It was

good to be back in town. He always took comfort in work when he felt troubled. Unfortunately, work did little to relieve his mind or body these days. His hasty departure from Eastcott had brought about a mood of brooding pensiveness that even Kim could not lighten. His friend had declared him beyond help, then stalked off in search of more amiable camaraderie. Not that Reave cared much. All his attention was focused on the little nobody who resided at his country estate.

"I will not be your mistress."

Her voice was so loud in his mind, he almost turned to address her. But she was not there, he reminded himself. His parting image of her curled up like a frightened child in her bed still tore at his conscience.

She was attracted to him, he did not have any doubt. Her response to his initial lovemaking could not have been feigned, she did not possess the guile or experience. Perhaps he had rushed her. After all, she was a virgin. It was one thing to pursue her quietly, quite another to parade her around London.

Lady Brackett had sent him two posts, both expressing her regret at his sudden departure. There was no mention of the lady who tormented him with inadvertent ease. Although he missed Tessa more than he would willingly admit aloud, there was his damaged pride to consider. Several seasons could pass before he willingly returned to her.

"Dear me, Hayden has been a most negligent host to leave you unattended for so long."

Reave ground his teeth, irritated he had been so distracted he had not heard Claire Quinn enter the room. Elegant and confident, she held her hand out to him, then leaned forward to kiss him on each cheek when he reluctantly stepped forward to claim her outstretched hand.

Adorning her wrists were a rainbow of gem-encrusted bracelets, each winking and tinkling with each movement of her hand. It reminded him that Tessa did not own any feminine trinkets with the exception of her precious locket with its broken chain. The thought of sending her a gold chain to replace her broken one mingled with his perfunctory courtesy.

"Claire." He greeted her politely, resisting the urge to cough. She smelled as if she bathed in her perfume; the fulsome scent of roses still clung to his face where she had kissed him. "Where is Hayden?"

"Oh, he's about somewhere. You know how he gets when a case bothers him." She touched her hair and sniffed. "You have not commented on my dress. Do you think it makes me look too matronly?"

She puffed out her breasts, stressing how well her enticing curves clung to the dampened fabric. Claire was a woman who knew her effect on men, and this was not the first time he had seen her ply her charms. She had just chosen the wrong man that night.

"As usual, you are stunning. If you looked any older, I might suspect you had just come out of the schoolroom." He had not meant it as a compliment, but he knew she would accept it as one.

"Thank you, darling." She tilted her head to the side, a predaceous smile thinning her painted lips. "May I boldly compliment you as well? I have never seen you look so arresting. Your coats should always be of this dark green. I am delightfully breathless from admiring all that sinewy muscle shifting just beneath. It makes a woman hungry to taste the prize within." Her finger tapped each of the gold buttons on his coat. Reave stepped out of her reach before she touched the last button.

"May I suggest we send someone after your husband?"

Her pout was genuine when she wiggled up to him. "I quite think it would not be as interesting, unless the idea of inviting him excites you." She lifted her hand to his cheek. Reave grabbed it before she touched him and gave it a hard squeeze.

"Don't." Reave released her hand. "If I am in need of a woman, I do the asking myself. I am not of the habit of dallying with another man's wife, especially when she happens to be married to my business partner."

Not deterred, she brazenly pursued him. "If you think he cares, you are wrong."

"Madam, Hayden could sell you nightly on the streets and it would be of little difference to me," he said. "I am not interested in what you are offering." He poured a much-needed drink.

"Lying bastard." Her laugh dwindled to a choked-off sob. "I have seen the way you admire my body. You want me."

"Good Lord, when have I ever given you such a misconception? True, I have dined occasionally at your house, but it was business with Hayden that brought me, not you." He took several gulps from the glass.

"I am surprised?" Claire drawled.

"By what?" Reave snarled, rapidly losing patience.

She gave him a calculating stare that met his eyes, then lowered to his groin. "Why, a man of your captivating power and handsome looks could be only half a man. I was not aware you had lost your manhood when you lost your wife." She practically purred her triumph at his restrained stance.

"Claire, darling, have you been properly entertaining Reave while I was detained?" Hayden entered the room, a drink, obviously not his first, in hand.

"You know me, husband, I have offered everything within my power." She sighed. "He is a difficult man to please." She glanced back at Reave, daring him to deny it.

Nothing would have given him greater pleasure than to strangle the bitch Hayden called his wife. Alas, he was not in a position to gratify himself, or he would have turned heel and left the house when she first rubbed up against him. It was Hayden's latest news on the Lathom case that kept him still.

Forced by rank to escort Claire down to dinner, Reave had to fight back the desire to squeeze a bruise or two onto her powdered flesh when she pretended to stumble, giving her the opportunity to touch him indecently. Reave glanced back at

Hayden, but the man was too occupied steadying himself on the stairs.

The dinner was as uneventful as the food. After the plates had been cleared, Claire bedeviled the two men by lingering longer than expected.

Exasperated, her husband brought her to task. "Be a good girl and leave us to our vices, love. Reave and I have business to discuss."

Pushing her chair back, she frowned at his firm dismissal. "What am I to do while the two of you discuss your boring cases?"

"If there is nothing to amuse you, why do you not seek your bed early?" Hayden staggered to his feet. Reave followed his actions.

"There is no sport when I have to be there alone," she said, slyly casting a side glance at Reave.

Hayden crudely clasped her by the neck. Pulling her tight against him, he planted a hard kiss on her lips. "That will 'ave to satisfy you till later. Off with you now." Dismissing her from his mind, Hayden reached for his half-full wineglass. With his attention elsewhere, Claire paused to blow a kiss to Reave. She stomped out of the room when he did not react.

"Claire is in an unusual mood this eve," Reave said. He watched Hayden pour more wine into a glass with unsteady hands. It was unusual for Hayden to imbibe so heavily on a night they planned to discuss business.

"Someone in the family, a cousin, I think, passed away, and she has taken the news poorly. Never mind her, let us discuss more important things." He wobbled, balancing himself only with the aid of the table.

"Hayden, perhaps we should have our discussion another time."

"Nonsense, a li'l wine won't numb my keen mind. Sit and join me in a glass." He slumped into a chair before dismissing the footmen with a wave of his hand. "What shall we discuss first?"

"What of Lady Lathom? Have your men uncovered the whereabouts of the man who sighted her?"

Hayden appeared dazed, his thoughts directed inward. Reave called his name. "Pardon? Oh, yes, the Lathom chit, verily a bloody mess, if you want my opinion."

"What of the man?"

"No luck, I fear. I've had people search everywhere, and the bloke has vanished. Do you think there is a connection?"

"Hardly," Reave said dryly. He had assumed the man had been in his cups and his sighting the effects of the spirits. "Was the statement taken?"

Hayden weaved his hand in the air. "You know these types. All they want is their coin and then they scurry back to the gutters, where they belong." He made a face and belched. "He swore she is about town somewhere. She could be hiding anywhere, and most would never think to search for her in the poorer rows."

"How would he know the countess from the average courtesan?"

"The painting, of course."

"What painting? I was led to believe none was ever commissioned." Why did no one tell him these important details? Hayden's slapdash work irritated him almost as much as Claire's whorish advances had.

"None was," Hayden scratched the back of his head and yawned. "There was a miniature painted when she was a child. Care to have a look at it?"

"Is there a doubt?"

"Not really, but t'will have to wait until morning. I left the trinket on my desk at the office."

When Reave entered one of his clubs, his mood was more dour than it had been before his meal with the Quinns. It was not just Claire pestering him; he had dealt with her bold advances in the past. Rather, he was troubled by Hayden's appearance.

Perhaps they were having marital difficulties. Lord knows, the woman could drive any man to drink. Reave shook his head. If he had remained in town instead of pursuing Tessa, he would not have such a sticky mess to handle. When Kim caught his attention with a wave, he returned the gesture. He did not bother joining his friend, because he was not in the mood to play cards.

"Wycke!"

Reave's gaze circled the room until he saw Densmore motioning him closer. He was not exactly in a sociable frame of mind, still, one does not insult a duke even if he is a friend.

"Bryson." Reave shook the man's hand as he cordially greeted him.

"Damn me, it's worse than I heard." The duke cuffed him across the shoulder, amusement playing across his face. "Have a seat. Philmore, go find some other corner to sleep in." He pushed his drunken companion off in another direction before he could pass out in the chair he was offering Reave.

"What have you heard?" Reave asked, his expression guarded. He sat in the empty chair.

"I've heard you have been curiously absent from town of late. And there is talk of a certain lady who would love to have your manhood in a vise. I do not envy you if she is able to gain what she dearly craves."

He, too, had heard Maggs was still in a snit about him severing their relationship. Making it a public performance was her subtle way of exacting her pound of flesh. "Isn't it always like a woman to accept the rules of the game while one is playing, but the moment it is over, she vehemently cries foul."

"I suppose so. Still, I suspect Lady Pratt was not the true reason for your timely absence." Densmore's eyes narrowed speculatively. " 'Fess up, who is she?"

"Why do you assume there has to be a woman involved to encourage me back to Eastcott?"

"Nothing has ever drawn you down there before. Sorry,

didn't mean your son wasn't a good reason as any other." He awkwardly attempted to apologize.

"Forget it." Reave shifted in the chair, acutely aware his friend was awaiting some sort of explanation. He liked Densmore, tolerating him almost as much as Turnberry. He suspected Lis and Bryson's relationship had been tumultuous even before she had been charged with treason a few years earlier, but whatever their problems, they had put them to rest. Perhaps of all his friends, Densmore would understand his plight.

"When you began courting Lis, was it managed with ease?" The duke's outburst of laughter drew curious stares from nearby club members. "I assume not," Reave wryly replied.

Densmore slapped his palm on the table. "The first time I met Lis, she thought I was trying to kill her. By our second encounter, I was certain one of us would end up a candidate for Bedlam. As you know, she can be exceedingly stubborn in matters of the heart, although I cannot complain about the results." He paused to finish off his snifter of brandy. "May I be forward and assume you have been experiencing a similar dilemma?"

Reave found nothing except sympathy in Densmore's expression. "She's a complicated little minx," he confessed, evoking more laughter from his friend.

"The ones who matter always are. Who is the fortunate woman?"

"Miss Tessa Belanger."

"Belanger. Belanger. I have heard the name." Densmore tapped his left temple, trying to conjure the memory. "I believe the name is linked with trade or something. Damn, what's good about having a brain if you cannot recall significant information!"

"I doubt the people you are thinking of are related to my Tessa."

Reave decided to tell him everything he knew of her. How she met Turnberry and arrived unexpected at Eastcott. He spoke of his initial dislike and frustration, which evolved into an undeniable attraction between the two. He concluded with her refusal to attend him in London. When he was finished, he felt as if a great burden had been lifted from his chest.

"So is it love?"

Reave stared at his clasped hands for a moment. "I never thought I would ever love anyone as much as I loved Elise. Her death took a part of me with her. I never imagined I would meet someone like Tessa and feel—"

"Lust? Passion? An incredible longing when she is farther than an arm's reach?" Densmore cheerfully supplied.

Reave chuckled. "All I fear! What did you do when you were plagued by these feelings?"

The duke raised a distinguishing brow. "Why, I married her, ol' man!"

Chapter Seventeen

There was no word from Reave. Tessa kept telling herself she did not care. She strolled about the land south of the house beyond the granary and bakehouse, attempting to meld mind and heart. If Lord Wycke could affect an air of indifference, so could she upon his return.

If he returned.

She felt responsible for chasing him from his home, particularly since his relationship with Jason had been improving. It broke her heart to see the boy missing his papa so, when she could have prevented his leaving. No, she reminded herself, it was his duty as a barrister that had called him away, not their disagreement. Then why did she feel so guilty?

The weather had gradually improved. With the passing weeks, the snow was almost a distant memory. But there was still a distinct chill to the air, and the sun never remained out long enough to dry up the mud. She frowned, noticing the hem of her skirts were covered with the mud and dripping water. Fortunately, she had chosen the gown she had originally arrived in at Eastcott. Still, she had not expected to come tromping home like a mischievous child at play. Picking up her sodden skirts, she changed direction and headed back toward the house. Jason would have awakened from his nap. Besides, she knew how Sims worried about her when she went walking unescorted.

She did not understand why the house felt so confining since Reave's departure. Sometimes at night, Tessa would sneak down to the library and sit in his leather chair. The room still held his scent. It was there that she thought of every word they exchanged, attempting to find—what? Some hidden meaning to help her understand him.

She had never felt like this with Edmund. With Reave she felt more. The driving need to melt her body into his, taking what he promised and giving all of herself in return.

Lust.

The full impact of what she had been willing to give Reave frightened her more than the beatings Edmund had threatened but never delivered. Her fear fed her disturbed husband more than anything exacted from her flesh.

Reave was not Edmund.

Her fists flew up to her temples, forcing her mind to accept what in her heart she already knew. Reave would not hurt Tessa Belanger. Her fear was for what he would do to Lady Lathom once her caught her.

Approaching the house, she noticed there was a carriage in the forecourt. For a brief second her heart sped up its beat at the thought of Reave returning. She glanced down at her gown, dismayed she looked more like an ill-kept child than the lady she was. Switching direction, she headed for the servants' entrance, hoping to slip unnoticed into the house. She nodded to Cook as she ran through the kitchen. He answered her greeting with a wave of his knife, then returned to the task of peeling potatoes. Pleased she had reached the stairs unnoticed, Tessa gathered up her sodden skirts.

"Miss Belanger, I was about to send someone out after you."

She slowed her pace, saying over her shoulder, "Yes, yes, Thorne, tell his lordship I—"

"Oh, no, it is not Lord Wycke who wishes to see you, but the vicar."

Her disappointment was plainly on her face. Halting, she turned to Thorne and gestured at her skirts. "Very well. First, I must change out of this gown. Please tell Lady Brackett of my return. I shall be down shortly." She picked up her skirts at his concordance and hurried to see to the task.

An hour later, with the help of Sims's abigail, Tessa was able to walk into the drawing room and properly greet their guest. "Sir, it is a pleasure to see you again. Forgive my tardiness."

"Not to worry, my dear lady, it is I who has rudely intruded upon you ladies. For this I apologize. I heard from various members of the flock that Simona was up here as your chaperone." He ignored her ladyship's grimace at the use of her Christian name and continued. "Of course, there was the usual speculation 'bout the village when his lordship whisked you away, but I now understand you have been tutoring Master Jason."

"Yes. Although, I dare say my abilities of governess border on average, there was a need for my presence until a more suitable tutor could be found."

"The chit is too humble, Jacob. Why, Tessa has worked magic with the boy. Even Wycke has noticed her abilities, and if I am not mistaken, she has worked a little magic on him too!"

The vicar wagged his finger at the older woman. "Cease this prattle about unnatural workings, Simona, else the more superstitious of our flock may think she has bewitched the entire household, including yourself." He had more to say on the subject despite her unladylike snort of disbelief. "You know of whom I speak, and the dear girl will have the mark of the devil if you persist in this manner."

"Fret not, my dear." Sims patted Tessa's arm and offered her a biscuit. "It is true there are one or two who see demons in every shadow, though no one could mistake you for what you are.''

Not bothering to comment, Tessa bemusedly bit into the biscuit she was holding. Her ladyship poured her a cup of tea and handed it to her.

"La! My forgetfulness. I have the most exciting news to share. The vicar has brought wonderful news from the village. There is to be an assembly next Tuesday, and all will attend. Think of the music, the dancing and conversation. It will be an opportunity to meet everyone in the parish. Your lavender gown will be perfect for the evening.''

The cup was still poised inches from her lips at Sims's casual announcement. "I doubt I will attend," Tessa said, "I have not found much opportunity lately to practice the steps to the more popular dances. I would shame you.''

"It would take more than a few bruised toes to make me give you the cut, Tessa. To ease your fears, we shall review our steps if it will please you," Sims offered.

"I doubt Lord Wycke hired me to dance the night through till dawn.''

Sims held out her hand. Tessa clasped her friend's hand, drawing comfort from the gesture. "My dear, Lord Wycke never imagined you would cease to have a life here. If he were present, he would encourage you to attend." Her hazel eyes brightened at a sudden inspiration. "I wonder if I sent a post out immediately, if I could receive a reply from his lordship. I am certain once he reads of your—''

"Notifying the earl will be unnecessary. I will be happy to attend the gathering," Tessa said, resigned.

Reverend Leach smiled. "I am pleased you have had a change of heart. You shall not regret your decision. Everyone is eagerly awaiting an introduction. Now that the weather has been kinder, we shall see more of one another." He stood to state his farewell.

Tessa followed behind the couple as they walked down to the front hall. She was frustrated she was obliged to accept the invitation to the assembly, but she feared her absence would cause further speculation. It had been rather high-handed of Sims to haul Reave into the matter. Since the woman had only her best interests at heart, Tessa could forgive the subtle threat. She forced a smile as she said farewell to the vicar, praying this decision would not be the one of her undoing.

"What an extraordinary turnout!" Sims whispered to Tessa as she fluttered her fan in front of her face. "I feel as nervous as a gel at her coming-out ball." She nodded to a couple who had caught her attention. "Perhaps you should seek the ladies' dressing room and give your cheeks a pinch. You look a trifle pale, my dear." The older woman patted her cheek with gloved fingers. "You are as regal as any queen in the lavender gown we chose. If this was a London drawing room, you would have nothing to fear. This evening everyone has come to see you."

The observation did not settle too well with Tessa. "I am no one of significance. Why would my presence be of importance?"

"Don't be obtuse," Sims chided. "You are a stranger to our parish who has caught the most eligible man in the countryside's eye. I am certain there are quite a few young women gnashing their teeth and fluttering their fans at the sight of you. You are truly lovely this evening. More's the pity Wycke has missed this event. You would have made a handsome couple."

It was true, Tessa acknowledged, she had received one or two unfriendly stares from a few of the ladies present. She had not associated their behavior with Reave. Naturally, it would not have been unusual after a proper period of mourning for Reave to select another bride. The lady's bloodline would not have been so important since he had his heir. Tessa was certain with his good looks, half the women from the ages of five through eighty were smitten with him. Sighing, she supposed she should add herself to the list as well.

"Who is the woman staring so intently, Sims?" She gestured

with her fan of plumes and ivory, attempting not to draw too much attention to herself.

"Oh, her." Sims's expression soured for the first time in days. "Ignore the squinting ol' crone. That is Lady Rodengove. She claims to be the highest-ranking matron in the area. Pity, she has a particular memory lapse when it comes to recalling my husband quite clearly outranks hers." She raised her lorgnette as if scrutinizing an insect. "I would avoid her if I were you."

Just then the music commenced. A young man, a Mr. Robert Cox if she remembered his name correctly, approached her to claim the first dance. She eagerly accepted his offered hand and joined the whirling couples on the floor. It seemed almost a lifetime ago when she enjoyed the light-headed reel of a country dance. Colors flashed by as she and her partner weaved through the couples, then moved out of her vision when she was tempted to admire the various gowns.

When the dance ended, Mr. Cox confessed as he escorted her toward the refreshments, "You are as pretty as the description I was told." A light blush colored his ears.

"Thank you," she demurely replied. Secretly, she was pleased by the compliment. "Was it the vicar who mentioned me?"

"No, Miss Belanger, I believe it was Leath Williams."

Tessa crinkled her brow and nose, attempting to recall the man. "I do not remember encountering Mr. Williams."

"You didn't," the young man replied, eager to have an interesting topic to discuss with his partner. "It was Franklin Morris who mentioned you to Leath."

"Ah, I see. So it was Mr. Morris whom I had met?"

"No, I don't see how it was possible, since the man spends most of his time with pigs. Begging your pardon, Miss Belanger. I meant he tends his animals and rarely has time to be sociable."

Tessa nodded her head in understanding, but in truth she had no idea where this discussion was leading. "Why do we not skip all the people I have not met and come right to the person I did encounter."

"Now, that's odd, considering he'd be the one you did actually meet after all."

"Mr. Cox!" The boy was as thick as suet pudding. "Mr. Cox, please." She glanced about for Sims.

"It was Tanner Ralley, the blacksmith. He told Lady Rodengove's servant you were looking for a coach. Of course, that was before his lordship showed up to claim you at the vicar's."

Tessa resisted the urge to bite her lower lip at the reminder of how she had left the village. It was no surprise the little scene had been repeatedly discussed about many hearths these past cold months. Gratefully, the music commenced. She thanked Mr. Cox, leaving him to claim his next dance partner, and hurried in the opposite direction to locate Sims. She spotted her friend, but her next dance partner claimed her hand and she was off again to dance among the whispering colorful whirls of fabric.

Hours later, she was still dancing. Another gentleman held her waist in his hand. She did not remember his name, nor did she care, because she was enjoying herself too much to pay attention to the particulars. Sims had pronounced her the belle of the assembly, and for the first time, she actually felt like it.

She was certain her well-connected peers would have found her partners too common. Offensive. She had even danced with the elusive pig farmer, Mr. Morris. Regardless, she discovered their lack of social connections mattered little to her, nor the fact their glittering ballroom was a dim room with a rather uneven wooden floor.

The evening would have been perfect if she could have danced with Reave. She could imagine him in his best black attire, something she had never seen since he saved such formal dress for London, but she imagined he looked extremely handsome just the same. His boots would be polished to the highest gloss. He would, of course, be waiting impatiently to claim her as he watched her with restrained tension move about the room in the arms of another.

Tessa glanced toward the doorway, almost expecting him to

be there. She stepped on her partner's toes when she noticed Reave was actually present, glaring at her with such an intensity, it exceeded even her active imagination. Murmuring her apologies for her sudden awkwardness, they danced close to Reave, then whirled out of his reach.

He stood there, unmoving, yet there was a certain air of violence about him. She noted he still wore his greatcoat, though his hat was absent. His dark, curling hair glistened in the light, dampened by rain or sweat. Tessa thought he never looked better.

What was he doing here? Her heart raced in her chest when the music stopped. Sims was beside him, gesturing furiously behind her fan, but she was ignored by the earl. Reave removed his greatcoat, tossed it to the nearest man, and stalked onto the dance floor to claim Tessa. He had not lost his angry expression when he scooped her into his arms and began to dance, the beginning notes of the waltz clumsily lagging behind them.

"Was this an attempt to make me jealous? Odd, I never thought you the type."

If she had not seen his lips move into an awful sneer, she would have thought his tense, firm expression quite unyielding.

"I told Sims you would never approve of this outing, you are too possessive, although I wonder why you believe you have the right to make such claims." Her own eyes were beginning to shadow in anger.

"What right?" he demanded sharply, squeezing her hand so tightly, she gasped. "What right? You reside in my home, eat my food. Hell, even the gowns covering your luscious skin were purchased by me. I believe I have valid reason for my claims." His stern expression softened when he realized he was frightening her. "Tessa, I have thought of nothing except you since my departure, and when I saw you in that man's arms . . ." He did not finish the sentence. "It drives me insane knowing others have touched you, when it is my right." His expression hardened again, angered he had been forced to make the vulnerable confession.

"I only danced with them, nothing more. I confess, before your arrival, I was imagining how nice a waltz would be encircled in your arms." She laughed at his amazement. "I do not understand why you are so surprised. I rarely am of the habit of almost going to bed with men who are not my husband."

He instinctively pulled her closer, gaining a few disapproving looks from some of the older women, and a few of the men. So Tessa had bewitched the entire village in his absence. "I thought you were through with me," he said mildly into her hair.

"I thought I was too," she admitted much to her chagrin. "I suppose I was beginning to miss the dour visage you generally sport when we are together." Another thought struck her, and she did not hesitate to ask. "What did she write to encourage you to come this time?"

"Who?" Reave lazily asked, enjoying the fragrant oils she had rubbed into her soft skin. It was a heady combination, and he wondered if she would be shocked if she knew he would like to be the one to rub the oils onto her flesh. His body reacted accordingly at the thought of caressing her.

"Oh, stop this jest immediately! You know very well of whom I speak. This is not the first time Sims has meddled."

A little bewildered, Reave replied, "Tessa, I never received word from Lady Brackett."

"Why are you here tonight, if not from her request?"

He did not like her tone. It was disturbing enough to accept the reasons for his return, especially since he had sworn he would not speak to her until she had asked for him, and now she was accusing him of insincerity. Pure stubbornness made him keep silent, which further angered his little angel-witch.

"Why does it take several painful lessons before I truly understand the nature of deceitful men," she muttered, looking like she dearly wished she could kick him.

"Again, you are indulging in sweeping generalities, Miss Belanger. Forgive me if I boldly point out that if anyone has been deceitful, it has been you." His voice was carefully controlled; still, he was angry enough not to temper the hostility in his eyes. "Shall we discuss your vague past and your obscure associations with dead aristocrats?"

Her lashes fluttered up, and fear blazed fiercely on her paling features. "What do you know?"

He was not immune to the terror seizing the softness from her beauty. She felt vulnerable to him, so her reaction was self-explanatory. But more than that, it spoke of something else, which brought him low.

She still did not trust him.

The realization rasped against his tender male pride, its blade sharper than cold metal newly polished from a stone. He had assumed that in time, she would tell him of her sad upbringing. It angered him she still believed he would use the knowledge to hurt her. The last notes waned in the distance. Reave stopped dancing. Repulsed that the sweetness of their reunion had turned bitter, he stepped back.

"Reave," Tessa called out, acutely aware she might have mistaken his intentions. His reaction was not the one of a person about to expose a murderess; rather, it was one who hurt. She raised her right hand to touch him. The coldness of his next words froze her hand in the air.

"It appears I have again misunderstood your feelings, Miss Belanger. I suppose, like you, it takes several painful lessons before I, too, understand. I shall relieve you of my presence and seek out another who would warmly welcome my attentions. Good evening." He stiffly bowed and retreated to the other side of the room, where a large group of men were enjoying something no doubt stronger than the weak punch being offered.

His rejection ravaged her pride. It took all her strength not to break down into a fine fit of tears. Another partner claimed her for a dance. Reave's cut stripped away all the pleasure of the assembly, leaving her feeling cold and numb. Reave approached a beautiful dark-haired woman and ask her to dance.

Miserable, she watched him dance with the beauty and the

next three ladies who followed. In her opinion, he held them indecently close, but no one appeared to notice. The brunette who had been glaring at her during their arrival tossed her a triumphant smirk as she whirled passed Tessa in the arms of her earl.

Reave did not even acknowledge her.

"You are making a spectacle of yourself, my dear," Sims softly admonished, appearing at Tessa's side. "You are permitted to sulk, for it is evident to all that the Challis chit has stolen Wycke's attention from you. To save your pride I would seek out a partner and paste a smile on your face. There will plenty of time later to cry in your chambers."

"Oh, Sims, I was so foolish!" Tessa managed to tear her gaze from the couple and choke out. "I thought I cared about the reasons for his presence this eve, forgetting the fact minutes before I had been assiduously praying for such a miracle. I should have been grateful you meddled and sent for him. Instead, I attacked him, accusing him of insincerity. Now I have turned him away forever." She knew it was for the best. Then why did it hurt so much to see him dance with other women?

"Tessa, I am not the reason for his presence."

The fan she was using to cover her stricken expression shook in her hands. "You threatened the day the vicar was at Eastcott to write Reave on the matter of the assembly."

"This is what you deserve, old woman, for your empty threats!" Sims scolded herself, then addressed Tessa. "I mentioned the letter because I did not wish to see you not accept the invitation. You have literally closed yourself off from everyone, and I thought mingling with people your age would help. I highly doubt Wycke would have received my post even if I had been intent to send it. To be present this evening means he had already made the decision to leave London."

Sims lifted her lorgnette to peer at Reave. " 'Tis obvious you have come against his injured pride, my dear. It is a formidable obstacle, worse than any silly, frivolous goose he may choose to show his indifference. Let him rage for a few hours, then seek him out. He may be approachable once he thinks the situation over and comes to the conclusion, as you have, that you were just being foolish."

"I never thought it would upset me to see him bestow his smile on another, but I swear, all I want to do is pull that woman's hair out."

Tessa glanced back to the dance floor. She was startled to catch Reave glaring at her. He quickly reverted his attention back to his partner when he noticed her regard. If his anger was any indication, Sims might be correct. She might have a chance at mending their rift. He certainly was not as indifferent as he tried to portray. Cheered by the consoling thought, she gave a weak smile to her friend.

"You are quite correct, Sims. I believe I shall salvage what is left of the evening and seek out my next partner." Determined, Tessa went off to do exactly that.

Chapter Eighteen

After her illuminating discussion with Sims, Tessa felt not nearly as confident when she walked onto the dance floor with Mr. Mason Timms.

Reave had danced several more dances with the Challis chit, knowing well his attentions would not pass unnoticed by the doting mamas. His wickedness was stirring up exciting speculation, blast his soul, and Tessa was not pleased at his flagrant attempt to humiliate her. He might as well have slapped her across the face. Lady Lathom would have hidden herself away to nurse her wounds, but the countess was dead. Miss Tessa Belanger was indifferent to Lord Wycke's exploits, and Mr. Timms was just the man to prove it.

It was selfish to use the man so unjustly. Mr. Timms's adoration made it so simple for her to execute her own mischief. Another waltz had been played. Tessa suspected it had been Reave's doing so she could watch him hold the brazen hussy close. What he would not expect was his trick to turn up trumps in her favor.

When Mr. Timms placed his palm on her lower back, she

took a step closer, knowing their proximity might be subject
to criticism. She did not care if anyone disapproved, except for
the particular man she was hoping to irritate. It was wicked to
encourage her partner, though he did not seem to mind the
attention. Emboldened by her actions, Mr. Timms's hand eased
a little lower than even Tessa could accept. She was about to
remove the hand practically cupping her derrière, when another
couple slammed into them, dislodging Mr. Timms's unwelcomed appendage. The man was knocked off balance and fell
to the floor.

"Sorry, my friend. I suppose the combination of liquor and
the intoxicating beauty in my arms made me miscalculate the
last turn."

Reave's voice was congenial, his stance challenging. Tessa
did not doubt the horrible man had bumped into them on purpose! Before she could open her mouth and tell him what she
thought of his brutish tactics, he excused himself and resumed
dancing. She would have given everything she possessed if she
could have wiped the smirk off his partner's face! Mr. Timms
straightened his clothes, and this time when he turned her about
the floor, he behaved in a more gentlemanly manner. From the
corner of her eye, Tessa could have sworn Sims was laughing
from behind her fan.

Several dances later, she had had enough of their little game.
Excusing herself from her partner, she joined Sims. It had been
a quarter of an hour since she had last seen Reave.

"He's gone, you know," Sims said in place of a greeting.

"I do not care," Tessa snapped, the fan dangling from her
wrist whipped dangerously about her.

"Really?" was all Sims asked. Cackling like an old hen,
she followed the seething Tessa out the door in search of their
cloaks.

Tessa peeked in on Jason when they returned to Eastcott.
He was fine. Without care to what she was about to do, she

tiptoed up to Reave's chambers and unbiddenly listened at his door. The room was silent. She stealthily opened the door and glanced at the bed. It was empty.

With miserable thoughts as her companions, she walked passed her chambers and headed down the stairs. What she needed was a few moments in the cold air to compose herself. Opening the door, she slipped into the night and began her short walk along the foundation of the house.

On the ride back to Eastcott, she had come to the conclusion that she could not remain another day. She had not collected a pound for her duties at the house, but she felt secure Reave would double the amount due her when he learned he would soon be rid of her. His life could revert to its uncomplicated, cold, structured form as if she had never been there to stir it up. She rounded another corner. With tears blinding her vision, she ran into a wall. She shrieked when the wall grabbed her by the upper arms and shook her.

"Damn you, Tessa, what the hell are you doing out here by yourself," Reave raged. "You have no sense of the consequences to your actions, now, do you?"

Tessa could not miss the smell of brandy heavily lacing his breath. He staggered slightly when he adjusted his grip, making no attempt to release her.

"I did not expect to encounter anyone at this time of the night," she weakly replied.

"Well, do not consider yourself fortunate you came upon me," he muttered. "You might be safer with the average lot of thieves."

She opened her mouth to tell him his thoughts were drunken rubbish, then recalled the reason that brought her outside. Stiffening in his arms, she had to tilt her head back to give him the baleful glare he deserved. "Are you alone? Or perhaps you just finished rutting in your coach or the nearby woods." Anger renewed her boldness. She tried to shake her arms free from his tightening hold.

Reave blinked several times before answering. His expression displayed his confusion. "I? What did I do to justify the manner in which you acted. Good God, you allowed that fop to practically make love to you on the dance floor!"

"I did no such thing. Was it fair of you to knock poor Mr. Timms to the ground when you were practically grinding that black-haired hussy to your loins?" Tessa blushed as much for her reference to his intimate parts as for her anger. How dare he question her actions, when he began the wicked sport! His soft chuckle caressed her forehead.

"Ah, so you noticed Miss Cup." He sounded amused.

"Challis," she corrected him. "Was it not the point?"

"It was," he said, expelling a breath. "But I thought you were enjoying yourself too much to notice." The anger was returning to his voice at the reminder of her flirting.

"I was, that is, until you—you—" Tessa slid her hands up to his chest. Despite the chill in the air, he was incredibly warm. She did not want to fight. Nor did she want to think about Reave making love to that smug chit.

"Why were you punishing me at the assembly?" She winced at how pathetic the question sounded. Had she not learned her lesson with Edmund?

"Why do you insist on keeping me at a distance?" He countered her question with one of his own. He reached up and plucked a pin from her hair, then another. A fat curl struck her shoulder. It rolled to her back when she shifted.

"Your assumptions are incorrect, as usual. I seem to be quite close to you, if you are not too sotted to notice." She tried to slap his hand away. Nimble as a thief, he stole three more pins.

"I noticed." Reave pulled back and tilted her chin up, peering down at her face. "What confuses me is the reason for this privilege?"

Tessa stiffened, then begrudgedly moved out of his embrace. This time he did not make any effort to stop her. Chilled, she pulled her cloak tightly across her breasts. "There is no sinister motive, I assure you. In fact, before I had noticed your presence, I had been wishing for you to come."

"Then, why, Tessa?" He came up behind her and hugged her to his chest. "If you did not mind my—"

"Call it pride, I suppose. I wanted you there by your choice and not because of Sims's matchmaking." She turned in his arms until they were face-to-face. She sensed what he would say next and cut him off by placing a finger to his lips. "I know. Sims told me she had only threatened to send for you to get me to agree to the invitation. You gave me what I desired. I was too stubborn to see it."

"You still haven't answered why you are here now." His voice had grown husky, caressing.

Tessa wet her lower lip with a flick of her tongue, wondering if she should confess the truth. She had lied to him about so much. She felt she could push her pride aside for the answer he obviously craved. "When we arrived home, I tried to seek you out. You were not in your chamber so"—she sucked in her breath—"I thought a walk in the cold would help clear my thoughts."

Reave plucked the remaining pins from Tessa's hair, savoring its softness as it cascaded down her back. He knew what she had thought. There was no doubt Miss Challis would have been an eager participant to any suggestion put forth, but Reave could think of only one. He had escorted her back to her mother. "I was never interested in her. From the moment I saw you, you captured my full attention."

"It was upsetting to see you dance with her. I never knew I could feel so possessive."

"Possessive, eh?" He gave her a crushing hug. He loosened his hold when she gave a protesting squeak. "I suppose if you are willing to make your dark confession, then I can reciprocate. I purposely slammed into Timms because I could not tolerate his hands on you."

"You brute! I knew it was no accident. Do you realize I—"

"Shut up, Tessa," Reave muttered against her mouth, then silenced her next remark with a gentle kiss. He pulled back and lightly stroked her face with both hands.

"There are other things I'd rather do than freeze my arse off rehashing an evening we both would like to forget." To demonstrate his intentions, he drew her closer and began a full assault to her senses. He kissed her intimately, his tongue pressing through the soft barrier of her lips and boldly mating with her tongue.

Initially, stunned by his actions, Tessa attempted to pull away, but he persisted by running his tongue down her cheek to her arching neck. She groaned and instinctively pressed closer. Her little sounds excited him as much as her cool body pressed tightly to his. Reave ground his arousal against her. Only their clothing kept their intimate heat from igniting.

Frustrated by their barriers, he groaned as he removed his greatcoat. Freed from the heavy wool, he reached for her cloak and tore the ties. It fell unnoticed at their feet. Pushing her back against the stone wall of the house, he gave in to the pent-up desire that had been riding him since the day he met her. This time Tessa did not protest when his tongue claimed hers. She mimicked his actions, growing bolder, fencing each of his thrusts. Hotter than white metal in a fire, a burst of excitement shot through him. She wanted him. His hands slipped from her head and began to squeeze and knead her swollen breasts. Her hands came up to block this latest action, but he grabbed her hands and brought them to his manhood.

"This is what you do to me every time I think of you." He saw the whites of her eyes as they widened in amazement or shock from touching him. "I want to love you, Tessa," he pleaded huskily. Pulling her close again, he made small gyrating movements as his tongue demonstrated what his body craved.

Tessa closed her eyes, relishing the shocking sensations he was creating with his movements. She never knew one could use one's body in such tantalizing ways! Her mind told her she should end this madness and go to her chamber, but her body kept telling her just a few minutes more, then—what? She was not certain what was supposed to happen after this, yet it did not frightened her. Whatever Reave wanted to do was nothing similar to what her husband had tried to exact from her body. No, this was certainly different.

She gasped when he tore the front of her gown to free her breasts. Embarrassed by her nudity, she pressed her body into his to hide her breasts from his hungry gaze. He interpreted her actions as acceptance to his lovemaking. Dropping to his knees, he kissed each breast.

"Reave, I think I . . ." her words trailed off, then melded into a moan. Her nipples hardened in his hands, causing pleasure to radiate through her body. Tessa felt his hand slip under her gown and slowly slide up her leg. The night air chilled her. She felt vulnerable. Was she not supposed to do something? Reave kissed her knee. He boldly grazed her legs with his nails, each stroke lengthening, drawing closer to the heat between her legs. She brought her legs together but not before his fingers had reached their goal. He stroked the curly hair that no one except Reave had explored.

"Your were so responsive that night in my chamber. Let it be like that again for us. Tessa, your beautiful body was made especially for my touch. Let me love you."

Allowing her skirt to settle back over her legs, he sought another target. First, a few soft, featherlike kisses on her torn bodice, then his seductive trail moved up to her breasts. He licked and stroked her with his hands and mouth like a starving man offered a banquet. Such tribute was overwhelming to Tessa. With her eyes half closed by his seductive onslaught, she remained motionless, allowing him to coax the fires of passion within her into an all-consuming blaze.

Reave nipped her neck before returning to her already swollen lips. He licked and bit the succulent fruit of her mouth, deepening each kiss until she thought they would merge into one. Unfurling her hands from their tight fists, the last of her resistance faded. She worked her hands up his chest and around his neck. Tessa clung to him, accepting and returning everything he offered.

Reave rejoiced in her surrender. He did not consider himself

the conqueror and she the vanquished. Rather, they both were
giving up a part of themselves in order to become complete.
His knee had separated her legs, but the long gossamer gown
barred him from what he desired most. The thought of burying
himself into her warm softness almost sent him over the edge
like a nervous young man touching his first mistress. Heavy
with need, he grappled through the layers of fabric, pressing
her into the stone wall. He wanted to feel her legs wrapped
around him. Too soon, his mind warned. He did not wish to
frighten her.

"Oww, that hurts!"

It was not exactly the words he expected to hear. "I know
there may be pain the first time, but I—"

"No, no. The stone is cutting into my back. I shall perish
from loss of blood before we finish. And did I mention it is a
mite cold too," she complained, her laughter ruining her serious
charge.

Reave had not felt cold since she had stumbled into his arms.
Pulling her from the wall, he reached down to collect her cloak.
He was shaking from the unspent tension coiling within him.
He knew if she touched him again, he would lay her down and
make love to her heedless of their cold, wet surroundings. So
much for bloody patience. With a sigh, he placed the cloak
over her torn bodice. "Better?"

"Your body provided ample service of keeping the chill
from me," Tessa replied shyly. "Perhaps we could seek something softer to lean against. Like a tree."

Reave groaned, pressing his forehead to hers. He reached
for her anew, despite his good intentions, wrapping his muscular
arms firmly about her. Her cloak slipped unnoticed to the ground
when they began to kiss. Their movements became frantic as
their kiss intensified. Imitating his previous movements, Tessa
trailed her fingers down his torso until she reached the most
intimate part of him. Tentatively, she felt him through his tested
breeches. His body convulsed, constrained by her untutored

hand. Reave could tolerate no more. He scooped her up into his arms and headed for the door.

"Is something amiss?" Tessa asked in a weak voice.

"Yes. When I make love to you, it will be on my soft bed with a raging fire to pinken that delectable skin of yours. If we linger here further, I fear all there will be is damp leaves and earth with the night chill prickling our backs."

"Is it cold?" she posed, snuggling her face against the crook of his neck. She knew what she was about to let him do to her went against everything she once believed. Once, she had tried it the proper way with an aristocratic husband. It had been hell. Let her be marked a whore; it could not be worse than what others already perceived.

Reave did not hesitate with his precious burden when he reached the stairs and agilely sprinted two steps with each leap. Miscalculating the step at the top, he stumbled. Grasping her securely, he landed on his knees. He buried his face in her shoulder to muffle his vehement curses.

"Are you hurt?" A nervous giggle overlaid her query of concern. Thank goodness, no one had seen their flight, for she was quite certain they had appeared ridiculous. She stifled her laugh when she noted he was breathing heavily and had not bothered to answer her. "Reave?"

"Not to worry," he bit out between breaths. "I may not be a young man, but I am stalwart enough to withstand a few bruises." Still tenderly cradling her, he attempted to rise to his feet.

"A man of two-and-thirty is not old and feeble. However, I do think you have been more than chivalrous. I shall cherish this romantic gesture until my last breath. Still, for your sake and mine, if your gait is any source of sound judgment, please let me walk," she demanded as kindly as she could. The stubborn man shook his head.

"I have dreamed of this time together longer than I can remember. If I let you down, you may prove to be a vision of my liquor-sodden head, and I couldn't bear the empty feeling that would replace your warmth." He staggered to his feet and moved to his chamber.

She wistfully smiled, brushing a stray lock from his forehead. "My dear man, I cannot abide this madness between us. There is a keener hunger that licks at both our souls. It demands consummation, and I have not the inclination to deny either of us."

No matter the consequences.

His voice thick with desire, Reave vowed, "I swear you will not regret this. I will make it right for you." Reaching his door, he kicked it open with his foot. Once they were inside, he pushed the door closed with his back.

Tessa was not certain what he planned to make "right" for her. Every time he touched her, it seemed right. Even when he set her down and bolted the door, she did not waver in her resolve to remain with him this night. Mesmerized, she watched him remove his shirt, which was damp from his exertions. The light from the hearth cast shadowed planes across his torso, and she almost licked her lips in anticipation at exploring each hidden area.

Taking a step forward, she glimpsed her own image in a mirror. She looked like a doxy with her torn gown, disheveled hair, and high color in her face. Feeling awkward, she tried to salvage her dignity by pulling the tattered fabric together.

"Don't." He tossed his shirt over a chair and pulled her closer to the hearth. She was shivering despite her proximity to the fire. "There is no shame in what we are about to do."

Tessa slowly nodded, then offered him her back. Eagerly, he undid the tiny pearl buttons, placing small kisses where he had exposed her tender flesh. The act was needless, since the front of the gown was torn. But she enjoyed his caresses too much to protest. Feeling the weight of a hair pin brush her ear, Tessa reached up to remove the irritant. Noticing her intention, Reave grabbed her hand and kissed her palm.

"Allow me the privilege." His warm breath teased her ear. "Often I have thought about your fragrant curls, wondering what it would feel like as your hair brushed along my skin as I made love to you.''

''You find pleasure in the oddest things, my lord.'' Her voice cracked as he pushed her gown until it fanned around her ankles. He made quick work of her petticoat and stays. Only her waist-length hair remained to conceal her from his impatient eyes.

''A rare treasure indeed!'' he exclaimed in awe. ''What sin did you commit, dear angel, that caused you to be cast from the heavens.'' He lightly placed his hands on her shoulders, but she shrugged off his touch.

''Fie, I am no angel, sir. The places I have resided were decidedly of the warmer clime.'' She glanced back, knowing he must think her fickle. When she dared to look in his eyes, she saw only compassion. She felt vulnerable in her nudity while he still wore his breeches. Darting passed him, she jumped onto his bed, burying herself deep into the covers. She could hear him attempting to control his amusement. He soon lost the battle and his laughter filled the room. Peering over the blankets, her mouth went dry when Reave slid his breeches over his hips, then kicked them next to her gown. She drew the blanket over her eyes so she did not have to see the front of him as he approached the bed. The bed dipped accepting his weight.

''Must I unwrap you again? I confess I find pleasure in undressing you.''

She threw the covers aside, exposing herself to the waist. ''Fine, you cruel man. Enjoy your privileges now, for I doubt my embarrassment will gain you another,'' she warned, her body tingling under his hot scrutiny. He must have sensed her response and without warning pulled her so that she lay on top of him. She swore she could feel his heart beating, or perhaps it was her own. ''W-what should we do now?'' she stammered, noting his hardening arousal pressed into her upper thigh.

''Stop thinking,'' he muttered, then kissed her passionately, making her forget her disconcertion. She moaned against his mouth. Moving higher on his chest to reach his mouth easier, her legs naturally separated and straddled his hips. His hands slid down her back until they cupped her buttocks.

"I imagined you like this . . ." he began, not finishing the thought. The little minx was using her tongue to trace his ear, and it was driving him insane. He instinctively slipped his hand between her legs to feel if she was ready to accept him. He closed his eyes in ecstasy when he felt the telltale wetness of her desire. She arched against his hand, allowing him to caress the swollen bud of her flowering excitement. His fingers became slick with her precious honey as he slid one finger, then two, feeling her virginity. She tensed slightly at the invasion but soon found that this also offered her pleasure. He gently mimicked with his fingers the thrusting motion his arousal craved. Reave gritted his teeth against the raging need threatening to consume him. He wanted to be certain Tessa was ready to accept him. Slowly, he slid her down his body until he was positioned at her fragile barrier.

Tessa was barely aware she had moved, and her stomach still tingled with the sensations Reave had built within her. Her body craved for a release she did not comprehend. All she wanted was for him to place his hands back down between her legs. She had thought she would have been embarrassed by his bold caresses. However, there was little to ponder when her mind blanked and she enjoyed the pleasure he gave her.

Without moving her, he pushed his backside up the bed so his chest was raised up on the pillows. The calculated action caused her to slip farther down his torso until she felt his arousal press against her. Before she could shift away, he pulled her lips to his and sampled the sweetness there. He tentatively entered her, quickly withdrawing when she tensed. Repeatedly, he continued his tender assault until she accepted more and more of him.

"It stings," she said, tensing.

Reave kissed her, in part as an apology, the rest a distraction to ease her discomfort. Boldly, he thrust only to meet the slight resistance telling him she had never known a man.

She gasped, weakly attempting to still his movements. "I think you are too big," she said, squirming away from his invasion.

"Hush, sweet," he crooned, and stroked her back. "Your body will accept me in time, I assure you. The soreness will soon pass." He pushed her hair to the side and kissed her shoulder. His rubbing seemed to relax her slightly, so he continued to coax the tautness from her muscles. "That's it, trust me."

He buried his face in her neck, teasing the sensitive area. When she slumped against him, he renewed his gentle thrusts. Her wetness told him she still wanted him, the thought causing him to quicken his movements. Without warning he grabbed her buttocks and pressed her firmly down on his arousal. Her barrier gave way and he was buried deeply inside. Sweat broke out on his upper lip as he waited for her snug passage to accommodate him.

"Blast you! I would consider it a little more than soreness!"

He could hear the sound of betrayal in her voice, and it tore at him. Panting, he attempted to belay her accusation. "Only the first time . . . I promise. Now pleasure." To prove it, he slowly retreated and then reentered.

Initially, his movements burned. As he increased his tempo, a quickening of pleasure replaced her discomfort. When she attempted to meet his thrust, he groaned and increased his speed. His hands were all over her, on her buttocks, her breasts, her thighs, encouraging her to meet his frenzied thrusts. Suddenly, he placed his arm around her and flipped her on her back. Without breaking stride, he continued to press deeper and deeper into her until she thought she was going to burst. She did. A blinding flash blanked her vision as her body shuddered with each radiating climatic wave.

Sensing she had found her fulfillment, Reave allowed the last threads of his constraint to sever. Her tight, constricting passage was enough to send him over the edge. Burying himself deeply, he tensed as his own release claimed him.

A log in the fireplace dropped into the glowing ashes. Neither of them said anything. Reluctant to release her, Reave eased off her, settling down at her side. Her body gleamed with perspiration. He traced an indistinct pattern on her stomach, then around her left nipple. She flinched at the teasing caress, but her eyes remained shut.

"Do you regret our lovemaking?" he asked her, his words finally forcing her to open her eyes and acknowledge him. The last traces of euphoria faded as his body calmed. His eyes focused intently on her searching for a reaction.

"Lust," she said succinctly.

"That and more," he replied, a knowing grin surfacing then fading.

Her eyes were dilated, swallowing the inviting blue and replacing it with an unfathomable blackness. Despite their joining, Tessa was closed to him. She might as well have given him her back. Absently brushing his hand over his jaw and neck, Reave searched for the proper words to reach her. If he could not have her joy, then he would take her anger, for it was preferable to her damnable silence.

Tessa slowly sat up, wincing at the effort. She appeared stunned at the bloodied smears on her thighs. Her mouth dropped open, words failing her.

" 'Tis normal the first time to see a little blood."

She gave him a contemptuous look. "How fortunate I was to choose an authority on virgins." Her eyes were becoming shiny with tears.

"I was married before," he explained. "Don't belittle what happened this eve. It took Elise many tries to find her release as you did tonight."

She hopped off the bed, pulling a blanket around her naked body. "Damnation! Do not compare me to her. What do you want me to say? Am I supposed to compliment you on your prowess?"

"I wasn't—" Reave's jaw tightened as he sought control over his growing irritation. "I did not haul my dead wife into the bed with me, but you do have me wondering whom you invited."

A flash of guilt seeped into her eyes, then was gone. "Oh," she puffed with renewed outrage. Intending to quit the room, she gathered up her blanket and headed for the door. The wool blanket was cumbersome. Stepping on the fabric, she slipped on the wood floor. Her right arm caught the brunt of the fall before Reave could catch her.

He pulled her into his arms and kissed the pinkening bruise on her arm "Does it bother you so much to let me close?"

"Yes!"

There was a wealth of bitterness in that one word. It spoke of humiliation, fear, and pain. He did not understand how any of it concerned him. "Tessa, what we did was something wonderful. There is no place for shame."

He had managed to startle her when meant only to comfort. Cocking her head to the side, she smirked. "You are either a fool or as innocent as I was an hour ago." Her insult gained the release she craved. She scooted a few feet, distancing herself from him. "There are consequences neither of us have begun to consider." She shook her head. "Lust," she uttered the word as if it meant something vile. "For a few hours I convinced myself none of it mattered. But it does. It does." She covered her face with her hands and wept.

Chapter Nineteen

"You sleep like a princess."

"Is it morning?" Her gaze moved from the cold fireplace to the closed curtains.

"Dawn or there thereabouts," he murmured.

"I should go." Although reluctant to lose his warmth she tried to sit up. He settled her feeble movements with a gentle hand.

"Not yet. We won't be bothered for hours." He did not speak until she snuggled back into the bedding. "How do you feel?"

"Sore," she confessed, then wondered if he was referring to her hysterical blubbering.

Her reaction to Reave's lovemaking had turned their evening into a debacle. She had considered herself quite blasé when she had decided to give in to her passions. Her joy had been brief. The culmination of her release and the reality of what she had done had turned her into a watery stew.

"Did you sleep at all?" There were more pressing questions she would have rather asked, but this was the least threatening.

"Nary a wink, I fear. Dreams would have paled in comparison to the pleasure I received cradling you within my embrace." He ignored her look of disbelief. "Do you know what I was thinking while you slept?"

She shrugged. "I imagine the worst. I was not at my very best last evening."

He regarded her, a curve of amusement contorting his lips. "No, no, you were not. It made me ponder why you acted so abominably. To consider what I had done to make you cry as if all were lost to you. Do you want to hear my conclusions?"

"Not particularly."

"Pray, indulge me, love," he said, kissing her hair as if to reward her for not arguing. "I do not regret our lovemaking. I had imagined you a thousand times in my bed, the white-hot passion kindled between us." His eyes glowed with remembrance. "The feel of you, the taste, a hunger that equaled my own. I did not think of the price." He clasped his hands together, appearing truly bothered by his thoughts.

Tessa rolled toward him to her side. Curious, she asked, "Pray, what price?"

Reave caressed her cheek with a finger. "I turned you into what you feared most. My mistress."

She had forgotten about her dramatic declaration. In truth, her ruined status was minor compared to her other problems. Sighing, she rolled away from his hand and stretched out on her back. He was not in the position to understand her reasons or fears. "We cannot undo what we have done."

"No."

"Then we shall wipe it from our minds and never do it again."

He laughed. "Now, I know that is a promise I shall never keep." He positioned his body over hers, bracing his weight with his arms. "I want you now as much as I wanted you last evening. Mayhaps more."

With a heated glance he could make her want him too. "I could leave Eastcott."

Reave kissed one breast, then the other. "I would only hunt you down and bring you back." He kissed the valley of her neck. "No. There is just one way to rectify the situation, and that is for us to marry."

Marriage.

The very deed had scorched a black mark across her heart when she had wedded Edmund. Cleaving herself to a man again would be foolhardy. Edmund had seen to it that it had almost proven fatal. What had she been thinking when she told Reave she would entertain his proposal? Surely, it had been a ruse to escape him. That was it. A breath of idiocy uttered to escape his masculine persuasion.

"What are you doing up there?"

Tessa craned her neck, catching a glimpse of Sims rushing toward her. She must have looked a sight, standing on the chair, a blank look on her face while she clutched silver snuffers in her fist. Sims most likely was trying to decide on whether her charge was planning to jump to break her neck or gouge herself with the snuffers.

"Good day, Sims. Sorry I missed breakfast. I was not hungry."

"Tessa Belanger, we will not speak until your feet are treading the rug," Sims commanded. "You, sir"—she gestured at the startled footman who entered carrying several candelabra— "help her down before she breaks her leg."

"Sims," Tessa complained, exasperated yet complying. "Thank you, John. You may take the others on the table." She went over to one of the candle branches the footman had brought in and began snipping the wicks. "Did you hear? According to his lordship, the new housekeeper shall be arriving any day. It was too early for Jason's lessons, so I thought Thorne might need an extra pair of hands to put this household in proper order," she prattled. "No point overwhelming the poor woman before she has had a chance to warm herself by the kitchen hearth."

Tessa did not see the look of pity Sims bestowed upon her. "After our failure last evening, I would have not condemned you if you had chosen to remain in your bed until Wycke departed."

Snip-click. Snip-click. The briskness of the snuffers in Tessa's hand replied where her voice had not.

"Any sensitive soul would have been shattered by his dismissal. And to have taken up with the Challis gel!" Sims's outrage swelled with each breath. "I will confess, Wycke's moods can be darker than blood pudding, though I never expected him to carry on like a London rake. If he will attend me, I shall upbraid him as his good mother would if she had witnessed his devilment."

"Goodness, Sims, Lord Wycke is not a boy who needs a sound ear tugging. Forget the incident, as I have."

Not satisfied with Tessa's nonchalance, Sims drew the spectacles she wore bound by the ribbon around her neck up to her face. Moving them back and forth as one would a fan, Sims adjusted her spectacles until she could gain a crisp image of her friend. "You are not angry?

"Do not allow her docile demeanor fool you, Lady Brackett," Reave said, surprising both women with his unexpected appearance. "I am fortunate she has not demanded the pillory." He turned toward Tessa, who clutched the snuffers to her chest. "Shall they cut off my ears and slit my nostrils, or will you be satisfied if I was assaulted with the refuse from the local slaughterhouse?"

"Lord Wycke," Sims exclaimed, horrified by his crude speaking.

Tessa's lips twitched. "If that was your attempt to tease us, my lord, then you have gone beyond your means."

A rueful smile appeared. "I thought you might smile at the thought of having me tortured."

"You have spent too many years at the Inns, Lord Wycke," Sims charged. "Your tales are better told at your clubs than to a gentlewoman's ears.'' The reprimand was there, so she said nothing more.

Tessa returned to the candles she had been snipping. "Leave us, Lord Wycke, so we might recover from your presence." She bowed her head so he could not see her smile. She had never known Reave to publicly jest about anything, and his first attempt had been quite pitiful.

"Miss Belanger can be heartless, Lady Brackett. But, alas, I deserve each verbal thrust." He smiled again, knowing his presence was making her uncomfortable. "Would you allow me to make amends by escorting you both to breakfast?"

"No."

"Tessa, you are being rude." Sims's gaze glided from Tessa to Reave, reevaluating the couple. "Forgive this old woman, Wycke. I have already eaten. Pity, since I am certain the discourse shall be quite entertaining."

The moment Sims departed, Reave spun Tessa into his embrace and kissed the frowning objection from her lips. He wanted to claim the sweetness from her lips. However, the determined look in her pretty blue eyes made him suspect her mouth was full of vinegar.

"Enough, you wicked man. Sims will soon know what you are about if she bears witness to your imprudence," Tessa warned against his lips.

Reave sighed. She was too preoccupied with irrelevant issues to appreciate his clumsy attempts at romance. Deciding to set her fears aside, he confessed, "Tessa, I wouldn't care if the Regent himself knew about us. Let her have her fun."

"The reason for her presence was to protect my reputation, and to keep us from . . . well, from doing what we did last night."

He could barely hear her words, yet understood her concern. "And this morning," he added just to provoke her. She placed her hand over his mouth to keep him from elaborating. He chuckled and kissed her palm. After all the hours he had spent showing her with his body how much he wanted her, she still did not comprehend his commitment to her.

"You are no gentleman," she said, laughing, shaking the snuffers in his face. He snatched the snuffers from her and placed them on the table behind her.

"I was a gentleman this morning when I allowed you to leave my bed without first gaining your reply to my proposal."

Realizing he was serious, the laughter left her eyes and was replaced by a more guarded expression. "Your proposal was about as appropriate as your pillory quip. Neither rewarded you with the desired response."

"Don't be impertinent. What exactly deluges your senses, Tessa, the fact that you have a lover or that I happen to be the chap?" His jaw tensed as he awaited her answer.

Tessa tucked an errant blond lock of hair behind her right ear. "This is your damnable honor speaking to me."

"The hell it is. If I married every woman I had bedded since Elise's death, I would have one or two brides to spare."

"You do not need a wife," she argued. "You need a steward, a tutor for Jason, a good housekeeper, and maybe a few more maids."

"You speak of the household. I am speaking for myself." He cut her next words off with a hand gesture. "Accept my offer and we will announce our betrothal to the household this afternoon."

She had the look of a wild animal caught in the trap, trying to decide whether or not it should chew its foot free or bare its sharp teeth to its attacker. "I will not permit you to ruin your life because you feel honor bound to marry me. No one needs to know what we have done."

"There is the matter of the sheets," he kindly pointed out.

"Good heavens. The sheets!" she screeched. Breaking away, she rushed out of the room.

By the time he had walked out of the alcove, he saw only a flash of her skirts as she raced up the stairs. Rather than chase after her, he headed for his library. There was work to be done, and he understood she needed a few minutes to accept her fate, for there was little doubt the entire staff would know by the day's end that she had done more than sleep in his bed.

"Jason."

"Hello, Papa." Jason smiled, glancing up from his plate, a trace outline of milk still ringing his lips.

Reave's quick search of the nursery ended at the empty chair and untouched plate belonging to Tessa. He had expected her to seek him out hours earlier. There he would have offered her comfort after she had discovered her attempts to hide their affair had been futile. Where was she?

Too absorbed in his own conflicts, he barely heard his son call to him. He frowned at the wounded expression he saw in his little boy's eyes. It appeared he could not make anyone happy this day. Kneeling beside Jason's chair, the lines around his mouth and eyes softened. He tousled the boy's locks, gaining a faint smile from Jason. "Tessa seems to be playing a game with your father. Is this empty chair for Tessa or one of the maids?"

Content he was not the reason for his father's stern face, Jason wiggled in his chair, his hand outstretched for the plate of bread. Reave reached over and slid the plate closer. Jason bit into the bread, nodding as he chewed. "Tessa," he said, her name was garbled between his tongue and the thick chunk of bread.

Not having the patience to play this new game with his son, he asked another question. "Was she with you this morning?"

Again Jason nodded. He struck the legs of the chair he was sitting upon with his shoes, creating an irregular measure. "We had lessons," he said between mouthfuls. "I learned that—"

"Where is she now? 'Tis very important," Reave added when he noted the hurt expression was back because of his abruptness. He would make it up to Jason later, but now he had to find Tessa. He had to be certain she was not trying to leave him.

"She asked to be excused. Lady stuff, you know," Jason confessed. It was apparent he was as mystified by the phrase as Reave was.

Reave took a deep breath. "Was she ill when she left?"

"No. But she had a sad face when she left. Do you think I did something bad?" The thought distressed him.

"Not likely," Reave assured him. *Since I am the one responsible for her sadness.*

Reave found Tessa in her chamber. The unguarded, sleepy expression she wore changed to fury when she saw him. She slammed the door, expecting an end to their confrontation. Undaunted, he blocked the closing door with his foot and entered as if he had been invited. He glanced at her rumpled bed, relieved she was not packing, as he feared.

"Get out before someone discovers you here!" Tessa flounced away from him, plopping on the small bench in front of her dressing table. She seized a silver brush off the table. Her glare nurtured a spark, revealing the growing temptation to throw it at his head.

"I would not resort to such high-handed tactics if you would stop acting like a child and come when you are asked." He closed the door behind him, then turned the key to prevent anyone from entering, or her from escaping if her expression was any intimation. "Did you not get my messages?"

"Yes, you cocksure devil, but I wanted time to think. I assume you know." She looked miserable.

The sheets.

Yes, he was aware of the rumors circulating through Eastcott. Tessa had arrived too late to stop anyone from finding the evidence of their night together.

"It was inevitable. It is difficult to keep secrets with so many servants about."

Pain slashed her features. She pinched her brow as if the action could ease it. "Do not even pretend to feel regret, when

I know if given your way, you would have hung those bloody sheets over the banister for all to behold.''

He walked over and pulled her into his arms. "Ah, love," he sighed into her hair. It was damp from a recent washing and smelled of lavender. "Many couples sample their marriage bed before the holy words are spoken over them. We could plan a wedding within the next few months that would satisfy all." He thought he was being reasonable, but when she choked back a sob, he was all the more puzzled. Pulling back, he noted her strained features. "If you are worried about a babe being born too soon, I could talk to Densmore about a special license. He might have the influence to—''

"Baby!" she gasped in horror, her hand instinctively settled on her stomach. "I did not consider—it was only one night." Fear and accusation heightened the blue in her eyes.

"Tessa, Elise conceived Jason and his sister on our wedding night."

With a broken heave, Tessa dropped the brush she had been clutching and brought her hands to her face. "Is the notion of carrying my child so distressing?"

Various thoughts reflected in her expression like frightened swallows striking against a glass window, but Reave could not interpret them. "I would very much like to bear your children," she replied with a deliberate slowness. "Oh, Reave, is it terrible of me to wish they were born after a respectable amount of time after our wedding?"

"No, but babies don't know how to count," he teased, his eyes not quite matching his tone. He rubbed her back, becoming thoughtful as he studied her reflection in the mirror. "I know what you are thinking."

She gave up the pretense of smiling. "Indeed? Well, wise seer, read my mind."

"You are thinking about how I lost Jason's mother. She died because I was not there to protect her from that butcher." His throat locked up on him, and his vision blurred. "I swear, I will not allow anything to happen to you."

Tessa twisted on the bench until she faced him. She cradled his face with her hands, then brushed his lips with her own. Some of the fear ebbed in her gaze. "What of your feelings?"

He expelled a ragged sigh. His hand moved from her back to her arms, where he began to absently stroke the sensitive flesh. Now that she seemed willing to accept his touch, he could not get enough of her.

"I swore, when I lost Elise, there would never be another woman to take her place. I had my heir. It was enough." He fingered a stray curl before tucking it behind her ear. "The first time we met, I understood you were to be my test. The first one to challenge my oath. I was determined to fight you with all my will, heedless of the aching expostulation from my traitorous flesh."

"Expostulation?" She wrinkled her nose at the unfamiliar word. "Sounds like a word better used in court, Lord Barrister."

"Protest, love." He gave her nose a playful tap. "I lusted after you long before I realized I wanted to possess more than your body."

Tessa rose off the bench. Reave followed, not about to let her escape him so easily this time. A seductive nudge of his hip moved her backward until the backs of her legs bumped against the side of the bed. She glanced over her shoulder to see what she hit, giving him the opportunity to knock her off balance. Laughing, they fell back on the mattress.

"What are you about, sir?" she charged.

"An experiment." Reave wriggled his hand into her dressing gown, attempting to tease the already hardened nipples straining against the thin fabric. He could feel the gentle swelling of her breasts against his chest. "Feel good?"

"Mmmm." She nodded. Without thought, she linked her fingers behind his head and pulled his head to her breasts. He obliged her unspoken command by peeling back her dressing gown, then kissing and laving every inch of exposed flesh.

"Reave?" Her voice had a dreamy quality to it.

"Hmmm?"

"You mentioned an experiment," she prompted, then gasped when she felt his hand slide between her thighs.

"Quite right." He smiled when he felt her warm bare skin beneath the gown. She shuddered, her body rising to his own under his skilled ministrations. "I am curious to see if loving you on this particular bed is any different than my own."

For once, Tessa did not argue.

"Whatever has been said is a lie," Tessa said, her chin held high, daring them all to call her a liar.

Reave pulled her trembling body against his. He silently cursed himself for not anticipating the vicar's arrival. "I have little use for gossip," Reave replied, dismissing the subject.

"I, too, have never been one to pay heed to idle chatter. Even so, this concerns Miss Belanger's reputation. There has been talk of an expected child." The vicar had the forethought to take a few steps away from his host when he repeated the village gossip.

Reave's bellow of rage shattered what little composure Lady Brackett maintained. Her cup slipped from its saucer, breaking into three large pieces on the rug. "I should summon Thorne," her ladyship began but was silenced by Reave's pinning glare.

"Leave it!" he snarled, then turned his wrath on the vicar. "Who has been whispering in your ear besides God, old man?" he demanded. Glancing at Tessa, he noticed she was the color of chalk. Someone was going to pay for this insult! "I think a well-worn brank and a brisk walk through the village for all to see should satisfy me." Reave could think of one or two women who deserved the iron head brace with its nettlesome mouthpiece. His gaze alighted on Lady Brackett.

The vicar nervously flexed his fingers on his knees. He considered the command. Shaking his head, he said, "I cannot do that, my son. It would not be right."

"Yet it is appropriate for those righteous gossips to spread malicious lies." He rubbed the tension in his jaw. "Give me the names and I will make a generous gift to the parish."

"Reave." Tessa placed her hand on his sleeve. "You cannot ask this of him."

"The hell I can't! I will not tolerate their slander." He focused on the vicar. "Well?"

"Forgive me. I cannot."

"Damn you, sir," he sneered, then walked away. This had not gone very well. Where was the man who could speak with such eloquence and logic that he rarely lost a trial? He felt consumed by his rage. He flinched when Tessa came up from behind and gave him a quick hug.

"I know what you are about, and I love you for it. You know this is not the way to handle the situation. These are your people, you must be their lord and not a sullen child."

Reave exhaled. Taking up her hand, he gallantly kissed it. She was truly an angel. Despite her embarrassment, she would not allow him to punish the lot of them. She would make him a fine countess. "You are correct. I suppose I fell apart like Lady Brackett's teacup when I saw the look of shock on your face. It pains me to see you so sad and hurt."

"I learned long ago it is possible to survive such insults. Their words cannot do any more damage to my life than I have not already inflicted by my own hand. Tell the vicar you will not seek retribution," she pleaded.

"I shall do what I should have done from the beginning." He glanced over at the older couple, who appeared extremely interested with the pattern of his rug. He did not doubt they were straining to hear every word exchanged, not that it mattered much, for soon all would know his mind.

"I am a private man, and rarely pay heed to the gossip directed my way. Still, I must pause and reconsider my actions when someone I have grown to love is being punished for my insensitivity to the issue." He heard Tessa's quiet intake of breath, knowing he had stunned her with this public proclaim. Dammit, he was tired of hiding his feelings. "Therefore, it is my decision we end this scandal by immediately posting the banns of our forthcoming marriage."

"This is splendid!" exclaimed Sims.

"You have made a wise decision, my lord. Miss Belanger, by all accounts, will make you a good wife." The vicar expelled a ragged sigh of relief.

The only one who was silent was Tessa. She sat in the chair with her head bowed. The sole indication that she had understood his announcement was the white-knuckled grip holding her to the chair.

Reave was not unmoved by her silence. He had hoped she would be pleased he wanted more of her than her body. Ignoring Lady Brackett and the vicar, Reave brushed past them and knelt beside Tessa's chair. Ever so gently, he cupped her chin, lifting it so he could see her face. He imagined there would be relief in her eyes and gratitude. Most of all, there would be happiness.

His hands fell away when he saw the glittering fury in her eyes. *Betrayer.* The word hung between them as if she had spoken it aloud. He wanted to deny it, but even he had to confess that he had acted once again in a rather overbearing manner. He would make her understand his motives were true to his heart. He loved her. When the others were gone, he would make her understand. "Vicar, understand this. My decision has nothing to do with the gossip. I had every intention of marrying Miss Belanger."

"I never doubted it, my lord," the vicar replied cheerfully.

"This will be a favorable match. I shall write my husband forthwith, and soon all of London will know of your betrothal!" Lady Brackett bubbled with enthusiasm. "We shall order the best of everything. Wycke, your pocket can withstand the lightening, if the rumors are to be believed. This will be the affair of the season!"

"Enough," Tessa cried, jumping to her feet. Her mournful plea capped the effervescence of everyone present. "Must I sit and watch you all build a house of cards that will easily be felled by the first bout of ill wind?" She brought her hands to her mouth to choke off the anguish.

Sims placed a protective arm around her. "There, there, my dear. Here we ramble on about our plans as if you were not an important part of it." She accepted Reave's offered handkerchief and dabbed at the tears on Tessa's cheeks. "You must feel quite alone without a family to share your wondrous news. Never fear. I want you to know I think of you as if you were my own. Allow me to help you as if you were."

"I care little about the gossip, and if I must, I shall leave this eve. There will be no banns. No marriage. Ever.'' Taking advantage of everyone's varying degrees of shock, Tessa picked up her skirts and fled the room.

"Tessa!'' Reave roared, catching her on the steps. Too many times he allowed her to run from him. This was too important to allow her to escape. ''I demand to know where you are leading me with this madness?'' He was not prepared when she whirled her fist around, nearly striking him across the face. Losing her balance, she fell forward. He caught her easily and held her close to his pounding chest. She fought him as if her very survival depended on her release.

"Demand. Decide. Release me, you arrogant arse,'' she hissed, gaining her immediate freedom. ''You are not my father. He, at least, had the right to hand me over to the richest man willing to tolerate me. Heedless to the concerns that the man might be the vilest of creatures.''

Puzzlement and fury melded, leaving Reave with burning frustration. ''I want to be your husband, not your father. What did I do to cause this upset? You knew I wanted to marry you, and you have repeatedly shown me you are not averse to my attentions.'' She kicked him in the shin, causing him to yelp in pain.

"Are you so arrogant to believe all you have to do is satisfy a woman in bed to make her marry you?'' she taunted.

"You said you loved me. Was it a lie?''

"Love is not everything.''

"Fine. Let us assume you are correct on that fact, Miss Belanger. What other ingredient would you add to make a sound match?''

"Trust,'' she blurted out. ''You promised me time to become accustomed to our relationship. Then, without care to my feelings, you announced our betrothal.''

"Have a care, Tessa. The ground you tread is about as fragile as pastry. You speak of trust when you give nothing of yourself.''

"That is not true. I trusted you to give me time, and you

lied!'' Her eyes glowed with desperation. ''If you care for me, you will call off the banns.''

''No.'' He threaded his fingers through his hair. Softening his tone, he tried to justify his decision. ''I have not broken my word. Exactly.''

''How odd, I thought you just announced our imminent marriage.''

''Listen to me, you little termagant!'' He drew an intimidating step closer. ''I may have told them we are to marry. I did not state the date, if you recall. That should give you proper time to polish your lies, so then perhaps I, too, may believe them.''

''If you think I am such a fraud, perhaps you should find someone else to marry. From what I have discovered about you these last few weeks, I would not have been surprised if your precious Elise died to escape you and your blasted arrogance!'' The telling flush of rage crept up his neck, stopping her cold. Even she recognized she had gone too far with her taunt. ''I was heartless to speak of such things. Please forgive me.''

''Get out of my sight,'' he said quietly. Too quietly.

''Reave, I was thoughtless.'' She reached out to soothe him.

''Are you deaf, or mayhaps you are ignorant of your proximity to imminent danger. Run away, which you do rather well, or face my wrath. I suggest you do the preceding,'' he grimly announced.

Before she could react, there was a pounding at the front door. The door swung open before Thorne reached the foyer. Viscount Turnberry sauntered into the hall.

''Hello, Thorne, where is Wycke?''

Thorne cocked his head. Kim's gaze followed the direction, settling on the solemn couple on the stairs. ''What have I missed?'' he jovially queried, strolling to the bottom of the stairs.

Tessa glared at them, then ran up the remainder of the steps until she was out of sight. Both men listened to her footfalls until the slam of her door left them in eerie silence. Kim raised a brow and turned to Reave for an explanation. "Care to let me in on it?"

Reave stared blankly at the spot where Tessa had stood, then acted as if he had just noticed his friend's presence. "You might as well come along and congratulate me. Lord knows I could use a drink," he muttered.

"What shall we drink to?" Kim asked, glancing once more at the empty staircase before he followed his friend.

"Why, naturally, to my impending bloody blissful marriage," he austerely replied. It sounded like a curse more than a wish for eternal happiness.

Chapter Twenty-one

A knock at the door shook the contemplative expression from Tessa's face. Another knock, this one more persistent, made her glance at the door. Rubbing her eyes, she grimaced.

Her unwelcomed visitor swore. He pounded again on the door.

"Give over, Lord Wycke," she called out when he jiggled the latch. Tessa almost laughed when he grunted and kicked the door. Good! She wanted him angry. He was less likely to talk her into being reasonable. "Go away before I do open the door and give you the fight you most definitely deserve."

"For God's sake, Tessa. It's Kim. Now, open the damn door before I drop this tray."

A stab of disappointment knifed her as she walked over to unlock the door. Reave had not come after all. The door swung open, and Kim rushed in with a large tray, overburdened with a teapot and covered platters.

"Took you long enough," he groused, searching the room for a place to set the tray.

"I thought you were Wycke."

"Obviously," was his droll, succinct reply. Setting the tray down, his gaze fixed on a chair. "At present, this should do nicely. Why not come over to the table and eat a little while we chat. I hear Cook made you your favorite dish of veal."

She joined him at the table, covertly watching each plate as he removed the silver covers. There was not a single item she would have turned away if she were not feeling so deplorable. "I am not terribly hungry."

"Well, I am, so why not talk while I eat." He cut a piece of veal and popped it into his mouth. His eyes rolled heavenward. "Mmm. You really should try it." He cut another piece and offered it to her. Reluctantly, she leaned over and took the meat. "Much better. You should eat more. I swear you've lost a little flesh since last we visited."

She shrugged and accepted another bite. What could she say? Worry had been her persistent companion since she left Edmund in their town house. "Why are you here?"

"Well, I always make a point of visiting Jason when I venture from town," he explained, misunderstanding her question. "Of course, I wanted to check on you too." He winked.

"No, I meant why are you here with me in my chambers?"

"Oh, that." The knave actually dared to be amused by her discomfort. "Well, someone needed to look after you, since you are too stubborn to see to your most basic needs."

"Must you always play the clown? Have you ever been known to be serious?" She gripped the table to push her chair out, but he stilled her movements.

"Must you always be so serious, so afraid?" he countered. "What has put fear in your eyes? Was it Reave? No," he answered the question himself. "It was there when I first met you. I naturally assumed it was the robbery that had frightened you so."

"Since you arrived hours ago, I assume you have been around here long enough to hear of Reave's high-handed dealings." She released her hold on the table and sunk back into the chair.

"Actually, he has been rather closemouthed about the affair.

I had hoped you could explain what has happened in my absence." He offered her another bite. She waved it away.

"You should talk to Cook. Jason says the man knows more about this than I do."

"Which is," he prompted.

Tessa studied her nails. "We have become close of late."

"You and Jason?"

"No—yes, of course, I have grown exceedingly fond of the boy." Uncomfortable, she shifted in her chair. "I happen to be speaking of Lord Wycke."

Kim tapped the fork to his chin, suddenly understanding the situation. "I see. He cares for you. I bet he is finding it difficult to settle with the past. I am not surprised, since he blames himself for Elise's death."

"No, I believe he has accepted his feelings for me." She frowned, comparing silently the differences between herself and Reave's virtuous, beautiful dead wife. The only mark in her favor was that she was living and the woman who held Reave's heart for so long was not. "Whether or not he holds himself accountable for his wife's death is a subject you must take up with him."

Puzzled, Kim's brows came together. "I do not see the dilemma. He loves you."

She rose from the chair and began to walk about the room. It felt confining. "He betrayed a trust," she said simply.

"Reave? Nonsense. The man is stuffed full of those honorable virtues until he is positively choking on them. Who did he betray?"

"Me! He told the vicar the banns were to be posted."

Kim choked on the wine. He covered his mouth with his napkin, unable to calm the fit of coughing that overtook him. Tessa rushed over and pounded him on the back. When he dropped the napkin, she saw that it was laughter, not distress, that kept him from speaking.

"Enough," he rasped. "You'll crack my rib if you continue to abuse my flesh."

She shoved his shoulder, expecting to push him out of his chair, but he was as rooted as his blasted good humor. "Next time I shall use the bed warmer if I find you amusing yourself at my expense again. Why not seek out the other child in the house. Check the nursery."

"Tessa, I would never mock you. However, I must confess I have never heard a woman complain that the man she loves was willing to marry her. Or is that the problem, you have no love for him?"

Tessa took a deep breath, then held it, as if she could hold the feelings she held in her heart. Love flowed forth uninhibited, limitless, on the air leaving her lungs. "My feelings are not in question, Kim. I had asked for time. He consented, only to break his word."

"I heard the rumors being exchanged in the village. Reave was trying to protect you."

She opened her arms in mock surrender. "I knew you would take his side. You might as well go back to him and tell him his plan did not work." She marched to the door and swung it open, awaiting his departure.

He joined her at the door, then pushed it closed despite her wordless protest. "Hear me out and then I will leave you to this wondrous display of childish sulking. Ah!" He placed a finger on her lips to silence her next words, then firmly grasped her elbow and guided her back to the chairs. "No one sent me here to manipulate you, nor did I intend to repeat our conversation to Reave. I do feel that when two people are in love, they should marry. Unless you can convince me to the contrary, I can see no reason why announcing the banns would be considered a betrayal."

He raised his hand to quiet her next objection. "True, he should have discussed the matter with you. But consider this— not many are fortunate to find this elusive love. Whatever your differences, you can work through them. Tessa, is it truly worth losing what the two of you have found? When you met, each was wounded. Together you have found a way to heal."

He strolled to the door, his hand poised lightly over the latch. For the first time, he allowed her to see into his heart. Tessa glimpsed the pain he kept within. There was loneliness too. She did not know its source, but it did not keep her from understanding.

"God, how I envy you." With a dramatic bow, he slipped out of the room, leaving her to wonder what secrets the handsome viscount kept hidden behind the depths of his green eyes.

The clock chimed one as Tessa held a taper over the small bed to check on her young charge. He almost looked like a baby, all flushed and warm buried under the blankets. Giving in to her urge, she flipped her unbound tresses over her shoulder so they would not wake him and placed a light kiss on his cheek. She felt unbearably alone and would have liked nothing better than to have crawled into bed with him as a mother would cuddle her child.

Tessa could not escape her restlessness this eve. She suspected she had been subtly manipulated by Kim's dramatic exit, though the notion did not dampen the impact. She knew everyone thought she was insane to throw away her chance to become Reave's wife.

She knew better than anyone what she was walking away from if she refused to play out this cruel charade. She also doubted she could bear to witness Reave's full reaction to her betrayal when he learned how much of what she told him were lies.

Backing away silently, she turned and ran straight into Reave. The candle fell from her grip and extinguished with a hiss on the rug. She immediately tried to squat down to make certain the wick was doused. Reave reached out from the darkness and held her close.

"Leave it." Reave's warm, husky voice, flavored with his favorite brandy, tickled her ear. "I want to talk to you." He led her out of his son's room and down to his own.

A warm fire greeted her in his room. She noticed the empty glass and the almost depleted decanter on the table next to the chair he positioned near the hearth.

"I know what you are thinking, and you are once again incorrect in your deductions." Her eyes widened on him expectantly. He obliged. Gesturing toward the table, he said, "I have had enough to warm my aching gut but not too much to befuddle my senses. I expected you earlier."

Did she detect hurt in his voice? She shifted her bare feet on the wood floor, uncomfortable to be standing beside him almost naked in her thin night rail when he still wore his evening clothes. He had loosened his cravat. Still, he looked every bit the man about to enjoy the night pleasures of London. "I had planned to speak to you but lost my nerve several hours ago."

"Why, Tessa?"

His guarded expression vanished, giving way to the vulnerable man she had come to know so well. She tenderly cupped his jaw with her slender hand, and he eagerly met her caress as a cat would easily accept the hand of a human. He kissed her palm. When she attempted to retreat, he held her hand, pulling them down onto the chair. He settled her on his lap. The minutes passed; still, neither spoke. He absently stroked her back, watching the crackling and shifting embers. Tessa allowed her head to drop on his shoulder, she, too, absorbed in the hypnotic glow and warmth of the fire.

"Were you aware of Kim's visit to my chamber?" She felt his muscles beneath her tense.

"No. Turnberry forgot to mention your little chat to me. Was he the reason for your sudden softening toward me?"

"Goodness, no!" She knew better than to fall into that trap. Reaching up, she rubbed the tension from his jaw. "I was bound to come to my senses eventually, once my temper cooled. Nevertheless, Kim could not resist prying and called me a fool for sulking." Whimsically, she rubbed her nose against his cheek. Satisfied to see the rigidness slowly ease, she tenderly smiled at him. "I love you, my lord. That has never faltered. I let my own fears almost turn you away."

Reave gathered her to him, giving her a fierce hug. "Never," he hoarsely whispered in her hair. "I wondered if you would forgive my indiscretion this afternoon. It was rather arbitrary, but at the time seemed the best solution all around."

"Well, I have not quite forgiven you. I shall need at least another day of sulking before I can put it aside and consider you in my favor," she teased. "I have decided you were correct all along."

"In regards to what, love?"

"You had mentioned that announcing our engagement does not mean the time I asked for was disregarded. I still insist I am given appropriate time."

He shifted his position to study her face closely. "Why is this time so important to you? Was it worth destroying us?"

"I explained all of this to you. I want to assure both of us that this match is more than relieving a winter's boredom."

"Bloody hell, Tessa. At the rate we've been making certain our match is sound, you will be giving me another son come winter," he said, exasperated by her stubbornness. She buried her face in the warmth of his neck, muttering something uncomplimentary about his outrageous boast. He pulled back to show her he was beyond finding amusement in their predicament. "I have never been one to be reckless with my heart."

"True, but who says what we have transcends the pleasures of the flesh?"

Reave replied by shoving her off his lap. Surprised, she did not try to prevent her backside from hitting the floor. He ignored her indignation. Stepping around her, he strode to the fireplace. Silent, he pressed his palms against the chimneypiece. She could sense he was struggling with his emotions, although his arm concealed his face from her. Suddenly, he pushed off the mantel, marched over, and pulled her to her feet.

"Reave?" His name came out in a rush of startled breath as he dragged her to the door.

"Not this time," he growled. "You are too good at this game of deceit, but I am on to your tricks!" He jerked the door open with his free hand while holding her tightly with the other.

"You make no sense!" Her eyes darted anxiously for a means to escape.

"Oh, I do, my love. You have confounded me at every turn. It will cease this night if you do not wish to end up in a locked room till our wedding."

"You still want to marry me?" she squeaked.

He rolled his eyes upward, raising his free hand in surrender. "At last, there is understanding." He linked his hands around her waist, lifting her off the ground. "Listen, you exasperating witch. I want you. Despite your stubbornness, your sharp tongue, your obscure parentage . . . even your damnable secrets!" He softened his tone, adding, "I will take you just as you stand before me, for life without you would condemn me to a life filled with shadows and strife. Tell me you feel the same, tell me that you will marry me!"

"Must you make this so difficult for me?"

His loving expression vanished, and a more imposing one took its place. Without warning, he pushed her outside into the corridor. Before she could open her mouth to apologize, he slammed the door in her face. She knocked on the door, whispering his name.

"You know what I want to hear," he shouted behind the closed door. "Don't bother to speak to me until you have come to your senses." The lock clicked, signaling the end to further discussion.

Tessa pressed her ear to the thick wood, striving to hear his movements. "Reave?" Silence answered her. Disappointed, she slid to the floor, pressing her back against the barrier separating her from the man she loved. No, this was only an obstacle; she was the true barrier. She laid her forehead on her knees, contemplating the day's events. Whatever she decided would shape the outcome of the future.

Their future.

Did she have the courage to fight for him and his son, who could be hers as well? Most of her life, people had made decisions for her. Now Reave was asking her to decide. Could she say the words to free them both from the past? Or would her choice only delay her inevitable fate?

"Yes."

Tessa had not realized she had spoken the word aloud until the door swung open. She toppled backward, her arms flailing to keep herself from hitting her head on the floor. Warm, familiar arms scooped her up and carried her into the room. "You misunderstood."

"Hush." He kissed her lightly on the lips. "It took you an eternity to make up your mind, and I have much to do before dawn."

Bemusement shone plainly on her visage, and a wry smile tugged at her lips. "Indeed? What matter demands your attention so late at night?"

"Why, I must set about proving to you once again how sound our match is." He dropped her on the bed and eagerly began removing his shirt.

Tessa gathered her night rail and pulled it over her head. She tossed it in his face and ducked under the covers. Laughing, he covered her nude body, trapping her, teasing her, until she could do nothing more but wait blissfully until he released her so she could show him that she, too, thought they made a sound match.

Chapter Twenty-two

"From your expression, I gather you and the elusive Miss Belanger have reconciled."

Reave raised his brow, then nodded to Kim leaning in the doorway. "No thanks to your meddling." Kim only laughed and without waiting for an invitation, sauntered into the library.

"I cannot imagine why she would want to put up with you for the rest of her life. You are getting grouchy in your old age." Kim plopped down into the chair across from Reave's desk, his legs casually splayed out in front of him.

"I suppose I have one or two redeeming values that make her willing to overlook my faults." Reave gave him a conspiring smile that was infectious.

Kim chuckled, shaking his head. "Bedding her may have solved her immediate reluctance, but what happens the next time? Do you plan to keep her in bed for the next few decades?"

"If I must. I cannot think of a more congenial method of ending a domestic squabble." He leaned back, his thoughts reflective of last night's lovemaking. It had been the best of his life; she had given herself completely, readily accepting all he had to offer. For once there was nothing between them except their love. Each had slipped into slumber, sated and content. If he had to, he would keep her in bed with him forever.

"I wish I felt that was all there was to the problem," Kim continued, interrupting the thought-filled silence.

"Why? Did she say something to you last evening to cause you to think otherwise?"

"No, she mentioned everything I would have expected. It was what she did not speak of that makes me worry."

Reave crossed his arms, resting them against his chest. "Kim, she was frightened. I never considered her parents' disastrous marriage or lack of would cause anxiety to surface when faced with her own nuptials. I blame myself for pushing her into something she was not ready for."

"I see you are accepting what you were spoon-fed." His friend resignedly sighed. "You must be in love." Kim stood up to leave, but Reave jumped up, meeting him eye to eye.

"You have never been one to dance lightly about an issue with me. Do you know something about her? Something you are reluctant to speak of because of my involvement with her?"

"Don't be an arse."

"Then why are you standing there like the hangman when I tell you I will marry her regardless of the past?"

Kim's face grew speculative. "I guess it was her eyes. You know, I have never seen anyone so frightened at the prospect of marriage. There must be more to it."

"Her eyes." Relaxing, Reave chuckled. "Now you are the one being an arse. Hell, if I may remind you, sir, you were the one who brought her here. I wanted nothing to do with protecting a waif. Yet, you trusted her enough back then to foist her off on me. So what has changed your opinion?" What disturbed him the most was he had asked himself similar questions and could not come up with rational answers. He told himself he was willing to wait until Tessa was ready to trust him completely. The risk of losing her had made him reckless.

Kim shrugged, then jammed his hands into his pockets.

"How was I supposed to know you would lose your head over her? I asked you to offer her employment, not your title."

"I think you knew exactly what you were doing, rotter. You thought, why not stir up your dull friend by pushing an irresistible fragile beauty into his arms and see what happens. I should beat that arrogance out of you."

Reave reached over the desk and grabbed Kim by the coat, forcing his friend to steady his balance on the desk as he was pulled halfway across it.

"I should," Reave threatened. "Just once, someone should give you a few bruises to dampen your spirit. Today you are in luck." He suddenly released his grip. Kim slid off the desk, taking half of the paperwork over the edge.

Reave laughed outright at Kim's irritated "Bloody bounder." The man deserved a little abuse after all he had done to bring him and Tessa together. The only reason he did not kill him was that, despite everything, he was grateful. "Do you need a hand?"

"Not if you are offering," Kim shot back, wincing as he gingerly touched his backside. "I think you broke my arse."

"I highly doubt it. It's about as hard as your head." He walked around and offered his hand. Grudgingly, it was accepted. He pulled Kim to his feet.

"Only to be matched by yours." Kim dusted off his coat, then slowly eased into the nearest chair. "If I had known you would be in such a mood, I would have sent my news by post."

Reave poured a drink from the decanter, then gestured to Kim. Receiving an enthusiastic nod, he filled another glass with the amber liquid and brought the glass to his friend. "What news? Don't tell me—you have gotten yourself in another scrape and need my help to get out."

"Really," Kim drolly replied. "Your faith in my abilities to get in over my head astound me. Frankly, I came to save you from a wasted endeavor. My news should free you to delve into your beloved's past if you desire, though if you would rather mock me, then—"

"Enough, you win. What are you saving me from?"

Kim raised his glass to the light, studying the crystal facets as he turned it. "What if I told you the Lathom case has been closed." He struck the rim of the glass with his finger, enjoying the reaction his news had created.

"They found her?"

"Yes, but—"

"Damn, I should have been there! I had hoped my contacts would reach her before the locals had a chance to parade her through town." He rubbed his eyes, as if suddenly weary. "Have you heard anything more?"

"I wouldn't worry about her well-being, since she turned up dead."

"Dead!" Reave bellowed, then added in a softer tone. "Hell."

"Very appropriate sentiments considering they pulled her out of the Thames. From what Hayden described, she'd been dead for some time, her face bloated beyond recognition."

Dead. A tragic beauty ruined in death, as her husband had ruined her in life. Reave closed off the grisly image in his mind.

"Hold." Reave tried to collect his wits. "How was she identified if the body had deteriorated beyond recognition? No one had seen her leave, so she could have been wearing a disguise."

"Hayden explained that besides being the correct height and weight, not to mention her gown marked her as a lady, she had one piece of jewelry difficult to discount. She wore the Lathom crest on her third finger." Kim cast a shrewd glance at him. "Damn me if you don't look disappointed she was found."

"Ridiculous." Reave took a healthy swallow from his drink. "I was just thinking about all the time I dedicated to the investigation. I was never certain she had actually done the deed."

"Odd you came to that conclusion. The general assumption was the ol' girl couldn't live with herself after slaughtering Ed and Mums, so she decided to take a dip in the frozen river,

thus saving everyone the trouble of hanging her." Kim smirked.
"I suppose you could say you lost this one on a stipulation. I
doubt any of us will count this against your sterling record."

"Could you be serious just for a minute and let me think?"
Reave snapped. He opened a drawer in his desk. Taking out a
narrow box, he removed the lid and pulled out a miniature. He
dangled it by its gold link chain, studying it as if it held the
answers to his questions.

"A gift for Tessa?"

Reave slowly shook his head, his attention still focused on
the miniature. He popped open the case, gazing at the small
painting of a young girl. "No," he absently replied. "This
belonged to Lathom's wife."

"Really? Might I see it?" Kim caught the gold miniature
tossed to him. He inspected the painting. "I thought this was
the countess. This is a mere child," he complained.

"She must have been about ten when it was done. I suppose
she has changed quite a bit since the sitting," Reave said
apathetically.

"Obviously," Kim muttered. Disappointed, he tossed the
miniature back to Reave. "I have never seen a murderess. I
was wondering if it was something one could recognize on a
fair face."

"If that was true, we would have tried and hanged you ages
ago," baited Reave. He opened the gold lid, studying the young
face again. There was nothing extraordinary about the girl: a
chubby, babylike face, straight blond hair, her expression
almost pinched, as if uncomfortable. It told him nothing about
her. Distracted and frustrated, he pinched the lid shut and
slipped the locket back into its box. "I suppose we will never
know the truth."

"Most likely. The ton has made up its mind declaring her
guilty. Let it rest, there is nothing more to prove."

"I suppose so."

"I would place your energies toward convincing your
betrothed that she should marry you."

Reave's lips moved as if to stifle his smile. "I have it on good account, the dear woman will have me. Tessa just wants to be the one to chose the date. She just needs a little encouragement to see this year would benefit both of us."

"And your unborn child," Kim quipped.

"My thought exactly," Reave replied.

Entering the music room, Tessa noted Kim and Sims were sitting entirely too close, their heads bowed. Nigh deep in controversy, she gathered. Considering their history, neither she or Reave would be safe from their machinations this evening.

Seemingly oblivious to their schemes, Reave sat at the piano, softly playing a melody unfamiliar to her. He looked troubled, distracted, but she would wait until they were alone before she asked him what bothered him so. Sensing he was being watched, he met her gaze. He glanced at his companions, then cocked his head in their direction.

"Gossiping, no doubt," Reave replied, then returned his attention to his hands.

"Come join us, my dear. Kim has been kind to inform me of the latest news from London." Sims waved her over to the seat closest to her left.

"So you *are* gossiping. You surprise me, Kim. I was not aware men relished such endeavors," Tessa chided. She sat in the chair, primly straightening her skirts.

Kim winked at Sims, causing the older woman to blush. "In truth, I brought word from Sims's husband. Only fair, since it was I who encouraged her to remain here with you. As for gossiping, one can hardly avoid the current talk circulating through town."

"Indeed? Pray what couple has set the town on its ear this week?" Tessa inquired, looking forward to a little distraction from her problems. The ton was as frivolous as it was fickle, and she was certain the news would be entertaining.

Kim looked surprised. "The Earl and Countess of Lathom,

of course. They have been the current rage since the ol' boy was found dead in the arms of his wife's mother. The whole affair was rather torrid, I must say.''

"It all sounds like a good novel. What do you think, dear?'' Sims turned to Tessa. "Are you well? Shall I fetch Thorne for something?''

Tessa's lips felt numb, and there was an odd tingling in her hands. It took all her concentration to speak without a tremor. "No, no, do not bother. I suppose it is all this talk of murder. Sims, I was there at the inn with Kim when someone announced the murders.'' Taking her handkerchief from her sleeve, she dabbed the moisture from her face. She ignored the knowing looks Kim and Sims exchanged. They probably assumed she was breeding, which was certainly more acceptable than the truth.

"I had forgotten we were together when I heard the news,'' Kim remarked. "I do recall the man had an unusual enthusiasm for the grotesque. Do not upset yourself with the memory. Most likely he embellished the details to entertain and shock his audience.''

"I know little of the Lathoms. What were they like?'' Sims settled down, ready to hear the entertaining tale. "Were they admired among the ton?''

"On the contrary. They were mocked and despised as much as they were a source of amusement when their affairs turned to the absurd,'' Tessa said with enough bitterness to draw even Reave from his stupor.

"I am surprised you know of them, love.'' It was the first time since the conversation began that Reave was interested in their discussion.

Tessa fidgeted with a fraying piece of lace at her sleeve. Her frustration made her want to tear it from her wrist rather than try to repair it. What had she been thinking? This case mattered greatly to Reave. Any knowledge of the Lathoms would gain his attention. If swallowing her unguarded tongue had been possible, she would have taken it with a pinch of salt. "My lord, I had mentioned my short residence in London while searching for my father. The people from whom I acquired my rooms were not unfamiliar with the fashionable. I must confess, many an evening was spent discussing the various people who stirred the tongues and imaginations of the ton.''

Her explanation only fueled further questions. His music forgotten, Reave prodded, ''Was this couple acquainted with the Lathoms?''

''Good God, Reave,'' Kim chided, ''stop interrogating her. The case is closed.''

''I do not understand,'' Tessa said, reluctantly removing her attention from Reave to address Kim. ''The murderer, he has been captured?''

Kim made a sound akin to disgust. ''I should have known you would share his views too. What makes you both so certain the killing was done by a man?''

Failing to possess a credible lie, Tessa bit her lip and glanced away. Reave, however, did not hesitate to answer.

''I said,'' Reave bit out, visibly irritated from having to explain himself again, ''I doubted she was capable of the crime. Nevertheless, I would not dismiss the notion a woman could have done the killing. A knife is an easy enough weapon for a woman to wield. What perplexes me is how the woman was powerful enough to overtake Lathom. He was a rather large man, if the description I culled was accurate.''

Tessa listened anxiously to the men's conjectures of how a woman could kill two people and not be heard, until she thought she would faint from the terror of it all. Her bitten lip cracked from the stress and she tasted blood. ''Why is the case closed? You said no one has been charged with the murder.''

Kim spoke first, cutting off Reave's reply. ''It appears the lady could not live with her sins and took her own life. Perhaps she thought she had better odds in the higher courts.'' He and Sims chuckled at his wit.

''What?'' Tessa whispered, stunned. Dead? She clutched her

heart as if further explanation would undo her. "There must be some mistake."

"Not likely, since she was identified by someone who had a distant association with the woman. Her body was badly decomposed." He hesitated at Reave's look of warning. "Uh, my apologies, ladies. She was identified by the Lathom ring she wore upon her third finger. The family crest was unmistakable."

"Tessa, is this not the most intriguing tale you have ever heard?" Sims gushed. "It is certainly the most tragic, unless you count the Laney affair. I was told the husband butchered three of his children before someone wrestled the ax from his hands!"

"I believe he murdered two of the tikes and was in the process of hacking the legs off another when . . ." Kim's correction of Sims's account of the tragic tale faded for Tessa and was replaced by the accelerated heartbeat pounding in her ears.

They thought the countess was dead! No, that was not quite right. London thought *she* was dead. She shuddered from a chill in the room. Heavens, who was the unfortunate woman possessing the family crest? Another mistress, perhaps?

Tessa had never worn anything that connected her to the Lathom family, not even the family jewels. Only once, early on in their marriage, had Edmund forced her to wear a ruby-and-diamond necklace. It had belonged to generations of Lathom women. To Tessa, it was a fancy collar that seemed to tighten around her neck as the evening wore into morning.

When the evening was over, Edmund tore the necklace from her throat, vowing that never again would she wear the family jewels. She was not worthy of them. The Lathom women were remembered for their beauty. He had called her an swinish, ugly commoner.

After the years had passed, and her weight had long since been a moot issue, he found other matters to criticize about her. By then, wearing a token of his affection seemed a mockery.

Glancing up, Tessa was grateful her silence had gone unnoticed by her companions. They had moved on to another gory tale, one in which she could not even pretend interest. Touching the crumpled rag that had once been her handkerchief to her temple, she caught Reave's gaze on her. He looked as if he had been watching her for some time, his expression unreadable. Discomposed, she gave him a weak smile. "All this talk unsettles me. I have never commanded a strong stomach for others' misfortune."

He grunted, saying nothing more, but his full attention remained on her. Wondering if she had said or done something to deserve this speculation, she thickly swallowed, pretending to join in on the others' conversation. She could still feel his brooding stare on her face, giving her no explanation for his present mood. Perhaps when the others had retired, she would be privy to his thoughts. For the moment, she was not so certain she wanted to know them. She had enough to bear. As it was, it took another hour before she could discreetly stand and escape the room.

Chapter Twenty-three

"I find activity intolerable under this baking sun." Sims fanned her face and bosom, looking as if she were close to collapsing. "I cannot fathom how those two can romp through the mud and water like a couple of mongrel pups." She gestured in the direction of Reave and Jason. "I feel faint just watching them."

"It may be warm for May, Sims, but the water holds a winter chill that could set your teeth on edge." Tessa smiled in the direction of her men. Her men. Ho, what flights of fancy! Her men indeed! She could not prevent the warmth that filled her breast every time she watched father and son any more than she could keep the feelings of possessiveness at a distance. The climate was not the only element to have warmed in the past month and a half.

With the Countess of Lathom believed dead, Tessa could almost accept this life at Eastcott. It was so simple when all the land was abloom with nature's colors and the land smelled sweet from the nourishing rains. Darkness had no place here.

She kneeled to pick several pale violet cuckooflowers at her feet. Standing, she inhaled the light fragrance of the delicate blooms. Without looking back, she said to Sims, "You would be more comfortable if you chose lighter fabrics, I think. I promise not to tell a soul if the sun blackens your arms a bit," she teased.

"Heaven help me if that were to happen," Sims panted, and fanned herself with increasing frequency. "I would not blemish my husband's good name by running about the countryside dark as a Nubian slave. Upon hearing the gossip, he would petition for a divorce."

Tessa cocked an innocent eye on her companion. "Surely, you do not think the same people who had only our better interests at heart when they spoke cruelly of my relationship with Reave would speak ill of you?"

Time had not eased the anger that had led to the events of her betrothal. Reave rarely pressed her on the subject, but she saw the question in his eyes.

When?

Frowning, she brushed a small beetle off one of the flowers. She had told him that she would wed him in autumn, knowing in truth she would be gone from their lives. She could have left weeks before, except for the money. Reave had yet to pay her as he had promised. He always made certain her needs were met when it came to clothes and other women's frippery, as he called it. Yet when she asked for money of her own, he found various reasons for withholding her funds. Tessa suspected he knew her too well to trust her with the full sum. A prickly lady with a heavy purse might be less inclined to set a wedding date.

A shout called her attention back to Reave and Jason. Both were drenched from head to foot, though neither seemed bothered. They were crouched in the mud around the crude sailboat they had built. It was having a few difficulties making its maiden voyage. Every time they released the vessel, it rolled to its side and slowly sank. She could not tell which one was more frustrated.

"It is a handsome family you will be marrying," Sims said, joining her.

Tessa bent and broke off a wood anemone at its stem, adding it to her bouquet. "It is a lucky woman who captures their hearts." She tried to keep the wistfulness from her voice. What she did not tell her friend was that sometimes capturing the heart was not enough.

"You are responsible for bringing them together when others doubted it was possible. I have never seen a stronger bond between father and son." Sims's gaze followed the two as they attempted to launch the boat again. "Have you thought about setting a date?"

Tessa opened her mouth to awkwardly explain Reave's promise, but masculine outrage gave her a chance to escape. Setting her cut flowers on the ground, she ran to the water's edge. The reason for the roar had nothing to do with pain, but, rather, frustration. She searched for their waterlogged vessel. It had capsized and was gently floating out of range with the current. Jason kicked at the water before running after his boat.

"Damn boat," Reave cursed, throwing up his hands. "It's wood. The bloody thing should be floating like a rotten log!"

Tessa glanced back at Sims, who appeared to be preoccupied with cooling herself, though the flush on her cheeks told Tessa she had heard every word. "My lord, remember the rule about the delicate sensibilities of women and children?"

Reave whirled around, finally noticing she had inched as close to the water's edge as she dared. "Hell," he muttered, wiping his wet locks backward. "Sorry. Things are not going well."

"Have you tried to weigh it down with something?" she suggested, receiving a glare that told her he had considered everything that would come to the mind of a woman. "I just wanted to help."

"Papa?" Jason ran back to them, breathless. "What if we put some rocks into the center? Perhaps that would keep it from tipping."

Tessa smirked, taunting, "Thank goodness, there was a *man* around to think of such an idea." She fluttered her lashes, then picked up her skirts to rejoin Sims. An arm shot out to stop her.

"Oh, no, Miss Pert." Reave jerked her arm. She lost her balance, but he deftly caught her before she fell. He grinned when she looked uneasily from his face to the cold water under her. "Not feeling so cheeky, now, are you?"

"Come now, Reave, it was just teasing. 'Tis not worthy"— she anxiously eyed the water—"o-of such vengeance." She squealed when he pretended to lose his hold and drop her. "Reave!" She clung to him as if climbing to the top of his head were her ultimate goal.

"Call me beloved," he prompted, his wicked smile grew wider.

"Beloved," she instantly replied. "My dearest, sweet, loving beloved!" she yelled out.

"Say you will marry me next month."

Tessa halted her struggling and opened her eyes. Gone was the teasing delight from Reave's face. This was not part of the game but a moment for truth. With a desperateness she could not understand, she wanted to say the words he desired. The search for the missing countess had ceased, and if she remained at Eastcott, perhaps no one would ever reveal her secret. A chance at a new life. She had left Edmund and London for precisely that reason. Inhaling deeply, she said in a rush of breath, "I shall marry you in a month's time."

At first, he did not seem to trust his ears. She answered his unspoken question with a quick nod. She would marry him! He let out a yell that shook a few leaves out of the trees. Whirling her about, he hugged her close to his chest. What he did not take into account was that the stones at the bottom of the brook were covered with slime. Reave lost his footing. Instinctively, he protected her from hitting the bottom as they collapsed. His actions did not prevent her from getting as soaked as he was. The yards of fabric making up her gown soaked up the water, and soon her teeth were chattering. Reave and Jason laughed at her attempt to stand in the water-sodden gown. Her wobbly gait forced her back into the water.

Tessa glared at him. "P-perhaps I was hasty with my decision and should r-reconsider." Reave pulled her to him with amazing agility considering their condition, fiercely hugging her.

"Attempt to retract your promise and I swear I will lock you in your chamber with only stale bread and weak marrow broth to drink until you come to your senses." He placed his cold, wet hands on either side of her face, stilling her shudder. "Let me take care of you."

The tenderness in his expression overwhelmed her. He could make her forget about her past. With one kiss, he healed a thousand scars that took years to inflict. Tessa knew he deserved better than she could give. She was just too selfish to take back her words. Placing her own wet, chilled hand on his cheek, she gave him the words he had wanted to hear these last few weeks. "Let us set a date, one month from this day."

His serious features lightened to boyish delight. "Do you mean it? You know I would never lock you up, or at least if I did, I would make certain I was with you. Honestly, Tessa, is this what you want?"

She did not need to think about it. She did not want a new life if she could not have him and Jason. "Yes." She clung to him. "You are everything I have ever dreamed!" She hungrily accepted his kiss, oblivious that she was losing the feeling in her legs from the cold water. Vaguely, she heard Jason call his papa. How could she have forgotten their audience?

"Papa, does this mean Tessa will marry you?" Jason asked wide-eyed at the passionate kissing he had just observed.

Reave fondly gazed past her shoulder at his son. "Rightly so, my lad. Soon we will be a family in truth." He widened his embrace so Jason could share their hug. The three of them stood in the middle of the brook, laughing and hugging, joyfully unaware of their discomforts.

"No one will ever believe the date was set in the middle of

a brook while the betrothed couple turned a delicate shade of blue!'' Sims said, standing at the water's edge. ''I hope you do not expect me to wade out there in order to congratulate you,'' she huffed. ''If not for me, I doubt the two of you would have ever gotten down to the business of marriage,''

Sims might believe they had forgotten it was her meddling that had brought them together, but Tessa had not. She would be eternally grateful for the older woman's mischief.

Hand in hand, the sodden three pulled one another onto the dry land. Despite Sims's protests, all of them wrapped their wet arms around her and included her in their joy.

Reave trailed his finger slowly down Tessa's back, smiling as she shuddered under his tender assault. They had spent the last few hours making love and cuddling. Both were too sated and lazy to do much else except sleep. Despite the late hour, he was wide awake, his mind reeling with their wedding plans. A month was too long to wait to claim her as wife. He stroked her again, causing a sound that sounded remarkably similar to a snore before the noise abruptly stopped and she shifted deeper under the covers.

He would marry her tonight if it were possible. Still, he would wait out the month, knowing she needed the time to prepare. He wished he could understand why time seemed so damned important to her. It was the only subject that caused them to argue, yet he loved her enough to remain silent until she was ready to explain.

His thoughts flicked randomly to the conversation he had with Kim before he departed for London. The viscount had suggested that if Tessa's past was so important to him, he should have her investigated. He had been angry at the suggestion. Privately, he had to admit he had considered the thought himself. She could be so tight-mouthed about her past, and he wanted to know everything about her so he could prove, once and for all, her secrets meant nothing. His love was constant.

Once he showed her he would not leave like her parents had, only then would she completely trust him.

Before he gave in to the temptation and woke her again, Reave rolled off the bed. Putting on his dark blue dressing gown, he quietly left the room. After he made a quick stop to check on Jason, he went to Tessa's chamber.

There was nothing remarkable about the room. It revealed little about the woman who resided there. The room was meticulously clean, and at first glance it looked as if no one had occupied it. There were a few perfume bottles. He picked up the largest one and smelled the contents. Its aroma instantly reminded him of Tessa. Capping and returning the glass bottle to its place, he picked up her silver-handled brush. Reave tugged at the bristles until he had freed the tangled strands of hair. He wrapped the silken threads around his first finger. Bringing them to his lips, he placed a loving kiss on his bound finger. He was truly in love to worship even the lost strands of hair caught in her brush!

His attention wandered until it settled on the small drawer under the table. Without hesitation, he tried the drawer. Becoming stuck halfway, Reave tugged harder, shifting the cosmetics and brushes within. Undaunted, he reached deep into the drawer, groping to clear the obstacle. Intrigued, he removed a small leather pouch from the back. He shook the contents into his palm.

Ah, he had forgotten about her locket. The last time he had gripped the ornate oval, Kim was threatening to whisk Tessa away. At the time, he had been too furious at his desire to have her remain in his household to pay too much attention to the necklace.

Cool metal shifted in his palm, the chain a twisted clump of gold links. Delicately, he brushed the tangled links aside, revealing the engraved surface of a locket.

An uneasy feeling washed over him.

Slipping his nail between the edges, he popped open the hinge and looked at the miniature. The painting was of a little girl he did not recognize. She was a pretty child. Reave assumed she was a relative, perhaps even Tessa's mother. A locket was a common remembrance. With a final glance, he snapped the locket shut.

Tomorrow he would go to the village and have someone repair the broken chain as a surprise, then he would present her with his betrothal ring. He had given Elise a family ring. It would not be so for Tessa. Their marriage meant new beginnings. He did not want her wearing a ring that would remind him of another.

Flipping the locket over, Reave rubbed the scratched gold surface with his thumb, studying the delicate engraving. It was two drooping roses intertwined with a small fox sitting at the base. Recognition pricked the back of his neck like small, cold needles. He recalled another time when he had held its twin, another locket, in the same palm over a month before in his library. Gripping the locket tightly, he slammed his fist against the fragile dressing table. The mirror vibrated, blurring his reflection.

"No," he cried out in anguish. His mind refused to accept the possibility. The woman was dead! He dropped the locket back into its pouch and placed it in the drawer. Slamming it shut, he stalked off, seeking the answers his breaking heart refused to acknowledge.

"Wake up."

If Tessa heard Reave's command, the warm cloak of sleep kept her from stirring. He said her name, but this time it was punctuated with a shove.

"Hmm?" She rolled over, quickly blinking away the haze clouding her mind. "Reave?" Her throat, unused, sounded raw and strange. "Is something amiss, my love?"

She seemed so innocent, so beguiling, lying there with her honeyed tresses splayed all around her. He wondered what it would take to shake her fragile composure. "I have been thinking," he replied without betraying the conflicting turmoil churning in his gut. *Deceitful, perjuring bitch.*

"Indeed." Amusement animated her face. "And you thought to wake me with this news." She covered her open mouth and patted away a yawn.

"I was thinking about our upcoming nuptials. You do not know the full extent of my feelings when I think of us becoming husband and wife," he said in a dangerously silky tone. His hand shot out to caress her cheek. He froze the gesture by balling his hand into a fist and shoving it into the pocket of his dressing gown.

"I—I am happy you are pleased," she stuttered, finally awake enough to notice he was acting odd. Sitting up, she wrapped a blanket around her nude body.

"Yes, well, this is truly an auspicious occasion, since I had sworn to all that no one was likely to capture my heart again. Elise was a generous, honest, and loving woman. Our marriage went well beyond a good match. We loved each other with an intensity that—" He halted, disappointed his words had not brought forth the reaction he desired. "Never mind, it is the past. I am indeed fortunate to have been blessed again with a woman who deserves my complete trust and loyalty." She did pale at that comment.

He smiled. "I have been selfish keeping you locked away only for my pleasure. This day my selfishness ends. On the morrow, I shall send out invitations to all of London, inviting them to Eastcott. You shall be presented and we will announce our betrothal at a ball in your honor. No expense shall be spared for you, my love." He was not surprised when panic destroyed her guarded expression. It only confirmed what he feared.

"A ball?" Tessa lowered her gaze, and her eyes darted back and forth across the bedding as if it held the answers for her. "No, no, I cannot do this." She met his gaze. Whatever she beheld simmering in his dark blue depths silenced her. She took a deep breath and glanced away.

"Why not?" he demanded. His edged brevity made her

blink. "You are a true prize, love. I wish to share you with everyone."

"Reave, I have lived a sheltered life, and the thought of facing half the ton makes me—"

He dismissed her excuse with a wave of his hand. "Fine. Perhaps, you are not prepared to come out and need more time." Reference to the excuse she had used for months set his teeth on edge. "A house party with my closest friends in attendance will accomplish my purpose. Even you could hardly object to that." He scowled at her, daring her to protest.

"Could we not wait until after the wedding?" She wildly gestured with her hands. "There is so much needing my attention. I can barely think." She sounded desperate, almost begging. "Would you not reconsider?"

He forced his expression to remain stony. He watched her squirm under his silent scrutiny, drawing no satisfaction from what he must do. He had to know the truth even if he had to tear it out of her. It could destroy their fragile love. Reave prayed his assumptions were incorrect. He would spend the rest of his life compensating her for his cruelty. Please, let him be wrong!

"I think not," he said. With her shoulders slumped, she seemed almost childlike in the large bed. Swallowing the urge to comfort her, he continued. "I confess, I am ignorant in the ways of preparation for this wedding, but the women attending will be of immeasurable help in this endeavor, since both are married. Densmore's duchess is only a few years older than you and undoubtedly will be able to sympathize with you, since she had a rather rushed marriage herself."

"Densmore?" Her head lifted at the mention of the name.

"Yes, are you acquainted with the family?" he asked, keeping his voice casual.

"Ah-oh, no. Well, the name does sound familiar," she lamely admitted. "How many shall we expect?"

Reave raised a brow at her immediate acquiescence but did not comment on it. Instead, he answered her question. "Let's see. The Densmores, my law partner and his wife, and Kim. That makes it five, unless Turnberry picks off the streets another chit in peril. It seems the only manner the gent finds women willing to bear his company.'' He forced himself to laugh, an attempt to lighten his demeanor. He was not willing to share his suspicions with anyone until he had proof. Nor could he have her running off blindly, for he knew her well enough to predict that is exactly what she would do if she suspected he knew the truth about her past. If she was the one. He did not realize he was lost in thought until she swept by him clothed only in a sheet. ''Where are you going?''

''To my chamber to change. I have much to consider with the arrival of your friends and a wedding to plan.''

Tessa looked so lost, he did not bother to detain her. She shuffled out the door, heedless of her state of dress. Reave wearily sank onto the bed where she had sat bleakly accepting his decision.

He did not know what he had expected. Did he think she would have jumped up from the bed confessing she was Lathom's wife? And where did the dead woman fit in to all of this? She was found wearing the family crest. He did not think Tessa was responsible for the woman's death. She was too soft for the bloody business of killing.

Too soft to kill the husband who betrayed her?

He rubbed his eyes, pressing back the stinging wetness threatening to unman him. He had lost one wife, and it had nearly cost him his son. If he lost Tessa, he was certain he would lose his soul.

Chapter Twenty-four

"Have a care with that cloth," Sims warned the seamstresses, and received a discreet glare for her unnecessary instruction. "This gown must be worthy of the future Countess of Wycke."

Tessa turned, finally glancing at her image in the cheval glass. Her focus was not on the willow-green gown being altered for her wedding. Instead, her gaze blurred on her cynical, pinched reflection. She could draw little enthusiasm for the delicate gold beading at the short sleeves and hem, nor for the vandyking around the petticoat. Sims carried enough excitement for them both.

These last few weeks, Tessa had walked about Eastcott in a state of unremitting wretchedness. Reave barely spoke to her. For reasons he kept to himself, he left for London the morning after he announced the house party. He returned ten days later, his dour mood worse. She had tried to speak to him to see if he doubted his decision to marry her. He reciprocated her questioning with an expression so filled with bitterness and pain, it devastated her.

He reminded her of the man she had first encountered when

Kim had brought her to Eastcott. The man who might have lusted after her but had no desire to keep her in his life. Sadly, her reflective gaze met Sims's.

"Do not worry about him," Sims assured her as if understanding what was occurring between them. Reverently, Sims touched the exquisite round collar created with pearls and gold wire. "The days before the wedding are the most trying. It will all pass when the vows are spoken."

Tears welled in Tessa's eyes. Her voice cracked with emotion. "I think he regrets his hasty decision to marry someone like me and cannot think of a polite manner to rid himself of the arrangement."

"Off with you—we need privacy." Sims hustled the shocked seamstresses from the room. She took a scrap of fabric off a chair and covered Tessa's front so her tears would not ruin the bodice. "Hush, now. I have never seen a man so smitten."

Sims handed her a handkerchief. Tessa wiped her eyes, then blew her nose. Fresh tears soon replaced the ones wiped away. "This happens to all brides," Sims said soothingly. "Why, it would not be wedding if there were not a few tears shed."

Tessa shook her head. "Something is very wrong, Sims. This goes beyond tattered nerves." She sniffed, blinking away the tears clinging to her lashes. "He avoids me, and I doubt I have gotten him to utter more than four words to me since his return from town."

The older woman patted her hand. "My dear, you have much to learn. Men loathe these trimmed events. It takes the attention off them and makes them churlish. I suggest you give him some special attention, and he will brighten up." She smiled and rapped Tessa lightly under the chin. "I will call the seamstresses back so you can get out of the gown. From the looks of things, you have much to do."

Tessa's strained smile fell the moment Sims close the door. She did not believe Reave's behavior was the result of feeling ignored. He was the type of man who would have demanded attention if that were the reason. No, there was something else on his mind. Sims was correct about one thing, she did need to seek him out again.

The fire had almost burned itself out. Reave was too drunk to notice or care. Thorne had notified him Tessa had been inquiring about his whereabouts again. Always a resourceful man, he had managed to elude her. Unfortunately, it took the numbing effects of his good brandy to banish her image from his mind.

Being summoned to London regarding the Lathom case had not eased his thoughts. The case was officially closed. Not deterred, he hired men to search for information that others might have missed. His attention served him well. However, it was not what he had expected.

He learned Lady Lathom had been to a disreputable apothecary in one of the lower districts, inquiring about a poison guaranteed to kill rats in an expedient manner. Rats! Reave expelled a bitter laugh, then drained the contents of his glass. One had to appreciate the irony of it all.

The countess had killed husband. His vision blurred and Reave shook his head until it cleared. He had to remind himself the poison did not prove anything. After all, it was the numerous stab wounds that had killed Lathom. Why poison him too?

He pushed back from his desk, knocking himself backward in his chair. The unexpected crash sobered him slightly as he staggered to his feet. Of course! He moved to his desk and began shuffling through his papers. One of the reports noted that there was broken glass strewn about Lathom's chamber. The countess could have poisoned the liquor. Instead of killing him, she discovered the poison had rendered him unconscious. Stabbing him would have been a simple task, while he lay helpless, sickened by the drink. The scenario would explain how she could have overpowered a man of his size.

Another drink was needed, Reave thought, dropping the crushed papers. Squinting about the room, he searched for the cart. It was there, where it had always stood, but in his condition he miscalculated the distance. Several of the decanters shattered when they hit the floor. Bloodred liquor mixed with amber. It pooled and flowed down the hardwood seams. Transfixed, he watched the liquid seep around a freshly murdered Lathom, his blood trickling from his mutilated body and soaking into his fine Axminster rug.

He did not know how long he stood staring at the horrific image conjured by his drunken inspiration. Perhaps he dozed, he was not certain. The sound of the door opening behind him startled him awake. He glanced at the floor. All that remained was broken glass and good brandy ruining his wood floor.

"I do not recall summoning you." He did not have to turn around to know it was Tessa.

"We—I thought you might be hurt. I heard a noise and . . ." He glanced back to see Tessa standing in the doorway. She was abusing her lower lip again as her wary gaze scanned the room.

She remained silent so long, Reave began to think she, too, was a vision from his sodden head. He focused on her, his body slightly weaving with an imaginary breeze while he tried to see through the illusion. When she refused to vanish, he snapped, "What do you want?"

He swung his right arm out to ward her off, forgetting he held a half-full decanter. The counterweight of the liquid sloshing within the crystal caused the decanter to slip from his relaxed grip. It shattered at his feet. "The bloody thing was cracked." He chuckled to himself. Taking a step away from the cart, he lost his footing and landed on his back.

If she was frightened of him, she ignored her feelings and rushed to his side. Kicking away the glass beside him, she sat on the floor and gently cradled his head in her lap. "Have I done this to you, my love?" She took a portion of her skirt and wiped the brandy and splintered glass from his cheek.

"I vaguely recall breaking my arse for your benefit once before," he muttered. He lifted his head off her lap and sat up.

She did not attempt to halt or assist him. He tensed when she gasped.

"Your back is bleeding," she said as if the pain were her own. "There might be glass still buried in your flesh. Here, let me—" She leaned forward to examine his wound, but Reave pushed her back.

"Leave it be, *Miss Belanger!*" he roared like a wounded animal. "I feel nothing."

Tessa did not move. Her assessing gaze narrowed in disgust. "Hardly surprising, if the stink of you is any indication to the amount of spirits you have consumed." She demurely lowered her lashes, concealing what he suspected was tears. "Is the thought of marrying me so dispiriting, you must drown the very thought from your head?"

She sounded hurt and confused by his behavior. Was this the guise of a cunning bitch, or was she as angelic and fragile as she appeared on her knees before him. He stood, steadying his gait on the nearest chair. "Ah, Tessa," he sighed. "Why must you tempt me now, when I have tried to hold true to all my beliefs." He sank into the chair. "You are a witch."

He mumbled the last few words, slipping into unconsciousness with his next breath. Drawing her knees up to her chin, she watched the steady rise and fall of his chest. Satisfied his sleep was the result of too much drink and too little sleep, she rose to tend the fire. The nights still held a chill, and she did not want him to be cold.

The fire blazed, heating the room. Dusting off her hands, she frowned at Reave's ungainly position in the chair. The uncomfortable posture would have him hunched over in the morning. Locking her arms around his legs, she dragged the unyielding dead weight from the arm of the chair to the front. Tessa stood. She took the time to adjust her lace cap while she assessed her efforts. Noticing a small stool under one of the numerous tables, she slid it across the floor to Reave's chair, then proceeded to prop his legs on it.

Next, she went about removing his boots. He moaned and

turned so his head rested on the bony wooden arm of the chair. Taking pity on him, she stuffed his discarded coat under his head.

Convinced she had done all she could, she swept the hair off his sweating brow and kissed him lightly on the mouth. "Despite everything, know this. I love you," she said softly, then left.

At the click off the latch, Reave's eyes snapped open. Too drunk to move but not enough to sleep, he stared blankly at the ornate legs of his desk, considering her parting words. Tomorrow, when his head was clear, he would decide what must be done.

The chance to speak to Reave never came with the early arrival of his houseguests. Tessa peered through the lace curtains in mute horror as she watched the Duke of Densmore help his pregnant wife down from the coach. They had not traveled alone. A gentleman she assumed was Reave's business partner, and a woman, his wife perhaps, descended from a second coach. She became more daring with her vigilance when the husky timber of Reave's voice welcomed his guests.

As if sensing her presence, Reave glanced up to her window. Tessa retreated into the shadows. He would be angry at her for not joining him in the courtyard, but the choice between insult or recognition was an easy one to make.

She pulled out from under her bed a small black bag. It held her locket, a shawl, and a few coins she had managed to collect. She had considered searching Reave's chambers for additional coin to compensate for the money he had held back, except she did not want him to think her a thief as well.

Stuffing the bag back under the bed, she cursed Reave's guests' premature arrival. Their presence complicated her escape. Instead of departing by the light of day, she would now have to wait until everyone retired. It was risky to travel alone.

Nevertheless, desperation had a way of making even the least courageous bold.

Tessa groaned. She had avoided their arrival. What was to be done this evening? Reave would expect her to join them for supper. He had made a point of avoiding her all these weeks, and today, when she counted most on his absence, the man was going to demand her attention.

A knock at the door quieted the hysterics she was fighting. She jumped up and grasped the bedpost for support. "A moment, please!" A slightly higher version of her voice rang out at the more persistent knocking. She opened the door and was surprised to see Thorne. She had anticipated her transgression of etiquette would hail the beast of Eastcott himself!

"Forgive me, Miss Belanger. His lordship is rather concerned about you. He has requested you join him in the drawing room," the butler explained in his diplomatic fashion.

Tessa was not fooled by the invitation. "I suppose he is quite irritated with me and most likely demanded my presence or your head."

"You give a fair account of the situation, miss." He had trouble keeping his bland, bored expression. "May I suggest you hasten to his lordship's side?"

"No, you may not," she replied curtly, stubbornness setting her chin a notch higher. She laughed outright at Thorne's shocked expression. "Tell his lordship that I am indisposed."

"I would rather not." The butler mournfully shook his head. "Lord Wycke has been in a sour disposition of late, and I doubt your stubbornness will cheer him."

"You tell me nothing I am not aware of. But do not fear, Thorne, his lordship is a fair man and will place the blame on the rightful head. Might I suggest we give him a note, so you may depart immediately upon its delivery?" She had already started for her small writing desk.

"A practical solution to both of our problems, Miss Belanger." The bored expression was back in place. "May I recommend a place or two to hide until his lordship has cooled his temper?'' She laughed again, and began penning her note.

The long-case clock in the great hall had struck three when Tessa began her silent walk down the stairs. Motivated by her growling stomach, she headed for the kitchen in hopes of securing a quick meal and a few provisions for her escape. She would have rather skipped rummaging through the pantry, but her funds were low and she did not know when she would next be able to acquire a decent meal.

The warm, mellow aromas of roasted meat still lingered in the now-silent vacant kitchen. She lifted a cover off a basket and was rewarded with hard rolls. Eagerly, she helped herself to one, biting through the thick crust to the soft center. It was heaven! She had not eaten since the morning meal, and then she had taken a small tray in her room as she plotted her flight. She stuffed the remaining rolls in her reticule.

Her plan was to head for the village. There was bound to be someone who was heading out, and she would be less obvious, mixed in the village activity, than if she tried to walk one of the country roads. She choked, the dry, thick roll stuck in her throat. Frantically, Tessa glanced around for something to wash it down with.

''It might go down easier if you put some butter or preserves on it before you swallow it whole.''

His voice echoed all about her. She blinked back the tears in her eyes as she swallowed the swelling bread. ''If you were a gentleman,'' she coughed, ''you would offer me some wine or water before I choke to death!'' Flustered, she wondered how long he had been watching her.

A bottle was suddenly placed in her hands, and Tessa quickly swallowed the mysterious liquid. She choked and spit out the remainder in her mouth. Her insides burned and knotted. ''Thunderous hell! You could have warned me you were handing me this vile brew.''

Reave chuckled again from the shadows. "You insult my finest brandy, my lady. I thought you asked for something to drink."

"You are the devil to torment me so. If you had not warned the staff with certain death or dismissal if they brought me a tray, I would not be down here in the middle of the night, foraging for a piece of stale bread." She crossed her arms, satisfied her reasons for being caught down in the kitchen were justified. Thank goodness she had the foresight to drop her bag out the bedroom window instead of bringing it along. It certainly would have been difficult to explain that away!

"If you had come down when I called for you instead of hiding like a coddled, sulking babe, you would have had more than enough to fill your belly."

Tessa turned to face the scratching sound behind her. She was most interested to see Reave's face, since his bland tone revealed nothing. Light filled the room, cast off by a small candle in his hand. Cupping the candle to protect the fragile flame, he joined her at the roughened and scarred worktable.

His expression was as enigmatic as the contents of the room hidden in the shadows. Irritated and feeling ungracious, she said, "You accuse me of sulking when you have been nothing but a moody brute since we set a wedding date. I tried numerous times to get you to tell me the reason for your coldness, yet all you did was avoid me and drink more than the village drunk." She took another bite of her roll. Swallowing, she continued. "So you are angry I did not present myself to your rich, noble friends. Well, I did not invite them, so you can amuse them by yourself." She would have marched off, except his iron grip prevented her from taking another step.

"Oh, no. We are not finished with this discussion. First, Miss Belanger, I do not need your permission to invite my friends to my estate. I think most of my friends would consider it odd that I would marry without the briefest of introductions to my bride."

"Do you think it matters to me whether or not I meet the

snobbish, overbearing lot?'' She was exaggerating a bit, but she was too defensive not to attack. ''And on that concern, do you think I want to marry an arrogant chap such as yourself? Pay me what you owe me, and I shall immediately depart with your blessing!''

His grip tightened on her arms. He shook her, then out of character to the anger he was repressing, he gathered her up into his arms and gave her an unyielding hug. ''Why, you little witch—you call me arrogant? I should have you beaten for the grief I have endured on your behalf!'' He set her aside and picked up the bottle she had abandoned on the table. He took a deep, gratifying swallow and considered her request. ''Tomorrow I expect to see you in the morning room with the others, dressed appropriately, or I shall give you reason to truly fear me.''

Tessa thought his threat of a beating was absurd. What sobered her was the notion that he did wield a power. Although unknown to him, she feared it more than anything she could conjure in her blackest nightmares. ''I will not do it,'' she said quietly, awaiting his bellow of rage.

He surprised her by replying in a reasonable tone. ''Why? What do you fear? I swear these people are kind, and except for Hayden's wife, I would say all do not emulate the ways of the ton.''

''Please do not ask this of me,'' she begged. ''I am not well. I thought my note explained it all.''

''Like hell it did. You have told me nothing from the moment we met. I demand the truth. What do you fear? Tell me.''

Feeling trapped, she glanced from side to side looking for a way to escape. He blocked her body with his own, insisting on an acceptable answer to her odd behavior. She had to tell him something. Anything. Never the truth. It would destroy what remained after the ravaging lies.

''I—I am with child.''

A look of shock washed over the anger coloring his face. His eyes narrowed speculatively to her flat stomach. ''At least

I suspect I am,'' she amended. This was a lie that time would soon expose. There was the slightest possibility she could be speaking the truth, but she was not late. Nor was she experiencing any symptoms to hint toward the delicate condition. "I— I think this is why I have been feeling so ill of late,'' she prattled, her anxiety increasing each minute Reave was silent. "And why I have been so upset. At first, I thought it was the preparations for the wedding. Later, I thought it might be more.'' She closed her eyes, daring not breathe until she heard him speak.

"Is this why you—never mind. A child.''

She had never seem him so shaken. So incoherent. Taking a few distinct breaths to collect his thoughts, Reave said with his usual lucidity, "Tessa, nothing would please me more than to see you carry my child. I swear, I will never let anything happen to you. I will protect you,'' he vowed.

Reave hugged her with such a fierceness, it stole her breath. She suspected the gesture was to conceal the misty sheen in his gaze, but it did not prevent her from reveling in his embrace. He was thinking of the dead wife he failed. She was heartless to use his weakness to distract him.

Tessa closed her eyes, wishing her lie would come true so he would never discover what a cruel, desperate woman she had become. She buried her face into his neck, savoring his scent. Reave held her tightly, seeking comfort as much as giving it. A shudder escaped her body. Reave was not hers to love. She muffled her denial by pressing deeper into his warmth, a feeble effort at banishing the black coldness of her fate.

Chapter Twenty-five

Thunder rumbled overhead, rattling the glass panes of the windows in Tessa's bedroom. The storm echoed the restless undercurrent of emotions that randomly struck her like lightning arcing through the dark clouds.

She endured Sims's dressing-down with the practiced ease of the skilled liar she had become when the older woman had visited her room that morning. Tessa expressed remorse for provoking Reave and embarrassing him in front of his guests. She then begged to be excused. From Sims's disapproving cluck of her tongue, Tessa knew her friend did not approve of this latest game. Still, the older woman held her tongue and departed to join the guests in the morning room.

Tessa had not lied when she had told Sims she felt ill. Guiltily, she recalled the night she had spent in Reave's protective embrace. After her confession, Reave had reached out for her. He had touched her like a man driven by fierce hunger, yet he was tender, considerate of the life she had sworn was within her womb.

The memory made her tremble, and she tipped the hot tea

from the cup she held, burning her hand. ''Oh,'' she gasped, snatching a napkin to blot the expanding wetness. If only the mess she made of her life were as simple to resolve.

The thunder sounded overhead, reminding her of the approaching storm. Holding her injured hand, she walked to the window to see if the rains had begun. A muddy road would be more difficult to traverse, especially if it rained throughout the day as the dark clouds promised. Glancing down at the hedges below, she suddenly remembered.

Gracious, her bag!

She had been too preoccupied with Reave the previous evening to retrieve it from the bushes. Assuming everyone was in the morning room, eating, perhaps she could slip unnoticed outside. Opening the door, Tessa ran straight into Thorne's thin frame and grunted.

''My pardon, Miss Belanger,'' the older man said in a labored breath.

Her unexpected appearance in the doorway had visibly shaken him. Tessa was about to offer him a glass of water, when the object in Thorne's right hand caught her attention.

Noticing her eyes had widened at the sight of the satchel he held, Thorne raised it higher to explain, ''His lordship felt you might prefer this in your room. He said that you had become forgetful and had left it in an odd place.''

Tessa accepted the outstretched bag with unsteady hands. Reave knew. He knew what she was about last night and had laid in wait to catch her in the act. ''Thank you, Thorne,'' she barely choked out, for the fury in her almost strangled her. His pledges of love and trust—ha! It was all a game of manipulation. It hurt all the more because she had believed his lies.

''Shall I tell his lordship you will be joining him shortly?''

Had she actually been feeling guilty for the lies she had uttered to Reave? His mastery of the game left Tessa speechless. Well, almost. ''You may thank his lordship on my behalf and tell him that I will meet him in hell!'' She slammed the door on the stunned, openmouthed butler.

*   *   *

The morning room was rather sedate for such a joyous occasion. Except for Lady Brackett's occasional attempt to draw someone into conversation, everyone ate in silence. After a while, even she declared the atmosphere hopeless and quietly finished her meal.

Reave sat at the head of the table. Sipping his coffee, his gaze never strayed from the doorway while he waited for Tessa to join them. After last night, he had thought he had settled matters. She had been so yielding and passionate in his arms. Perhaps he was acting the arrogant fool she had called him to believe he had swayed her with seduction.

Thorne's sudden appearance was a welcomed distraction. Reave signaled him closer, hoping he had word from Tessa. Ignoring everyone's blatantly curious expressions, Thorne bent down to whisper in Reave's ear.

Reave listened patiently to Thorne as the man explained the strange encounter that had just transpired with Miss Belanger. When Thorne finished, Reave laughed, although there was little humor in his expression. "I wager she was, Thorne. That will be all."

After dismissing the butler, Reave glanced at his guests. Everyone had ceased eating and awaited some explanation to the cryptic outburst. Reave was not feeling particularly accommodating this morning. Lady Brackett cleared her throat, plainly losing her inner battle to question him. He frowned at her until her lips thinned, sealing her obvious question. *Where was Tessa?*

Hayden, his business partner, was more forthright. He wiped his mouth, then casually tossed the soiled linen on the table. "Well, Wycke, when will your lady make an appearance? If she does not appear soon, I shall believe this is a costly ruse."

"She has been unwell of late," Reave replied. His gaze locked with the Duke of Densmore's. He saw understanding in his friend's eyes. "The strain of the wedding."

"Or she's breeding," Hayden countered. "Shame on you, Wycke, for not keeping your hands off her until the nuptials. The gossips can certainly count to nine," he baited, but no one joined in on his amusement.

Lis deigned to ignore Hayden's remark and instead asked, "I thought Kim was to join us?"

Reave shot her a grateful look. "He was. Yesterday, I received a note expressing his regrets. His reasons are his own. Kim, however, has met Tessa on several occasions. In fact, he brought her to Eastcott."

Everyone demanded at once to hear the details, so Reave began to explain the circumstances that brought Tessa to Eastcott. He kept the tale to the barest facts, for he was not in the mood to explain why he knew so little about his bride, or, rather, what he knew. Hayden, forever the solicitor, questioned him further about his mysterious betrothed until Reave grew tired of being interrogated and excused himself from the room.

"Stay out of it, Lis," Bryson ordered his scheming wife who sat innocently on their bed, rubbing her growing abdomen. "If Wycke wanted your help, he would have sent for you."

Lis's eyes gleamed mischievously. "Oh, but he did, my sweet, when he summoned us to meet her. Something tells me there were problems before we arrived and—"

"And, naturally, you feel duty bound to help them," he finished for her.

"We owe him for my life, Bryson. If it had not been for Reave, I might have hung as a traitor," she argued. "I think he would not mind if I meddled a bit."

He looked at his wife's pleading face and sighed. It was difficult to deny her anything when she used that look on him. "Fine. Meddle if you must. However, be forewarned. If Reave asks me to beat you, I shall oblige him," he said sternly as his arms eased around her swollen belly. Both knew he would never lay a hand on her.

* * *

Tessa reread the note once more before entering the dimly lit conservatory. The message stated that she was to be there at precisely midnight and was signed with an elaborate *W* at the bottom. She wondered why Reave insisted they meet there rather than in her chambers, but with guests in the house, he might have wanted to avoid further speculation. Or the temptation of having a bed close at hand.

She made a face as she settled on one of the stone benches. Crumbling the note, she stuffed it into her sleeve. She did not feel up to another fight, nor the questions he was bound to ask. Finding her bag outside her window was too damning for Reave to dismiss lightly.

Tessa jumped up at the sound of someone entering the conservatory. Assuming all had retired hours before, she softly called out, "Reave, I am here." He did not reply. The sound of footsteps grew closer. She heard a potted plant fall from a shelf and break on the stone floor.

"Reave?" Her voice was so soft, he would have had to have been next to her to hear it. She sank back on to the bench, wondering if she had made a mistake coming. The leaves rustled nearby, and someone stepped from the shadows. Tessa peeked out from her hiding place, then stifled a scream when she saw a face that looked as shocked as her own.

"Great ghosts! Saffron, is that you?" Lis grabbed a wooden shelf to steady herself.

A wealth of buried memories engulfed Tessa at the mention of her name. Most had called her Countess, but there were a close few who understood her dislike of the name and resorted to calling her by variations of her second name. When the duchess spoke her name this time, the fear was evident. Not too surprising, since everyone believed she was rotting in some cold grave. She stepped from the shadows. "Lis, stop looking at me as if I am a ghost. You know very well that if I were a spirit, I would be scaring Lady Foxglove until her bounty of black hair was bleached stark white.''

Some of the tension eased in Lis's stance. Hesitantly, she returned Tessa's smile, both enjoying the image of Lady Foxglove being tormented by a vengeful spirit. The woman in question was one of the cruelest women of the ton Tessa had encountered. The woman had never uttered a kind word, and she had specifically found pleasure attacking Tessa. Edmund had ignored the lady's insults. And if the gossip was true, he had even encouraged the vile she-cat.

Lis took a faltering step forward and embraced Tessa. "I never believed you had killed them. Yet, I would have been at your side if you had.''

Tessa's tears glittered like fractured diamonds in the soft light at the unexpected offer. It had been too long since someone had believed in her innocence. "I might have left him, Lis, but someone hated him more than I to butcher him and my mother.'' Tessa returned her friend's embrace, then retreated a step. "You must go. Reave is coming and if he figures out you and I—''

The duchess shook her head. "He will not be coming tonight, at least not here. I sent the note.''

"You?''

"Do you mind if I sit down?'' Grabbing her lower back, Lis sat. "No one warned me about this damnable back pain.'' Tessa moved to the side and offered her the bench behind them. "Much better. Well, now, where do I begin? I suspect my presence is simpler to explain than yours. This evening I was attempting to repay a debt to Lord Wycke.'' Briefly, her eyes became unfocused, recalling the past. She shook her head to clear her dark thoughts and concentrated on the present. "It was obvious to all that Lord Wycke and his lady were having difficulties, especially when she refused to put in an appearance. So I thought I owed him enough to meddle in his affairs.'' She looked calculatingly at Tessa's waistline. "Are you truly breeding, or is it a ruse to get him to leave you alone?''

Her grace was nothing but direct when it came to important

matters. Tessa watched her caress her swollen stomach, making small circles on each side. She instinctively placed a hand on her flat one, wishing she could have carried Reave's child. "I spoke not from certainty. Lis, I was desperate. I would have said anything to prevent him from dragging me downstairs."

"The fear of one of us recognizing you must have been dreadful," she said, her voice laced with sympathy.

Tessa looked upward through the dusty panes of the glass ceiling at the sky. The fear of discovery and the loss of the people she loved had taken its toll. She felt trapped in the deceit, and it sickened her. "I never meant for any of this to happen, nor was anyone to get hurt." She met Lis's expectant gaze, knowing she wanted to hear every detail.

Taking a deep breath, she began her tale. She told Lis about the poison, her threat to divorce Edmund, which he never believed, then of her flight to avoid his wrath. The duchess listened intently to Tessa's first impressions of Reave when he had rescued her from the footpads and how the news of the murders had eventually led her to Eastcott. She spoke of the deal she struck with him to care for Jason, and of his generosity. It was awkward to speak of the love that grew between them, and more painful were the lies that were pulling them apart. When she had finished, she was crying again, something she could not seem to stop. Lis held her hands and gave them a reassuring squeeze.

"It sounds like he loves you, Saffron—I mean Tessa. Perhaps if you explained—"

"No!" Tessa released Lis's hands when she noticed she was gripping them too tightly. "He asked me too many times to trust him. All I did was feed him more lies. No, he is a prideful man, the truth would make him hate me."

"Saffron, he is a powerful man, he could—"

"Have me sentenced to the gallows," she finished bleakly. "Lis, I have heard him speak of the case. It was decided long ago that I was guilty, and my denial would not change his judgment. Then, there is Jason. What will he think of me when he learns the truth. I will be just another woman who promised him love and failed him." Thinking of Jason renewed her anguish. All her senses were heightened by emotion. She felt pain as keenly as if she had fallen upon the point of a sword. The hair on the back of her neck prickled. Tessa cocked her head to one side and listened. "Did you hear something?" Rising, she searched the room.

"No." Lis also stood and inspected their surroundings before returning to the bench. "It was a rat or just nerves, and justifiably so. What can I do to help?"

"Swear you will tell no one of our encounter. Lady Lathom must remain dead." Tessa was asking much from her friend. There was no doubt to the duchess's loyalty. It was the ton's censure Tessa feared if Lis was associated with a murderess. If the duchess was exposed, Tessa prayed Reave would protect her as he had in the past.

Lis rubbed her stomach. Shifting her position, she said, "I have survived a few scandals during my life, and another could not add much more tarnish. After all, I am a duchess!" There was enough haughtiness in her tone to make them both laugh. A machinating gleam warmed her expression. "Tessa, I think the way to keep your secret is to let me tell the others I have met you."

"No."

Lis ignored her. "I will describe how charming I found you, but, alas, so terribly ill. I will suggest we end our visit so you may rest." Lis paused with her finger on her lips. "I am a little confused about how you plan to marry Reave without accidentally being discovered. Eventually, he will insist you come to town. However will you keep your secret then?"

Determined, Tessa held her chin high. " 'Tis quite simple, really. I will not marry him."

"Saf—Tessa, Lord Wycke loves you. If you leave him at the altar, it would devastate him. And this lie about a child. You are aware of how he lost his first wife?"

Tessa nodded her head while misery shredded her heart. "I

think you would agree, the humiliation of one of England's finest barristers wedded and bedded to a murderess would be a crueler fate. He may never forgive me for leaving, but as the pain lessens, he will come to understand that I truly did love him."

Lis nodded, frustrated she was unable to help. "What if you complete your new identity? You have chosen another name; now all you have to do is alter your physical appearance. Have you ever considered becoming a brunette?"

Tessa shook her head. "I thought about the woman lying in my grave, wondering if her death would give me another chance at life. No, changing my appearance would cause Reave to ask more questions than I am prepared to answer. Besides, I have learned no matter how well a consummate liar you become, the truth will surface eventually, for there will always be at least one person who knows your secret. Yourself."

Creeping through the silent passageway, Tessa feared any noise she made might stir the curious to inspect. She paused at Jason's room, wishing she could look in on him and give him a kiss. Too risky. With a heart full of regret, she headed for her own chambers. She reached for the latch, but the metal was jerked from her grasp. Reave. The familiar scent of him assailed her senses, and she wanted to fall into his arms and forget. It was the murderous intent in his eyes that forestalled her. She took a step backward to distance herself from his wrath. He firmly grabbed her by the wrist and unceremoniously hauled her into the room.

"Did you forget your bag this time?" he sneered, and with a flick of his wrist she fell on the bed.

Tessa scrambled to her feet. "I was not leaving. As if I could, sir. I noticed you have posted a few men to watch the grounds. I am so glad we have *trust* between us!"

"Do not even start me on that subject," he warned. "Where have you been?"

Relieved at the change of topic, she did not hesitate to tell him the truth. "Actually, I was in the conservatory, meeting you. No"—she cut him off before he called her a liar—"I did not discover until later that it was her grace who sent the curt message. By the bye, you have a loyal friend in her. She vows you have no flaws. Not to worry, I set her straight."

Reave visibly relaxed his stance. Encouraged, despite his frown, she gave him the version of the encounter she and Lis had agreed to relate. He looked confused when she had finished but did not press her for further details.

"I suppose I could have Bryson beat her for meddling in our lives." He pretended to consider the proposition thoughtfully.

"Why would you want to torment the woman? She actually did what she set out to do," Tessa defended.

"And pray, what was that?"

"To show us there are few problems worth fighting over. She reminded me, I must have admired one or two of your fine qualities to agree to this betrothal." She playfully tugged at one of the buttons on his shirt. That burning intensity was back in his irresistible blue eyes. This time it was not fueled by anger. The emotion she saw there made her move closer.

Reave's gaze dropped to her stomach. Gruffly, he asked, "How do you feel?"

Tessa did not have to be asked twice. She showed him exactly how well she felt by grabbing his shirt and pulling him onto her bed.

When sleep had claimed her, Reave slid from the bed and quietly began to dress. Slowly, he opened the door. He gritted his teeth when the hinges creaked, but Tessa remained undisturbed in sated bliss. He slipped through the opening barely wide enough for his body and did not breathe until the door was shut. The candles had burned out in the passage hours earlier; even so, he did not need them to find his way back to his chamber.

He had intended to remain the night with Tessa. After hours of turning about on the bed, plagued by unanswered questions and doubts, he decided to seek his own chambers. It was difficult to think impartially and logically with her so close to his touch.

What bothered him most this eve was her encounter with Lis. Unfortunately, Bryson would not appreciate a knock at their door at this late hour, so he had to accept what Tessa had confessed as truth. He wanted so desperately to believe the two women had never met before that night.

Still, Lis had acknowledged knowing Lady Lathom. Would she risk her reputation and family to protect Tessa? He ran his fingertips along the wall, counting the doors. He quickened his pace. Sorting through the lies was driving him mad. Women and their bloody secrets!

He clicked open his door and strode into his room. A fire welcomed him, a telling sign Thorne had checked on him before retiring. He was grateful for the warmth and light. Without breaking stride, he began unfastening the few buttons he had bothered to connect and removed his shirt. Sinking onto the end of his bed, he pulled off his boots.

"By my faith, if I had known what a magnificent specimen of hard male flesh you are, I would have at least waited until you had removed your breeches before I announced myself."

A sleepy, familiar feminine voice came from a chair near the fire. Claire. She peered over the edge as if it were a game. It was partly true. She enjoyed playing the game of cat and mouse, but Reave was not in the mood to tangle with her claws.

"I suggest you return to your room before your husband awakens. My apologies if I do not feel obliged to act as your escort." He shrugged into his shirt again, fastening all the pearl buttons so no one could misconstrue his intentions. He tucked the ends into his breeches, then turned away to fasten the buttons at his waist.

Claire pouted. It was a predicable device she used often. Awkwardly, she climbed out of the oversized chair and swayed toward him. "Pooh! I never thought you the shy sort."

Reave knocked her hand away when she tried to touch his cheek. Everything about her disgusted him. "I see you found my private stock."

She gave him a seductive smile, then strutted in front of the fire. Her filmy night rail was almost sheer in the firelight, and she knew it. Reave doubted there were many men who had refused what she offered when she whetted their appetites with a teasing glimpse of promised pleasures.

"It was not kind of you to make me wait so long," Claire purred. "I became bored and needed a little comfort. Now, I possess enough fire to make our night rewarding." She opened her arms, willing him to take her. Reave walked past, not bothering to acknowledge her offer.

"I have never doubted your boldness, Claire, but choose another man to ply your charms. There is nothing you can offer to hold my interest," he coldly stated. There was no denying she could be quite alluring; he knew many who had succumbed to her charms. Her debauchery repulsed him.

His thoughts flickered to a dimly lit room where slept the only woman who stirred his lust. When he had left her, she had curled herself into a tight ball. Even with her cheeks pinkened and puffy, he thought her the most beguiling. He cast a side glance at Claire. She, too, was a little flushed.

"You cold, impotent, self-righteous bastard!" she spat out when she could bring the words forth. Fury had contorted her beauty into an ugly mask. "How dare you turn away from me? No wonder your betrothed refuses to stand at your side. You are a piece of male mockery!" She curled her hands until they resembled claws, then lunged for his face.

Reave latched on to both her wrists and leaned out of reach every time one of her sharp talons drew too close. With one move he flipped her around so she was facing away from him and her hands were behind her back. She keened in powerless defeat. "When I want a whore," he growled, "I know where to find one. However, if I were you, I would not wait for my card. I have chosen a bride whose passions equal my own," he whispered cruelly in her ear. Claire thrashed about in outrage, but he held her firmly. "I recommend you focus your, ah, energies on your husband in the future. Have I made myself clear?" He rushed her to the door.

"Do not underestimate me, Wycke," she raged while she twisted from his grasp.

Reave held her with his left hand while he opened the door with the other. "Madam, do not mistake my gentle handling of this situation for ineptitude. Cross me in this manner again, and I shall show you how ironfisted I can become. I am certain there are others who can attest to your obsessive appetites, and I shall have you committed. I daresay your devoted husband would not object if he learned of your nocturnal habits."

He shoved her out the door and slammed it after her. Claire did not leave until she told him once more what she thought of his questionable manhood. Driving the bolt into the frame, he listened until he could not hear her distant footfalls. "Rabid bitch," he muttered, noticing she had cut into the fleshy part of his palms. Thin red seams of blood filled the broken skin. Bringing the stinging wounds to his mouth, he sucked his hand, wondering if he had finally ended the game. Lord, he hoped so!

He considered telling Hayden. Such an attempt could backlash, and he could find himself at the other end of a dueling field. No, it was best to let the matter die. Claire was a clever woman. She knew when to accept defeat. It was a deadly game she played. He began to unbutton his shirt again, then thought better of it. Instead, he reached for his boots. It was too late to think about dead issues. Reave wanted nothing more than to return to Tessa's bed. After what had just occurred, it was for the best he was discovered in bed with the correct lady.

Chapter Twenty-six

"Lord Wycke, you are kind to forgive our rude departure."
Lis placed her gloved hand in Reave's palm, allowing him to
assist her into their chaise.

"No more than you were to forgive the elusiveness of my
betrothed. I understand you sought out the introduction I was
unable to deliver."

Densmore laughed, joining them. "I warned Lis her charade
would be revealed to you. You have an uncanny knack for
unearthing all our secrets."

Reave gave his friend a faint smile, although his gaze
remained on Lis. "My abilities are culled more from practice
than from aptitude. Not to mention, I dislike losing." He saw
nothing except sympathy in the duchess's gaze. If she was
keeping something from him, she hid it well. "Did my lady
receive you favorably?"

"Indeed, sir. She accepted my deception with more gracious-
ness than I deserved. I wish you both happiness." She brought
her handkerchief up to her nose and sniffed.

Densmore returned Reave's hearty handshake with an

equally forceful whack on the opposite shoulder. "An unusual house party, my friend, and the shortest on record." Lowering his voice, he added, " 'Tis the babe who distresses her, not you. When can we expect you and your bride to call on us in London?"

Reave glanced up at the windows to Tessa's chamber. There was a flicker of movement in the one on the right. Dismissing its source, he said, "I have discovered I am a most selfish man, and plan to keep my bride tucked away for my personal amusements."

"Say no more, Wycke," the duke laughed, his attention turning to his wife. "I, too, am most selfish." He climbed into the chaise beside his wife. "Farewell. Farewell, Lady Brackett!" He signaled the coachman their departure.

Lady Brackett clutched her heart as she tried to catch her breath. Her cap was lopsided, revealing her haste to join them. " 'Tis no bread and butter of mine, but never have I seen guests behave in such manner. Scarcely here a day, then off without apologies. And at an indecent hour for all! Densmore should know better."

"One would think," Reave mused, watching the chaise until it was beyond his vision.

Lady Brackett gave the departing chaise a final curt, dismissing nod. "Well, there are the Quinns at least."

"I regret Mr. and Mrs. Quinn brushed and loped before dawn, or so I was told."

"Simply shameless," her ladyship muttered. "Never have I met someone quite above oneself as that Mrs. Quinn. She scarcely uttered one kind word to anyone. And poor Mr. Quinn, a fine example of a man living under the cat's paw. Tessa was quite correct to take herself off to bed."

Reave's smile held a twist of irony when his gaze shifted back to Tessa's windows. "Saved her from excessive suffering, eh?"

"Someone of Tessa's virtuous nature cannot comprehend the evil in others. She is a veritable angel whose wings Mrs.

Quinn would have enjoyed plucking.'' Lady Brackett hesitated when she saw Reave's expression. "It is rude of me to speak of your friends in this manner. Forgive this old woman's impudence.''

"I cannot hold you accountable for speaking the truth," Reave lied, wishing he were as convinced of Tessa's innocence as Lady Brackett.

"Tessa. Open up, we need to talk," Reave commanded when she asked who was there.

She cracked the door and smiled at the sight of him. He had just returned from his morning ride. "Your valet will weep at the sight of those muddy boots, Reave. Not to mention Thorne when he follows your muddy footprints to my door." Opening the door wider, she reached up and wiped away the beaded line of sweat above his upper lip. He stepped into her room when she danced a few steps away. Giving him her back, she said playfully, "I was about to call Sims's maid. Would I unman you by asking you instead?''

Tucking his riding gloves into the waist of his breeches, he said, "I thought it was my job to do the unfastening."

"Most of the time I would agree. However, I am feeling well today and wish to enjoy some air."

He quirked a contemplative brow at her extraordinary ebullience, something he had missed since pressing her to set a wedding date. "Am I to guess from your cheery disposition that you know what news I bring? Ah, of course.'' He slapped at the grime on his breeches. "You must know. Otherwise, why would you be willing to remove yourself from your chamber?'' She lowered her gaze to the floor, although not before he saw what his mocking tone had diminished. He had pinched the twinkle from her eye as readily as snuffing a candlewick. He was a damn fool.

"I heard the horses. It was not difficult to conclude everyone was departing," she said in a small voice.

"It was considered best."

"Are you disappointed they are gone?" Anxious blue eyes met his own.

"Not entirely. If I had known I would have lost you as a result of their presence, I would have never sent the invitations." It was a small lie. It barely measured up against Tessa's omissions. He cupped her waist, drawing her close, then placed a loving kiss on the tip of her nose.

"Illness kept me from your side. Truly," she added, sensing his doubt.

"Ah, yes. Our babe. How foolish for me to forget. Shall I send for someone to confirm your suspicions?" he politely offered.

"N-no, I would rather wait a while longer. It would be embarrassing for me to be examined while not bearing your name. There will be little the gossips can do but count on their fingers and snicker after we are wed."

Even though her concerns were understandable, her face gave her away. There were other unspoken worries she kept to herself. How he wished she would trust him, or at least pretended to convincingly!

His irritation flashed briefly on his face before he buried it behind a mask of a composed demeanor. "Quite so, my love. Now that I have you fastened properly, I am off to attend to my work. I am certain there are preparations you must oversee yourself."

"Well, yes." She watched him warily as he headed for the door.

He paused in the doorway, finally recalling the reason that brought him there. "I almost forgot to tell you—I have found a suitable tutor for Jason. He shall be arriving within the week."

"Indeed? You are certain he is right for the position?"

"I had the man checked thoroughly, and he exceeds all my expectations. You look almost disappointed."

"I have enjoyed my time with Jason. I know in my heart he will learn more under another's guided hand."

She looked as if he had told her she had to give up her child. Understanding her feelings, Reave returned to her side and gave her a comforting squeeze. "You are not losing Jason. Soon you will be his mother, a position that wields more power than any tutor, I assure you." She gave him a brave, trembling smile. He kissed her tenderly before closing the door.

Blurry-eyed, Tessa reached for a handkerchief. Blowing her nose, she sadly thought of the plan that would take her away from the people she loved most. There was nothing to do but act.

Odd, it had been rather easy to leave the house unnoticed. The sullen thought did little to ease her fear as she carried her bag down the muddied road. The staff had been bustling about, preparing the house for their new mistress, and had paid little attention to her when she walked out the front door. One of the footmen, someone she had not met, politely held the door for her.

It took only an hour of walking the lone road to the village to decide she might have been a little hasty leaving the house on foot. The spring rains had flooded the road in sections. It smelled of earth and dung, and each foot sank into the horrid mire. Several steps later, she realized she had lost one of her shoes. Limping back, she searched frantically for her missing shoe. How could she travel without proper protection for her feet?

On the third hour of her escape, Tessa caught sight of a small wagon turning onto the main road that headed for the village. Tired and wet, she did not contemplate how she looked as she limped toward the distant wagon, waving her arms and shouting for him to halt.

Fifteen minutes later, she was perched next to her kind savior. A horsehair blanket was thrown over her skirts and provided a little warmth. She was grateful there was no need to walk the entire distance, although she doubted she would have been given ample opportunity. With every step she had to resist the urge to glance back, fearful she would see Reave charging forward, dark and resentful at her fearful flight. What could she have said? Nothing.

By dusk, she was on a stage-wagon headed for London. Although the fare was cheap, the conveyance was not very comfortable. The slow-moving wagon was better suited to carrying luggage and merchandise than passengers. A heavy canvas stretched overhead was all that protected her and the three other passengers from the cold. The movement of the wagon swung a small lantern, their sole light source, to and fro.

Their destination was London. Tessa was not foolish enough to return to town. Instead, she hoped to depart at one of the posts in hopes of finding another means to take her closer to her father's estate.

Her brows drew together and a frown creased her forehead. She wondered how she would be received by her father. She held no great love in her breast for her sire, especially after she discovered the type of man he had wedded her to without thought. However, she knew him to be superficial, and the disgrace of the family name could not be easily ignored.

"Was that a pistol?" asked the woman beside her.

Her frightened outburst stirred everyone from their various states of dozing. Two more shots rang out overhead, and the wagon, which was already hindered by the mud, began to slow.

" 'Tis thieves to cut our purses and our throats!" the woman cried out.

"Should they not try to outrun them?" a nervous, foppish gentleman asked.

"A crate this size, an' the road would surely be the cause of many's demise at a great speed. It is best to empty our pockets, an' be on our way," another man said with some authority.

Tessa's eyes widened at the sound of angry voices. There were no more shots, but the nervous horses jerked the wagon forward and the movements jostled the occupants inside. Sud-

denly, the canvas flap was lifted, allowing a burst of early
evening air to freeze all motion. A darkly garbed head poked
through, and she recognized the ruddy face of their wagoner.
He scanned the dim interior as if searching for someone.

"He be callin' the womenfolk out. You two, heed yer step."
Then he was gone.

Tessa bit her lower lip as she followed the other frightened
passenger. They crawled over the shifted luggage to get to the
opening. Gritting her teeth when she scraped her bare calf on
a wooden crate, Tessa was forced to remind herself that she
had experienced a robbery and had survived. She had nothing
to offer these rogues. They probably called for the women to
insure the men complied with their demands.

She grasped the edge of the wagon frame, preparing herself
to jump to the ground. Strong, firm hands locked around her
waist and dragged her from the wagon.

"Release me, you filthy—" Tessa twisted in the arms of
her captor, cold and frightened, thinking only of the ways they
planned to harm her. The wagoner coughed and raised the
lantern he was holding higher, illuminating the rogue's features.
The sight of him only heightened her fear.

"If I beat you now, I doubt anyone would deny me the
pleasure." Reave's eyes glittered dangerously. "Unfortunately,
we are losing the light. We will discuss this latest inconvenience
at Eastcott." She winced at his words. Temporarily pulling his
attention from her, he thanked the wagoner and without further
word hauled her onto his horse.

Their journey was made in silence.

Without the burden of a coach, they made amazing progress.
Still, she had expected him to stop at the village to seek shelter
as the last of the sunset slid into the horizon. The question was
on her tongue, but she did not possess the courage to speak.
If she did, he just might feel obliged to answer, and she was
not certain she was prepared for what he had to say. As the
land blurred past, she was tempted to leap from the horse and
run far from his wrath. A foolish fantasy since she knew there

was no place she could hide that he would not discover. Their bond would not be so easy to sever.

Tessa did not know when she had given in to the rhythmic canter of the horse. Startled awake by the sudden halt of the beast, she blinked away the grogginess, realizing they were at Eastcott. Reave swung his leg off the horse, sliding down to firm earth. He raised his arms out to her, expecting her to comply. As she accepted his help, she saw the anger had not left him. The confrontation she had avoided for so long would be addressed. Dreading her fate, she limped slowly behind him, defeated.

Reave frowned, staring at Tessa's back as she hobbled through the door. She acted as if he had beaten her. Not that he was not furious enough to contemplate the task! Tessa had left him. Without a word, she had actually walked out the front door, forgetting she was taking their child with her. A rush of white hot violence washed over him, and he bit the inside of his cheek to prevent himself from grabbing her like the madman he felt he was and shaking her until her teeth rattled.

Tessa rubbed her eyes at the bright interior. With a joyful shout, Jason and Lady Brackett rushed into the hall to greet them.

"Thank heavens you are safe," Lady Brackett exclaimed, hugging Tessa fiercely to her generous bosom. "All of us had such a fright when it was discovered you were gone."

"Enough!" The one harsh word sliced through the happiness of the reunion. He knew everyone was looking strangely at him, but there were matters to discuss with Tessa in private. Jason pulled on his sleeve.

"Will she be taken to the shed like Mr. Luke used to when I was bad?"

Innocent, curious eyes gazed up to his. He also noticed the question caught the attention of both ladies and each held her breath, waiting for his reply. Tempted to lie to prolong Tessa's discomfort, he truthfully replied to his son, "She is too heavy for my knee, so I will have to think of another manner of punishment." Reave smiled, tapping his son on the nose. His amusement vanished when he stared into Tessa's frightened blue eyes. "Tessa, join me to the library. Thorne, see to it that we are not disturbed for any reason."

"My lord, surely you can see the dear woman is shivering and would welcome a warm bath and dry clothing." Lady Brackett stepped in their way, halting him from removing Tessa to his private sanctuary.

Irritated by the obvious protectiveness Tessa had stirred in the woman even while he battled his own feelings to shield her like a undaunted knight, safeguarding his own, Reave pushed past her. "There are more pertinent concerns to address beyond the lady's simple comforts," he barked, angered he felt the need to explain his actions.

"I could send in some hot tea and a tray." Thorne's waning voice trailed off, when his daring rewarded him a flash of his lordship's wrath. The butler swallowed thickly.

They were protecting her. From him! Some of his control slipped as he lashed out, "Have I a house of deaf idiots, or perhaps there is the need to speak plainly. No one is to disturb us. I do not care if the house is ablaze and I am sitting in a room doused in brandy. The person who dares to misunderstand my orders shall deal with my wrath and unemployment. Have I made myself clear?"

The immediate compliance from everyone present soothed his pride. Taking Tessa by the elbow, he guided her into the library, briefly satisfying his primal urges by slamming the door shut, thus allowing the others to know they had angered him by questioning his commands. Releasing Tessa, he walked to the small table where a decanter of brandy sat. He poured himself a liberal portion, then tossed it to the back of his throat. He splashed more into his glass, and another for Tessa, before joining her. She refused the glass he offered. Undaunted, he pressed it into her hand, saying enigmatically, "I predict we shall both need a glass or two before this evening has ended."

He downed the contents of his glass and walked away to pour another.

Tessa set her glass down. She watched him drink his third glass. "Please, my lord."

He studied her above the rim of his glass, noting her agitation. Lord, was she a mess! She presented little resemblance to the lady he knew her to be. Somewhere on their journey she had lost her bonnet, and her hair had unbound into a tangled, muddied snarl. He was not certain how she had managed to smear mud on her cheeks, but it made her appear like a girl of sixteen. Her gloves were missing. Confound it, where was her shoe? He felt guilty he had not noticed until then that she wore only her right shoe. Did she think him such a brute? If he had known, he would have found something to wrap her bare foot. His gaze flickered to her discarded glass. "You should drink your brandy. It will warm your insides."

"Please, Reave." Her lip trembled when she attempted to speak. "Can this not be said without brandy. I have seen the effects of it on some men and—"

"I am not every man, and it takes more than a few drinks to numb my senses. On the contrary, my lady, I need all my wits when dealing with you."

Not knowing how to accept his words, she made a feeble attempt to straighten her hair. It was so tangled by the wind and bound with mud that her nervous fingers could not penetrate it. Giving up, she sat down in the chair farthest from him. Taking a deep breath but avoiding his eye, she wearily began, "You must be wondering why you found me on that wagon."

He walked around to his desk and pulled open a side drawer. "Actually, my thoughts were more in the direction of what took you so long to leave, when it has been your fondest wish from the beginning." He pulled out a wooden box, opened it, and removed the leather pouch from within. "I believe you forgot something in your haste to depart." Reave turned the bag upsidedown and a gold locket fell onto his desk.

"My locket!" Tessa recognized her property before she

reached the other side of the desk. She regarded him with a wary eye, so he gestured her to take it. She snatched it up before he retracted his offer. The golden links coiled around her fingers as she lovingly caressed the engraved surface. "How did you take this without my knowledge." Her eyes returned to her precious locket, and she allowed herself the indulgence to open and peer at the small portrait.

Shock arrested her expression when she gazed at the miniature. Recoiling as if it had bitten her, she dropped the locket. It hit the desk, then slithered to the floor. Tessa's hands covered her mouth, and she took several steps backward, not quite believing what she had held.

"I always wondered about the girl you treasured so close to your breast. I had guessed it was your mother in her youth, but then, we both know the tale was a lie." Reave's frigid tone brought her wide-eyed gaze up to meet his hardened, cynical expression.

Her mouth worked, but no sound came forth. With great effort, she stuttered, "H-how long?"

"I assume the one you just dropped was you, and the other, who? A sister? Could you have possibly spoken some truths?"

"I never wanted to lie. I was afraid."

His wounded angel had fallen.

Reave slammed his glass on his desk. Its contents sloshed from one side to the other like storm-tossed waters. "Afraid? Whom did you fear? Your husband lay in his dark chamber, madam, his heart literally minced in his chest. Or was it your mother whom you feared? She looked as if she drowned in her own blood!" He mercilessly matched each step she took backward to escape. When she did not answer but crumbled to her knees, he pulled her up and shook her. "What did you have to fear here, when all I offered you was my heart, my life, my soul. Damn you for making me love you!"

His curse made her cry harder. Lifting her head, she tried to explain through her tears. "All assumed me guilty."

Her words seared his soul. He did not bother to conceal his

anguish when he released her. She had finally acknowledged her true identity, and despite all the clues, he had not wanted to believe it.

Tessa dried her cheeks with the cuff of her sleeve, obscuring the muddy lines her tears had dredged. Raggedly, she said, "Yes, I am Lady Lathom. Though I curse the day I was wed to that monster. You see, everyone knew of his cruelty. Except me. Not when I might have been able to save myself. In the end, there was little I could do but flee from his sadistic custody."

Her confession settled in his stomach like ground glass. "Did he hurt you? Was that why you . . ." He closed his eyes; he could not speak the words.

"Killed him?" Tessa tossed her head back, a bitter laugh escaping her lips. "Yes, I murdered him. Every night I slayed him in my dreams, each time more painful and disfiguring than the last. His cruelty gave me the right." Sorrow softened her sarcasm. "After knowing me all these months, Lord Wycke, I thought perhaps you might have understood I did not possess the taste for killing."

She let him see how much his doubt hurt her, then shuttered her emotions. "I left my husband after I realized he would never grant me a divorce. I might have been the one found dead if I had dared to remain and face his wrath for standing up to him that night." Her voice held a dreamlike quality as she spoke of her last night with Lathom. "But I was too frightened of him, so I ran away. I thought if I disappeared, then he would let me go." Her gaze suddenly focused.

She faced Reave, wanting him to understand. "I hated Edmund, Lord Wycke," she said, using Reave's title to distance herself from him. " 'Though not enough to murder him. Not my mother."

Never in his life had he wanted to believe in something as much as he wanted to believe in her innocence. He could not ignore the damning evidence against her. "Tessa," he said, not able to bring himself to call her by her true name. "The poison. I have witnesses who will testify it was purchased by your hand."

She took the glass of brandy she had cast aside and eagerly brought it to her lips. Not used to the taste, she choked. Straightening her shoulders, she turned to face him. "I may not be the cleverest of women, but I do know that poison does not leave gaping wounds."

"You could have used it to render him unconscious so that—"

"I beg you, do not speak so!" Her voice rose to the point of screeching. "The thought never occurred to me! Yes, I did purchase a poison. I confess I would have done almost"—she stressed the last word—"almost, anything to free myself from him." She took another swallow of brandy. "I corrupted the decanters in his chambers, placing the poison in all of them for fear he would choose the wrong one. I told you once I was a coward. I spoke the truth. I could not stand before him and watch him swallow the vile brew. The glass was to his lips. so I taunted him. Edmund smashed his glass and all the decanters and he would have destroyed me, too, because I could not do it!" She crossed her arms over her breasts and shuddered. "I wish I had killed him." She watched him, measuring his reaction. "For if I had, I would be worthy of the condemnation I see in your eyes." She took another sip, and this time she was able to swallow it without gagging, though she grimaced as it settled in her stomach.

She looked so proud, her movements almost mechanical, he thought as he watched her raise the glass to her lips a fourth time. His hand reached out to comfort her. He forced his arm to drop impotently at his side. Everything he knew about her, everything he had grown to love, had been a fabrication. This woman, this countess, was a stranger. Yet he wanted to close his eyes, honor be damned, and believe her. He glanced at his own hands. He clamped them tightly into fists to cease the tremors. "If not you, then who could have killed them?" he asked quietly.

Tessa rolled her eyes upward. "Who indeed?" She shrugged. "Even you should know Edmund was not liked by many. Heaven knows there must be at least a handful of cuckolded men who would have dearly wished to snuff out his hateful existence."

His eyes narrowed at her speculation. "You knew of these liaisons?" Her laugher tinkled around the room. Obviously, she was feeling the effects of the brandy.

"He never made a secret of his conquests," she explained. "In fact, he used to seek out my chamber when he bothered to reside with me. I took up the habit of bolting my door against his nocturnal visits. My defiance did not deter him. He pressed his lips to the seam of the door and frame to taunt me with his wickedness. He relished describing in explicit detail what he did with his women. Naturally, I thought he whispered lies to hurt me, for I was ignorant of the lusts between a man and woman." Tired, she closed her eyes.

Reave's eyes narrowed on the shallow pulse at her throat. He knew she was thinking about his hands and mouth on her body. Hell, he was too. His muscles tensed, resisting the urge to pull her close and lick the rapid heartbeat, tasting the salt on her flesh. It was lust, but something more, much more.

Collecting his fraying threads of sanity, he forced his thoughts back to her words. He came up from behind her until he could feel the heat of her body caress his. "You were a virgin," he said, swallowing the rasp in his throat. He leaned a fraction closer, indulging himself with the womanly scent in her hair. "I do not understand how you could be. You had been married to Lathom for years."

The glare she shot him held more venom than a viper. "I suppose you believe I faked my virginal pain," Tessa accused. She shrugged off his hands on her shoulders, taking a few steps out of his reach. She did not want his comfort. Nor did she acknowledge his soft denial. Keeping her back to him, she continued. "You must wonder why a man of Edmund's appetites would leave his wife chaste. Well, he did not want me.

Simply, Edmund married me for the money my father could provide. He had no desire to bed the soft-fleshed child he took as a bride."

"Tessa, you speak about the child he married. What of the woman you became?"

"He hated me." Sensing his next question, she replied with a shrug. "I existed, it was reason enough. I also fought him, sometimes in front of all and sundry. I displeased him often," she said with a rueful smile. Absently, her fingers kneaded the knotted scar at her temple. "See this? You once asked how I gained this unsightly mark, and now I shall give you the truth you so dearly covet." She lifted her matted hair so he could get a better look at the scar.

The scar did not belong on someone like Tessa. It represented pain, an emotional breach that might never heal and a tale he did not want to hear. "You do not have to speak of it."

She scratched her dirty head, then waved away his objections. "'Course I do. I was almost free from him that night." She leaned back against a table. "One evening, when one of his mistresses disappointed him, Edmund decided to seek me out. He was drunk and mean, and when he found me, he got it into his sodden head that perhaps it was time for our wedding night. We fought. Now knowing his true nature, his touch would have sickened me. He tore my clothes despite my efforts and forced me to the floor. I prayed for death while he loosened his breeches and his sour breath curdled my stomach—" She took a few deep breaths; the reminder of that night was strong.

"But you escaped him?"

Her eyes finally met his. "Yes. It must have been the drink, or perhaps he truly could not summon up his body in lust at the sight of me, but his, his ... body refused to respond. Angered beyond reason, he blamed me, shouting I had used witch magic to unman him. He grabbed me by the neck and swore he would banish the demons from my tempting form, all the while striking my head against the ornate post of my bed." Tessa rubbed her scar, frowning. "I have no memory of this. I lost consciousness after a few blows. The physician who cared for me said I would have died if not for the servants. They heard my screams and rushed the door. When they broke through, he was still striking my bloodied head against the wood. It took five of them to pull him off me. They thought I was dead.'' She gave him a weak, mocking smile. ''As you can see, I survived.''

Agitated, Reave rubbed the beard stubble on his jaw. The thought of Lathom trying to claim his rights in Tessa's bed made him want to kill the bastard himself. The thought stunned him. What had happened? Where was the man who saw the world with cold logic? He could barely think without battling the desire to strike out at someone. He stared wearily at Tessa.

''Run along. Damn the hour and have a servant carry up enough water for a bath. Eat something too. You must think of the child.'' He brushed past her, pausing at the window to peer into the night.

''Hold, sir. I lay this damning evidence at your feet and you tell me to wash myself? I must know your thoughts.''

Reave pivoted, towering over her. ''Must you? Do you truly want to know my thoughts at this moment, madam?'' He was acting like a menacing bastard but it did not prevent him from admiring her courageous quick nod. ''Lathom was a vile creature. He deserved to die. Have I said what you needed to hear?''

Tessa wet her lips before speaking. ''Do you believe I killed him and Mother?''

He hesitated. ''Tessa,'' he began.

''You should not have brought me back to Eastcott. I had a chance to escape the gallows.'' She valiantly tried to hold back her tears. ''Tell me, Lord Wycke. Will you watch them hang me?''

Reave wanted to pound the glass panes until they shattered, hoping the wounds would leech out the torment he felt. He could not tell her what she wanted to hear. She would never believe him anyway. He needed time alone to think. Tessa, finished with him, marched toward the door.

"Wash, eat, sleep. Do not presume we are settled with this subject and try to leave Eastcott. I will hunt you down. And you will not enjoy it," he threatened.

Tessa slammed the door.

Chapter Twenty-seven

"The Countess of Lathom is dead."

The significance of the statement brushed away the cobwebs of lingering sleep from Tessa's mind. She groaned, forcing her strained muscles to move. After yesterday's adventure, the simplest actions would bedevil her that morning. Not willing to open her eyes quite yet, she tried to sit up. Warm and unyielding, Reave held her to his chest.

Reave!

"I enjoy watching you sleep." He rubbed his knuckles against her cheek.

His face lacked the care of his habitual morning ablutions. She shifted in his arms to face him. Grimacing, she noticed he had not changed his rumpled attire. "Did you sleep?"

"Very little," he admitted. "And what amount I did was disquieting."

Although tired, he seemed reconciled with his thoughts. His subdued state increased Tessa's apprehension. "You have come to a decision."

"Tessa, I battled demons and judges within the realm of

frail dream fragments, and I lost.'' He added before she could speak, ''Not the battle. I have always won my battles. It was you I lost. You.'' He hugged her to his chest. ''I did not understand until that moment how much I was willing to sacrifice to keep you. Lady Lathom is dead.''

She pulled back to see his face. ''So you said. Your words will become truth once I am discovered.''

''No.'' He untangled himself from her and stood. ''The answer was before me, yet I refused to see it. Think of it. An unfortunate victim of fate has died. By providence someone has graciously bestowed your name on her. The case is closed. Let it remain closed. Lord Wycke will accept the good-natured ribbing of not solving the case to his satisfaction and find another intrigue to tease his mind. Miss Tessa Belanger will marry Lord Wycke and bear him a healthy child. It all wraps up rather nicely, I think.''

''Reave, what you are suggesting is illicit and would bend that rigid code of honor you possess, snapping it like a dry stick.'' Finally seeing him in the morning light, she thought he looked a little feverish. There was an intensity radiating from him she could not define. ''I blame lack of sleep for this spout of nonsense. It sounds nothing like you.''

Appearing perplexed, Reave said, ''When it was your plan, it was competent. Now that I concur, you—'' He stopped, his expression growing thoughtful. His gaze focused on her, sharpening in its clarity. ''It was never your intention to stay. You told me what I wanted to hear, what I wanted to believe, until you could flee.''

Tessa lifted her chin and straightened her shoulders. Grimly, she said, ''To act in such a manner would make me a very selfish, manipulative woman. Your superior barrister skills must be telling you such a woman could murder her husband and mother without remorse.''

''No.'' Agitated, he brushed his hair off his forehead. ''Tessa, you have tangled my words into such a knot. Even I do not know what I mean. Christ, I am here. Is it not telling?''

"Yes, my lord. It tells me you have yet to decide who shall be the sacrifice. You or me."

Reave left Eastcott that morning. He had not bothered to explain his pressing business in London. He had said only that it would take several days, a week at most. Tessa did not beg him to remain. Their mutual lack of trust had made them strangers.

"I warrant you have spent the afternoon here." Tessa turned to greet Sims as she waddled down to join her at the end of the gallery. "Your lips and hands are positively blue. You will be sick by morning if we do not put you to bed."

"I had not noticed the cold."

"What holds you here? If you are hiding from Lord Wycke, I fear it has been in vain. I was told he departed for London quite early."

"I know." Tessa adjusted her wool shawl. Crossing her arms, she tucked her hands under her wrap for warmth. She stared up at a portrait of Reave. "He must have been barely twenty when this was done."

Sims gave the painting an impatient glance. "Yes. Yes," she said, dismissing the subject with the flutter of her hands. "I did not join you in this frigid gallery to admire Wycke's ancestors. I came to attend you."

Tessa smiled, appreciating her support even if she did not deserve it. "Sims, all is as it should be."

"First, Wycke disappears without explanation. Now you stand here, acting deliberately mysterious. I shall not stand for it," Sims said, clearly upset. "Lord Wycke was beyond reason when he discovered you missing from the household, but I daresay not surprised. Then you return. I almost fainted at the sight of you. Your gown, your hair." She made a clucking sound with her tongue. "We all thought he had tied a rope to your waist, the other to his saddle, and dragged you back to Eastcott."

"Lord Wycke was not responsible for my disheveled condition, Sims." Her ladyship was not convinced. "Do not judge him for my foolishness. His hand was gentle, and what harsh words I did receive were duly deserved. He is a man of honor," Tessa said, her gaze full of love as she stared at the brush-stroked eyes of the portrait.

"Beg pardon, ladies," Thorne interrupted from the doorway. "There are gentlemen here to see Miss Belanger. I think their business is of an official nature."

Tessa could not seem to move or speak. Tessa Belanger was no one important. Blast it all, the woman was not even real! Why would gentlemen call on her?

Sims took control of the situation. "Well, Thorne, we will receive the gentlemen in the drawing room, if you please. I am certain their business concerns another, and we shall rectify it immediately."

Sims waited until Thorne had departed, then she reached out and pinched Tessa on the arm. Satisfied she gained a response, the older woman snapped, "It bodes ill to look guilty before one is accused, my dear. Straighten up and act the part of a gracious lady and the future Countess of Wycke!"

Both women greeted their visitors with measured smiles. Sims, recognizing one of the men, extended her hand. "Welcome to Eastcott, gentlemen. Why, Mr. Carden, I have not seen you since I saw you chasing the Glyn chit at the last assembly." Her smile grew genuine when her comment reddened his ears. "Tessa, do you recall our constable, Mr. Robert Carden? No? Well, it is so difficult to recall a name plucked from a sea of faces. Mr. Carden, this is Lord Wycke's betrothed, Miss Tessa Belanger. Now, I am not familiar with your companions." She adjusted her spectacles to scrutinize the grimy men.

The men looked from one to the other, then nudged the constable to relay their business.

"My apologies for our unexpected visit. These men"—Mr. Carden gestured with the small hat he held in his hands—"they have ridden straight through from London with charges

of a most serious concern,'' he said, looking around for someone
to corroborate his statement. He received several concurring
nods.

Sims focused on the larger of the two men. Clearing her
throat, she said, ''Indeed? I am confused, why you have brought
them here, sir. If you seek Lord Wycke, I fear he has departed
for London. Perhaps you may catch him there. Thorne, if you
could show these men to the door.''

''No, Lady Brackett, you—I—'tisn't Lord Wycke we seek,
but the young lady.'' His eyes briefly flickered to Tessa. ''Miss,
there have been some evil charges issued, an' a warrant has
been granted by the magistrate. You must come with us.''

Sims laughed at the absurdity of the events taking place.
One of the men stepped forward to take Tessa by the arm, but
Sims slapped his hand away. ''I am in charge of Miss Belanger
until Wycke's return, and no one shall remove her! Mr. Carden,
you are bedeviling an innocent woman. Whoever issued these
charges has been wasting your time.'' She drew herself up to
full height, daring anyone to gainsay her.

The forty-year-old Mr. Carden looked to his companions for
help. They ignored him. Instead, they watched Tessa, expecting
her to flee. The constable rolled his hat in his hand, crushing
the nap. ''With apologies, miss, I must ask you to come with
us,'' he politely commanded.

Sims clasped her heart as if it pained her. ''I will not hear
another word of this lunacy until Wycke can be summoned.
You would have treaded lightly, sirs, if his lordship was standing before you, but with a couple of helpless women, you think
nothing of terrorizing us!''

The constable swore. ''Simona, our families have known
each other for thirty years. I am no more terrorizing this young
woman than you are helpless.'' His hand swept in the general
direction of the men. ''They have a warrant and I have to
enforce the law.''

Sims took a protective step to shield her friend. ''Charges?
What has Tessa been charged with?''

"Just take the wench an' be done w' it!" One of the silent muscles found his tongue.

"No, this is my jurisdiction, an' I be doing this by my time," Mr. Carden snapped. The creases around his eyes deepened when he spoke to Tessa. "Miss Belanger, there has been questions raised about your identity. They're saying you are the Lady Lathom who murdered her husband and mother. Since the person who recognized you is a member of society, his word was not questioned."

Member of the ton. Knows who you are. Tessa was certain the Duchess of Densmore did not call for her arrest. *A man of honor.* Tessa gasped. Reave had chosen his sacrifice.

"Miss?" The constable hovered as if she were about to faint.

Sims's voice cut through the numbing fog, trying to claim her. "What horrific blather! You should be ashamed of yourselves to frighten us so with your stories. Away with you!" She pulled Tessa to her side with a crushing hug. "Away, before I call the staff and allow them to give you the proper dusting you all deserve!"

Resigned, Mr. Carden signaled the two men to take the prisoner in custody. Sims cried out as the men not so gently pried Tessa from her grasp, separating them.

"Tessa! I shall send someone to find Wycke; he will gain your release. I will not rest until I hear word!" Thorne struggled with Sims to keep her from attacking the men.

Tessa raised her head, bravely facing her friends. "I fear his lordship knows all too well my fate." She spoke through numbed lips. "His absence explains much." Fingers dug into her upper arm. There were no tears this time, no resistance. Tessa glanced up at the night sky. Clouds concealed the moon, shielding her indignity. In the distance she could hear Sims sobbing. Stones crunched beneath her feet, but the noise did not block Sims's unanswered questions.

"Why?" Sims cried out. "Why does she speak such madness? Where is Wycke? How could he have left her?"

Her grim guards pushed her into a wagon. She was shackled

at the ankles and the wrists. The constable protested the need for chains. His reward for his kindness was a large fist to the back of his neck. His limp body was tossed in the wagon beside her. Tessa did not consider the guard's actions odd. Nothing seemed real. Tugging on the short chain, she brought her hands to her face.

Reave had betrayed her.

The sight of Eastcott in the distance caused Reave to urge his horse into a gallop. Home. It had been a long time since he thought of this place, or any, for that matter, as home.

His parting from Tessa five days before had been solemn and strained. He had handled their confrontation in a clumsy manner. Reave hoped she would forgive his sudden journey to London once she learned of his intentions.

Spotting Jason arcing a stick back and forth through the tall grass, Reave signaled the horse to slow as he guided the animal off the road in the general direction of the wandering boy. He called out a greeting. Jason stopped his movement and waited.

"Something amiss?" Reave asked, noting his son lacked the exuberance he had grown accustomed to seeing since Tessa's arrival into their lives. "Are you ill? Have you been dipping your grimy fingers in Cook's batter again?"

Jason shook his head.

Irritated by the lack of response and in particular the lack of enthusiasm for his sudden arrival, Reave grumbled, "Are you being impertinent, or has someone split your tongue? By the bye, where is Tessa?" He glanced around, the leather saddle creaking with his shifting weight as he wondered if she was hiding nearby.

"They took her," Jason cried. Not waiting for a response, he ran toward the thickest section of forest, knowing Reave would never be able to pursue him on horseback.

Reave urged his steed after his son. Deciding the pursuit was futile, he changed direction and headed for the house. Alarm coursed through his veins as he struck the horse's flank with his hand, urging the steed to run faster. Tessa was at Eastcott. He had left orders with the staff she was not to leave. Thorne would know where she was. He imagined her sitting in the drawing room, having tea with Lady Brackett while they discussed the lace on her gown, or music, or some damn insignificant bit of nonsense.

Both rider and horse were breathing heavy when they rode into the courtyard. Leaping off the horse, Reave tossed the reins to a stable boy and ran into the house.

"Tessa?" His voice echoed in the hall. He counted, waiting to hear the swish of her skirts, and the melodic, heart-warming sound of her voice calling his name in greeting. She did not come. "Tessa!" He roared a mixture of torment and fear.

"Lord Wycke."

Reave blinked back the moisture in his eyes and turned to greet the butler. He was alone, and the expression on his face told him he was not going to like what he was about to hear. "Perhaps you will join me for a drink, Thorne. I doubt I can stomach whatever you are dreading to tell me."

Silently, they headed for the library. Reave poured each of them a healthy dram, then held the drink out to him. Both immediately emptied their glasses, and Thorne boldly held his glass out for another. "That bad, eh?" He refilled Thorne's glass. "First, tell me that no one is lying cold in the shed."

"What, milord?" The butler's brows furrowed together. They twitched upward when he recalled their conversation of the deceased Mr. Lawson. "Ah, no, milord. No one has died." He emptied his glass.

"Then I must believe this bad news involves my bride. Jason ran off into the woods, crying that someone had taken her away. Is this true?"

Thorne would not meet his gaze when he said, "We tried to send word to you. I assume the lad missed you."

Reave gave him a curt nod, leaving the butler no other option but to continue. "You see, we were desperately trying to reach you 'cause the constable arrived with two rather brutish-looking gents and they took her away."

Reave stared at him in disbelief. "You mean, when men you were not familiar with knocked on the door requesting Tessa, you simply handed her over without question?"

He had spoken calmly; still, Thorne was not fooled. "N-not exactly, milord. Lady Brackett was very single-minded about her purpose and told them they could not have her. The constable said there was a warrant from the magistrate, so there was little we could do. They were quite large—the gents, I mean."

"Did anyone see this warrant?" The butler shook his head. "Damn!" Reave ran his hand along his jaw and began to pace. "Did you not consider it could have been a bluff, man? How many days have passed since she was taken?"

"Three days, milord. Lady Brackett did ask them to tell her the charges."

Reave froze, his expression incredulous. "And pray tell, what were they?"

Thorne twisted the tip of his immaculate gloved finger. "Well, they said Miss Belanger murdered her husband. That she was the Lady Lathom. None of the staff believed the charges, my lord." He interjected at Reave's sudden bellow of rage.

"If you had doubts, why did you allow her to leave," Reave roared, lashing out. He should never have left her. "You should have made them wait for my return."

"Lady Brackett tried every plausible reason to detain them, milord. She could not sway them. In the end, your lady willingly walked out with them."

He closed his eyes, and a vision of Tessa came before him. Tessa! God, how frightened she must be, wondering when he would come for her. If they had touched her—he blocked the thought from his mind. He managed to choke out, "Do you know where they keep her?"

"Unfortunately, all of us were too stunned to ask," Thorne miserably confessed. "There is more."

"What darker depths can be reached? I have already plummeted into an onerous abyss."

"Well, it was what Miss Belanger said when she was taken. She said that you were aware of her fate, and your absence explained everything."

Reave turned away from Thorne. "Leave me." He stared at the cold hearth until he heard the door quietly close.

Damn! She believed he was responsible for her arrest. Her faith in him was so weak, she thought he could take her body and love, then leave her to the authorities. Not only was he a traitor in her opinion, but a coward as well. Reave smashed his empty glass against the wall, heedless of the splinters of glass striking his face. He would find her. Storming out of the library, he called for a fresh horse and food. His sole thought was to find Tessa. He would then deal with the soon-to-be-dead men who dared to take her.

Chapter Twenty-eight

"Here you go, your ladyship. An 'umble dwelling to rest your sore head and companions to ease your loneliness." Her guards sniggered.

Tessa thought the imposing iron-spiked four-foot-thick oak door sheltered a rift, exposing mortals to the portals of hell. Her deduction was accurate. They had brought her to Newgate.

After traveling the countryside for days, their destination was this abomination. None of her guards' actions had made sense to her since they had dumped the badly beaten body of the constable out of the wagon. She did not even know if the man had survived his injuries.

One of the guards nudged her toward the open door. "Don't get queer on us, your ladyship."

Entering the lodge, a tiny high-roofed apartment, Tessa used her hand to block the fetid stench in the room. Its source could not be ascertained, since the foul haze permeated everything. Secured by irons, she was led to a small room on the left.

Her guards were replaced by an unsympathetic female warder who ordered her to strip. Tessa refused. Did they not realize that if she possessed a weapon, she would have dispatched her guards days ago? A heavy-handed cuff to her left ear extinguished further womanly protests.

Nauseated, and with a persistent ringing in her ear, Tessa attempted to remove her gown. Not satisfied with her feeble attempts to disrobe, the warder removed the shackles from her wrists, then tugged the gown from her trembling frame with practiced efficiency. Once she was nude, the woman made a cursory search of her limbs and other places, which until then only one man had dared explore.

Once the humiliating examination was completed, she was told to dress. Tessa did not argue. The warder's harsh voice halted her movement when she reached for her gown. She could not keep her gown.

Blinking in disbelief, she listened as the warder spoke of the entry fee, which was fifteen shillings, and of simple comforts such as a bed, linen, candles, and food, all of which cost money. The gown was of fine quality and would pay her entry fee and for a little food. If she wanted more, she would have to get word to the outside and pray there was someone charitable to lend her the funds. It was one thing to sleep on the damp floor without the friendly light of a candle for comfort, but it was quite another to die slowly of starvation. The dead dropped in the quicklime over the "bird cage" walk daily were a harsh reminder it was easy to be forgotten in this dark prison.

Dressed only in her cotton chemise and petticoats, she was led through an oaken door faced with iron. The stench of unwashed bodies and death overwhelmed her as the door was opened. Retching into her hands, she was pushed into the darker depths of the prison. The door was locked behind her, diminishing all hope with the turn of a key.

She did not know how long she sat in the darkness once she was thrown into the ward. It was not a large place; certainly Eastcott had chambers larger. One of the prisoners to her right held a precious candle. She counted twenty shadowy figures, although none of it mattered. There were no beds, only a few wooden benches, and all of them were occupied. She leaned against the cool stone wall, wondering if it was possible to fall asleep standing upright. The thought of rats, vermin, and filth on the floor did not make the alternative appealing.

The women around her shuffled past her as if she were not there. When she was first brought to the ward, the clamor of jeering and teasing was such that it muddled her senses. Now, a part of the darkness, she did not exist.

Icy cold fingers clasped her ankle. Tessa screamed, stirring the other prisoners in the ward. Some blistered her with colorful oaths for disturbing their peace, while others added to the din with their tortured, eerie howls and moans. Tessa sank to her feet, covering her ears to block out the maddening noises.

Her head snapped up at the brush of fabric across her arm. She shrank away from the light caress on her tangled tresses. Losing her balance, her hand touched the oak floorboards, settling on something wet and slimy. A strangled whimper rose in her throat as she wiped her hand across the damp stone to rid her hands of the filth. A chuckle broke the silence near her left ear.

"Bitty likes pretty things. A little dirt hurt n'one," the almost lyrical voice whispered in her ear.

Tessa decided it was best not to answer, praying the woman would grow bored and leave. Drawing her knees to her chest, she recited the alphabet in Greek, pretending she was not locked up in a ward filled with starving, half-mad felons. The voice in the darkness laughed again.

"Yers brains than most, but 'twill not block the noise and stink. Once the gut speaks, the mind slips fast," the voice teased.

"I do not mean to be rude, but I would rather keep my own counsel," she said sternly, the quiver in her voice ruining the effect. She scooted away from her new tormentor. The voice scurried to her side.

"Bitty pays no mind. So, what pretty do to play behind the gate?"

"I have no comprehension of what you speak."

"Mus' be bad, very bad to lay head here. Who ye prick?" the voice pressed.

"No one! This has been a dreadful mistake. Once I can gain someone with a little intelligence, I shall be removed from this hole forthwith." The awful stench of her companion made her stomach churn. Everything she said amused this woman, and her announcement of escape was no exception.

Bitty bubbled with laughter. It was so contagious, others joined in her amusement.

"Oh, pretty, many 'av said the words, an' many tasted the lime on their escape, 'Tis the way here."

"I will find another course besides death to leave this place, I assure you," Tessa said, not believing her foolish boast but too prideful to keep silent.

"Ewwww, sounds like we have a real lady in our grasp." Another voice in the darkness sneered. "Killing one was what brought me here. Remember, missus, they can hang me only once."

Her warning was only too clear. Tessa shut her mouth, swallowing her tart retort. "I think it best we retire before we anger the wrong person," she quietly suggested to Bitty.

"Tha' one's all spit an' piss, pretty. Her lady beat her once too many. No more," she gleefully cackled. "Bitty let no one harm ye."

Tessa winced, not knowing how to keep Bitty's bloodless hand from petting her hair. Seizing upon the strange woman's fondness for chat, she asked, "What circumstances brought you here, Bitty?" The woman's indistinct figure moved closer.

"A swap o' sadness, is it?" Bitty's excited voice questioned. "Well, well, not much to tell. A flasher I was—"

"I beg your pardon, a flasher?"

"Pretty lacks manners to wait quiet for the tale to be spoken," an annoyed Bitty scolded. "I worked in a grand house, offering games of luck to those willin' to play. 'Twas my task to see others heard of the big wins from the tables."

"To encourage these newcomers to empty their pockets."

"Yeah, I helped to lighten the pockets by pick or by die. Only when a young pretty's papa stormed the house, demanding the gel's coin, that luck turned bad for Bitty." She paused, waiting for the young woman to interrupt. When Tessa remained silent, she continued. "This man fired his pistol at poor Bitty, gleaning a bit o' flesh from my cheek." She lifted her greasy hair from her face to show Tessa her scar, oblivious to the fact her features were lost in the shadows. "I was mad. Not like Bitty hurt the pretty. When I fell, I grabbed a stool an' struck the bastard when he turned his back. I kept hitting, hitting till he could not move to hurt poor Bitty."

"Oh, I am sorry, Miss Bitty. It appears we are both a victim of fate," Tessa said compassionately, not able to bring herself to touch the woman.

"Weaving your tales on another innocent, Bitty," an amused masculine voice queried through a small grate in the door.

"A swap o' truths, nothin more," Bitty grumbled, moving away from Tessa.

The turnkey chuckled as he opened the door. The candles he brought lit the room, and many squinted against the brightness. Spotting Tessa, he kicked prone bodies aside. The victims groaned but rolled away, else risking another vicious kick. Raising the candles to her face, he admired the tantalizing view her dirty underclothes offered.

"I'd keeps to meself in this room of vicious hags." He grinned, exposing his lack of front teeth. Tossing his head in Bitty's direction, he warned, "That one 'specially. She hacked her mate and cooked him in mincemeat pies she sent out to her kinsmen. That's how she got her name—hacking her man to bits!"

Bitty tried to spit on him. Her aim was off and her insult landed on another. The guard thought this was funny. From the corner of his eye, he caught Tessa trying to sneak away from him, so he leaned a stocky hand on the wall, halting her useless escape. "They say she likes them pretty. So do I."

He leaned closer, and Tessa could smell cheap ale on his breath. Turning her head to avoid his lips, she tried to slip under his braced arm. "Please, sir."

Moving his arm, he blocked her. "I come as a favor to all the new prisoners. A few nights with me pressing that slim backside of yours into the floor, and I promise you will be carrying my babe in your belly."

Disgust distorted her face. "I do not believe this!"

The turnkey's eyes roamed the gentle curves of her body. Desire flared in his dull brown eyes. "Oh, I swear that where I plant my seed, there yields a harvest. My wife has twelve, and there have been many here who have delayed the hemp by pleading their bellies," he boasted. He placed his hand on her breast. She yelped. Ducking under his arm, she moved out of his reach.

"Lay a hand on me, and I swear I shall do what I have been accused of," she threatened. Miserable, she conceded to herself that if he decided to rape her, there was little she could do to prevent it. "Plant your harvests on some other misfortunate. Beast!"

"Stupid bitch!" He made a move to knock the defiant glare from her face. Curious eyes throughout the room made him hesitate. She had drawn too much attention to them. "There will come a time, and this time will come, you haughty bitch, when you will eagerly spread your legs for me and pray I plow your belly till I get you with child." He stalked toward her. When he was against her, he lowered his voice so only she could hear his words. "I think when you are on your knees, praying for my prick, I think then I shall have you." He pressed a wet, punishing kiss to her lips, then swaggered away.

Tessa wiped the kiss from her lips in between retches. She would never be desperate enough to beg his stud services. Never! Finding a vacant spot in the far corner, she claimed it for the night.

Warily, she watched the turnkey. He had dismissed her as this night's quarry and was searching the room for an eager victim. His light shone on a woman who looked no more than six-and-ten. She did not protest when the large man awkwardly knelt at her feet. Setting the candle to the side, he loosened his trousers, then flipped her faded skirt over her head. He spat on his hand, then touched his sex. Tessa glanced away, realizing what the man was planning to do. Tightly closing her eyes, the image of him leaning over that poor girl burned in her mind. Turning to the wall, she listened to his beastlike grunts as he thrusted into her. His roar of release made her want to vomit.

Finished, the turnkey rose. He must have seen her curled in the corner. He chuckled as he left, taking the light with him. The key clicked, and his footsteps faded. The room was dark, and Tessa could hear the soft weeping of the abused girl.

It was her fault the girl had taken her place. Guilt possessed her, but she could not even think about accepting his offer even if he decided to shine his light over her again. She would rather die a slow, agonizing death. Laying her head on her knees, she tried to sleep. It had been almost a day and a half since she had been allowed to rest. Her stomach growled, but she ignored her hunger. She feared these miseries were minor inconveniences compared to what she was about to face when she would be summoned to court and forced to face her lover as he offered evidence to her guilt.

"Any word?" Kim Farrell asked in lieu of a greeting. Maxwell glared at the viscount, then slammed the door.

Reave did not comment on the polite war between his friend and servant. He might have if this had been an ordinary day, if he had never heard of the Lathom case, if Tessa were not missing, blaming him for her incarceration. Weary, Reave allowed his head to fall against the cushioned back of the chair where he was resting. Three days with little sleep and even less food was beginning to take its toll. "Nothing I want to hear," he said, his voice hoarse from raw fear. "However, there are one or two agents who have yet to send word to me."

"Might I recommend a few hours of sleep. You look terrible."

Reave shook his head. "I doubt Tessa is getting much sleep wherever they are keeping her." The thought of her suffering wrested his insides. He was failing her. He had spent days scouring the countryside, checking every country jail. She and her captors had simply vanished. "The search would be easier if I possessed accurate descriptions of the men. The constable has yet to recover from their beating and was of no use," he said, still enraged by the man's incompetence.

"I have visited my clubs, and no one has mentioned capturing the notorious countess." Kim had the decency to look sheepish at Reave's piercing stare. "Good Lord, man, you cannot fault me for being amazed I protected a criminal! She appeared so fragile, so innocent."

"Exactly," Reave ground out. "You know very well, once you became acquainted with Tessa, there was little doubt she was innocent of the crime."

"True, true. All the same, I cannot help but feel used. She was quite clever in her deceit. I swallowed her entire tale about her being the bastard of an aristocrat. It sits unwell in my gut."

"Shut up." He did not need to be reminded of her lies. Part of him understood the direness that drove her. Still, it hurt she could not have trusted him with her secrets. Trust had always been an issue with them, and now she was somewhere alone, frightened, and believing he was the fiend who betrayed her. "She has disappeared without a trace, so I can only assume the true murderer has found a means to dispose of her." He would not consider her dead.

"Why not just turn her in and allow her to take the blame?"

"Our killer might be worried about her association with me. If I believe her, and I do, the investigation would continue, and that might make him nervous. First, a body was given over to end the case, then our killer somehow discovered Tessa's whereabouts and removed her. He knows I cannot publicly search for her without revealing her true identity. I only pray

I find her before—'' His throat moved convulsively, unable to finish his grisly thoughts.

Kim glanced away, affected by Reave's distress. "If she lives, we will find her."

Tessa screamed at the departing turnkey, "How am I suppose to pay for food and ale if no one will allow me to send word to my friends outside?"

The loaf of bread and pint of ale she clutched was the last of what her gown had credited her. She had been demanding the last two days for someone to send a message to the Duke and Duchess of Densmore, but the simpleton did not believe she was so highly connected and laughed in her face. When she asked what she was supposed to do for food, it was suggested that she sell her body like the others. She had spit in his face at the crude suggestion and was promptly rewarded with a slap across the face. Damn the brutes!

Yesterday, a woman had tried to snatch her precious loaf of bread. Being with these animals had begun to wear on her, and immediately she attacked the woman. While they bit and scratched each other, the two guards who came to check on the screaming and cheers placed their own bets on the winner.

They had chosen the wrong woman.

With a handful of black, greasy hair, she picked her soiled loaf of bread off the floor and limped to the area she considered hers. There was a rather nasty bite on her calf and an equally appalling scratch to her bruised cheek, but she had won her meal back. She had hungrily sunk her teeth into the stale, filthy bread, not thinking of where it had been.

"You. She-cat." The turnkey who had witnessed the fight the other day stirred her from her musings. "A room change has been ordered. Hurry along." The door swung open.

Tessa stuffed her bread under her arm and carefully cradled her ale so not to lose a swallow. Was it time to face the magistrate and Reave? God, what would he think when he saw her like this? She looked worse than any street whore! She did not bother to ask questions. This was a place where nothing was volunteered, everything had a price, and she could not pay.

"Godspeed, pretty," Bitty called out as the door was locked again. "Don't fight the hemp! If yer nice to the guard, 'e might pull on yer limbs to make it speedy like!"

"Where am I?" The turnkey pushed Tessa into a small cell, and her ale spilled down the front of her petticoats. Ignoring her loss, she pleaded for an answer. "What will happen?"

"Seems you have an angel watching you."

He refused to explain, and the door shut behind him. Bewildered, she scanned her new accommodations. It was a small room containing an old chamber pot with a crack down the side and a small bed with—oh, could it be possible—sheets! Reverently, she touched the clean bedding but jerked her hand back when she realized how dirty she was in comparison. There was even a small window. Oiled paper covered the opening, so she did not bother to look out.

Why was she there? Was Reave aware of her presence and decided out of guilt to see to it she was offered a few simple comforts? There were too many questions disturbing her, and no one was willing to give her answers.

Curling up on the bed, she welcomed the little pleasure it gave her. At least, she was away from those horrible women, she thought, allowing the gentle currents of sleep to cast her into dreams. She welcomed them, for it was in her dreams she still walked with the ones she loved. Reave, a loving smile on his lips, gathered her into his arms. Jason was close, running with a stick, his mightiest sword in his hand battling imaginary beasts. Sims was smiling behind her paper fan, wiping joyous tears away and congratulating herself on bringing all of them together.

Thud! Twice more something hit her door. The assault to the door crumbled her pleasant dream as if it were made from old parchment. It fluttered away on wind currents as consciousness claimed her. She cried out, reaching out to capture the fragments. Another thud against the door shook the remaining effects of her sleep. Rubbing the wetness from her eyes, she waited wide-eyed as the key whined, turning in the lock. Low, angry words were exchanged outside before the door swung open.

Reave wiped his abraded knuckles with a handkerchief, then he tucked the cloth back into his pocket. In a place like this, he discovered physical persuasion was as useful as gold. Searching the dark cell for signs of life, he finally noticed the small figure coiled up on the bed. Sticking his head out the door, he demanded some light, which the guard immediately supplied by offering him a lantern. Dismissing the man, his attention returned to the silent figure in the cell.

"Tessa?" he called out, not certain if this poor soul was her. He knelt down near the poor excuse for a bed and studied the woman. She had kept her head lowered all the time he had been present, and her tangled, filthy hair hid her face. Tentatively, he reached out, lifting the hair from her face.

Tessa attacked the moment her face was revealed. She struck his face, his chest, anything she could reach. He suddenly wondered if she understood who he was.

"Tessa, it's Reave! Please, you will only hurt yourself." His words spurred her fury. She kicked him in the abdomen, quickly bringing him down. Gasping, and in pain, he lost his temper. "Bloody hell, I am the one trying to save you!"

Scrambling to her feet, she leapt off the bed and pressed her back to the opposite wall. "I would not need saving if not for your decision to turn me in, you faithless blackguard! What was it? Did your sense of duty finally overrule your lust, or were you lying to me all along so I would not try to flee?"

Slowly, he rose, supporting himself with the bed to confront her charges. "Has this place addled your mind so much that you can believe such evil of me? Faithless? You silly idiot, I have been living on hope for thirteen days, praying I would find you alive. Yet, when I find you, I am charged with betrayal." He straightened, giving her his full attention. "I have walked away from everything I believed for the sake of you, risking my reputation and my profession. How dare you believe otherwise.''

If he had expected to intimidate her with his stance, he was mistaken. Tessa matched his posture, fury flushing her grimy face.

She sneered. ''I was once fooled by your smooth words, and look what happened. I have fought off the advances of both men and women, I have eaten filth I would not feed a dog, and have lived with cold darkness longer than I care to remember. I know I should be grateful to you for moving me out of that harpy pit and giving me a bed instead of the stone floor to lay my head. Your kindness does not balance your justice, and I fear you have wrung all the love I have protected in my heart for you!'' She sobbed, not taking her teary gaze off him.

Reave reached for the lantern. Raising it, he wanted to get a closer look at her. My God, what had they done to his beautiful, innocent love? She wore only her chemise and petticoats. Both were filthy and torn. The face he knew by heart was bloated; her arms bore scratches and purple bruises. He had to fight back the urge to kill the person responsible for this abuse. The waiting. He was so close.

Physically, he did not recognize her, but he knew the woman who loved him was somewhere beneath the pain and filth. He had only to bring her out.

''Please do not look at me that way,'' she murmured.

''In love?''

''No! I do not seek your pity, nor want it. I deserve all that has occurred. I should have—''

''I know you did not kill them,'' he flatly stated. ''Nor are you here at my request.'' He saw a small spark of hope light her eyes, and he tried to fan it with his love. ''Tessa, whoever did kill your husband and mother discovered you were at Eastcott and ordered you to be kidnapped. No one knows you are here.''

Doubt furrowed her brow. ''Ridiculous. The constable came

with the men. He held a warrant for my arrest.'' Her eyes widened. ''The constable.''

''There was never a warrant. The constable was used to add credibility to the arrest at Eastcott. He was beaten so severely, no one has yet been able to talk to him. The killer must have been nervous to find you under my protection. I suspect he had you buried here to give himself time to dispose of you properly.'' He inched closer, pleased she was not backing away. ''Perhaps he hoped you would be accommodating and simply die.''

Tessa moved over to the bed and sat down, her expression thoughtful. ''No one knows I am here. How did you know where to find me?''

''Not the way you think.'' Reave joined her on the bed. He stared at her, his eyes hungrily memorizing her face. God, she was a mess. He did not care. He was just elated she was alive and he had found her. ''Forgive my rude staring, love. I confess after searching the countryside for days and never uncovering a trace to your whereabouts, I began to fear the worst.''

''I was moved from place to place the first few days before I was brought here,'' she said. Her eyes took on a suspicious cast. ''How did you find me, Reave?''

''Ah, I see you are as trusting as ever. Never mind, I suppose I deserve your suspicions,'' he grumbled. ''I decided to come to London and use my underworld contacts here.'' He gave her a rueful smile. ''This may surprise you, love, but once I was rather good at applying my intellect to solving puzzles. My problem was, I could not see past the crimson haze of rage when I thought of you out there alone, nor could I tuck away my feelings for you.'' He resisted the urge to pull her into his arms. Looking at the door, he said, ''Last evening I received word from one of my contacts within Newgate. He sent word a lady was being held, and no one was talking much about her. It was the only break I had. I was not even certain it was you.'' Risking rejection, he gently caressed her dirty cheek. Tessa pulled back, giving him a gauging stare.

"Am I free to leave with you?"

His expression full of regret, Reave pulled his hand away from her face. Distracted, he rubbed his jaw. "I have bribed the entire prison to get to see you, but that is all. Whoever placed you here is generous enough to keep his men loyal. Fortunately for me, they are also greedy to add a little more gold to their purses. In truth, you are a prisoner. If I tried to free you, your identity would be revealed, then you would be formally placed here."

"Then there is no hope," she whispered, sorrow leadening her posture.

"No," he said, taking her hand. "As long as we love each other, there is hope. I have a plan—it will take some time. There are men to contact. With luck I hope to know the identity of your enemy soon." He kissed her pouting lips lightly, and when that was not satisfying, he captured the sweetness again, this time reveling, plundering, until they were both breathless and aching. He pressed a few coins into her palm. "Use prudence, love. I wish I could take you from this cell and surround you with all the comforts you deserve. We must convince the killer he has hidden you well. He must not learn of my visit." He kissed the tears clinging to her lashes. "What I can promise you is this: I swear the next time you see me, you will walk out of Newgate a free woman."

Chapter Twenty-nine

Another week had passed since Reave's visit to Newgate, and his mood had darkened with the ending of each day. There had been no word from his contacts, which further blackened his outlook. He longed to return to Tessa but did not dare, for just as he had spies behind the prison walls, the killer might as well. He could not risk placing her in jeopardy, not when there was so much at stake.

Woodhouse, sitting to his left, reminded Reave it was his turn to play. Reave signaled to fold despite the high cards in his hand. He thought getting out to one of his clubs would serve to distract him. Waiting alone in his London town house, sifting through his notes and evidence, was bringing him no closer to the killer. Nor was sitting there at the club, pretending nothing was wrong.

Movement at his side caused him to look up. Hayden. Reave considered telling Quinn about Tessa, hoping he could offer some insight. Immediately, he dismissed the notion. His partner talked too much to the wrong people, and this had caused problems in the past. His lips formed a half-smile. ''Good evening, Hayden. I was not aware you had a membership at this club.''

Hayden dismissed the veiled insult with a wave of his hand. "I frequent only the ones that interest me, though I concede it has been some time since I have attended this particular one. I thought you were at Eastcott?''

"Some business opportunities arose demanding my attention, else I would be still hiding in my library while the servants and the ladies attempt to upturn my household.''

Hayden could not hide his surprise. "You left your betrothed behind, depriving her of the privileges and quality only London can provide?''

The urge to escape seized Reave. He rose. Thanking the gentlemen at the table, he collected his winnings. Determined to discourage Hayden's curiosity, Reave said, "Tessa has all a bride could require. I have people running to town whenever she desires, and she quite frankly seemed pleased when I announced my intentions to reside in London.''

His friend nodded, giving him a look of concern. "Is everything well? I mean no intrusion to your privacy, but there appeared to be trouble between you and your betrothed.''

"I have yet to hear of a prospective bride and groom not having a few, ah, let us say, misunderstandings while plans are made. I think this is the reason men are asked to keep to their own affairs.'' His smile lacked sincerity. Another night, and no word had left him no tongue for idle chat. "I will not keep you from your evening. There are a few cases I should attend to before I return to Eastcott. I shall take advantage of my restlessness and see to them.''

"Well, good night, then,'' Hayden called out, his scowl becoming more evident as he watched Reave depart. Remembering the men who awaited him, he reluctantly went in search of his companions.

* * *

"A word if I might, milord?"

Maxwell, his manservant, interrupted Reave's ascent to his chamber. Pausing on the stairs, he waited for the man to continue. "Well?" he snapped, the anger borne from frustration.

"Lord Turnberry was seeking an audience earlier this evening, milord. When I explained you were out, he insisted that you read his note upon your arrival. He stressed it was most urgent."

"Where is it?" Reave demanded, already descending the stairs. The question was inessential, since all correspondence was placed on his desk. The servant confirmed his query by telling him it was in the study. He rushed past, allowing the door to end their dialogue.

Impatiently, he broke the seal and scanned Kim's letter. It said little save that the report enclosed would interest him. Discarding the note, he broke the seal of the report, allowing himself to settle into his chair while he read. His hands shook as he read one sheet, then the next.

Within his grasp he held the means to free Tessa. He would have to move cautiously. His prey was cunning and would not simply place his head through the hangman's noose. His plan would have to be subtle. Reave reread the last line of damning evidence. He wondered if he could preserve his polite civility without exposing to the killer his desire to choke the life out of him. He could have lost Tessa; he still could if he handled the confrontation badly. It was too late an hour for confrontations, too late for the chilling control he needed. Tonight he would devise a plan of attack.

It was early evening when Reave entered Hayden's private sanctuary. Heavy, overwhelming odors of stale cigar smoke and liquor hung in the small room. A fire burned in the hearth, making the room uncomfortably warm.

"Good God, Hayden, are you sweating out a poison or just trying to kill yourself?" Reave exclaimed, heading for the

nearest window. Without permission, he drew back the draper-
ies and flung open the windows. "Are you unwell? I was a
little surprised to received your invitation."

"Forgive me for not giving you proper notice." Hayden
gestured for Reave to join him, offering the opposing wing
chair. "I did not intend to sound so mysterious. It was long
after our encounter the other evening that I concluded you
might be feeling lonely without your betrothed." He studied his
drink with a small smile playing on his chapped lips. "Drink?"

Reave sat down, refusing the offer. His friend looked like
he had not slept. His rumpled, stained shirt and breeches were
the remains of last evening's attire. "You look unwell."

Hayden dismissed the suggestion. He rubbed the drink-
reddened rims of his eyes with his thumb and first finger. "I
suffer from too much indulging and too little repenting. I had
intended to change but thought we should have our little chat
before Claire comes down. She abhors all talk at the table that
does not center on her. Ah, but you are aware of her fits."
Hayden leaned forward, supporting his carriage with his arm
on his knee. "How is your lady, Reave? Bearing well the
indignities of her new lodgings?"

Reave's jaw tensed, the only betrayal of his emotions. "How
did you know?"

Hayden chuckled, swallowing another mouthful before
deigning to answer. He wagged a chiding finger. "Nothing is
secret in the streets when one has gold to loosen tongues. I
received word you had been dredging up matters that were
better left to the dead."

"You son of a—" Reave charged Hayden, knocking the
glass from his hand. The contents splashed against the cast
iron grate, and a small explosion flared the gentle fire to life.
Grabbing him by the collar, Reave pulled him to his feet. "You
killed Lathom and his mistress. Butchered them like animals,
leaving Tessa no choice except to flee once word of the killings
reached her."

Hayden chuckled, renewing Reave's fury. "Rather accommodating of the lady, was it not? Come, let's have off with this show of brutality. This side of you is positively raw and unique, strictly not your usual control and intelligence, yet I think this proves my point.''

Reave released him with a shove. Turning away, he pushed his tousled hair from his face while he tried to gain some of his control back. What had happened just then? He had not expected the man to eagerly confess to what had been only his word against Hayden's. Where was the fight, the cunning he expected? ''There is actually a point to this madness?'' Reave sneered.

''Remarkably so, I'm afraid.'' Hayden removed a cigar from a box on the small table beside his chair. Igniting a piece of wood from the fire, he lit the cigar, enjoying the smell and taste. ''I believe this is the first time I have witnessed a complete breakdown of your control. Extraordinary. Not even when your lovely Elise died did I see a breach in your composure. Nevertheless, you were willing to commit violence for our countess. How touching!'' Hayden stared into the fire. ''I, too, have been infected by that same all-consuming violence that blinds one's senses to consequences and such. Unfortunately, there was no one to slap me back to reality.''

He puffed reflectively on his cigar. ''You see, I discovered too late my beloved Claire allowed that rutting bastard Lathom to touch her. It had been over by the time I learned of their treachery.''

''Vengeance.'' Reave said the word softly.

''The fact he had already moved on to another misfortunate wench did not diminish my pleasure. I entered his town house that afternoon and hid in his chamber, waiting for him to retire. I had waited this long to execute my revenge. What were a few hours more? Then enter our countess, the aggrieved wife ready to play out her tragedy. Oh, you should have seen their fight.'' Hayden wet his lips, watching the flickering images in the fire. ''She was magnificent. And foolish. She threatened to kill him when he dared to touch her. The bastard, probably still bearing the hot stench of some forgotten whore, demanded his bed rights. Our countess threatened to kill him if he tried." Hayden smiled at Reave. "It was then I began to think. In my original plan I had imagined cutting his pretty face up a bit so he could not charm the ladies. When that sweet, adulterous whore of a mother slipped into his chamber an hour later to sample sinful delights, the notion of a more permanent exile began to congeal in my head. Watching the two of them rut on the rug, I realized the countess had handed me the knife herself."

"You left Tessa alive so her servants could testify she had threatened to murder him."

"Oh, yes. It would not do to leave suspicion open to others. The countess surprised me. I had not expected her to run. She had always been such a quiet, mousy creature. I assumed she would meet her death as uneventfully." Hayden rolled his cigar between his fingers, a chagrined expression replacing his thoughtful one. "I was very careful. I must know what detail I missed to direct your suspicions onto me?"

"Honestly, Hayden, I never considered you a suspect. I knew whoever did the killings was cunning, knew the Lathoms, and was affluent enough to quiet a few tongues. I suppose what has always puzzled me about this mess was the dead woman wearing the Lathom crest. Kim had brought me the news of the countess's death, details related to him by you. I never saw the connection." Reave shook his head. "Recently, I made a few inquiries I should have requested months ago. I learned you were the one who identified her as the Countess of Lathom. Then I recalled a conversation between us, when you acknowledged knowing her. If true, you would have never mistaken that unfortunate woman for Tessa. Hating Lathom as she did, she would have never worn his ring."

"Ah, so that was my mistake? Well, there were too many details and old conversations to remember all." Hayden crushed the rest of his cigar into a marble cup. "When the countess refused to play her proper role as murderess, and you spoke of foul play, I began to think she had been smarter than I had assumed and fled the country. It was simple enough to find a sweet bit of skirt at Covent Garden who bore similarities to her. I had killed once, so what was another whore? Luck would have it, she remained hidden beneath the frozen, murky depths of the Thames until it was difficult to gaze intently upon her visage. I had done the countess a favor by having her declared dead, though I doubt she would see it in that light, now, would she?''

The reminder of Tessa imprisoned in Newgate forced the anger he was concealing to the surface again. Through gritted teeth Reave said, ''Then I, in arrogant ignorance, trying to press Tessa into confessing what I had already begun to suspect was her identity, brought you to her.''

Hayden tugged the tattered remains of his cravat from his neck and wiped his brow with it. ''I must confess, I almost gave myself away when I realized your bride was the lady I had been seeking. I came upon her, quite incidentally, in the conservatory. When I dared to move closer, Densmore's duchess surprised me. I was surprised to hear the extent to which the esteemed duchess was willing to protect her hapless friend, but it was not enough to protect my interests. I could not risk the investigation to be reopened. I knew questions would be raised about the dead woman if the countess confessed her identity. You understand why I had to take her?''

Reave slumped against the bookcase, casually fingering a small gold tassel that hung down the spine of one of many books. Hayden was so matter-of-fact, so willing to confess, too eager. He spoke as a man who had nothing to lose. Reave felt in his back the sharp edge of the knife he had concealed in the waist of his trousers. It was a comforting to know it was there, yet it was no match for a pistol. A bead of sweat trickled from his temple to his neck, soaking into his cravat. ''Why lock her up, when it would have been more prudent to kill her?''

''And have two dead countesses? Ho, what a coil! Regardless of what you might think, I do possess a considerable measure of pity for the dear lady. Lathom was a vile bastard. She deserved better. Still, I could not risk someone recognizing her. Even you must admit, it was inevitable as your countess. Eventually, she would have been presented at court. I really have no idea how you had proposed to handle it, but I could not trust even your uncanny abilities to do the impossible.'' Hayden's smile grew taunting. "The countess was always a delicate, sensitive creature. You haven't thanked me for removing her from the crowded ward to a private cell, giving her an increasing chance of surviving. Of course, we both know that chance is slight."

Reave moved with amazing swiftness from his position at the wall for Hayden's throat. The barrel of a pistol aimed point-blank at his heart prevented him tearing out the bastard's throat.

Hayden winked. "This is much more appropriate, I believe. Soon enough, one of us would have had to cast aside the mask of civility, exposing the passionate animal beneath. Killing you does pose a slight difficulty. Never fear, I trust my creative instinct to solve the matter."

"Others know I am here, Hayden, and of your duplicity," Reave said, eyeing the finger pressing the taut trigger. At this range he had little chance of avoiding the ball. "Did you believe me so foolish as to walk into your custody without guaranteeing my safety? There is a letter bearing your name. It will be sent to the appropriate authorities if I meet with a sudden accident." The pistol wavered, then was slowly lowered.

"No!"

Reave took advantage of Claire's soul-piercing scream and lunged for Hayden. His head struck Hayden's soft middle, and both men crashed to the floor. The impact jarred the knife Reave carried from its hiding place. Hayden kicked it out of reach when Reave tried to grab it. The rage that had been simmering boiled, overriding reason. Reave punched Hayden in the face, releasing a satisfying growl when he heard the bones in the man's nose crack, and blood dripped from his chin.

Wiping the blood with the cuff of his sleeve, Hayden coughed. His eyes, glazed with pain, focused beyond Reave's shoulder. "Claire."

Not certain who Hayden was warning, Reave pivoted as Claire, her face mottled with rage, rushed forward. There was a bright flash in her hand, then she drove it into his chest. A knife. It was his damn knife. The crimson metal rose for another taste of his flesh. Reave rolled just before the blade struck. It missed its mark but not the victim. Claire buried the steel into the back of his shoulder, her eerie laughter discharging in the air around them as the darkness threatened to smother him.

"Claire, enough!"

Faintly in his mind, Reave heard Hayden shout. Unable to move, he blankly watched his blood ebb into the rug. Sluggish, but understanding he was bleeding to death, he moved his hand up to the wound to stanch the flow. The argument between husband and wife came to him garbled, as irritating as insects buzzing overhead, only bits of dialogue making any sense.

"He cannot live. Even you must realize that!" Claire's voice rose in volume with each word.

"You mad bitch! He had to be seen leaving here alive, so as not to cause suspicion. Look at all of this blood. The servants know he was here. Do you intend to kill everyone in the household?" Hayden yelled over his shoulder. His gaze returned to Reave. "Sorry, old friend. It had been my intention to make your departure swift. However, we cannot allow you to expire in our household. Too many questions, you know."

"It was Claire. All along." Reave gasped, a spasm of pain silencing him. He choked on the bile rising in his throat.

Hayden dabbed at the drying blood under his nose. "Your curiosity is bound to get you killed, my friend. Yes, it was Claire who murdered Lathom."

"Hayden, you foolish bastard," Claire hissed at her husband's confession.

Hayden cocked his head to see his wife's face. It was the worst he had ever seen her. The affliction had a strong hold on her. She bit her lips to keep from screaming, the resulting pink froth at the corners of her mouth enhancing her disturbing image. He loved her, but in truth he knew her to be insane. He had to protect her. Wycke would have to die, but not here . . . somewhere else.

"Claire, you have poked enough holes in him to hasten his demise. It harms no one to let him understand the reasons for his death." Hayden increased the pressure to Reave's wound, watching the excess blood pool around his fingers. The small handkerchief was completely saturated with the earl's blood. Time was Wycke's enemy now.

"Claire is not well," Hayden began, ignoring her outraged hiss. "Her mother had the affliction and it wasn't until after I had married her that I began to see the signs." Wycke's eyes were closed and Hayden was not certain if he was listening. No matter. "The past few years have been the worst. She did wicked things when it was upon her. Lathom saw her weakness and took advantage of it. He was always one to do such things: finding a weakness and twisting it for his pleasure. The bastard was reckless. Got her with child. When he learned of it, he denied knowing her. She almost died ridding her body of his brat. It was then I first learned of their deceit."

"Perhaps I would not have sought his bed if you had been more of a man," she taunted, then stepped back when he lifted his hand to strike. Smirking, Claire said, "Even our dear Wycke proved to be more man than you!"

This was the sort of nonsense Claire confessed to hurt him. Hayden tried not to believe her barb. Staring at Wycke's unconscious form, he doubted any man could resist such a delectable treat as Claire. He had yet to know of one who had. Hayden punched Wycke's wound. The earl moaned, his eyes flickering briefly before closing again. "Did you sample the sweet flesh of my Claire, Reave. Did she pant like a bitch, begging for more?" His fury mounted when Claire laughed.

"She lies," Wycke said, his voice barely audible. "Only Tessa."

Hayden studied his friend thoughtfully before nodding, acknowledging the fact. "You were always too scrupulous to take another man's wife. I believe you. It would serve no purpose to lie."

"Why? Why—you?" Wycke tried to speak, not able to complete the thought.

"Why did I admit to the murders, when it was my faithless wife? I knew she was angry the night Lathom appeared at the ball with his latest conquest on his arm. Everyone was watching for the countess's reaction, so only I saw the wrath my Claire struggled with. I almost wanted to warn Lathom. Almost. Later, when I caught Claire burning her bloodied gown, I knew we had both been avenged. I returned to the town house and removed any evidence that might have linked my wife to the murders. I knew the countess would be blamed, not that I cared. I did my best to convince all who would listen of her guilt. Everyone had seen her at the ball. There were servants who could testify the poor woman had reached her limit and had threatened him. Claire, also, had heard the threat and obliged her by carrying out the deed."

"Husband, your tongue speaks too freely, as does my hand," she chided. Hayden stiffened, his hand clutching his throat as he sought to remove the knife she had driven into his neck from behind.

Claire frowned. "Forgive me, Hayden, this entire Wycke debacle has muddled my mind. Here I was thinking, my, what a jaw-me-dead twit you have become. Or was it jaw-be-dead." She shrugged. "I think I have taken care of the problem at hand, husband."

A bubbling sound came from Hayden's throat. He took a step toward her before he pitched forward, landing next to Reave. Claire walked around the bodies, halting at Reave's head. He flinched when she gingerly adjusted a lock of hair matted to his forehead. "You know, Reave, you have always been my favorite. I used to wish you were my husband." Claire sat on the floor, primping her skirts about her. "Hayden was weak. I wonder why he chose you to be his confessor, when I suppose half the staff must have their ears pressed against the door, listening to us. Stupid bastard.''

Wycke stirred. Rolling to his side, he embraced Hayden's dead body.

Claire squinted her eyes, and they almost looked like children sleeping. ''I had thought to keep you for myself. In exchange for your precious Tessa's freedom, you would have become my husband. Naturally, you would have exposed my dead husband for the murderer he was.'' She raised a trembling hand to her temple. ''All is ruined. Hayden should have never told you. Never.'' Tears streamed down her cheeks as she raised the knife over his inert body.

''I love you,'' she whispered, bringing the blade down. A shot exploded between them, a startled expression on her paling visage. Horrified, she saw the red stain rapidly spreading across her heaving chest. Her gaze dropped to the discharged pistol in Reave's open palm, the smoke still curling from the barrel. She had forgotten Hayden had tucked the weapon in the front of his breeches when he checked Reave's wounds.

Claire felt like she was floating. She did not even feel pain when the side of her face hit the floor. Reave was watching her, his blue eyes condemning, yet too weak to move or call out. How had he taken the pistol without her noticing? She pondered the thought while the demons howled in her head. She would rest for a while. When she was rid of the tightness in her chest, she would ask him how he—

Dispassionately, Reave watched Claire's bemused expression become fixed and lifeless. She was dead. In the distance, he heard pounding at the door, then someone kicked it, breaching the lock. A veritable whirlwind of confusing voices spoke to him at once. He felt hands on him, checking his wounds. He had thought he had experienced the worst of the pain—until someone tried to lift him. Mercifully, he passed out.

Chapter Thirty

"Beloved, can you hear me?"

The gentle, persistent voice coaxed Reave to awaken. Gray shadows fused with rings of light. Tessa's fair image came into focus, pulling him from the dark depths of slumber. She was dressed as he had first seen her all those months before. Her long blond hair flowed over the simple cream-colored gown she wore, curling slightly at her waist. Once she had reminded him of an angel, as he had hidden in the shadows, watching her kiss his son. Now she was leaning over him, placing small, light kisses on his cheeks and forehead.

Was this a dream? He tried to rise, wanting to bring her mouth onto his for a more rewarding kiss to assuage his growing hunger at the sight of her. Something heavy held him down. Sucking in his breath, he tried to ease the burning sensation in his chest and shoulder.

"Hush, try not to move. We almost lost you, and I will not have you ruin our work. I have prayed for three days that you would open your eyes for me, and you have, just as the surgeon promised. Kim said that you loved me too much to allow a few paltry wounds to take you from me," she prattled on, then stopped and gave him a brilliant smile. "Forgive me for going on so. I have been so afraid since I had heard you were wounded."

Reave raised his good arm and brushed her tears away with his thumb. Tessa laughed and kissed his fingers. Moistening his dry lips with his tongue, he tried to speak. "Where am I?"

Tessa stilled at his question, then moved away to pour him a glass of water. "Everything will seem hazy for a time. It is just the effects of the laudanum. You have lost so much blood. The doctor thought it best to keep you sedated while you healed." She pressed the glass to his lips. Realizing she had avoided his question, he turned his face from the glass.

"Where?" he demanded. Damn, he was weaker than a day-old infant.

"This is Hayden's house, Reave." She pressed the glass to his lips. He greedily emptied it. Tessa stood to fill the glass again. Sitting beside him, she held his head while he drank. "The servants found you," Tessa said, observing his face to see if he recalled.

Reave grimaced, the pain in his head making it difficult to think. "I thought I died."

"And you did a fine imitation of it too. The servants were terrified finding the three of you lying in puddles of blood. There was little they could do but bind your wounds and await the surgeon. It was he who feared moving you might kill you, so it was agreed you were to remain."

Reave listened, digesting everything. His thoughts were jumbled in his head like a complex puzzle he could not solve. One thought, however, was clear. "Tessa, you are not in Newgate."

"So kind of you to notice." She smiled. "The servants heard Claire scream. Not certain what to do, the butler and one of the footmen listened at the door. They heard Hayden's confession. Please, do not blame them for not interfering. The Quinns' chilling confession frightened them. Besides, you had already been wounded. All they could do was send for the constable.

At the sound of the discharging pistol, they broke down the door and found you all.'' Tessa took a deep breath and sighed. ''The butler's testimony restored my good name, absolving me from Edmund's and Mother's murders. Fortunately, you had mentioned to Kim where I was being kept, else I would be still waiting for you in Newgate.''

''Hayden? Claire?''

''Both dead,'' she admitted. ''It troubles me. Although we were remotely acquainted, it astounds me they were willing to allow me to hang for the murders.''

''Passion, Tessa. Everything was done in passion.'' He grabbed her wrist when she tried to adjust his pillow. ''Can you forgive me for what I put you through? If I had relied on my instincts, I would have never brought Hayden to Eastcott. You would have never been taken.''

''Never mind that now. I escaped with a few scrapes and bruises. My gowns need to be taken in a few inches, but a week or so eating Cook's hearty fare and you will have to purchase another wardrobe.'' She tried to laugh away the pain and memories of the last few weeks, knowing neither of them would ever forget. Sobering, she lightly touched his cheek. ''Reave, he was your business partner. It was inevitable we would have met. Another time, another place.'' She shrugged. ''It was my secret that almost killed me, not you, love.''

''The hell it was! You were just protecting yourself from Hayden's deceit. Instead of trying to show you I could be trusted, I tricked you and demanded that you tell me your secrets. I loved you enough to ignore the inconsistencies in the past you created yet never cared to understand why you had to lie.'' Reave clutched his head. Wincing, he tried to will the pain away. ''I purposely set a trap for you, expecting in my arrogance that you would confess your sins to me. My actions forced you to use any weapon you could.''

''The baby,'' she whispered. Stricken, her gaze met his. ''I bled in the prison.''

Reave swallowed the lump forming in his throat. He was

silent, not certain how to offer her comfort. "I would like to believe there was no child." It was easier to accept her lying about her condition. Otherwise, he was responsible for his child's death because he neglected to protect her. It was all too painful. "We have another chance at love, a marriage built on trust, and passion with no ghosts or deception to tear us apart. A relationship in which I would like our child to be conceived." His gaze lingered at the folds of fabric concealing her flat stomach, then moved up to meet her tear-filled eyes.

"You still love me? Want me? I thought—" She brought his head to her breast, causing him to yelp in pain.

"You will have to be more tender in your ministrations if you wish to bring me to the altar!" Reave chuckled against her breast. The feel of her soft flesh against his cheek, the fast tempo of her heartbeat, were worth a little discomfort.

"I never dreamed you would still want to marry me, especially when all will know me as Edmund's wife."

"Widow," he corrected her. He glanced about the room. "Where is my coat?"

Puzzled by his unexpected request, she bit her upper lip, her gaze searching the room. "There was much blood; I doubt it is repairable. Ah, yes. Over there." She untangled herself from his grasp and moved across the room. Returning to his side, she held up the ruined coat.

"Check the inner pocket," he urged, trying not to smile when she reached into the lining and withdrew a document. It was stained with his blood. "Go on, read it."

Perplexed, she separated the blood-plastered paper, gasping when she realized what she held.

"I left you that day to secure a special license. Densmore owed me a few favors." Reave grabbed her skirt and pulled her closer. "I had been willing to marry you when I knew you were lying, and when you finally broke down and confessed the truth. Do you honestly believe after all of this, I would simply turn against you because a malicious few will toss us in the gossip mill. I think the last few weeks have proven that both of us are stalwart enough to withstand the wagging tongues. I love you, Countess.''

Tessa clutched the precious document to her heart. She had come to him with nothing . . . no name, money, nor position, yet miraculously he had grown to love her, desiring nothing except her love. Pressing her cheek to his, she tried to keep from weeping.

"I assume this means you will be my countess?" he asked, not really doubting her response.

"Yes, you arrogant, stubborn man. When you are capable of withstanding the rigors of our wedding night, I shall become your bride.''

Reave smiled at her challenge. His beautiful countess would be surprised how quickly a man in love healed when the inviting dark waters of passion beckoned.

ABOUT THE AUTHOR

Barbara Pierce resides near Atlanta, GA, with her husband and three children. She is presently working on her next novel. Readers may write to her c/o Kensington Publishing Corp.